# Stronger

A NOVEL BY

BRANDI FORTE

BASED ON A TRUE

STORY

For inquires please contact:
Social Media:
Instagram: @authorentreprenuerbrandi
Facebook: https://m.facebook.com/authorbrandiforte
Twitter: brandiforte78

Paperback ISBN: 9780578736310
Cover Design: Ben Osborne
Library of Congress Cataloging-in-Publication Data On File
Printed in the United States of America

*Dedicated to Juan*

. . .

You Made Me Stronger. Asante Sana Warrior
Angel!

# Chapter 1

## Stretch Mark Love

He was Amistad Black yearning to be Sankofa free. A Mandingo warrior enmeshed with a Zulu swag. He was Shaka strong and immortal, it seemed. He wasn't aesthetically beautiful, but he was continental beautiful – African beautiful. His ancestors could have come from perhaps the same West African village that my great-great-great-great-grandfather came from.

His eyes were Asiatic slanted. His nose was broad. His face had the roundness of the moon, and he had one dimple indented in his left cheek. His back was broadly arched, and his shoulder blades were shaped like pyramids. I knew upon meeting him that there was a destiny connection; just wasn't sure if it was for a season, reason, or lifetime.

Kenya was a breath of fresh air for a sista like me, who had experienced concaved darker days and ratchet-life staircases. There were no "crystal stairs" in my life. More like wooden stairs wearing and tearing on the bottom of my bare feet, making the journey callous. The corns on my pinky toe would never disappear. The pain was mine, but so was the happiness.

Our immediate connectivity was that he accepted me for me. I may have been the perfect Picasso to him with all my flaws and hidden baggage; however, he witnessed a perfect imperfection in me that I couldn't see in myself. In Kenya's Mind, he had found a rare ruby that had been exposed to a raging fire. Fiery "Ruby Woo" that had been tarnished and tried but unbelievably unscathed. Yet, he was like a li'l boy who found something so profound that he would savor it for a lifetime. I was-and still am- The Ruby.

Using the tips of my nails, I dug deep and found a diamond covered in coal, covered in soil, covered in blackness that protected its shine from the diggers sent to make a profit off of something so scarce. It may have been best that Kenya remained deeply hidden in a realm where no woman could find, and no man could recognize his value. For if the coal were removed entirely, strangers would rob, kill and steal for a diamond, and yet, I understood this. My goal was to rinse off the coal, the subtleness of the dirt, and let him shine forever. His aura was protectiveness, understanding, and real love – nothing else was missing in my mind.

We were so opposite from the beginning that our differences became our attraction. Kenya was raised by his grandmother, although his mom and aunts were influential. For there were no men in his family, and the ones that existed when he was a jitterbug had died before their time, making him the last man standing. My mama and stepdad raised me, and my great-grandma profoundly impacted my life. There were plenty of men in my family. Let him tell it, he was "surrounded and spoiled rotten by the women in his family, aunts, and cousins." He was his parents' one and only, and the neighborhoods' "golden boy." Contrarily, I would be the woman-child that was golden in my family's eyes as the firstborn, first grandchild, and the one that my grandparents, great-grandma, and uncles invested so much into.

We agreed that we had a few things in common, but our courses in life revealed a complete contrast based on the roads we chose. At 18, I would pursue my dream of becoming a great writer and college graduate of a HBCU in "Chocolate City." At 18, he was pursuing a career in juvenile justice that would plant him in "juvie." He loved Italian food and Scarface movies. I couldn't live without Mexican food and romantic comedies. In his four walls, he was reading author Teri Woods and Wahida Clark, as I studied in my dorm the urban-lit of Sista Souljah and spiritual writings of Bishop T.D. Jakes. While he never aspired to go to college, and I never aspired to go to prison, we both longed for REAL love, prosperity, beautiful babies, and a house on the hill. We loved God. We were human in every way.

I would meet Kenya during the remission of suffering from panic and anxiety attacks as a result of a broken heart. We would meet at a peaceful place in our lives with great anticipation of living again, a moment in my life where my presidential campaign fellowship was over, and I was confident that I would never love Solomon again. Didn't really know if there was even any love in me or if it was sugar water in my heart without the red Kool-Aid. Didn't really know if I could love anyone unapologetically and pure, but what I knew for sure was if I met LOVE, I wouldn't run away. Life surely was amazing for me and unbelievable for America. The ancestors had their prayers answered, and the United States of America had elected its first Black president. President Hope brought new energy to the country and to communities nationwide. The energy was fresh, bringing about positive change, progression, and restoration of an economy that had been deeply oppressed by Republicans. The floodgates of opportunities were pouring from the heavens, and my economy became stabilized.

Kenya was definitely a very important piece on my chessboard, but my pride, joy, and my sincere focus were making sure that my son, King, was and will always be, good. Surely, I made up in my mind that King would be raised with godly principles, love, strength, self-worth, and good values, and he would not use his father's absence to take a wrong detour or make bad decisions. King would learn from me how to deal with the deck of cards that was given to him, learning how to play and take losses like how you take your wins – essentially, riding the wave of life without drowning. He was my firstborn and only child, and he was spoiled rotten. My reason for spoiling King was to overcompensate for the absenteeism of his father. In my psyche, I wanted to love his pain away, his hurt away, his abandonment away, praying that a mother's love would cure all uncertainty or lack thereof. I will never forget the first day that I met Kenya. As a matter of fact, we both would never forget because it was his daughter, Nia's, fourth birthday. It was Black August…scorching hot and humid. Nia celebrated her birthday with a host of family at a local indoor splash park, which was perfect for the temperature.

Nia's birthday was embedded in my head because it was the same birthday as Ceddi's, one of my ex-lovers. Numbers don't lie, and the stars chose when they aligned. Ceddi was my beau, for real. As a matter of fact, he was the one I should have married when I was young, wild, and free. His life was cut short when he was gunned down in South Central L.A. while I was working in the Big Apple as a budding journalist. He was a victim of Gang violence. Ceddi was an Inglewood Blood who lived a double life because he was a gangsta in the streets but the perfect gentlemen to me. What was piercing to my heart is that his murder remains unsolved, and in my heart, I wish he were here.

Ceddi was a real one. We built so hard, and we were so connected on all levels. During my college summer break, we would spend every day together. We would hang out on the daily after my shift at an internship with a prominent hip-hop magazine. I met Ceddi during my summer vacation from college. I was entering my senior year of college, and in my mind, I wanted to be vulnerable and try love. He worked at a propane shop in my hood. We would just live life so free, like restaurant-hopping form the East Side to the West Side and even to Beverly Hills. Yet, we had ghetto-ish tendencies as we popped bottles of Arbor Mist and Alize.

Ceddi and I were California dreaming, from amusement parks to long walks in the park to setting lunch dates at Indian reservations. He would take me to so many places that I had never been before, and I felt safe in our element. Often, we would sit on Malibu Beach, and talk about what we wanted out of life and how we could not live without each other. To be honest, he was so dope I didn't even want to go back to college 'cause I felt like if I did, I would lose him. But during my senior year, my parents and family would have kicked my ass to the moon and back if I didn't graduate. I was his Black Pochaontas-fierce in every way, and he knew he couldn't stop me. Graduation was calling me, and my prayer was that we would connect somewhere in the middle of the road under a midnight-blue sky and sparkling stars. Yea, the stars would align again.

Like Kenya, Ceddi came to me during a period of great loss and after the passing of my grandfather and uncle in the same month. Ceddi was a real G, and so was Kenya. Ceddi had only one child, and so did Kenya. Ceddi was raised by his grandma, and so was Kenya. Both of their parents were in and out of their lives and had addictions to the darker side. Perhaps that was the reason why they found fixation and a thug love in the streets. There was something about the streets…being a gangsta, being a part of the lifestyle that encompassed mama, girlfriend, and wifey. It was an illusion that sucked them into a matrix.

The only thing that separated Ceddi and me was time and space. I was addicted to the culture of the East Coast, and he was loyal to the WEST 'til his dying day. It wasn't that I desired to forget where I came from. It was just that the aroma of my dreams was so strong that it was calling me in a foreign land. Kenya, perhaps, would be, my Ceddi reincarnated or the second wind of fresh air that I needed to run my next race. Deep down, I felt bad because I never came back to save Cedric from the dark side. I was propelled subconsciously to save Kenya and make him a complete square…or at least an octagon.

Ceddi had a daughter, and so did Kenya, but I never had the opportunity to get to know Ceddi's princess. Kenya's daughter, Nia, and I had a relationship long before I met her father. I met Nia through her play aunt, Niecy, who she spent a great deal of time with. I taught Niecy's children in both elementary and middle school, and we managed to build a relationship as Black women. Nia and King were the same age and played at Niecy's house on special occasions and later casually on some weekends.

King gravitated to Nia, and so did I. She was bashful, she had the cutest smile, and she was sneaky and clever but respectful. Niecy kept a lot of drama going, yet, at the same time, she was well calculated and smart enough to know when to remove herself from the drama. She was in everybody's business but never figured out how to keep her husband out of other women's drawers. Although she was a nurturing mother, she had several shortcomings, and the main ones were gossiping and manipulation. The positive was that she kept a clean house, she could braid her butt off, and her kids were always clean. Niecy was notoriously known for braiding hair, and on one particular hot-ass August day, she braided Nia's hair for her fourth birthday. Niecy could be messy, but when it came to the image of young Black girls, she was the "Hair-in-Residence." If you were in her company, she would ensure your hair was on fleek.

According to Niecy, Kenya's baby mother was a slouch and missing in action when it came to her own daughter. She would stand in the gap often because Nia needed support. Once Niecy completed Nia's hair, she contacted the mother to let her know that Nia was ready to go to her party. However, Nia's mother wasn't even willing to pick up her daughter to bring her to her birthday party. Niecy knew that I was fond of Nia and gave me a call and asked if I was in the neighborhood and could take Nia and a fellow cousin to the pool party. I agreed because I was doing one of my sweet deeds, as usual, and my water baby would have the opportunity to swim at the pool party.

Without a doubt, I packed King's trunks and my Ralph Lauren swimsuit, picked up Nia and her cousin from Niecy's, and headed to Nia's pool party. Nia was a bright light, Spanish-red li'l mama with a cute smile, sassy disposition, and according to Niecy, she had been through a lot and knew more than an average 4-year-old. I always gravitated to young survivors – 'cause life sometimes had a way of dealing babies a horrendous stack of cards. Like her name, Nia was full of PURPOSE. I hoped that one day it would fully bloom.

I pulled up my Batmobile to the North Side projects where Niecy, Nia, and their cousin, Cam, stood.

"Thank you so much, Ms. Angelou." Niecy always called me by last name. "I can't have my niece looking crazy so I had to do her hair for her birthday 'cause her mother is so doggone trifling." She held no punches.

"Understood sis. It's all good. You know how I am about the babies. Plus, King will have some time to get in the water."

"That's my boo. Hey, King!" Niecy waved to King.

"Hey, Ms. Niecy," King waved back.

"Okay, I got them." I opened the back door for them.

"Thank you, Ms. Dream," said Cam.

"No Problem, Cam."

"Hi Ms. Dream," Nia said politely.

"Happy birthday, li'l lady," I smiled and then pulled off.

"Thank you." Nia was so happy.

We cruised onto the sounds of ol'-school hip-hop 'cause it felt like one of those throwback days. The pool party was just 15 minutes away from Niecy.

Upon arriving, you could smell the synergy of things being slightly off balanced. Cam introduced me to Nia's family as Niecy's kids' teacher, yet, Nia's family were full of high yellow, 'easty-looking-ass females" who gritted on me as if I would be a wesside problem. I had a navy-blue Ralph Lauren halter two-piece hugging me softly, and King wore his polo shorts. Yes, "the girls," one of my best assets, always drew attention – I was used to it. Together, we stayed fresh and looked fresh, and I knew back then that the "haters gonna hate!" I kept my distance and dusted them dusty broads off my shoulders as I invariably did. My son and I were water babies. There was nothing more calming to our soul than evolving in water. I'm a strong believer in enjoying the little things in life, and King and I did.

While in the neon aqua pool, a dark-skinned brotha standing about 6 feet tall had the attention of Nia and several of her siblings. Nia was actually hugging on the back of his chocolate shoulder blades as if he were her father or uncle. The kids all rallied for a ride on his back as if they were baby turtles at sea. Even my son doggy-paddled to him to see what the hoopla was about. He smiled at me, and I smiled back. He locked his eyes all in my cornea and wouldn't let go. His spirit was interesting.

"How you doing?" he walked toward me.

"Hi," I responded.

"You can let your son come over here. I'm just playing with the kids, taking them down the water slide," he conversed.

"It's my daughter's, Nia's, birthday party."

"I know. I brought her here. My son plays with her all the time."

"Oh, you are Niecy's kids' teacher, right?" he asked.

"Yes. I taught two of her kids."

"Thanks for bringing my daughter. Niecy told me that you would be bringing her. My baby mama be tripping."

I signaled to King that he could play with Nia and the kids who attended. He got excited and paddled along. I crossed my arms as a defense mechanism.

"No worries. It's all good. It's Nia's birthday. You gotta do right by the kids."

He walked within a few feet of me. "What's your name?"

"My name is Dream. And yours?"

"My name is Kenya."

"That's a nice warrior's name."

"You have a beautiful name for a beautiful lady," he said. The kids faded away and got on the slides one by one as Kenya tried to make his way.

"So, can I get your number and call you sometime?"

"How you gonna ask me for my number, and your baby mama is standing right there?"

His baby mama stood in front of the Jacuzzi with her pastel-green one piece on, cornrows, and her right hand on her hip as if she felt some kind of disrespect. Her eyes studied Kenya's body language like an eagle. My baby mama has a boyfriend. Her concern should not be about me. She needs to focus on him," Kenya affirmed, turning his back to her.

"Yea, but that's not me. I don't like drama. But it was nice talking to you." I swam over to the Jacuzzi and unwound in the water. It felt so good just to relax. After about 30 minutes, I motioned my right arm to King to get out of the pool.

"But, Mommy, I'm still swimming and having so much fun!" exclaimed King.

"OK, you got 15 minutes. The party is almost over, and we gotta get going." I said with an attitude because, in this life, you gotta stay sucka free and keep the hoodrat drama at bay.

"Okayyyyy," He sounded like he lost his best friend.

King zoned out and began seizing the last few minutes in the pool by swimming with other boys his age. I hopped in the Jacuzzi for a few minutes to rest my body, soak my feet, and take the opportunity to chill. The water was so relaxing. It was just me, myself, and I in my Cancerian element. Kenya could not keep his eyes off me, but I avoided a conversation because I truly didn't know the temperament between him and Nia's mom. Soon, I walked out of the Jacuzzi and went over to Nia.

"Hey, Nia, we're getting ready to leave, but I hope you have a wonderful birthday!" I hugged her.

"Thank you, Ms. Angelou," she affectionately called me.

"You're welcome, sweetie."

I walked over to King to let him know that our time was up and that we would head out. He understood, so he gave Nia and a few other kids a high five and waved good-bye.

King proceeded behind me to the changing rooms. He was amped up, sliding and gliding through the changing room.

"Calm down, boy. I'm getting our towels and clothes out of the locker."

I handed King his towel and change of clothes; then I got myself together. King was 4 now and very independent. He knew how to get dressed, make himself a snack…toast or a bowl of cereal, if needed. He was such a big boy, and we both loved it. I greased our faces, arms and legs real good with cocoa butter. We were a chocolate bronze and all beauty in my book. King put his swim gear in his bag, and I grabbed our belongings and placed them in our big swim bag.

We were good to go and dashed to our big ol' Cadillac, a.k.a. the "Batmobile." The humidity held no punch lines – it was baking bits. As we walked to our car, Kenya, being advantageous, jogged toward me to get my attention.

"Hey, pretty lady, so I can't get your number? Seriously. I want your number."

"Like I said before, I'm not into disrespect. You have your baby mama looking at me like she's ready to fight. I don't know what type of relationship you have with her, but I don't think this is the right place," I said sincerely."

"But-but-but," he stuttered, "can we talk? Maybe the kids can hang out. I'm not a bad guy. Me and my baby mama have nothing going on," he pressed me out.

"Look," I scribbled my name and number on a small piece a paper and handed it to him aggressively, "call me. We'll talk," I smiled and walked away sassily.

He stood there looking at the number as if it were make-believe.

"Mom, did you just give your number to Nia's dad?" King asked.

"Yes, son, I did, and I don't know why," I laughed aloud. Then, King and I laughed together.

"Is that okay with you?" I asked my li'l husband.

"Yea, he seemed nice," said King.

"I guess we'll find out." I headed in the direction to King's favorite place, Mickey D's, to grab us a bite to eat.

Later that evening, Kenya would call, and we would have an interesting conversation on the phone. Although he had gnagsta written all over his persona, he had a protective spirit and a cool, calm demeanor that offered respect. He told me that he was raised by his grandma and a household full of women. He made sure that he interjected that he was the only male in his immediate family. I also learned from our phone conversation that he only had one child, which was a good thing because I always met dudes who had a zillion. Most importantly, he believed in God and held a J-O-B, working in the culinary field.

Kenya lived less than a mile away from me, so close that he could walk to my house, or I could take a nice walk to his. That day in August would change my life in a way that was much different than I was accustomed to. My therapist told me one time, "Meet a better man so you can get over the bad man." Maybe Kenya was the better man…or the worst. Or maybe we would just be cool being homies or lovers or heck – homie-lover-friends in that order. All I knew was that he was great with children; he had a warm, kind spirit; and the kind of heart that was all LION. He was tall, chocolate, and Mandingo. He was no pretty Rickaaaaay, but he was definitely MANDINGO.

From that day at the pool, we would bond and kick it. Kinda like how Ceddi and I used to be. We would break bread over his great breakfast, lunch and dinner feasts. We would bond over watching our children play together at playgrounds across town. We would bond over good love making, and I mean *good* lovemaking. It felt like sex on the beach all day, every day. He found G-spots, GG-spots, and GGG-spots. His Isis Pistol was the bomb.com. No other brotha could get in his business, and I think he may have been slightly arrogant about his sex game.

But even stronger than sex, Kenya took the time to listen to my fears, heartbreaks, and my dreams. Sometimes, I would have minor anxiety attacks because of just the simple uncertainty of life. I would pop a pill, an off-white one to calm down. There just wasn't nothing more affirming than to have a Black man cool enough to be cool. No games, no strings attached but simply okay with the possibilities of a Love Jones. He was my Larenz Tate, and I may have been his Nina Mosely, minus the Harley.

Kenya was a family man who introduced me to all of his dysfunctional family from the beginning. Always with my guard up, it would take me awhile to introduce him to mine, 'cause after that Solomon hell-on-earth storm, my mother, father, brothers, or BFFs weren't trying to see or hear another nicca sell a nightmare, or better yet, take me through one.

It was a new chapter, and I proudly completed my fellowship with the President Hope campaign, manifesting my due diligence for the struggle for my people. My life had gone from corporate, colossal, and community in just 2 years. I had a new gig that would move me past the poverty level into the middle class. I had a new love interest that would paint the rooms in my life from dark mahogany to ruby red and eclectic suedes.

Kenya was warrior strong. He was an intense spirit that would allow me to be a woman. He wasn't intimidated by my career or aspirations – he just let me flow. He was an alpha man who would cook, clean and fuck my brains to the land of no worries. I seemed stronger, but I knew I couldn't do it by myself; plus, being alone got kinda boring. My therapist taught me how to do the work and the effort it took to push through adversity.

With my hands slowly unfolding and coming down to face my silhouette, the waves came toward me, and I began riding the wave. My heart was guarded. Yet, I needed that protective spirit – like Ceddi. I needed that affirming spirit that was so strong and willing to love me in all my stretch marks, concaveness, brilliance, and resilience. Someone who'd wipe my tears but respect the elevation. Someone who could love the remnants of the pain outta me until I experienced the residue of agape. Yea, me, the complicated one. The one who was learning the genesis of self-love. Yea, me. I was looking for a stronger one, so invigorating that the strength would build organically. Something fa'evea!

# Chapter 2

## Activating My Dream

The struggle evolved and became beautiful. The hunger pains dissolved, and I had been from the desert, through the wilderness, and hence, to the mountaintop. Intuitively, I knew that I graduated from being a hothead and that the lessons from the previous level were learned. God saw fit to give me a preview of what was to come, and my future seemed so bright that I had to put my shades on. I tossed my speech-writing career out the window for the "Hopeful" campaign in which I was selected as a fellow for 7 months. All I knew was that this brotha was a Black man and that if I could give up a year's salary to contribute toward witnessing the first African American president take the oath of office, then it was worth it. My intuition always worked in my favor when I didn't suppress it. By the end of my tenure as a campaign fellow, "Our President," indeed, was sworn into office representing the US! President Hope was a Black man from Chicago with an astounding first lady who resembled sistas like me. She had melanin and wasn't the type who'd pass. She was like Oprah—you knew she was a Black woman, and we all studied her, yearning to know what was next. The first kids were so beautiful. President Hope had daughters who were innocently poised, and you could tell they weren't coached. Hailing from the South Side of Chicago, they reminded us of who we could be. Hope's cabinet was colorful, and the "colored" had a chance at obtaining or activating the "American Dream."

President Hope had the country on lock, and I was working for a community-based organization full of Black men that prided themselves on carrying out White House initiatives, to include fatherhood and youth violence. I truly wanted to work in the White House's Office of Communications or African American Affairs, but after speaking with my former fellow supervisor, José, I had to weigh my options. While I was a dreamer, my reality was that I was a single mother of color with a lack of real support. Based on the hours that were required by any position in the White House, I would have to have a nanny or a family member to help me with King, because of the demand of the position and the amount of traveling. Working in the community was my other option, and I took the opportunity as if our lives depended on it.

I remember having a real conversation with José like it were yesterday.

*"Whatcha gonna do, Ms. Dream? Have you applied for transition team positions like I encouraged you to do?" asked José.*

*"Yes, I did," I said adamantly.*

*"Are you ready to lay it on the line to work for the White House or in one of the key departments?"*

*"Whatchu mean? I got what it takes."*

*"Yes, but you know the demand for work is gonna be crazy. We are talking 60–70 hours per week. Not normal, Dream. You got a son too."*

*"Yeah, I know. But do I just give up on my dreams?"*

*"No. Do you have someone who could help you with your kid? Like a full-time nanny? A family member who will hold it down for you?" He had me thinking.*

*"Naw. Ughhhh," I sighed. "No one I trust. No one I will leave my baby with. All I got is my son. Is there something else I can do and still keep my goal in mind?"*

*"Yes, you can do community work," he responded.*

*"Community work?" I questioned.*

*"I can link you with a community-based organization that carries out White House initiatives. A place where you can thrive and be of good service."*

*"That's awesome. And, yeah, I can still have the connection. That works. I can still raise my son too," I reflected.*

*"Dream, I'm just a phone call away," José spoke kindly. "You got a bright future and believe in youuuuuuu!"*

I chose my son over the White House. He needed me more. And although I wasn't going, change was good.

I wanted access to success because I had worked so hard for absolutely everything that I had. It didn't have to be a slice of apple pie or even sweet potato. Hell, it could have been cheesecake or blueberry.

It felt so good to matriculate from being a hothead to learning my very own life lessons while passing the tests. God saw fit to move me to the next level, positioned at a fast speed, and at a unique incline.

I wore many hats working for the Men of Valor, a community-based organization in the nation's capital. From coordinating their educational program to advising the president on critical issues, and even creating a series of conferences with local and national reputable officials.

It felt like roller skates as I entered a new senior-level position, which blessed me with full power to make decisions. I was the only woman at the table full of powerfully seasoned Black men. I was the only young woman who had the opportunity to sit at the table and eat well with brothas and comrades who had a respectable love and adoration from the community for 21 years. I was paving my own way, but their guidance would get me there.

On my first day of work, I was greeted by dark gray chipped walls, the smell of urine on the basement office steps, and the scurrying sounds of mice and rats that occupied the office suite for probably their entire lifetime. My new office would be in the middle of the toughest, roughest, grimiest project in Northwest D.C., a.k.a.

Menace. My alma mater was within 2 miles of Menace, and I would hear horror stories of what went on in the housing project. I saw tidbits of a tough life growing up in Cali, but to be honest, I was not about that Menace life. In Cali, you saw beaches and crackheads, businessmen and gangstas, as well as aspiring actors and Hollywood's finest. But Menace was truly something that a sista had never experienced.

Men of Valor had run a series of youth violence prevention programs, gang intervention programs, truancy programs, and was awarded a local grant to run an educational program for youth in a high-risk community who wanted a shot at life. They selected Menace because there, youth were getting slain left and right, and they chose to position themselves to serve as a positive resource for the youth and families who resided there.

I often wondered why God would use me to go into the grimiest neighborhoods—maybe because I was unafraid. Maybe because my heart was in the right place. Although I was in the basement of the housing project, my office and classroom space had potential—I mean, *real* potential. I'm talking about maybe this would cultivate my own business or institution of higher learning one day.

More than often, I would have a seat at the table with the executives to receive guidance in terms of how to execute the vision of the organization.

"Ms. Dream, how's Menace? How's recruitment going?" I met with Mr. Light in his office.

"It's going well, Mr. Light. I made flyers and went door to door recruiting in the community. There are a lot of young people who could really benefit from our program. However, I need buy-in from them. They need to see relevancy and consistency."

"I agree. We gotta get this thing on the ball. The councilman will be visiting that project in just a few weeks. We also have a major conference that we are planning, along with a documentary," said Mr. Light.

"The program is picking up momentum. I'm on board. I know I have recruited 15 youth on just door-to-door canvassing. But I'm also gonna reach out to some of my folks who work in high schools who could essentially enroll their students into our program," I responded.

"Yes. That's the mind-set that you must have. Progressive. Forward-thinking. At the end of the day, that's what our funders want to see—the numbers. Then, it's all about service and meeting the needs of the young people," said Mr. Light.

"I promise we will get our numbers and max out. My concern is getting the place up to standard. Have you seen it lately? It needs to be thoroughly cleaned. We need desks, bookshelves, maybe a new paint job, and cosmetics so that the environment is welcoming. That's important."

"Certainly, young lady. I'll send my maintenance guys down there throughout the week to help get the job done. Also, connect with 'Big C.' You share the space with him. He runs the other day-to-day programs as well in the basement."

"Yes, Mr. Light, I sure will."

"Check in with me next week so that we can get the train moving. Also, I'll send our CFO, Mr. Raymond, to you as well to get the supplies you need."

"Thank you so much. I appreciate you." I understood his marching orders.
"I appreciate you too, Dream."

More than often, I would meet with Mr. Light, who was the president of the organization. He was tangible, long-winded, but he was an OG. I never tested him because I wanted to learn from him.

It would be weeks before I would see the maintenance crew. Yet, I bought cleaning supplies from the local Dollar Store so that I could start to take care of business. At the end of the day, it was my program, and I wanted the classrooms to reflect me. After an extensive cleaning of dust, spiderwebs, dirt, and mice droppings, I didn't mind working in the basement. I was my own department—no assistant, no intern, no crew—just me.

Mr. C was a big, chocolate, teddy bear who commanded the respect of the community. He was a super OG with a super heart for the people. He was a nice dude who wanted to know more about me. Monday through Friday, I gave him surface. His side of the basement was definitely renovated. Bright yellow and green colors, clean floors, computers, a nice office accompanied by polished wood desks, swivel chairs, and flat-screen TVs.

Big C was welcoming when it came to me. He was the first to open and the last to close.

"Hey, Dream," he would greet me as I would come in.
"Hey, C, how are you?"
"I'm blessed. Can I get you anything? We got some water and juices and snacks." He began grabbing stuff for me to nibble on.
"Thanks so much." I received it in gratitude.
"How are things going with your program? You need some stuff?" He was inquisitive.
"I need desks, two bookshelves, chairs . . . just the essentials, you know," I said.
"I got you. We got plenty of furniture in the community room. I'm gonna bring it to your classrooms. All you need to do is wipe it down."

"I appreciate that'cause I was wondering when I would get at least chairs for these classrooms. My program starts in a few days, and I need to set up. I'm starting to feel like I'm a janitor and not a program director."

"Oh, Lawd," he chuckled. "You gotta do what you gotta do. We all started at the bottom. Mr. Light wants to see what you're made of. A li'l pretty young lady like yourself may be scared to roll up her sleeves."

"Oh, trust, I ain't eva been scared," I laughed.

"Oh yeah?"

"Oh yeah, C. I'm from Cali. I'm from L.A. I ain't ever been one to run. I just need to be equipped." The hood girl in me neva pumped fake.

"Well, I'm gonna help you get some stuff in here so you can do what you need to do. That's why I'm here. I've been with the Men of Valor for 10 years."

"Wow! That's a long time. But I guess it's not if you love what you do."

"You get the picture." He began grabbing chairs and desks and moving them to the classrooms.

I felt relieved.

I would spend the next few days utilizing my connects at the high schools to enroll more and more students. Our maximum number required by our grant was 40 students. I had 30 students, so I was on my way. I figured once the program actually began, participants would tell their friends how good it was, and they would tell their friends. Word of mouth would give me favor, plus the program had so many benefits. It provided educational tutoring, mentoring, paid stipends, and college preparation for high school students. Sheesh, I wish I had those types of opportunities when I grew up. All I had was a "dollar and a dream," and my belief system would take me a long way.

My colleagues who were counselors truly helped me with promoting the program to their students, and enrollment was booming for me in that basement corridor. The schedule was in effect, and I was working with high schoolers, Monday–Friday, from 1:00 p.m.–6:00 p.m. I was a teacher, tutor, college applicant reviewer, counselor, and "auntie" to many. I was genuine and REAL, and even though I was raised on the West, my mind-set was of an East Coast woman.

Big C had a big mouth, and I know he was Mr. Light's eyes and ears. Next thing you know, all these other execs from the organization would pop up. It was a smooth, ol'-school brotha who was the VP of the organization who appeared to have seen the world and back. His name was Mr. Fab, and, indeed, he was fabulousssssss. He was so in tune with everything. He would pull up in the hood in his grandiose Cadillac, and he had RESPECT all over his name. Mr. Fab would often check up on me and shoot the breeze.

His stroll through the basement could never be duplicated.
"Heyyyyyyy, baby girl. How's it going down here?"
"All is blessed. As you can see, class is in session, and I'm working with our new students on their homework." I leaned over to review a student's paper.
"I'm so proud of you. It's just you, and you're running this program perfectly. The young people are engaged." He smiled and looked around to see five youth. The rooms were bright. Meaningful posters of Malcolm, "Biddy" Mason, Oprah, and Tupac were on the walls. I had a pretty smile but a revolutionary mind.

"Class, please say hello to Mr. Fab. He's the vice president of the Men of Valor."
"Hiiiiiii," the two young ladies and three young men lifted their heads and spoke to Mr. Fab.

"Y'all looking good. Keep up the good work. You're in good hands," said Mr. Fab.

I walked him out to the front of my office.

"This is working. They're engaged. It was dark down here, but now, there's a bright light. Keep keeping on. Mr. Raymond should be coming down here shortly to take inventory of what you need and to go over some financial components."

"Cool. We never met, but that would be nice."

"You never met, huh? You two will have a lot in common. He's a major key to this organization. Also, it's good that you're getting this program up to speed because a councilman and mayor are scheduled to do a walk-through."
"A walk-through? We just got here." I was nervous.
 "Yea, Dream, there has been so much killing going on in this community that we are here to revive it and put in place interventions like your program," he said.
"That walk-through will be major. You'll be a part of it. They are used to seeing us men. But to see a sista, a young sista, is pivotal."
"I'm honored to do the work. At the end of the day, I want to help change the negatives into positives and give these young people a sense of HOPE."
"And you are, baby girl," he said, shaking my hand.
"Okay, I need to get back to the classroom, Mr. Fab. It was good seeing you." I shook his hand and began walking to the classroom. The students were talking amongst themselves and appeared to be sharing notes, which was a good thing. I observed their conversation and body language for a few minutes. They were bonding. Two of them went to the same school and had seen each other in passing. I intervened.
"When I was your age, I didn't want to become a teacher. I wanted to be a journalist, a writer, or entertainment reporter. I wanted to be on TV. I wanted to be a celebrity." I grabbed their attention as I stood in the center of the classroom.
"For real?" Alia, who was a ninth-grader, responded.

"Yea, I wanted to be a celebrity."

"So how did you get here?" she asked.

"Long story. But I graduated from college, then worked as a journalist and writer. I wrote two books that were published and lived in New York for a short stint. I was young and free. Then I lost my job during the terrorist attacks and moved to D.C. as an adult and not a college student," I reflected.

"Wow, Ms. Dream. You been to a lot of places," said Martin.

"Yeah, I have, but when I came to D.C., the only jobs that were available that paid were teaching. I started teaching special ed. Then I taught badass high schoolers with behavior problems. Then I worked as a speech writer."

"Dang, how old are you again?" Alia asked.

"Old enough to be your auntie," I giggled.

"But at the end of the day, I chose to work back in the community. I could have worked in the White House, but I chose to raise my son on my own. And I chose to come back to the grit of it all and make an impact. So, that's the level of seriousness about your future that I want you to have when you come down here."

"Yes!" all the students said in unison.

"Man, that's respect," said a tall, slim kid named Terrence. "*That's* what's up."

"You guys have about 15 minutes left before you depart. Wrap up your homework. Make sure you respond to the journal on the board and clean up."

As I walked into my office to just sit and think, Mr. Raymond greeted me at the office door.

"You must be Ms. Dream," he smiled.

He was tall, dark, slim, and had a Colgate smile.

"Yes, I'm Dream," I smiled back and motioned him to enter my office. "Please have a seat."

"Thank you. I can see already that this place has been cleaned up. It has never looked this good. And I'm sure you had a lot to do with it. That's why I'm here. I wanna discuss the budget, a contract, and any supplies you may need. Plus, since you are a part of the executive leadership, I want to talk so we can build a rapport with you as well."

"Cool, let's talk."

"You have a budget of close to $100,000 a year. More than half of that is your salary. You have room to hire two more people. Or you can hire a strong assistant and budget the money for activities," he said, pulling out all spreadsheets with hella numbers.

"This is your salary. These are line items for a program assistant and case manager. Let us know what you want to do. You have a line item for supplies. I have a supply sheet for you to fill out. List everything you need so I can process it for you." He spoke fast and expeditiously.

It felt like Christmas in the business world.

"You gotta monitor your own budget. Here is a copy for your records. At the end of the year, you gotta spend everything because that are the terms for the grant."

"So, zero by the end of each year?"

"Yes, zero."

"Okay, I got it. I'll fill out my supply sheet now. We need basic stuff like books, a TV, and a DVD player so that everyone can stay abreast of current events. They could also watch relevant movies and documentaries."

"Yes, add everything."

Mr. Raymond was cool.

"So, where did you go to school?"

"I went to Bison University."

"Bisonnnnnn!" he chanted. "That's my alma mater, years ago. Then I know what you are made of. I know how hard you had to go. I'm a Proud Bison!" He did a bounce rock.

"So am I. I wouldn't change my college experience for anything. It was the best!"

"Mine too. You are cut from a different cloth, though. I watched you in your interview. You were poised, intelligent, unafraid, and full of ideas. That's why we chose you."

"There was an entire team in that interview. I don't remember seeing you."

"I was there, and you were the best candidate for this position. Plus, you're a young woman. We need balance at this point."

"I'm so glad I was chosen. There's so much history here. I did my research, and what this organization has done has transformed so many lives. That's what life is about if you can reach one." I continued to fill out my supply sheet. I didn't miss a beat.

"Yes. Are you ready to meet and see these politicians? They're coming through Menace and will want to see all the programs to ensure the funds of the city are being used properly," he said firmly.

"Yes, I stay ready. All I can do is be honest. In this short time, we definitely have made progress. Big C is doing his thing. I'm doing mine. It's working for the good."

"Excellent. I'm going to review your supply list and process it. You should have everything in a week, definitely before they come. Keep up the good work." He zipped up his briefcase and began his exit.

"Take care, Mr. Raymond. Thanks again."

I began organizing my desk. I placed the budget facedown for me to review over the following days. Then I went back into the classroom and reviewed the sign-in sheet and the sign-out sheet. The students pushed their seats in. I gave them all pounds, and they headed out. I wrote down the journal and activity for the following day. As I sat in one of the desks, I realized that I was living a purpose-driven life. I wasn't sure how long I would be here, but what was clear is that I would make a change in their lives.

Then I turned off the lights and grabbed my belongings. My son was in aftercare, and I only had 12 minutes to get up the street, but I'd get there. I turned off the lights and closed my office door. I made sure that I let Big C know that I was gone for the day. I damn near skipped to my convertible Cruiser. It seemed like time was never on my side, and deadlines were daily. If I could steal 30 minutes for myself, I would be a "bad mutha, shut yo' mouth."

King's school was within 2 miles of my job, and I was there in a jiffy. I refused to get a late fee, so I pushed as if I had a Maserati.

The aftercare aide always had my back. Ms. Lonnie was his day care aide when he was an infant and looked out for me at all times. She was thorough and admired from afar my determination as a single mother. As off the hook King was, she knew how to check him and get him together. There were 3 minutes left. She stood with four kids at the front door of the school.

"Hey, girl, how was work?"

"It was good. I can't complain."

"You all suited and booted. Look at you. No red lipstick today."

"No lipstick at all. Hell, today, I didn't even get a lunch break. I'm taking one tomorrow, though. This shit is taxing." I swung my ponytail like a white girl.

"Yea, you better eat. You can't be running on fumes. Your boi was actually good today."

"He was? Thank God."

"I was good, Mommy!" King said, excited.

"Mommy is so proud of you." I hugged my baby and put his backpack on his back.

"Have a good night, Ms. Lonnie. Thanks for holding shit down. You go in at like 8:00 a.m. to 6:00 p.m. You're a G."

"Girl, I try. We try."

I gave her a pound, grabbed my son's left hand, and we walked to the car.

"What we eating, Ma? Can we eat chicken wings and french fries?"

"Fa' sho' 'cause Mommy ain't cooking. I'll order it now so that by the time we get home, the Chinese people will be there."

"Yayyyy." King was always happy when you mentioned chicken because he loved fried chicken, especially from the carryout. I wished I were the type of mother that could prepare at least five home cooked meals for my son and me, but trying to build my career, raise my son, and advance in life wouldn't give me the energy to come home to cook daily.

Our house was about 35 minutes from school. Even in traffic, I was at peace. I just needed time to chew up the day and digest it. The music was low. The wind was brisk but not too cold.

Kenya texted me.

I'm at the house. Whatchu want to eat?

I'm ordering carryout. The day was long.

Cool. I missed you. I could whip up something for you guys, if you like.

I missed you too like shit. No, we're good, I texted back.

Missed you too. I just wanna love you, baby.

You can. I need it.

I'm here drinking, thinking about you.

What you drinking?

Some Clear.

Oh Lawd, don't drink too much!

I'm not, baby. Just waiting for you.

I never knew my destinations in life, but I was clear that God always had me, and in that, I was comforted. Didn't really see myself at the Men of Valor for a long time, but my goal was to soak up everything. I would be like SpongeBob, soaking up information, strategy, leadership, running programs, and learning how to take my career to the next level. Striving, thriving, and riding. Nothing was permanent, not a job, not a man, and not even life itself. I was far from the bottom. It was an upward movement, and it felt good to be empowered as a woman, as a Black person in America and as a mother.

As I pulled up to my house, I saw Kenya paying the carryout dude for our food.

King rushed out of the car to greet the food and Kenya at the door. Then my cell phone began vibrating.

I had a text message from Mr. Light.

Hi, Sista Dream. The councilman confirmed he would be in Menace next Wednesday. Be ready to rock 'n' roll.

I'm on board, I texted back, deeply exhaling.

Good and enjoy your weekend.

You too, I typed back.

I had a weekend to do me and to live a li'l. I was like Erykah Badu. My goal was "concentratin' on my music, lover, and my baby." My music was activating dreams.

# Chapter 3

## Shades of Love

I was brown, cascaded with yellow undertones with native American eyes and cheekbones. Adorned with West African lips and three rolls on my neck that are associated with beauty, according to other West Africans and elders that I would meet in the Western Hemisphere.

Chocolate-covered in the summers, but a pretzel-colored brown during the winter, and hazelnut in the spring. I was thick, not all over but in the right places. I had a slight FUPA credited to lazy weight gain, stress, and a C-section cut that made it evident. I had stretch marks that could walk away with the healing of shea butter, and if I had lost 20 pounds and went to Yoga consistently. My face was almost perfect. It had depth, expression, no wrinkles, no inconsistencies—it was asymmetric. I was beautiful with imperfections in size and portions. I was ALL WOMAN for a man that dated thick and loved a few rolls, a pretty face, and an amazing smile.

My lips were Akoma shaped and electrifying in every color. Men would lust in ways that read, "I wanna fuck her. I want her to have my baby. I can trust her. She looks good on my arm—but I may have to leave her 'cause she surpasses my level."

That part.

Loving the wrong man broke me into pieces that took years to mend, but God showed me how to fuel my pain and turn it into purpose. God also revealed that royalty can't mingle with swine, and that more than often, people are simple assignments and not assigned to my destiny. All was not lost because there was something much greater blooming in my womb and called through the offspring. Amazed at my own recovery, I wouldn't have traded my life for anything in the world.

My heart was healed and guarded. Kenya was good for me. He was a breath of fresh air. He adored me, loved me for me, and made me feel as though I always had an army behind me. Waking up to him was like "sex on the beach" every day. The conversations were cool, sometimes simple and sometimes spiritual and sometimes just plain crazy.

He was addicted to the street life, and I understood that I was his angel. I was addicted to broken-ass niggas, and he understood that he had to protect my heart. We had a quiet understanding. He never could understand how a man could leave his son for dead. He never could understand how a man could leave a woman like me to the wolves. Yet, he comforted me in ways that I never wanted to go away from him. It was hard making love in the mornings on a weekday and having the energy to go to work—yet, he motivated me.

Kenya was a beast in the kitchen by nature and a line cook by trade. He was an ambitious gangsta with a GED and G Code. Niggas from where we live previously either loved him or hated him. I never wanted to know why—some secrets in the streets I didn't want to be exposed to.

My weekends were cozy. It was spring, and the sun blushed on my face. King always went with his dad's mom, Coco, on the weekends, which offered me a much-needed break. It was hard balancing it all. Coco understood me. We were kindred spirits, but like most Black mothers, she loved her son despite his wrongdoings. Coco adored King to pieces, and I think whatever she had missed with raising Solomon, she comprised it in her love and quality time with King. She was tough, yet beautiful. She was of Native American descent with the fire of an African queen. My mama was 3,000 miles away, and I needed a mama figure . . . Someone who could love me unconditionally and motivate me to do better. Someone who could help me with my son and have a connection to the father. Even Kenya respected Coco, and she saw something in him.

I woke up from a deep sleep.

"Mommy, Mommy, Mommy!" King was up early this morning. I never could understand why this kid never would sleep to 11:00 a.m. or noon on a Saturday morning like most kids . . . Why couldn't he just savor sleep? He always was the first to wake up and the last to go to sleep.

"Mommy, it's Saturday."

"Yes, it's Saturday, baby."

"Yes! Can I go with Grandma?"

"You sure can."

"Yes! I'm gonna pack up all my stuff." King stood in front of my bed.

"Dang, champ, you pressed." Kenya got all in the business.

"Kenya, I was talking to my muva," King snapped back with his raspy voice.

"Yea, but I was just saying, champ."

We all laughed.

I laid in a fetal position with a cotton-candy pink comforter wrapped around my entire body.

Kenya was cooking up breakfast looking like Ving Rhames in *Baby Boy*, except that he wasn't naked. He had on boxers and chocolate-colored house shoes.

The aroma of honey butter biscuits, turkey bacon, scrambled eggs, and scrapple permeated the house. His food was always on 1,000 percent.

I was as simple as a Cinnamon Dolce Latte and a croissant from Starbucks, so I cherished full plates and great meals.

I rubbed my eyes to make sure that my lashes were still on. I saw Ruby Woo stains of MAC on my cotton pastel gray sheets. I tapped the crown of my hair to see if my hair was still perfectly wrapped. It wasn't. It was all over the place. But I had 22 inches of Indian straight hair parted down the middle, and my weave brush would get me together.

I was a tomboy in the bedroom who wore V-neck shirts and boy shorts. I was sexy in my own way. My eyes spoke in a language that a nigga's dick would stay hard, and my morning breath made me imperfect until applying Colgate. I was normal yet a beautiful canvas that only artists understood.

I ran to the bathroom to pee, brush my teeth, and wash my face. It was morning, and it would take me 'til noon to wake up. Some days, the grind mode exhausted me.

I walked into the kitchen. "Hey, Kenya." I went to hug him.

"Baby, you slept good. You was snoring and slobbering."

"For real?"

"Yep. You hungry, ain't you?"

"Yes, you know." I sat on our suede dining chair, waiting for my plate.

"Here's your plate, and here's King's plate." He laid down three placemats before placing our plates on the table.

"Thanks, beau, for everything. This looks really yummy." I kissed Kenya on the forehead.

There was nothing like breakfast on Saturdays. We all bonded over food, and when King would be gone, it was time for good loving. King sat his li'l self at the table.

"Can I get some milk, please?" This child could not survive without milk or water. Ever since he was an infant, he never liked juice. He just never had a taste for sweets, which means most of my money went to a Spartan diet. It was chicken, fish, vegetables, rice, chips, Cheez-Its, water, and milk. Every now and then, I would treat myself to a Diet Coke, and Kenya would grab his Oatmeal Creme Pies. King was solid as a rock.

"What time you dropping King off with Coco?" Kenya inquired while demolishing his food.

"In an hour or so."

"Ma, I already got all my stuff packed up," King assured me.

"Fa' real? You ready, huh, man?" I said.

"Yep."

"Well, let me chill for like an hour and get myself together, and then you'll be at Grandma's soon after."

"'K." He went into his room and began watching his Saturday-morning cartoons. As long as King's stomach was full, he was copacetic.

"How was work this week?" Kenya liked catching up.

"It was cool. A lot of demands."

"Like what?"

"Like the founders of the organization wanted to make sure that I met all my numbers. That the program got off the ground, and that the classroom spaces were set up. Plus, the councilman for that ward will be at my center soon."

"Politics. You know how that go. But you a smart woman. Do you like what you do?"

"Yes, I love it. I feel like I'm doing something rewarding. I feel like I'm in my element."

"That's what matters most. They keep cutting my hours on my job, and I feel like I wanna do something else."

"But you cook so damn good. You're a natural."

"Yea, but I need a position with benefits, Dream. You got benefits. I need it all. I need more money. I wanna contribute more. You know we looking at the bigger picture."

"It's not always about money. You cook, clean, make love to me, inspire me . . . I love you for who you are."

"Thanks, baby." Kenya leaned over to kiss and hug me.

We held each other tightly. Kenya was an intricate part of my life, and I was growing. We were growing together. He wasn't insecure. His very presence secured my future. He was loving, strong, and he listened. We both got up to get our outfits together for the day. We planned to bring King to Coco and then hit the town and just enjoy each other.

We took a blazing shower together. He would wash down every roll, every insecurity, not missing a spot of my externals or internals. He would lather my back, and I would lather his. Our energies were so connected and intertwined. He would dry me off and lotion me down like I was his child. He never missed a spot.

I put on all-black everything and a blazer. Black DKNY jeggings, an off-the-shoulder fitted top, and an old navy blazer. I rocked some Steve Madden ankle boots. I took pride in my hair, and it was together 95 percent of the time. I didn't have a full weave, this time. I had a few pieces of Indian straight hair that came to the middle of my back. The lipstick color of the season was Ruby Woo by MAC. Red just did wonders for me. It was striking, intriguing, and sexy. It was my way of saying "fuck you" to the naysayers!

King was always ready to go. He had his own sense of style—True Religion jeans, a turquoise polo, and his Jordans. He grabbed a polo hat as well and rocked it to the back. While King and I were vain as heck, Kenya was simple. Jeans, a fresh white T, New Balance sneakers, and a gray Ralph Lauren hoodie. I would buy him pieces of some fly shit, and he would simplify it, fa' real. King, in no time, had his Incredible Hulk suitcase on wheels with his clothes, pajamas, and a few toys. He was standing at the door with a look like, "Ma, come on."

"Okay, son, I'm coming. I'm coming, son." I grabbed my leather coat just in case the weather switched up on us. Kenya locked up the house.

We hopped in the car and headed to Coco's home, which was less than 5 minutes away. As soon as we pulled up, she was posted on the porch smoking a loosie. King could barely wait for the car to stop.

"Granmaaaaaa, Granmaaaaaaaa," King rolled down the window and yelled.

"Hold up, boy, we gonna stop the car." Kenya busted out laughing. I put the car in park to get him out of it; otherwise, he would have opened the door in excitement while I was driving.

"King, boi, get your stuff!" He ran out of the car into his grandma's arms.

I grabbed his suitcase anyhow and took it to Coco. They were hugging each other like they hadn't seen each other in a month of Sundays.

"Hey, Dream. You look cute. Where you going?" Coco was nosy.

"Prolly to grab a few drinks and maybe out on the town," I gleamed.

"You look cute. Well, you deserve it. You work hard, so you need some chill time. Hey, Kenya." She waved to him.

"Hey, Coco." Kenya got out of the car and stood against the car door. "How you been?"

"I'm good. You look good too." She blew out her cigarette smoke.

"Thanks, Coco."

"Well, you two enjoy yourselves." She leaned toward my ear. "You got you a thoroughbred. He's different, Dream."

"You think?"

"Yea, I've been observing him. He got some oomph to 'im," she said in wise judgment. "He not like the rest."

"OK. Well, if you like him, I love him." I smiled so hard. Her opinion mattered to me. Coco had seen life before and could get a good read on a person.

"Go 'head. I got King. That's my baby. Come on, li'l Solomon. I got some new toys and gadgets for you to test out. Let's play." She was ready for her g'baby.

"Thank you, Coco. Love you, King," I yelled.

Kenya and I both hopped in the car.

"Where you wanna go?" he asked.

"Let's go to Georgetown."

"Georgetown, it is." I began driving to the highway. We were about 30 minutes away. It was windy, but the sun was out.

Kenya put in an ol'-school CD with some classic Teddy Pendergrass, Al Green, and Chaka Khan. We jammed all the way to G-Town singing songs that our parents grooved to. In my mind, I was Chaka Khan or Chaka's long lost daughter. When "Sweet Thing" came on, I was in such a zone. I sang my doggone heart out. Kenya whispered the lyrics. We snapped together, rocked back and forth in our seats, and sang together,

*"Don't you hear me talking, baby. Love me now, or I'll go crazyyyyyyy."*

Life was good.

"Whatchu wanna go to, a bar or lounge or an actual restaurant?"

"I wanna go to a lounge. Something with a li'l flare."

"What you got a taste for? Asian, Mexican, or American food?"

"Let's do American. I don't want a whole lot of food, but a few appetizers and a couple of drinks will do."

We pulled up in front of a lounge called Sugar. I had been there once or twice. They had good juicy burgers and a variety of wings. I found a parking space a few feet away from the joint. We walked in, and the place had a crowd, but it wasn't too busy. We walked in side by side.

"Would you like to sit at a booth?" asked the greeter.

"Yes, we would," Kenya responded.

We followed her and sat down at a booth facing a window.

"Good to have you to myself, baby."

"I know. I missed you like crazy. It's just good to do me."

"Right." He pulled my wrists toward his. "Baby, where you think all this is going?"

"You mean us?"

"Yea, like, you think this is long term? At this point, I feel like you are really the one for me."

"Yea, I'm starting to feel like that too. I just wanna make sure you don't hurt me like the others."

"Why would I do that to you?"

"I don't know why dem niggas hurt me like that."

I began scanning the menu to see what I wanted. I had my eye on an avocado turkey burger with mayo on a toasted bun. I didn't need no fries. I could go with a salad.

"Baby, I just want this to be right. Like I wanna secure shit," I responded.

"Yea, I understand. I just want you to let go of the past when you dealing with a real nigga like me. Understand all I want is your heart and loyalty. And you have shown me that you rocking with me."

"Hi. Sorry to interrupt, but are you ready to order?" A cute li'l blonde came and took our order.

"Yes, 'cause I'm hungry."

"You know what you want?" asked Kenya.

"Yes, can I order the avocado turkey burger with swiss cheese and mayo? Toasted bun. No fries."

"Would you like a salad then?"

"Yes, a salad with vinaigrette."

"And can I get the steak burger with ketchup and mayo, a li'l lettuce and tomato. You can add swiss cheese as well," Kenya put in his order.

"Would you like fries?" the waitress asked.

"Yes, fries."

"What would you like to drink?"

"Can I have a pomegranate martini?" I jumped right in.

"Yeah, lemme get a vodka and cranberry."

"OK, I got it." She took the menus away.

"But, baby, back to what I was saying. I love you. I'm with you. I remember when I met you, it was just you and your son. You was at the end of your struggle. Now, you at the beginning of something great. I wanna be there when you rise, fall, in between, or you need a shoulder to lean on."

"I appreciate you, luv. I do. I just need something constant and stable. I can't afford another heartbreak. I don't think my heart can take it." I looked away.

He softly grabbed my chin. "I know he broke you. But you are so much stronger now. More beautiful—more everything."

"Yea, but like, let's dig a li'l deeper. Were you raised with your mom and dad?"

"No."

"You didn't see your parents married. Did you see anyone married around you?"

"Yea, my homeboy was married, but he killed himself a couple of years ago."

"My mom and stepdad have been married since I was 5. My real father and mom were never married. But I have a foundation. Even though their marriage had a lot of drama, they showed me love. I seen it."

"So, you feel like 'cause my parents weren't married, I don't know what love is."

"Kinda." The truth entered.

The waitress gave us our drinks. I couldn't wait to take a big gulp of my martini. I should have asked for two. This conversation was going somewhere else. I wasn't sure if Kenya was the love of my life, or if he was here at the appointed time. I wasn't sure if he was a wolf in sheep's clothing. My desire was to test him out and see if he was the real deal before taking a major leap. I guess I was cool with playing house. I was cool with the Barbie and Ken relationship. It was nice. It wasn't too, too deep. It made sense.

"Kenya, I love you, but I think we should pace ourselves. Hopefully, you are the one I marry and have my daughter or son by."

"We would make a beautiful daughter, wouldn't we?" Kenya was downing that vodka.

"Yea, we would," we both laughed.

"Well, it's about living. It's about living life. We young. We got so much to do in our lifetime if God grants us a long life. I'm happy to be with you."

"I'm happy to be with you too."

Our food arrived.

"But real talk. Even King's grandma like me. Your friends like me. I'm a real nigga. I ain't gonna let nothing happen to you. I'ma guard your heart."

I began eating my burger, just thinking like, *Is he the one? Is he* really *the one?* He seemed like the right one for me. But I didn't want to roll the dice and crap out. I wanted to find out if there were some skeletons or secrets or other crazy shit out there that I needed to know about him. I had to let this chapter play out. Yes, the love, the protection, the sex, the food, and the relationship were amazing. I just needed to validate it.

"By the way, my grandma raised me. She showed me and my big cousins so much love. So I do know what love is," he asserted.

"We got relationship goals, man. We gonna figure all this stuff out."

"At the end of the day, man, I'm tired of dealing with these whack-ass broads out here. All they want is a nigga's money, rep, and protection. They not genuine."

I listened.

"My baby mama is bogus, man. She's selfish. I was in jail for a hot minute, and when I came home, she had another nigga. She didn't even let the bed get cold."

"Dang." I tuned into him.

"Yea, it wasn't really sincere between her and me. She appeared like a ride or die, but she ain't. She's an opportunist, and I don't respect her."

"Understood."

"But you are genuine. You a good girl, Dream, that has been hurt by these dirty-ass niggas. You were green and didn't know any better. You were just looking for love and didn't know you were dealing with wolves."

"Yea, that was me. I'm not looking for anything anymore. If good comes my way, I will embrace it. But that fool shit is for the birds." I sipped down my martini.

"Just wanna enjoy this part of the journey. This is a good part of the movie that I don't wanna miss. You in my movie, though. You got a main role," I giggled.

"Whatchu mean I got a main role? I'm gonna make everyone come see the movie. They jealous now of you, and you can't even see it because you're sweet."

"Yea, it seems like people always been jealous. Like damn, bitch, even when I lost everything, you was envying an illusion. Can't even let people know I'm happy."

"I know you in a better place. Shit, ain't no mice running around in the new place like in the old place. You ain't got crackheads banging at your door like before. You got a peace of mind, and your son is always happy. I'm happy for you and for us."

"Thanks, Ken. Love you."

"So, I got one question." He was adamant.

"Yea, shoot it."

"Do you trust me with your heart?"

"The jury is still out." I spit my liquor out.

"Whatchu mean? You don't trust me yet?"

"Dude, I got trust issues. Like *real* issues. Other than my stepfather, I never felt like a man sincerely loved me. It always came with a price. I suffered. I'd give my heart out. Keep getting pregnant and having abortions 'cause these niggas lie so bad. I gotta read the label and pay attention to the signs now and not be gully. But you, I love you and fucks with you hard. Let's just flow."

"Yea, we gon' flow."

Kenya ate his steak burger in a matter of minutes. He engulfed it. After we had about two rounds of drinks, we were full and good to go. The evening was young.

"Watchu wanna do? You wanna check out some stores and walk the town?"

"That will work. I would love to grab a few things."

"Yea, I want a pair of Armani shades," Kenya nodded.

"I need a new bag. Let's go check out Armani, Betsey Johnson, and a few boutiques."

"Yea, I know a few Arab cats who own some stores down the street. They got real stuff, and they gon' look out."

"Cool. Let me drink the rest of this." I was savoring it all.

"Look at you. I could use another one. When we get on our side of town, I'ma buy me a bottle."

"Dang, alchy."

"This liquor ain't nothin'. You already know." Kenya stood up to signal me to come on. He paid the bill. I put on my leather coat and left the tip.

"Thank you," said the waitress.

We both smiled. We was nice and tipsy. I had a few hundred on me, and I was gonna spend. Shopping was my Zen. It was a place where I could express myself without speaking . . . my happy place. We walked toward the Armani store, but I had MAC and Betsey Johnson on my mind too. We held hands like a real couple. We were young and fly, and we stood out.

"Baby, look at those shades, man." He pointed toward the mannequins and walked straight in.

"Eh, where are your shades, man?" he spoke directly to the salesman.

"Right there."

"OK, cool." Kenya began trying on shades, posing in the mirror. He was smiling. He had a pair of shades and began perusing the V-necks. He was in his zone. After a while, he forgot I was even right beside him. I started trying on the women's shades. I was a bit thick, so I knew I couldn't fit too many things. Armani was cut for the European size 6 and below, and I was a solid 12.

But there were a pair of glasses that I could stunt in. They adorned my face pretty well and gave my face life. I walked over to Kenya as he grabbed like three shirts . . . black, gray, and white. He was so simple. I was like, "Grab a purple one and replace the black. Do something different."

"Okay, baby. But this means I'm gonna have to get purple shoes to match."

"Oh Lawd. Okay, you got it. What you think of these?"

I flipped my 22-inch hair like I was somebody.

"You fancy, baby. I love 'em. We gonna stunt tonight." We walked to the cash register. Kenya immediately took the tags off his shades and mine and was like, "We gon' be twins. Here, put yours on."

We giggled as we both looked in the mirror together to make sure we were on point. Then he grabbed my left hand and carried his bag with his right.

"What next?"

"The MAC store, pleaseeee."

"Oh, shucks. We gon' be in there fa'eva."

"No, I think I know what I want. I wanna try a few new shades."

"Like brown?"

"Naw, you would never see me in brown. But maybe nude, maybe a cotton-candy lipglass."

"It's your time to shine." Kenya walked beside me like a real G.

We walked down the pebble stone concrete like we were in London. We were in our zone. We were connecting kinesthetically without force.

There were levels to this.

Shades to this.

Unorthodox.

# Chapter 4

## *Seat at the Table*

Work was my lab. It was my heaven on earth. A place of solace. A place where I could recover from pain. A place where I would grow and never regress.

*Work was my science experiment on myself. I could mask my insecurities and cover them with accolades and overachieving. No one would focus on the illmatic parts of me. I would become a winner. I would soar in places where most women only wish they could go. I would tread in places where most were afraid.*

I was clear that "men ruled the world," but women made the world evolve. Women gave the world height and depth. We were the souls enriched in nurture and emotion. The Men of Valor needed me, and I was their most prized possession.

On days like this, I was more emotional than rationale. I contemplated loving harder. *Often throughout my day, I would think about Kenya. He would help me to recover over a past lover. I was starting to feel like he could take me to a place where I would never wanna come back. He secured my heart. Yet, I held the key this time. The key to my heart would be hidden in a mysterious place. A place of peace that would take me years to find. It was buried so that I could not even destroy it.*

I sat in my office, drifting. I knew I had a big week ahead of me and a long year ahead, but life was a game of chess, and I had to move my pieces strategically. At the end of the day, I wanted to be a powerhouse . . . maybe a public figure, but one who could speak on behalf of the underdog. I desired to teach and transform the minds of the young and inspire women to do better. A spirit of hopefulness dwelled in me that was ready to unleash. I was in the right place at the right time. There were no windows in my office, but I imagined them to be there.

My office walls were dingy and could use a paint job, but there were substance and depth in the atmosphere. To the right of me was a poster that said *HOPE*, and to the left of me, *FACE FORWARD*. When I looked behind me, there was a photo of the legendary Maya Angelou, and in front of me was a large, framed picture of Malcolm X. My office was truly an expression of how I viewed life.

I heard footsteps.
"Hey, sista, you ready for tomorrow?" Big C walked straight into my office and asked.
"I believe so."
"It's gonna be a really huge day, and it's also gonna be good for you because you have really transformed this side of the building. I've been watching you these past few months, and you have really put it down," he said. "That's a strong quality. We're a unit."
"Thank you. You think?" I smiled. "It was a task."
"I know it was for me. Nothing in life is easy. You just gotta put your best foot forward, and your heart gotta be in it. I've been with these brothas for a long, long time. It's been a decade. I love what I do. I love coming to work. I wake up every morning in the mind-set that I will make a difference," Big C spoke.
"Me too. I just wanna see people succeed and win at whatever they set their minds to. I'm just assisting with engineering the process. If we don't invest in these young people, then who will? If we don't invest in our own, then no one will."
"Yes, you right, sis. Tomorrow, you will meet the councilman for this ward, along with maybe a few other council members, investors, and community members. You will get to take them on tour on your side and explain to them exactly what you do. Basically, they gave

us money to get this community together. They wanna see that we are doing what we said we would do."

"I gotchu. I'll write a few talking points for myself. I got me a nice li'l business suit."

"Okay, I see you," Big C giggled. "However I can help you, sis. We in this together. And if your youth need to get on the computers to do their assignments, homework, or projects, send them to this side to sign in, and they are welcome. We in this together."

"Thanks, C. I'm wit'chu. I meet with Mr. Light and Mr. Fab later today so that I can carry out what they need me to do."

"All right, that's good. I'm down the hallway if you need me." Big C began walking down the hall.

I opened my Dell and began checking my emails. The blessing was that I didn't have my email flooded with tasks after tasks like my previous job working for the college. There was only one email from Mr. Light and a few press releases from news outlets. The email read, **Meeting at the main office at noon.**

That was the difference between being supervised by a man vs. a woman. When I worked for women, my emails were jumping with tons of details, paragraph after paragraph. My nerves used to be so bad because I would have to organize by priority. The nature of a man was step by step. The nature of a woman was driven by multiplicity.

Mr. Light's ultimate goal was to do the work for the community, problem solve, and create a real-talk dialogue. He also wanted recognition, and I understood his vision.

During the day, I used my time wisely to create lessons and activities that I felt would be relevant to the youth. I also communicated with colleagues of mine who wanted to bring satellite programs to their high schools. Most of my colleagues I met in college, and they would do well in their fields as educators, social workers, and therapists. We could pick up the phone, and our conversations would be so on point. Our mission was to save a few.

My roster would grow. I was learning the youth. They were learning me. Together, we were building a system of trust. It didn't take them long to realize that I was authentic. You could talk to me, vibe with me, ask me for advice—I wasn't a desk mannequin. I was very tangible.

I heard a light knock at my door.

"Yes, come in."

"Helloooo, I'm here to meet with Ms. Dream."

I smiled. "I'm Ms. Dream. How can I help you?"

"I'm Neka. I was referred by the agency to your program." She was dark brown, petite, and stood around 5 feet.

"Hey, Neka. Have a seat. What year are you in?"

"I'm a senior, but I only have half a day, so I have time on my hands. I need help getting into college. I gotta get out of this place. I can't be in this town forever." She jumped right on in.

"Well, Neka, I can help you, but you gotta be consistent and real. I'm a college graduate, and I was like you. I couldn't wait to get away from my town, my home. I wanted to see the world. Do you have your ID so I can add you to my roster?"

"Yes, I have a referral and my ID." She was ready.

"Cool." I took her information and began adding her to my roster.

"I go to Charles High School. It's not too far from here, and I gotta car. You don't got any office work I can do?"

"We gotta stay focused. One step at a time. You said you wanna go to college, right? So we gonna take the steps we need to take to get you in college. Then we can go to the next level. How are your grades?"

"My grades are good. I'm like a 2.8 GPA student."

"I need you to get those grades up. One C and the rest As and Bs. Nothing under a 3.0. So, the next time you come in, we'll look at your grades and figure out where to strengthen them."

"Wow. OK. I just learned something. I thought my grades were good."

"They're decent, but you're competing with the rest of the country to get into college, so you can't be average. You gotta be above average. You gotta be top of your class. You gotta stand out. We're gonna take you there."

"Well, I live with my aunt, and there's always some drama with her. Sometimes, it's hard to stay focused 'cause of what's going on at home."

"I understand. That's why we gonna get you to a place where you have options. A place where you can go to a college that will offer you opportunities. Give me some time. I'ma get you there." I held no bars.

"Thank you so much 'cause I need it. You pretty young, huh?"

"I'm 31. I'm not that young. I have a son."

"Oh, for real? Well, you look good for your age."

"You think so? Well, thank you. Appreciate the compliment."

"What will my schedule be?"

"Start reporting here between 1:00 p.m. and 2:00 p.m., Monday through Thursday. That way, I can work with you individually. I'm gonna show you around."

We began walking through the basement.

"Here is the main classroom. Then there's a second classroom, which is more of a study lounge. Here's the bathroom for the girls."

We continued walking.

"You know you in the hood, right?"

"Yea, I know it ain't no crystal stair."

"These dudes be beefing. Shoot-outs. To be honest, I didn't really wanna come over here, but I wanted to see what you had to offer."

"I didn't wanna come over here either. But you can't live your life in fear. And life is about taking risks. You gotta go to places that people won't go just to get ahead . . . and offer something."

"You right. It's cool down here. It looks way better on the inside than the outside."

"Yes, we got a stage and a kitchen too down this way." I showed her.

"This is nice."

I walked her to the other side, where Big C's computer lab and learning lab was set up.

"It's all bright on this side. Y'all even got computers and stuff."

"You got another student?" Big C got out of his leather chair to greet Neka.

"How you doing?" she smiled.

"I'm good. Welcome to the basement. We show nothing but love to the young people. You working with a good sista," he assured her.

"I see." You couldn't miss Neka's braces. She smiled from ear to ear.

We walked toward the front exit.

"So, now, you know where you are, my sista. I should expect to see you the day after tomorrow at 1:00 p.m., to be specific."

"Thank you so much." She hugged me.

"You got it and be safe."

"You too." She departed.

"You bringing them in, huh, Ms. Dream?" Mr. C didn't miss a beat.

"Slowly but surely." I walked back into my office and plopped myself back into my seat. Something about my destiny connected me to individuals who needed me to plant a seed and help them grow. In my heart, I knew Neka was a symbol of young ladies that I would reach in some fashion. It was inevitable. It was spiritual . . . planned before I even got here.

I closed my eyes, meditated and prayed quietly. I needed guidance. I needed to hear a word from God. I was thankful in the realest way. Silence was the best atmosphere for me.

After about 20 minutes, I wrapped up my laptop, notepad, and pen and placed them in my leather laptop bag and headed across town to meet the executive team. Not knowing how long this meeting was gonna be, I stopped at a Starbucks to grab a Venti Banana Chocolate Smoothie. It was the boost of energy that I needed and a snack replacement just in case my days were too long.

I pulled up in front of the company headquarters. Brothas were always in and out of the building. They indeed were a unified front. As a woman, it was just so good to see positive depictions of Black men, right in front of my face. They were always respectful.

One of the lead outreach workers came to my door. I paid attention to every staff person near and far. I watched their movements, their level of attentiveness, effectiveness, and how they carried out their duties. Lee was a native who was in his early 40s. He had experienced life, you could tell, but he had heart and was unafraid to go into the trenches. He loved his city, he loved the youth, and you could see him pull up in front of the building, bumping the local music, which was Go-Go. It was easy to see that Mr. Light and Mr. Fab had respect for him, and what I admired about him the most is that he was flexible and could assist any program. At times, I would see him cleaning the main building, assisting Mr. C with his program, checking up on me to see if I needed assistance, and even do outreach work in Menace. He had an openness to him. He reminded you of a big brother with an "uncle" feel.

"You need some help, Ms. Dream?" Lee stood on the curb like security.

"No, Lee, thank you. I packed light today."

"Oh yeah. What, you coming to the meeting?" he was aware.

"Yep, I'm here for the executive meeting." I flexed my she-power.

"Yea, I was briefed by Light and them. Y'all got that grand opening coming up in Menace. I'm going to get that place clean from head to toe, buff the floors, and move a couple of things around," he explained.

"*That's* what's up."

"Some days you will see me down there as support for you and Big C. However I can help, I will. I got y'all's back. I love how you helping the youth. I peeped your classrooms and all of the inspirational stuff I see on the wall."

"You pay attention, pay attention." I stepped out of the car and stood next to him. "I appreciate all support, brotha. Thank you."

"Lemme know if you need anything, anything." He was sincere.

"Yes, Lee, I'ma need you. What days you gonna be in Menace?"

"Monday, Wednesday, and Friday from 1:00 p.m. to 6:00 p.m.," said Lee.

"Perfect, 'cause that's when my program is going on. So, definitely come to my program side. Come sit in the classrooms, observe, introduce yourself to the youth, and you can assist them with their homework, do some tutoring, and just your presence as a positive male will be great," I explained.

"Bet. I got you, sis! I'm there. See you soon." Lee made it plain. It was like I was working in a '70s era where Black pride and Black love were relevant. That was the environment, and I loved it. I grabbed my laptop, purse, and smoothie and began walking up the building stairs. Midway, I stopped in my tracks and saw this brotha who was finnnnnneeeeee. He stood about 6 foot 3. He was chocolate brown with a hint of red undertones. He had a low-cut Caesar and a faded goatee. Although he had a fresh white tee, some blue jeans and nice sneakers on, his whole style had me floored. He was absolutely beautiful. I couldn't move. I needed him to know that he caught my eyes by surprise. I was stuck.

"Hi, how you doing? You are so gorgeous," he spoke. He was breathtaking. He spoke and stopped.

"Lord Jesussssss! Hi, how you doing?" I sang.

"I'm great. What's your name?" I couldn't believe a brotha that fine even spoke.

"My name is Dream." I was so unfocused that I forgot what I even came for. "And yours?"

"What a beautiful name. My name is Roca."

"Roca? That's unique."

"Yea, it's Spanish for 'rock.'"

"You Spanish?"

"Naw. I got Trini roots. You work here?"

"Yea, I do." I stared directly into his eyes. "I work with the executive team. I run the new program in Menace."

"Oh, okay. I'm with the truancy team. Your eyes are so clear," he said, looking into my eyes. "Where you from?"

"Cali," I gushed.

"I ain't met a girl from Cali. Wow. What made you come way out here?"

"Long story."

"Take down my number so that I can hear about your story." was so confident. "Put it in your phone."

I pulled my cell phone out of my bra. I was so nervous. I didn't know him from a can of paint, yet his positive vibrations had me at a standstill.

He said each number slowly, and I didn't miss a beat. I entered each number and pressed *save* twice.

"You got it?"

"I sure do."

"Good. So I hope to hear from you really soon. We work for the same organization, so we should be seeing each other often." He missed no punches.

"Roca, I'll be calling you. I'm gonna head to my meeting now."

"OK, love."

He walked down the stairs, and I took my time walking up the stairs to gather my thoughts. I needed a few minutes to get myself poised and professional before walking through the conference room. I placed my phone back into my bra, knocking that silly smirk off my face. I was dazed.

The hallways of Valor were heavy with traffic. Everyone was moving fast, demonstrating respect by speaking gently to one another. I walked into the bathroom to get myself together. Donna Karan pink button-down, Anne Klein slacks, and a pair of Enzo Angiolini black ankle boots—I was saucy and professional.

I never knew what to really expect when going into a meeting with Mr. Light. I said my prayers and walked into the boardroom. Mr. Light was getting settled, Mr. Fab and Mr. Raymond were already present, and so was Big C. There was a sista there who was a veteran for the organization and had been working for them for nearly 20 years. She was in my initial interview with Valor, and she was intimidating to most, just not me. She was black as coal, thick as a brick house, about 52 years old, and she wore shoulder-length locs.

Her name was Queenie. I sat directly across from her and adjacent to Mr. Fab, who sat to the right of Mr. Light.

"Good afternoon! God is great. He woke us up this morning, didn't he? And I'm glad. We've got to be glad because we are truly blessed." Mr. Light stood at the head of the maple oak conference table. "These are exciting times for the Men of Valor, and we are making a major difference in the communities that we serve." He made eye contact with us individually.

"Tomorrow, Councilman Small will be doing a press conference in Menace to discuss his plans for the community and also to address how programs like ours will highly focus on violence intervention and prevention. He will also tour the basement to see how we are utilizing the funds that his office has allocated and how the youth are benefiting."

"That's major. This is a major blessing," said Mr. Fab.

"So, we have to ensure that what we said we would do is *exactly* what we are doing," added Mr. Raymond.

"Yes, and we are really doing the work," Queenie chimed in. "I know in abscondence, we track the young people down and bring them back to safety. It's not a game with us. We got a 98 percent retention rate."

"Great work, Queenie," said Mr. Light.

"It's my job to ensure that we are fiscally responsible and that everything we wrote in our budgets is being spent and the funders can actually see the difference that we have made as an organization because the young people are benefiting," added Mr. Raymond.

"The community knows we are in the house," interjected Big C.

"We show them love, and in response, they show us love. It's about making positive deposits. We got the computer lab up and running. It's bright and colorful. The youth and their families can be comfortable. The learning lab is up. We have the flat screens up, and CNN and educational channels are running."

"That's it, Light. That's it, Raymond," Mr. Fab spoke. "They gotta see the work. We can't hide it because it's amazing."

"And, Dream, Ms. Dream Angelou has hit the ground running. She has indeed transformed the other side of the basement and given it life. It was dark. No one even wanted to go to the other side. But now, those teens are coming. They are engaged, and she has their full attention." Mr. Light showed me love. I was trying not to smile from ear to ear, but I couldn't hide it.

"Councilman Small will see that tomorrow. He will see the work that we are doing, and they will want to invest more," said Mr. Light.

"We the only ones doing what we do at this time," said Queenie.

"It's not a game. We in the trenches. You can put us in any hood, and we gonna make it work. We ain't scareddddd." Queenie's octave went up.

The men began clapping and shouting. 'Cause indeed, you could not be afraid working with the Men of Valor.

"It's called courage. It's about going the distance for those in need. It's about creating opportunities that some may never be able to obtain. More importantly for me, it's about making the investment into the lives of so many young people because they are our future," I said, opening my mouth and speaking truth. The room was silent. "As long as we stay committed, focused, and our hearts are in the right place, the flock will come."

"Young sista, you got a lot of wisdom. You get it. We are so glad you are on board and a part of the team. How many young people are now in your program?"

"Thirty-five, sir," I responded swiftly.

"What's our maximum?"

"Forty youth."

"So, we are near to hitting our maximum. That's great."

Everyone in the room began clapping in full support.

"What do you need?"

"Right now, just your support. I would like to take the kids on more activities and culturally relevant field trips. We have supplies, thanks to Mr. Raymond," Dream said.

"Put your request in and let's get it done. Mr. Raymond will make sure it's done," said Mr. Light.

"Thank you, and I will."

"What part will we play in tomorrow's press conference?" Mr. Fab was on target.

"We'll participate as a team. We'll sit on stage with the councilman. He'll probably ask me to give remarks. We'll answer any questions that members of the community or Councilman Small ask. Most importantly, we'll provide a tour of the Men of Valor Youth Programs. They really want to see what we're doing down there."

"Gotcha. That's simple," I responded.

"Things should be pretty smooth. I can lead the tour," said Big C.

"You sure can. Then let Dream tag team with you. You show one half, and she shows off her program," said Mr. Fab.

"Yes, that makes the most sense. Also, I want to let you know that we'll be presenting a conference on violence prevention in about 4 or 5 months. I've been meditating and reflecting. We have been doing this work for almost 20 years. We're in the business of saving lives. We have always been relevant, and the politicians and great leaders of this city call on us."

"Yes, they do!" said Big C.

"We're gonna do a conference. We're gonna give them our best practices, philosophy, and ideology on how to transform the minds of these young men and women so that they can be an asset to their community. The conference will bring about the community, leaders, politicians, and I would even like brothas in the prisons to participate in this conference via teleconference."

"Wow, OK, Mr. Light. You thinking big," said Queenie.

"Queenie, what we're doing is big. How we are transforming our communities is big. My goal is to be the organization in the country that other organizations in this line of work model after. What we have done works and continues to work," said Mr. Light.

"This is major. And the reality is that we are a game changer. We cannot minimize the work that we have done. Even organizations in Ireland have been calling us to discuss our methodology for preventing youth violence. This should be a national conference. An annual event," interjected Mr. Fab.

"What we pour into it is what we will get. So, we'll begin planning as of next week. We got some young energy, and I'm sure Dream will be a great asset," he signaled me out.

"This is exciting. However I can contribute, I'm there."

"Count me in," Queenie voiced.

"Big C is with you."

"However I can assist," Mr. Raymond added.

"Thank you all for being persistent and consistent. As you can see, our plate will be full. And with God on our side, ALL is possible. We gotta be prayerful and stay focused. I believe tomorrow will be awesome. Each of us will play a role in making the press conference a success. Let's flow with it. I'm thankful for you all!"

"Teamwork makes the dream work," smiled Mr. Fab.

"Yes, it does," said Queenie.

"Let's meet at 9:00 a.m. in Menace since the event begins at 10:00. See you tomorrow, looking sharp. Anyone have any questions for me?"

The room was quiet. We all looked at one another for feedback.

"Well, meeting adjourned."

We had our marching orders. We stood ready and prepared. We were in the realm of activation, and I was most comfortable realizing the dream.

# Chapter 5

*Searching for Happy*

My heart was racing. My nerves were on frantic. What the hell did I *really* get myself into? Did I bite off more than what I could chew? My insecurities began to aggressively attack my mind.

Was my position at Valor bigger than what I expected?

Would I have a meltdown and collapse if they asked me to speak?

Was I gonna really be able to fit in my suit? Would I look too fat?

Would I sweat so much that you could see the sweat residue in my suit jacket?

Lord, would I be able to articulate my program to the councilman, and he'd understand?

"Shit shit shit!" I screamed in the car. I was barely in my 30s. Just got off of receiving food stamps. Just got my life together. Had a little boy that I was raising. Had a boyfriend that had a li'l thug in him. Suffered from my own PTSD and anxiety. Panicked during transitions.

"Shit! Shit! Dammmnnnnnn!" I hit the brakes hard so that I wouldn't crash into the bastard in front of me. Wanted to call my granny, my mama, or my stepdad. My life was picking up momentum, and I began to feel like my destiny was fa' sure. I had been down for so long that I was slightly afraid of success. Hopefully, it would be a steady run of success without interruption. The plain truth, ya girl was terrified.

I skirted away from the office yearning for normalcy. It was 1:00 in the afternoon, and I needed my hair done and my mind right. The hair salon was a sanctuary for Black women. A place where you could lay your battles, worries, anxieties, and uncertainties right on the altar. You could lay your tracks and bundles there too. I couldn't be in the atmosphere of politicians, and my hair game be off, edges be all over the place, and roots be nappy. Although I had a partial weave, I needed a mean flat iron and lots of body.

Mama didn't raise no fool or give birth to an ugly duckling. My mama was an '80s fly girl who was one of the best stylists of her era. She was premium, loved and hated on, but you could not take away that she could do some hair. As a matter of fact, she did the entire community's hair. She styled professionals, Black women of all ages, seniors, and even white girls. Mommy was charismatic and so talented that dignitaries sat in her chair, including the late great civil rights activist, Coretta Scott King. Whether you were Black, white, Armenian, or somewhere in between, my mama would get your hair together, and she didn't discriminate. The love language my mama spoke was green, and best believe, she was about her coin.

I think I was the envy of the neighborhood when I was growing up. I had beautiful, long, healthy hair, and it was growing out of the seams. Girlfriend had inches for days, and my mom stayed getting my hair together, whether it was a typical Saturday afternoon in her salon or a late Friday night. At the end of the day, my mommy made me understand a few things at a young age:

1) Fake it till you make it
2) Look like something even if you felt like nothing
3) Present yourself in the cleanest and most professional way
4) Image is everything; and
5) Never step out wrinkled.

Most importantly, she would quote I Peter 5:6–7, "Humble Yourselves Then, Under God's Mighty Hand, So That He Will Lift You Up In his Own Good Time." I got the life points that my mom often serenaded in my ear, but I was lazy with an iron and was wrinkled most of the time. If I couldn't afford to take a few suits or dresses to the cleaners, then I would put my clothes in the dryer and select "wrinkle free" or "tumble dry." In my mind, heat could solve a lot of problems, including heat applied to my hair.

I was a product of my environment. I knew that being pretty, charismatic, and intelligent could get me a long way in life, and I used it to my advantage.

I got in my car and sat for a few so that I could text my hairstylist. I needed a quick miracle.

Hey, girl, can you pleaseeeeee do my hair? I just need you to flat iron it. I have to present before a councilman, and I gotta look on point.

I sat still in my car and turned on the radio while plucking my chin hairs with a tweezer.

Yes, I can do it. When? she responded swiftly.

Now.

**Okay, come now.** My stylist was always there for me. Desire was always accommodating. We had come a long ways together. We were friends for about 10 years, and she was consistent. She never looked down on me. She rolled with me when things were cool, difficult, turbulent, and crazy. She could make me look like a rock star, a princess, a businesswoman, a politician, and a porn star in one breath. It was whatever I wanted to give. Like my mama, she was magical with the hands. She was also outspoken and would give you a jewel or two and be genuine. She wasn't jealous. She wasn't a hater. She was a sweet soul, just like Sanai. When I would step into her salon, she would set me free.

**I'm on my way,** I texted back.

The office was just 10 minutes away from Desire's place. I drove off to a local sandwich shop and grabbed us both a turkey and provolone sandwich on toasted wheat bread with mayo, lettuce, and tomato. It was owned by Mr. Harry since the early '80s and was a staple in the area. I also grabbed two large, homemade lemonades 'cause I knew I would be in the shop for at least 3 hours, and we would be spilling tea.

I then headed to the salon in a jiffy.

In my mind, I knew that I would present well before the council, politicians, and the community. I was slightly nervous, but I would take my time to rehearse what I would say, and more importantly, I would be poised. My mom, when I was growing up, called it the ability to "code switch." That simply meant I was trained on how to speak according to my audience. I understood how to be professional, yet, when I was in the comfort of my homies, I was ratchet, hood, funny, dramatic, and simply Dream.

In the back of my mind, I wondered about that fine brotha, Roca. He was *so* fineeeee, and I wanted to know more. I wanted to be nosy. I didn't see any ring on his finger, so he wasn't married. He was fly, he was nearby, and I was curious. Yea, I had Kenya on my team, but I needed a nigga in the cut, just in case or for emergency purposes, 'cause at the end of the day, Kenya was gonna fuck up like most niggas do. I didn't know how or why, and even though things were going well and at a cool pace, he was human and imperfect. And I learned from Solomon that muthafuckas always got another side.

I pulled up at Desire's, put the car in park, grabbed our food, and walked into the salon.

"Hey, honey buns, how are you?"

"Girlllla, my plate is full." I took my jacket off, placed my LV bag in a chair, and placed her food at her station.

"This is for me?"

"Yes, I figured you'd be hungry."

"Yes, girl, you must really know me 'cause my stomach was growling, and I've been here since 8:00 a.m."

"Damn, for real?"

"Yes, I got bills to pay. The hustle is real. You know how the grind goes. So, what's up with you and this last-minute appointment stuff?"

"Man, this job of mine is taxing. I love it, but there's a lot of pressure. They in the light. Everyone is watching their footwork. I'm the new kid on the block. I gotta prove myself. They really like me, and I'm young, so they're banking on me."

"That's great, honey. You have always been destined for greatness. I only expect great things from you. Only great things."

"Yes, so tomorrow, the politicians from Menace are doing a tour of our facility. A part of the facility is my program, which is the newest program that they have." Desire walked me over to the shampoo bowl, placing a towel and a cape around my neck. She adjusted my head into the shampoo bowl and began massaging my temple and crown with a mintlike shampoo.

"You are educated, and God always seems to put you in a position of leadership, so you are where you need to be for a reason. Plus, it's better to be employed than unemployed. You not in the heart of the struggle, girl." She began scratching my scalp, getting all the gook out of my hair until there was a good amount of lather. I closed my eyes. There was something so relaxing about going to the salon. It was my form of peace and quality time with one of my closest friends. Being in the salon, I could be human. I could let my hair down and be myself while vibin' in a judge-free zone.

Desire thoroughly rinsed my hair, wringing out all the water and gently raising my head out of the bowl and in a position where she could dry it with a towel. She added some leave-in conditioner to my hair and combed through it.

"How's King?"

"He's getting big. He's doing good. He's healthy and happy, and that's what's most important to me."

"That's good, 'cause I remember when he had asthma bad. That was scary," noted Desire.

"Yea, it seemed like I was living in the ER. It was just me. Scary moments, not knowing if my baby could breathe or not. Jesus, I'm glad his immune system is doing so much better. I think the sports help it too."

"Is he still playing soccer?"

"Naw, he dumped soccer for football."

"Did he?" Desire walked me to the dryer so that my hair could dry for a few minutes. She put the temperature on low so that we could continue our conversation. I grabbed my sandwich 'cause I was starving.

"Well, I think he's gonna have a build like his father. Watchu think? All that boy drink is water and milk."

"Yea, that's it. Still no sweets. He's like a Spartan, for real. His muscles are so cute," I added.

"Dang, still no sweets. Well, that's unusual, but it's healthy. What about his dad?" she sipped her lemonade.

"Solomon is good. He's still with Amara. I guess they good. I haven't really heard of any drama. True and King see each other when they're at Grandma Coco's house."

"How do you feel about that?"

"I really don't care. They're brothers. I have to accept that. I had to move on from the bullshit. It is what it is."

"Wow, you are growing up, honey. Yea, I guess when you go through so much with a man, things like that don't matter."

"My life is so different now. Things have turned around for the better. What Solomon did is in the past. Hopefully, he will do better about seeing his son more often. I do know that he visits King when he's over his mom's house." I began devouring my sandwich. I lived for Mr. Harry's sandwiches. The sandwich was so simple, but it was organic, and I know he put something in it that none of us knew about. They were his ingredients, and we never questioned him.

"You and his mom have a great relationship. That's good."

"Yea, we do. I love her to pieces. She's like my mom away from home. We vibe, we connect, and at the end of the day, she keeps it so G. She know her son ain't right; however, she played a part in that."

"Wasn't she on drugs when he was growing up?" Desire asked.

"Yea, she was. She was young, a fly girl, in the streets and irresponsible. I think Solomon still spites her 'cause of that. He gotta respect that at least she got clean and gave her life to Christ."

"Yea, during the '80s and '90s, the crack epidemic was meannnnnn. My sister was heavily addicted, and my brothers too. Those around me were addicted. It was so hard seeing my loved ones get on drugs and lose their minds."

"Anything that makes you abandon your kids, abandon your livelihood, and just say fuck life is the devil. I'm glad she changed, though. Solomon may have not had her in his life, which he still holds onto, but at least his kids do. She's a helluva grandma. She helps me out tremendously on the weekends 'cause I be needing a break."

"She lives right up the street from you, right?" Desire began eating her sandwich.

"Yea, like 2 miles away. That was one reason why I moved close in proximity to her because I wouldn't be in a new area without knowing someone. On the weekends, she's always looking for her grandson, and I have no problem bringing him to her."

"I know that's right." Desire continued eating.

"How's everything going with your business?"

"Girl, I'm just glad my brother helped me with these renovations. I don't know what I would do without him. It was a lot of work, but it was worth it. This owner is shiesty as hell. My water bill be high as hell. It's as if I'm paying for the entire building. He has two tenants above me."

"Really? Yea, you better check on that. 'Cause when I lived Uptown, all my utilities were rigged. I was paying gas for the four-unit apartment complex, and my neighbor was paying electric for *all* the tenants. My shit was like $600 a month, and I only had a one-bedroom. Then I had the gas company come out, and they couldn't even read the meters 'cause it was locked in the basement." I sipped my lemonade and patted my hair to see if it was dry.

"Really? Yea, I'm gonna have to investigate further 'cause this ain't right."

"Yea, and you don't want to get caught up with a hefty bill, neither."

"You almost dry?" She lifted the dryer and tapped my hair. "Give it a couple of minutes."

"Cool." I began checking my text messages.

Kenya hit me with a text 15 minutes earlier.

Baby, how's your day going? he texted.

It's going pretty good. It's a lot tho.

He responded swiftly, Take your time. You in a good place.

The big day is tomorrow. I meet the councilman. I'm under pressure. I'm getting my hair done right now.

You gonna be good. You at Desire's?

Yea, she getting me together right now.

Hit me when you done.

Okay, I will, I love you. I texted back.

I raised the dryer head up.

I love you too, he responded.


"Come sit in my chair, Dream. You're dry now," Desire said.

I walked to her stylist chair. She took the wet towel from around my neck, removed the old cape, and placed a new cape around me.

"So, how you want your hair?"

"I just want it bone straight with a li'l body and a part right down the middle."

"Real presidential, huh?" she replied. She pulled two different flat irons out and put a li'l Moroccan oil through my hair. The aroma smelled so good. I loved the fragrance of burning flat irons, oils, conditioners, and shampoos. The salon was a sacred place for me. It was like the barbershop for men. I could unveil my kinks and coils. I could unveil what was jagged—what wasn't perfect about my image. I had no problem being open and vulnerable, and more than often, my hairstylist went beyond our friendship. She was like a therapist.

"Girl, that's the only way to do it. How's Devin? What's going on in your world?" I got in her tea.

"Devin is good. You know he's preparing to go overseas for a 12-month contract. But he brings home six figures, and the money is tax free."

"Overseas where?"

"The Middle East."

"Awe, hell naw. That's real. How are you gonna deal with not fucking for a year? Are you prepared to deal with being truly faithful?"

"Wouldn't you be faithful for a year if your man brought back more than six figures to your household?" Desire fired back.

"I guess I probably could, but it would be so hard. I mean, you gotta entertain someone, right?"

"I love him, Dream. I really love him. I think he's the one. I don't have to worry about all that mess that I was worried about before. He's not in the streets or from the streets. He's from New Orleans. He's a country brotha. He can cook, clean, make good love, and we have a great time."

"Well, what's wrong with him?"

"Humph, he's a Cancer, just like you. He's moody. Sometimes I gotta read in between the lines. He's quiet at times and removed. I be asking him questions, and he be looking at me like I'm crazy. Yea, that's my biggest pet peeve."

"Cancers can be the biggest assholes. 'Cause once we get in our moods, we remove ourselves from the world and go in our shell. It's not personal; it's just how we are. The worst thing you could do is knock on his shell, like 'Hello, are you in there?'"

"You hit that shit on the nose." She shook her head as she put clips in my hair to flat iron small sections of it.

"Yea, but you gotta let him be when he gets moody. Don't be insecure. It prolly ain't even him, or maybe it's prolly him. He'll come around. I'm sure he cares about you," I put her on.

"Yea, I know he loves me. We have a good time together. We just got our passports, so we're gonna be going overseas together. We both grind hard, and he has a wonderful work ethic."

"Which is good, 'cause all we ever knew was hustlers. If a nigga sold drugs and heavy artillery, we were on him if he had a net worth. We always been the good girls who liked the bad boys." I grabbed my cold brew tea and placed my cell phone in my left breast.

"We love the bad boys, but the bad boys don't mean us any good," Desire affirmed.

"Yea, I know. But wouldn't it be a bomb-ass ending if we could turn a bad boy into a productive, positive, and progressive returning citizen?" I was a hood romantic.

"That would be great but how possible?" she laughed.

"You laughing and shit, but that flat iron is hot as heck. Blow, girllll!" My head was hot.

"Okay, I gotcha. You are tender headed. I'm gonna blow. It got too hot?"

"Yes. Are you tryin' to kill me?" I was a big baby.

"No, honey. But back to what you were saying. Dudes gotta wanna change. We can't change 'em. They chasing fast money, fast cars, and fast broads. Where is it gonna end them?"

"Death or destruction. That's why I'm glad that I only have just one child. OMG, I would be in a messed-up predicament if I had more kids. This single mama life is like 'thug life.'"

"I can't imagine. So, you don't have any more kids in your deck of cards?"

"Yea, maybe 5 or 6 years from now. I need to be married, stable, and with a man who is gonna hold the fort down. I need to feel secured."

"What about Kenya?"

"He's a prospect," I giggled.

"Like, how do you feel about him?"

"He got a past life. He from the lifestyle. The streets made him. The whole nine. That 50-Cent type of shit before he got the bag. But I think he's done with it. At least, I hope."

"Oh Lord, what does he do now?"

"He's a chef. He cooks. And he cooks so good. Like his food make you wanna lick your fingers—every last one of them."

"Lawd, that's how he got you."

"Yea, he can cook, clean, tighten up my son, protect me, and fuck my brains to never-never land."

"You are crazy, girl." Desire was halfway done with my hair.

"Food and good loving—nothing beats that. He's family oriented too. My only issue with him is that he drinks a li'l too much."

"Devin does too. He drinks his signature Hennessey and watches his games, and he's done."

"See, that's cute, but Kenya like gets fucked up for real. He's a different person. He's a li'l aggressive, turned, and then there's no turning back," I reflected. "'*I drink, but I'm coolin'. I'm chillin' when I'm tipsy or drunk. I'm creative and intrapersonal.*' This dude get drunk, and he gonna cuss you, or he's ready to fight. Liquor should not make you feel like that."

"You're right. But maybe you can convey to him how you feel. Like really sit him down," Desire advised.

"Yea, I think I will." I looked straight ahead in a trance. The conversation made me really think about my approach with Kenya.

"I remember when I was dealing with Tip. I was overwhelmed. I didn't know if someone was gonna kill him or kill me. I would have over $100,000 of his cash stashed in my house. He would be drunk as hell by the time he came home. Ready to fight *me* for no reason."

"Yea, I remember," I responded.

"And he wouldn't change. The money was great, but he, as a person, would not change. He couldn't leave the streets alone. There were women. It was a bit much for me."

"I understand. I remember you coming to my house with dinner every night 'cause you would prepare dinner and Tip wouldn't come home some nights, or he would come home too late."

"Yes, that was so painful. I had all that money of his, and all I wanted was for him to come home from hustling and doing him, and he couldn't even do that. I was done. I had to save myself."

"Yea, you did. Kenya does come home. He loves me and my son. He's there almost every day. He's loving, but . . ." I said.

"He has his demons. They all do, girl."

"Yea, he got his demons. I got them too. Only time will tell."

We both were silent for about a minute. We had a girl code, and we fought off the demons sometimes together. We had both seen each other go through storm after storm. We cried together, were pregnant together, even had abortions around the same time. We'd been broke together and rode the bus together. Yet, Desire's gift was that she could take your ashes and turn them into a beautiful canvas. She could paint the pain. She was an awesome hairstylist and makeup artist, but she was human and no different from the rest of us. We could talk and spill the tea and the beans. We had come from humble beginnings, and Desire was a thoroughbred.

I met Desire almost 10 years ago in another salon. A Cali dude who was an excellent stylist with a wild-ass attitude introduced us. I would put him on to boosting his client base by referring him to the college girls on my campus who kept eyeing my tresses. He would silk my hair out where the wind couldn't breeze through it, and I was the envy of so many women in the DMV. I would share the jewel of who did my hair, and as a result, Tank had his clientele on lock. Desire was his apprentice and a skilled makeup artist who was finding her way. While on the spoken-word and celebrity-journalist circuit, Desire would do my makeup after Tank would do my hair for my performances.

I remember one time telling Desire, "You study that dude. Study how he do hair. If you learn how to do weaves and straighten hair better than him, you'll get all of his clients, and more, because you have a better attitude."

Years later, she would have her own salon, clientele, and women from all walks of life would be at her door for an immediate, magical transformation. She would have good Karma because she planted positivity.

"I like Kenya for you, though."

"Do you?"

"Yea, 'cause he seems really genuine. So, give him a chance. And any man who love the baby *and* the mama is a good man." We busted out laughing.

"Give him a chance, Dream," she advised.

"Okay, girl."

"But how do you feel? How's *Dream*? I know you got the good job, the good car, and the good nigga. But how are *you*?"

I turned my head to look back at her. She knew how to dig deeper than most.

"I'm in a zone. I'm in a good place. I haven't had any Xanax in over a year, so that's good. When I feel like I'm gonna have a panic attack, I just ride the wave, 'cause I know it will pass."

"I'm so proud of you 'cause you were on those zannies, and I was concerned."

"Well, I don't plan on taking any zannies unless I'm in real distress. And right now, I'm in a good place. Getting used to a new man, new job, new home environment, new car, and a new life."

"You found your happy place?" Desire asked.

"I guess this is happy for me. It feels like happiness. I know I wanna go to Yoga more often. I wanna exercise more, and I definitely need to go to spas and vacation more. But, yeah, I'm a li'l happy."

"I'm so proud of you, girl. You are blessed. God is all over your life."

"I know so. I was so addicted to those zannies. I didn't want to feel. I didn't want to hurt. I just was so tired of crying. You take a Xanax, and you don't feel shit. Like you'll be zombied out. But then not feeling nothing scared me too, especially when I knew I was in a situation that required emotion."

"What helps you not to go back to popping pills?"

"Kenya helps me a lot. He keeps me leveled and balanced. He takes the edge off. I let Solomon go. I forgave him. I didn't forget, but I let it go. My life is better, although I probably should check in to therapy every couple of months. I pray, I meditate, and smile."

"Girl, you could write a book about mental health, Black women, and anxiety. 'Cause I had it just as bad as you had it at one time. It's hard to overcome." She turned me around.

"I'm almost done. Is it straight enough for you?" She tilted my hair toward the mirror.

"Yes, it sure is. Just make sure you lay down those areas where my hair stands up like the Japanese."

"Lol. OK, miss lady."

"But can I tell you something? Something I've been thinking about?"

"Yes, honey buns."

"I don't wanna work for anyone. I want to be like you. I want to work for myself. I want to be my own boss. So, I'm gonna soak up as much as I can working for Valor. I'm gonna learn, learn more, and perfect my craft—but I won't be there long."

"I see you running your own company. You're bossy, independent, and ambitious. I see that for you. But are you giving yourself a time line?"

"Yea, by the end of the year, I'm gonna position myself to move forward. I'll save my money and start up on the paperwork aspects within the next couple of months."

"A year? That's pretty quick, isn't it?"

"Well, I'm giving myself 18 months to pull my plan off the ground, at max."

"Yea, the paperwork is the hardest. Obtaining a business license is time-consuming, but it's worth it. There's nothing like waking up when you want to and running a business the way you want to run it," said Desire.

"That's what I'm trying to do. I wanna wake up in my pajamas with a laptop near and make it do what it do. I wanna sip a Cinnamon Dolce Latte and run my own shit. I'm highly capable."

"Yes, you are. And whatever you say you are gonna do, you do. Just do your research. What kinda business?"

"Mentoring. Job training and educational programs. Pretty much what I do now."

"Yes, that's a no-brainer. And you can write your own grants 'cause you're a writer." We both laughed and giggled . . . 'cause I was on to something.

"But I got something else to tell you."

"What, girl?" She combed through my hair and began aligning my middle part. It was a li'l off-centered, as usual, but I looked better than when I came in there. She sprayed my hair with some sheen and olive oil.

"I met a guy today."

"Whatchu mean, a guy? And where? Here we go with this." She shook her head.

"I met him at work. He works for the same organization. He was walking out of the building, and I was walking into the building."

"You already in a relationship, though."

"That's why I'm being thrown off. I know that. But this dude like . . . took my breath away. He was so beautiful. He was finnnnnne. I just wanna . . . you know?"

"Ughhh—Kenya?"

"I love Kenya. He's not going anywhere, but I'm not married. I don't have no rings. And just in case he switch up, I need a runner-up!" I busted out laughing.

"So, who's the dude? Chile, you always up to something."

"His name is Roca."

"Roca . . . That sounds Spanish. Is he Black?"

"Yea, he's Black."

"Where is he from?"

"D.C., I think."

"You ain't had enough of these D.C. cats?"

"He looked different, like he stepped out of a *GQ* magazine. He wasn't rough looking. He was clean, pretty smile, a fresh haircut, nice clothes, clean shoes. He was smooth."

"Tall, dark, and handsome, huh?"

"TDH . . . You already know. He was Finnnnnnnnnnne with a capital F. I just wanna talk to him. Okay, it's tempting."

"Yea, and you work together?"

"But in different divisions."

"Okay, if you wanna put your hand in the cookie jar, then go ahead," she advised.

"I want a glass of milk. But if you seen him, you would say the same thing."

"Roca, huh? Roca gon' get your ass killed by Kenya."

"I didn't do anything."

"I know you, though," she laughed as she applied edge control to my hair and sideburns.

"Are you scared of love, Dream?"

"I'm scared of being broken. I don't know if I could stand another broken heart. Maybe never bounce back. But when you go through heartbreak, you don't think you will last. My focus more is about being happy. I wanna laugh, smile, giggle, dance, sip wine and spirits, and travel. I wanna sit and be pretty, like now."

"Are you happy now?" Desire had a way of getting to me.

"My hair looks beautiful." I avoided her question and swung my neck from left to right like a white girl.

"How much do I owe you?"

"Fifty dollars."

"Okay. I got you." I pulled out $55 and handed it to her. She smiled. "I know I'm not sad. I know I'm not depressed. I feel different. I breathe differently. I look revived. I feel hopeful. I'm arriving at a happy place. When you get there, let me know how it feels."

There was a mutual silence in the air. I don't think either one of us were happy, but we weren't far away. We weren't at the "bus stop sucking on a lollipop" anymore. We were growing; we were soaring, guarding our hearts, and watching our steps.

"Thanks for being honest. I'm not happy, but I think I'm getting there, Dream. I think I'm nearby," Desire chimed in.

"We gon' get there. But I accept and respect where I'm at in my life right now."

"Good stuff."

"Thank you, boo." I went to hug Desire. We embraced like sisters who truly knew and understood each other. It was heartfelt. It was a 30-second embrace. I sipped the last li'l bit of my lemonade and tossed it in the trash. Then I stood up in front of the mirror and put on a peachy colored lipglass 'cause my lips were cracked.

"Dream, are you ready for tomorrow? Just be yourself, and they're gonna love you," she spoke confidently over me.

"I hope so. At least, I look pretty. All I gotta do is get a good night's rest, wrap my hair up, and sleep like a princess."

"You crazy."

I put my jacket on and checked my phone to see if I had any messages. NONE. I pulled up Roca's number and began texting.

Hey, what's up? This is Dream. You met me in front of the job. Call me when you get some time. I was bold and curious. He texted back immediately.

Hey, luv. How are you? When are you free? Let's have some lunch.

I smiled from ear to ear. I was ecstatic behind a man I didn't even know.

Sure. Just let me know. My fingers hit those keys quickly.

"Okay, honey buns. I'll see you in about 2 weeks or so," said Desire as she ushered in another client.

"You sure will. Love you, boo."

"Love you too." Desire waved to me as I walked out of the salon.

I was looking good, and I felt good. I needed to make a few runs before I grabbed King from school and headed to the house. I would use the evening to review any talking points and at least run through my program goals. Overall, I was ready.

My phone began vibrating. It was another text from Roca.

Are you going to work tomorrow? he asked.

Yes. I'll be in Menace for a press conference, I typed back.

I'll be in the field. But give me a call when you're done, luv. Maybe I can meet you.

Okay. I gotchu.

I was a free agent in my mind. I didn't sign no deal, nor was I offered millions. I was the best thing I eva had.

# Chapter 6

*Momentum*

"Baby baby baby." Kenya was my alarm, and it was 6:30 a.m.

I was in a deep sleep.

"Baby," he rubbed my back.

"Yeaaaaaaa?" I was dreamin' too good and wasn't prepared to wake up.

"Today is your day. The councilman is coming, remember?"

"Yeaaaaaa." I rolled over to my right side as if I didn't hear him.

"You want breakfast?" Kenya was persistent.

"Ken, it's too early. I'm tired. I'm so tired."

"I know you are. I'm gonna get up and make us some breakfast."

"OK." I pulled the covers over my head.

I needed another good hour of sleep. I was working so hard that I knew Kenya needed me and some attention. I felt sort of sleep deprived, and every minute counted. Every morning, I was rushing to get myself dressed, to get King dressed, and if I could remember to grab a bowl of cereal or some turkey bacon, that was good for me. It seemed like my life was always on the go. My thoughts were on the go, my food was on the go, and so was my life. So, sleep and I needed to become friends.

By the time I got home each evening, it was 7:00 p.m. The routine was to unwind, work with King on his homework, give him a bath, spend time with him, watch part of a movie with Kenya, and fall asleep on the Kenya's lap. I was quite boring, but my hunger and thirst for never being poor again was real.

When I was on Clay Street, I either couldn't sleep because my anxiety was high, my heart was racing and palpitating, or I was so depressed that I would sleep all day due to being unemployed and having the single-mama blues. My new house sleep felt good. I would wake up to the smell of fresh paint, sometimes breakfast in bed, or the aroma of amazing food prepared by Kenya. Sleep was a necessity because I was moving and grooving. I enjoyed lying in a spoon position where Kenya would hug me tightly. He would caress my body and listen to the repetition of my snores. When some evenings permitted, he would lay me on my stomach and make sweet love to me until I came to the land of no return. He'd penetrate every insecurity and convince me that he was right for me and would never leave me like before.

It was the comfort of having a strong man on my team that believed, adored, cherished, and demonstrated that he was into me. I felt protected when Kenya was around. Although we lived together, there were not any promise rings, rumors of engagement, or disclosures of commitment. I was scared to outline any demands. It was more important for me to let time tell everything.

Some days, he didn't come home, and deep down, I questioned his whereabouts. Generally, he would have an alibi. He said that he was at his cousin's house or with his friends, partying drunk and wasted.

He was still a man, and it was hard to trust him, or anyone, for that matter.

The days that he was home, I valued them. The day or two that he was a no-show would more than often have me on edge because I would immediately have a "news flash" of how life was when Solomon decided to walk out of my life without a word of closure. If Kenya left me, my heart was prepared, but emotionally, I wasn't sure how well I could cope. I knew that I wouldn't be broken as bad if he vanished or left me for another woman because, for me, the worst had passed. It couldn't have possibly gotten any worse than what it was—I was damaged goods.

Thirty-five minutes had passed. The smell of eggs, bacon, scrapple, and fresh fruit greeted me on my nightstand. King was still asleep, and I was moving in slow motion.

"Baby girl, don't you think you should get up? You got a big day ahead of you. You gotta put on your lucky brown suit and act like a boss in front of those high-profile politicians," Kenya announced from the kitchen.

"I know, I know. This bed feels so doggone good, though. I'm getting up. I'm getting up," I whispered.

Suddenly, I jumped out of bed and ran to the bathroom to pass my water, to contemplate my day, and decide how I would flow. I sat on the toilet, rubbing my eyes, checking to make sure my scarf was in place, ensuring that my hair was still gently wrapped, wondering if I should wear my lucky brown suit or the black suit that I recently bought. I chose black.

I flushed the toilet, brushed my teeth, put on my shower cap, turned on the shower, hopped in, and let the hot water permeate my back. I inhaled the steam for 8 seconds, and then I exhaled, slathering my skin with Yardley's lavender soap.

"Baby, you good?" Kenya barged into the bathroom to be nosy.

"Yea, I'm tryin'a rinse this soap off my face." Kenya snatched the shower curtain back and kissed me on my forehead and rubbed my back.

"Baby, I wanna back shot so bad," he whined.

"Naw, boy. You know I gotta go in focused. I can't be all sleepy and tired going to this press conference and tour." I came out of the shower, and he handed me a towel.

"Lemme dry you off then."

"Dang, boy, you pressed."

"You making me hard, girl. I love looking at you naked," he laughed.

"You crazy, Ken."

He began drying my back off. He embraced me, and we hugged each other tightly.

"I love you." He started pecking me.

"I love you too. I missed you. I know we haven't sat down to build and bond in a while. I've just been working so hard, and I be tired by the time we get home. It's a lot."

"I understand, baby girl. Right now, you're on another level. The struggle was real on Clay, but you ain't struggling anymore. God blessed you. Look in the mirror." He grabbed my chin and stared into my face. "You are creating a name for yourself—a brand. The organization that you work for has already done their research. They know who you are, and that's why they have you on their team," he spoke firmly.

"You think?"

"I know. You are college educated, you are highly intelligent as heck. You are someone who they can depend on. You don't even use your sick leave or personal leave. I know that about you. And anyone that is around you can observe and see that about you. This is just another stepping-stone, and a major one."

"I believe it is."

I walked into my bedroom and sat on the end of my bed, just kinda staring into space. Kenya brought my food to me.

"Take a bite." He held a fork with cheese eggs and scrapple.

"Ummm, this is really good. Ummmmmm, *really* good." I started chewing, savoring the taste.

"I didn't want to put too much on your plate because I know you needed something filling but something light. You got turkey scrapple, cheese eggs, and a few fried apples."

"This is so good. I appreciate you so much, 'cause I was hungry as hell."

"I figured you were because you took about two bites of your dinner, you talked to King, said a few words to me, and fell out. I knew you were exhausted."

"Dang." I shook my head and devoured the rest of my plate. "Is King up?"

"Yea, I hear his footsteps in the bathroom. He's probably getting dressed for school."

"Good." I put the plate on my dresser, wiped my hands on a few baby wipes, put on deodorant, greased my face, arms, and elbows with cocoa butter, and dabbed some Chanel perfume on my neck. I took my size 12 black suit and white blouse off the hangers and snatched the tags off them. It was a Calvin Klein suit that gave a professional edge with a slight flair because it was fitted. I felt like I was growing up because I had more business casual attire than my everyday wear and going-out gear. My swag was changing. When I was in college, I majored in business initially and had to wear suits 3 days a week and hated it.

In my eyes, professional attire had no depth, took away one's personality, and was too stuffy. After going to a few department stores and trying on different styles of business attire, I began to develop my own style and added more color to my look.

"Where you going, Ma?" King questioned.

"I'm going to work."

"You look real nice." He flattered me.

"Thank you. I see you are dressed already. Did you eat?"

"I'm about to eat. I'm trying to get to school on time, Ma, so please hurry up."

"OK, boy, let me get myself together." King and Kenya knew I struggled with time. And time was of the essence for everything in life. Money was my motivator, and paychecks were my incentive to get to work, events, meetings, and appointments on time. King was right. Getting him to school on time was a must that I could not renege on.

"So, you chose to not wear your lucky brown suit this time?"

"Naw. I'll save it for something special."

"It seemed like every time you wore that suit, you would win at whatever," Kenya remembered.

"I know. I love that suit. One day, I'll be a millionaire, and I'll still keep that suit in my closet."

"Well, you look nice in all black. You look sexy, baby." Kenya turned on the news.

"Thanks." I sprayed my hair down with olive oil and began brushing it down with my weave brush until it was perfectly in place with tons of body. I would put on a few dabs of Mystic, something light and refreshing. My white gold stubs were in my ears. I put on a comfortable pair of Calvin Klein pumps and kissed Kenya on the cheek.

"OK, I gotta go. Say a prayer for me."

"I already did that this morning. You good. You'll be fine. Remember what I said. You are branding yourself."

"Yep. Got it."

"Ma, I'm ready." King had on his backpack, his jacket, and skater hat to the back. My child stayed ready. He was an early bird, and he was also proactive to be just 7 years old.

"Let's go, baby boy. I'm ready. I think you'll be on time to school today."

"Finally," he laughed. He rushed to the car and signaled me to unlock the door. He hopped in the backseat, took his backpack off, and locked in his seat belt. I turned on the car and let it run for about 2 minutes.

"Ma, can you turn on the radio, please?"

"Yes, son, give me a second."

I ran in the house and grabbed my briefcase and my cell phone and charger, placing them in the front passenger seat of my car. I cut the radio onto an R&B station. Erykah Badu's "Certainly" was banging, and it fit the mode for my day.

Her voice brought on a connectedness.

*"The world is mine*

*When I wake up*

*I don't need nobody telling me the time."*

Badu's music made so much sense to me. If more people learned to embrace the world every morning when they wake up, they would feel a sense of reassurance.

King and I nodded our heads to every song that was on the radio. We were so much alike, that, for the most part, we just vibed off each other as we rolled out to our first destination, which was school for him and work for me. It would take me about 30 minutes to get him to school each day, and today, he would be on time.

"Ma, you got here quick. You were flying." King smiled as we pulled up to his school.

"You think so?"

"Yea, you got here real fast, and I'm on time. You gotta get up early like this every day."

"OK, li'l man. I'll try. I ain't gonna promise you, though." I put the car in park and gave him a hug and high five. He got out of the car with his belongings and walked with one of the many school escorts. I waited a minute to ensure that he went into the schoolhouse. I had a man-child, who was my only child. He was what I worked so hard for—he was my motivation on so many levels.

For the last 7 years, it was King and I. Limited family, limited friends, limited money, and sometimes limited resources. Yet, God made it possible to see days like this—where we both were happy. I felt so blessed, and only God and I knew about those underground talks that we would have. It was all good.

I was headed straight to Menace, which was only about 3 miles away from King's school. My stomach kept fluttering with anxiety. It was showtime, and I was prepped and ready. We were scheduled to meet at 9:00 a.m., and I had arrived around 8:30 so that I could do a walk-through of my program classrooms and ensure that they were clean and presentable.

As soon as I walked to the basement, Big C was already there, suited and booted. He greeted me with a cheery smile.
 "Hey, sis, how are you?"
"I'm good. How about you?"
"I feel really good about today. You know I had to come down here and make sure we are airtight."

"Yep, me too. I'm a team player. I'm gonna check on this end." I pointed toward my classrooms.

"That'll work. Mr. Light and the rest of the executive team are on their way from the headquarters."

"Let me hurry then."

I walked from classroom to classroom, spraying Febreze and using the Clorox wipes to wipe down the doorknobs and desks. I added a few large decals to the hallway that included meaningful words: RESPECT—TRUST—TEAMWORK—PROMISE—DREAM— LEGACY. Each word was in a different color, thus, giving life to the work we do without saying too much.

I went into my office, shut the door, and gave thanks to God Almighty for ALL things. It was the sacredness of being in a closed room and humbly getting on my knees and going before the Lord in thanksgiving. I closed my eyes and both prayed and meditated. I needed to hear a word that could speak to my heart deeper than a human tongue. God was all-knowing and all-seeing, and there was so much more than the day represented. Hearing his voice gave me so much confirmation. You would have to be still in the moment in order to hear.

*The Best Has Yet to Come. Go! Don't Be Afraid.* His instructions were clear. The mandate came.

"Dream, come down to this side," Big C yelled down the hallway. "They pulling up, and Mr. Light is gonna brief us on this side."

I raised my head, came out of a posture of prayer, and said, "Thank you, Jesus. Thank you, Jesus," as I walked down the hallway to Big C. Mr. Light, Mr. Raymond, Mr. Fab, and Ms. Queenie, along with other members of the organization, walked into the basement. There were about ten of them, and they were dressed to the nines . . . real dapper, smelling really good, and seemed pretty prepared.

"God is shining on us today!" Mr. Light came in with authority, and the others followed right behind him.

"The sun is always shining," said Mr. Fab. "It doesn't matter how things may appear."

"What's happening, Sista Dream? What's happening, C?"

"Hello, Mr. Fab and Mr. Light. Hi, everyone," I responded.

"Hey, brothas." Mr. C began dapping up all the brothas.

"I understand that everyone knows what to expect. Basically, the councilman is gonna come with his chief of staff to give remarks to the community about his plans for Menace. And other politicians and council members may be in the house. He may or may ask me or Mr. Fab to speak as well. We're gonna just flow with him. Lastly, what everyone wants to see is what we are doing for the youth in this community so that violence will not be an issue in this community," he explained.

"Our organization is a safe haven for this community. We will lead a tour of the basement for Councilman Small's office at the very end," Mr. Light added.

"Also, be prepared to take questions from the community and from the council," said Mr. Raymond. "Big C and Dream will lead the tour. Be prepared to discuss the wonderful work that you do. This is how we get more funding and more programs." Mr. Raymond never missed a beat.

"Let's say a prayer. Hold one another's hand and get on one accord." Mr. Light was a God-fearing man. He immediately grabbed my hand. We bowed our heads, and he began praying.

"Dear God, maker of heaven and earth. We wanna thank you for waking us up. We wanna thank you for guiding us. We wanna thank you for loving us and never giving up on us. We are not worthy, but you saw fit." He began tapping his foot. "Yet, you shine upon us. Help us to hold out. Help the Men of Valor to do better. Plant us where we need to be planted. Give us your blessings today. In Jesus' name. Amen."

"Amen," we said in unison. They began clapping and shouting like we were at a Baptist prayer service. I observed the full spectrum. This was a nontraditional work setting for me. I appreciated a true spiritual aspect to the world of work. It kept us grounded and humbled.

"We better get going." Mr. Raymond looked at his cell phone. "The councilman has arrived."

He led the way to the stage. There were about 100 white chairs for the community. It was a small podium. Chairs for the councilman and his team were to the right of the podium, and to the left, it was

Men of Valor. Mr. Light requested Mr. Fab, who was the VP, and Mr. C and I to sit on the stage with him. My spirit was leaping. I followed Mr. C because he had been around long enough to know how the story goes. The home team was in all black, and that brown lucky suit of mine would have thrown everything off, so I was glad to have chosen the black suit.

There were no women on that stage. I stood alone. However, Mr. Light had a 20-something-year-old executive assistant named Kiana. In meetings, Kiana was the one who you would see sitting near or in the cut, taking solid notes. You could tell that Mr. Light entrusted her with a lot of responsibility, even though she was so young. She had the keys to all the offices, she was the one who opened up the main office, and she worked closely with the chief financial officer. She was petite and quiet. Although she didn't have much stage presence or customer service, she was stoic, somewhat professional, and effective.

Kiana was brown, and her weaves were always on point. Her bundles looked like they were growing out of the seam. She never said too much other than, "Hey, Dream. Everything good with your program?" Then she would add, "I'll email you when your checks are ready for your program or when your supplies come in." Every staff and visitor knew that they couldn't just walk up on Mr. Light. We had to book an appointment with Kiana's young, tight-lipped ass before you could even have a conversation with him. However, as she saw me growing in my leadership role and becoming a part of the executive team, Kiana was observant of me, and sometimes we would have a short and cute conversation—nothing major. She understood her position. I respected her because she was young and had the juice but was humble.

The men appeared to be 45 years old or older. I was barely 31. Councilman Small hugged Mr. Light and Mr. Fab like he had known them all his life. He was a short and stubby white man with big ol' glasses with a pastel-green bow tie. He was unique and not what I expected.

The community was present. There were more senior citizens and a few middle-aged Black women and men in the crowd. Most likely, the parents in the community either worked, were still asleep in their houses, or were uninspired. There appeared to be a few other politicians in the crowd who were ushered to the very front row.

The chief of staff for the councilman came straight to the microphone. He too was short, but he seemed middle-aged, focused, and perhaps a block boy who had been reformed.

"Good morning," he spoke to the crowd.

"Good morning," the crowd echoed back.

"Councilman Small is very proud to be here this morning to share with you his plans for this community, as well amazing things that are being fostered as we speak. As you know, I am no stranger to this community. This is like home to me. I am Chester Williams, the chief of staff to the councilman," he smiled.

You could tell by the body language of the crowd that they were fond of Chester.

"Let's give a warm welcome to Councilman Small." He introduced him immediately. They had no time to waste. The crowd was warm and began clapping as he approached the podium.

"It feels good to be here today. It really does. This is a community that is filled with so much hope, despite what people may say. The crime is down, the violence is down, the dropout rate is down, and we wanna keep it that way." Small held no punches.

"I'm thankful for this community for standing together. I'm thankful to organizations like the Men of Valor for creating programs where youth can now have somewhere to go to Earn, Learn, and Grow. Our young people don't have to stand on the corners anymore. They now have a place that Men of Valor, I understand, has fully renovated that will serve as the fiber of hope and educational programs for this community."

More people began clapping.

"As you know, I have had a 2-year plan for this community. We started almost 2 years ago, and we are not far off." He pointed to tall posters that stood to the right of him, triple his height.

"My goal was to upgrade these units and buildings and bring in a developer who could create an atmosphere of affordable housing that was viable and vibrant. The construction will break in 30 days. I said there would be community gardens which we completed just last year, and they look beautiful. You can now get fresh fruit and vegetables from your own community, grown by your own residents."

The seniors all began clapping. You could tell they took some part in that project.

"We have collards, kale, tomatoes, potatoes, strawberries, and blueberries. And I have tasted the freshness myself. I am indeed pleased." Everyone laughed.

"The aquatic center and new state-of-the-art recreation center is almost completed. This will promote healthy living, the performing arts, and programs for all residents in this community. Our young men can hoop somewhere safe. This is what we need, and I'm sticking to what I said."

The crowd got excited. Mr. Light and Mr. Fab were clapping and shouting along with other members of the community. The community would greatly benefit from everything he mentioned.

"This community is transforming into a community that will be known for good outcomes and good things. I love serving you. We are so close to meeting your needs. That's my job. I said that I would invest in your youth and create a hub that focused on education, workforce, and technology. A year ago, I brought on the Men of Valor who have served the community for 2 decades to get the job done. They were committed from the beginning." He looked at Mr. Light. "When we met with Mr. Light and Fab, they said that they could get the job done. And they did. I understand the education center has several programs up and running, as well as a computer lab, and the basement is fully renovated. I'm excited to see it."
"We can't wait to show you," Mr. Fab responded.
"Yes, sir," Big C added.

Councilman Small faced the crowd. "We have about another year to get all of these plans completed, and I know we can it done. Most importantly, I don't want to hear of another youth dying to gun violence. It breaks my heart . . . it really does. It's senseless. As a result, I have met with the commander for this area and the department and you will see our police officers walking the beat and patrolling. You'll see a community police presence, and you'll see officers also participating in our town halls and community events. Safety is #1—education after that and viable living are the focus for my platform. We'll get there if we work together."

People began standing up in agreement with the councilman. You could tell that even though he was white, he had been around Blacks for a while. He was sincere and genuine.
"He was in AA with me," Big C nudged me.
I smiled. "OK," I whispered.

"We all want to live in a good environment where we can work together, our children play together, and we can build together. It's onward from here! Now, let's take a tour of the community. We'll start with the Education Center in the basement, and then proceed with a map of central areas that demonstrate progression."

He was clear and concise. He didn't roll numbers or discuss budgets. He came to see how the money was used and to let the community know that they were not forgotten. He didn't ask anyone for remarks, either. He gave the microphone to his chief of staff and walked over to Mr. Light and began a conversation that none of us could hear.

"Thank you, Councilman Small, for your remarks. As you can see, this community is doing great things. Progress is being made, and soon, we'll hear the success stories," Mr. Williams added. "With that being said, the Men of Valor will lead the tour to the basement, and we'll follow suit. Councilman Small will take questions at the very end of the tour."

Big C got up and guided me to walk with him to the basement. I followed him as he walked swiftly.

"Dream, it's showtime. We'll start off the tour on my side, and then I'll walk the councilman and his team so that I can introduce them to you. We should expect folks from the community too."

"OK, cool. I got it, Big C."

"We a team," he affirmed.

"Yea, we're a team."

We walked straight to our corridors. I ran to the bathroom to release my nerves and to also ensure that I looked fine. I was more confident than nervous. I could hear voices and footsteps trailing into our program. I walked down, standing at the entrance of my youth program side. Looking right across from me was a poster of the late great educational trailblazer, Mary McLeod Bethune. The ancestors were with me. I was in the right place.

I listened quietly as the councilman was ushered to meet with Big C. I heard them chuckling as they embraced each other as if they were real good friends beyond politics.

"Boy, oh, boy, C, it's so good to see ya. You have always been one that you could depend on to make sure these young people have someone rallying for them." Mr. Williams stood next to him like a guard.

"Thank you, sir." Big C was humble.

"Oh, don't 'sir' me. We've come a long way together. We're from the same place." He patted him on his back. Mr. Fab, Mr. Light, Mr. Raymond, and other staff members surrounded Big C in support.

"So, tell me about what's going on down here and the great work you have begun."

"Councilman Small, as you can see, we have already begun planting the right seeds into this place. When we first came down here, it was vacant. No one even wanted to come down here. It was called the 'dungeon.' It was a dark place for young people. But now look at it. We painted it bright yellow and lime-green so that the youth could feel the love and excitement down here." He walked them to the study resource area. "This is our resource area where our youth who come in for educational support can come to study, research, and complete their homework with the proper resources. We purchased a catalog of books, graphic novels, business magazines, self-help books, a thesaurus, and dictionaries. Over here, you can see we purchased the latest desktop computers and created a minicomputer lab with printers," he boasted.

"This is awesome." The councilman walked around to touch the computers and skim through a few books. Mr. Light and Mr. Fab were smiling from ear to ear.

"So, what are the ages that mainly come to your program?" Councilman Small asked.

"Ages 6 to 13. We have the elementary and middle school youth from this community," C answered.

"Do you have any special activities for the youth?"

"Every month, we have a monthly themed activity. And if it's a holiday, we generally include the families in the celebration. Our goal is to give them some exposure as well and take them on field trips out of the community so that they can have a different outlook on life."

"This is good news. The atmosphere feels like a place that any kid from this community would want to come to. You even have leather couches and nice mahogany desks and bookshelves. I see you have a flat screen on PBS. This is good." His chief of staff handed him a bottle of water. There was a table with light refreshments, including water, iced tea, fruit trays, and muffins. It was very continental. You could see others filling their plates.

"So, Light, tell me about this new program that I've been hearing a whole lot about. It's a pilot, I understand."

"Yes, it sure is." Light was caught chewing on a piece of fruit.

"This is a pilot that is empowering our teens to go the distance. It has after-school tutoring, college prep, career exposure, and life skills training. It's amazing."

"Well, let's see it." Councilman Small was eager, and so was I. Mr. Fab led the pack.

I stood at the entryway, ready for the handoff.

"This initiative is being led by one of our brightest. Her name is Dream Angelou, and she's a Bison University grad. Her insight and motivation are awesome. Let me introduce you to her." Mr. Fab had on a mean fedora hat.

Councilman Small and I made contact.

"Dream, meet the distinguished Councilman Small. Dream is the director of this youth program, and she can tell you much more."

"Greetings, Councilman Small. I'm happy to meet you, and I'm glad that you're here to catch a snippet of the awesomeness of the Men of Valor." I shook his hand.

"Dream, what a beautiful and unique name. Let me tell you, I've been around for decades. And this part of the basement has never—I mean *never*—looked like this. So, first off, I wanna commend you for taking a big risk and giving this particular community a chance."

"It's an honor to be able to serve in this capacity. The name of this program is 'Activate Your Dreams.' It's no coincidence that my name is a part of it," I said to loosen up the crowd, and everyone began chuckling.

"Seriously, our teens growing up in this city are born with so many barriers. Three out of five of them will not be raised by their fathers. In most cases, their homes will be led by a woman, and more than likely, the same three out of five will be raised in poverty. So, what chances do they have at succeeding? How are we going to put them in a position where they are at an advantage and not a disadvantage?" I spoke directly to the heart of the crowd.

"She's onto something," Mr. Williams said, nudging the councilman. "We owe them a path of advantage. Programs like 'Activate Your Dreams' are imperative. We serve youth ages 13 to 21. This is a pivotal period in their lives. What they do now will determine if they will be dead, incarcerated, teenage parents, or caught in cycles of abuse by the age of 21."

"So, what does your program offer, Dream?" he asked.

"Academic tutoring, college preparation, life skills coaching, career exploration, financial literacy and management, as well as entrepreneurial development."

"I love this. This is empowering our youth for today's world and workforce!" He was intrigued.

"Let me walk you into our first classroom." He followed. "This is our learning lab. This is the place where students are tutored, prepped for tests and exams, provided test-taking strategies, and viable information." More people from the community started entering the classroom.

"Very good. This is very good. They're getting academic support in this room. It's quiet, so they can focus, am I right?"

"Correct," I responded.

Mr. Fab winked his eye at me to let me know I was doing well.

"Now, please walk with me to the second classroom. This is more of an activity room. When students don't have homework or other assignments for school, I give them food for thought. There is a lot of journaling, free writing, researching, and creative assignments that go on in here. And you can see the students' work on the walls."

"Yes. I see vision boards. Looking good, looking good."

"Thank you. Our last room is a multipurpose room. This room will be used for events, productions, guest speakers, and counseling if students need it. This is an open space, and we plan to have a few presentations in the up-and-coming months."

"How many seniors do you have?" Councilman Small asked.

"We have seven. Most of our youth are in the ninth and tenth grade."

"Do they want to go to college?" he pondered.

"Yes, they do. And our goal is to get their grades up so that they can get there."

"Let me know so that we can provide scholarships for young people from this community. I feel like there are gonna be huge success stories here."

"That's right. Real success," Mr. Light echoed.

"This is our program in a nutshell. We're just in the toddler stages, but we're picking up momentum, and we're happy that the teens are coming here so that we can help them achieve their aspirations. We have bathrooms down the hall as well."

Councilman Small whispered to his chief of staff. He looked around for a few minutes and most certainly zoomed in on a photo of Biddy Mason.

"I know everyone on these classroom walls except for this lady. What's her name?" he said, tapping me on the shoulder. Mr. Light and Mr. Fab both looked clueless as well.

"That's Biddy Mason. She was a pioneer, real-estate tycoon, and philanthropist who challenged her master and sued him for her own freedom—and won. She was also a midwife and nurse who saved her money and purchased land in what we know as downtown Los Angeles—she organized the first African American church . . ." He got me started.

"Wonderful, wonderful. Go, Ms. Mason. I see you are well researched, Ms. Dream."

"I try to be, and I try to instill that into the youth."

"This is a safe haven, a culture of learning and thriving. Now, it's *our* job to let the community know that the Men of Valor are here, and these programs are for their children and get them enrolled. Light and Fab, I love what I see. I feel the energy, and we're gonna build on top of what we already have," he spoke energetically to the crowd. "Thank you, Dream. I see you going so much further," he whispered.

"Thank you very much, Councilman Small, and I hope to see you again soon." I shook his hand and the hands of the members of his team.

"OK, everyone, the councilman is going to take a 5-minute break. Please meet us at the garden for a tour and for questions," Williams announced. Councilman Small grabbed a poppy seed muffin and some tea as he walked out of the building. Mr. Light and Mr. Raymond walked beside him. Big C was networking with community leaders and residents on his side. I wasn't sweating. There was no hair out of place. I was just fine.

"You did fantastic, baby girl." Fab stayed behind to talk to me. "You just flowed with it. You have a gift, and it stood out. You made me so proud of you and us."

"Thank you. I'm glad I did well. I was kinda nervous," I said.

"Well, no one could tell. You're gonna go far. The moon and stars are in your alignment. I want you to know this. This is a blessed start, and I heard Councilman Small in your ear. He's right. So, while you're here, we're gonna get what we can get from that amazing mind of yours," he laughed. Mr. Fab was always so jazzy, real, and optimistic. I hugged him.

"Thank you. Thank you."

"You're welcome, baby girl. I'm gonna head over to the garden with Light and dem."

"Okay. I'm gonna grab a muffin or some fruit, whatever is left, and take a breather."

"Yes, hon, take a breather."

I walked over to the refreshment table, and, of course, there was not a muffin in sight. At least 20 people were in the room, though, hanging out and politicking. I grabbed a few pieces of melon and pineapple and a bottle of iced tea and went back to my office to reflect.

That day was beautiful and significant. I felt a glimpse that I would do even greater things. Visions of meeting men and women in high places, from governments, from other counties even, and different societies. Maybe I would be like a younger Biddy. I would be different. I would stand out. I knew deep down that I wasn't going to retire at the Men of Valor. I was clear that I wouldn't be there for long. In the end, I would spend a little more than 2 years learning how to run a business, how to write grants, how to speak at large engagements, how to create large conferences, and how to present before politicians. I was a jack-of-all-trades. Mr. Light truly got a good run from me during my tenure.

Working with men, you would have to pick up the slack, sometimes baby them, hear them out, do their job, and still let them feel like *they* were in charge. I had long days, stressful days, and some days, I just was like, "fuck it."

I spent 60 percent of my time running programs and events and probably 40 percent of my time advising the leadership of the organization. God was good. He gave me insight, foresight, and even hindsight.

I think my best days at the Men of Valor were paydays and my private lunches with Roca. He was such an interesting brotha who was both intriguing, authentic, caring, and respectable. It was just good to talk to someone who was genuine, with no strings attached. After talking to him almost every day during our lunch breaks, it wasn't hard to decipher him. He was a young brotha who had experienced both sides of the grass, being raised by his father and grandfather, who were from Trinidad. Yet, the balance came from his mom, who heavily influenced him—she was from the city. Meeting a brotha who was raised by his very own father was rare, better yet, foreign, even. A few days a week, we would go out for lunch and have a chat and chew about our relationships, our goals, and just "LIFE." He was a great communicator, motivator, and encourager. I expressed to him that I saw myself starting my own company. He said that he saw me doing that as well. He would always say, "The organization needs you. If you leave, what dey gonna do?" I would respond, "But *I* need me. And if I don't got me, who's gonna take care of King and me? No one. *I'm* all we got."

Roca was so freaking handsome that most of the time I just was staring into space, wondering what life would be like if he were my man. Or what if I had met him before Kenya or even Solomon. He was so thorough and tangible. Yet, he was just as passionate and compassionate about people and youth and wanting a better way for the community. Roca was edgy. There was a mysterious side to him. Most Men of Valor had a story. Roca didn't share that other side with me, and to be honest, I had my share of "thug life." We both protected our interests and guarded our hearts, subconsciously knowing that if we got any closer than lunch—it would be a total wrap. We both drew the line of RESPECT and left it there.

Time didn't waste for nobody. I found myself most of the time missing the bus, missing the boat ride, or the plane ride . . . and landing on the sidewalk.

The worst part is that my opportunities began arriving on the second round, and it was like "flying standby." You never knew when you could board or when they would call your name. But once I boarded, there was a destination. I understood this lesson clearly. I would hit all focal points and pass all tests. I studied my instructors' instructors. I learned from my leaders' leaders.

I was gonna give this part of my life a good run. At Valor, I would get a crash course on learning how to write proposals and grants through the executive team assigning me to shadow the senior grant writer during deadlines. Most of my responsibilities included reviewing previous grants, understanding the history and past performance of the organization, as well as conducting rigorous research to help compile the grant. Although I was a writer by trade, technical writing was a skill set that was acquired. More importantly, studying the writing mechanism would position me to obtain a few mini grants while working for Valor. Valor was highly respected and had an endowment of $5 million which came from earmarked local funding, grants, and foundations. Realizing that a young Black girl like me from the hood could assist a nationally recognized organization to obtain millions of dollars gave me a sense of confidence about my own future.

It was time for me to become well researched, say my prayers, launch into the deep, and see that the waters were turquoise and crystal clear. This dream was mine—all mine. This dream was Biddy Mason. This dream was Oprah. This dream would make me a millionaire or billionaire. It was *Above the Rim*, like Tupac. It was enterprising.

Men of Valor would become a phenomenal chapter of my life, leading me on a journey to the White House, the Capitol, and to Congress. I would help lead confidential meetings with congresswomen, statesmen, and ambassadors. I would dream in color. Yet, in the presence of great men and women, there was something divine that dwelled beyond the present.

It was a bittersweet departure from the MOV. They were like big uncles to me. I knew they did not want to see me go, and I could have stayed as long as they needed or I needed to; however, I smelled a sweet aroma of "next level" in the atmosphere. There was a shift that had to occur in order to reach my very own greatness. Wouldn't miss this second chance for nothing in the world. I was obedient. No man could stop me.

# Chapter 7

## Black Boy Joy

"So, what's your greatest fear?" Dr. Keema, my therapist, asked.

"My greatest fear is failing at being a mom." I looked away.

"Question."

"Yea."

"Why are you afraid of something you do every day? You have never stopped. You never quit. You keep pressing your way even in the darkest hour," Dr. Keema assured me.

"No matter where I am in my life or how successful I become, nothing matters but my son. We are all that we have. You feel me?"

"Yes, I feel you."

"We all we got. Me and King. When my family switched up on me for having him in an intense situation, I was left to raise my son alone. So many nights I cried, not really understanding parenthood, but God gave me maternal instincts to guide me along the slopes. King is older now, and he's watching my movement," I said adamantly.

"Dream, you have already overcome. You are still here, loving on your son, nurturing, and supporting him. You are his example, and you are a shining light. More importantly, you are riding the wave.

*You have learned to cope with life and not fold when things get*
*tough. Nope, there is no failure in you. Remind yourself." Dr. Keema*
*always put things in perspective for me.*

*"I guess I'm doing OK, huh?" Small tears ran down my right cheek.*

*"Yes, you are." Dr. Keema smiled with her hands to heart.*

*"I can't afford to fuck up."*

*"You are not gonna fuck up." My therapist had a li'l hood in her,*
*and that's why I connected with her so hard. She was like a shot of*
*tequila with no chaser.*

*"Dream," she said, commanding my attention.*

*"Yes?" My eyes confirmed that I was listening.*

*"Stop being hard on yourself. You will* not *fail."*

As I stood on the sideline of the Astro Turf field of Charles Drew
High School, I reflected on my last conversation with my therapist.
It had been over a year since our last session, yet, her last words to
me were being rehearsed in my head. I hadn't fully adjusted to being
my own boss, but it felt good to have free-flowing time to attend my
son's football practice without feeling like I was gonna pass out on
the field because of exhaustion from working to execute someone
else's mission.

King was in his last years of elementary school and preparing for
middle school. He was growing up before my eyes and learning how
to become independent. He found his passion in football, and as
aggressive as he was, a contact sport was good for him. King found a
way to channel his thoughts and even his frustration with his own
father while on the field. He loved to exceed. He loved to win, but

that boy needed to learn how to take his losses without losing his mind.

The football field was his universe, and his coaches were young Black men who were so passionate about developing our young boys. Many of the coaches were in their 30s, former athletes who could have gone pro, but for some unusual circumstances, they didn't make it to the NFL. All the coaches had good jobs, mostly working for Metro, Department of Public Works, or a sector of a labor-intensive industry. A few were police officers. As a mother, it just felt good to know that King had positive male role models that cared about him and his teammates. They would volunteer their time to teach the youth every component of the sport.

The field was King's heaven on earth, and he owned every practice and celebrated every game. He was excited about where football could take him.

He stood at the 30-yard line with Coach L as he began drills. "Check this out. We not playing today. If you on this field, you gotta listen. And the moment I see you running around or playing, you on the sideline. Straight like that. You gotta put your heart and soul on this field or stay home!!! We're gonna work on conditioning and agility. It's eight of y'all, so spread out." Coach L began setting up five cones, four forming a square, each 10 yards apart, with the fifth cone in the middle.

The teammates were fully suited in their blue and white helmets, jerseys, and practice cleats. King was completely in tune with Coach

L and vibed off of his good energy. He stood fourth on the defensive line.

"Pay attention. Once I signal, the first player in line will sprint up to and around the first cone. Still facing the same direction, he will shuffle to the right to the second cone," Coach L demonstrated. The players were watching.

"After going around the second cone, the first player will backpedal at an angle toward the cone in the center. Who's the first player on the line?" he shouted.

"Devonte, Coach!" the teammates shouted back.

"Devonte, you up first. Observe what I'm doing so you can set the example to those who will follow you."

"Yes, Coach!" Devonte was attentive and had played with Coach L for 3 years, so he knew the drill and how to set an example for the other players.

"You gonna loop around." He demonstrated the loop. "Then you gon' backpedal to the fifth cone. One more time around that cone and then shuffle back to the first cone where you started. All right, let's go." He picked up the clipboard from the grass.

"Let's go, Devonte." He had his whistle in his right hand, eager to blow.

Devonte, standing 5 foot 1, took off sprinting to the first cone and around, speeding up to the second cone, and then shuffling to the center and around perfectly, making his way to the fifth cone.

"Look at that. That was smooth, Devonte. Pick up your pace pedaling back, though. Don't take your time. That was good! Who's next?"

"Caleb!" the teammates responded loudly.

"Let's go, Caleb, hustle up." Caleb was a li'l husky fella, but the team depended on him to hit. He was short, but there was power in the hit if he could get a hold of you. The other kids chuckled because Caleb was slower than most, but he followed directions.

"I don't know why you guys are laughing. I wanna see what *you* can do."

Caleb tried his best to get to the second cone, struggling with his loops, but he made it to the fifth cone.

"Go, DayDay, hurry up." The teammates were eager to get their own turn. The adrenaline was picking up.

Coach L blew his whistle. "Eh, DayDay, wake up, brotha. It's your time to sprint." DayDay took off, but initially, he was in a daze. His sprints were fast, and his looping around the second and center cones was precise.

"Go DayDay, go DayDay!" The teammates got excited because once he took off, nothing was stopping him.

Coach L was warming up, and so was the team. As DayDay pedaled backward, King made eye contact with me as he always did. He felt less confident when he didn't see his mama. It was the lioness energy that I gave to my son when he was on the field. When his eyes locked with mine, he felt invincible on or off the field.

"Come on, King, take off!" Coach L yelled, and that's all that King needed.

King sprinted up and around the first cone, shuffling to the second cone and around, and then backpedaling at an angle to the center, forgetting to loop around. Coach L blew his whistle. "King, you forgot to loop around." King was already at the fifth cone.

"All right, Coach. I got it on the fifth," he smiled.

He continued backpedaling to the fifth cone and looped for the last time. He finished off smoothly by shuffling left back to the first cone.

"Good work, King." He blew his whistle for the fifth player to proceed with the drill.

You could see King's smile beam across the field, and I smiled back to him. King began talking to the other players as his teammates completed the drill. One thing he was challenged with was his mouth. King was talkative wherever he went, and it could be for good or for bad. In school, it was an issue because I had constant calls from the teachers and the dean about him having difficulty following directions and shutting his mouth. However, he revered his coaches, especially Coach L. Since he was 5, he treated his coaches like his uncles, and if they said, "Jump," he would say, "How high?"

Another young coach, Rocko, came on the field to assist Coach L with agility drills, which was good. Coach Rocko was loud and obnoxious, but he kept the energy up, and the kids loved him. He had a Colgate smile, a nice body, and a great respect for the parents who were, all but one, single moms. I knew nothing about football other than the fact that I wanted Michael Vick to be my baby fatha.

I followed Vick from the Falcons to the Eagles to prison to the New York Jets, and lastly, the Steelers. He was mesmerizing, fast, handsome, chocolate, thick-arched eyebrows, and a nice smile. His shoulder blades and back were perfect—he was just, all-around, my prototype of a man. Not to mention we were both the same astrological sign and the same age. I felt like when he elevated as an athlete and role model, that the powers that be decided to humiliate him through that dog-fighting incident. He was a target like so many successful Black men in America, irrespective of industry. Had Vick been a white man, those charges against him would have been reduced to probation or community service. What I most admired about Vick was that he took full accountability for his actions, did his bid, and came home. And although they tried to break his spirit, he still rose to the occasion and retired from the NFL gracefully. I would always show King clips of Michael Vick, hoping he found something relative in his career. I'd invest in the aspirations of my son.

"Hey, hon," one of the team mothers on the field said, walking up to me.

"Hey, how are you?"

"Sis, I'm good. I'm just trying to keep the team organized. I see your son is doing well."

"He's trying. He loves the sport, and he's happy with this team."

"Yes, these boys love football. Some of these mothers, though, get on my damn nerves. They so messy. Wanna run shit but have no experience being team mom." She tooted her own horn.

"Oh, you know I don't get caught up in the messiness. I speak to everyone, but I mind my own business. And I pay my dues when requested." I rolled my eyes 'cause I didn't have time for the shenanigans of dealing with the football moms and their drama amongst themselves. Didn't know who was sleeping with the coaches so that their son could get the quarterback or running back position. What I knew for sure is that the coaches wished for a conversation with me because I was fly, thicker than a Snicker, reserved, and stayed in my lane. I never slept with a man for advancements, and it was against my principles to hit any man off to get a spot, whether it be for my son or myself.

"Yea, girl, you don't talk to no one, Ms. Antisocial," she faked giggled.

"Yea, I don't get caught up in the hype. Just here to support our boys and roll out. That's how you stay outta shit, you know?" I began checking my emails from my phone to avoid her commentary. Couldn't really get into politricks of Pop Warner.

"Well, okay, let me check in with the other moms," she said, waddling away.

The coaches had moved the players from the cones to a balance drill to improve agility and footwork. All the players grabbed a football and were spread out so that they had plenty of space around them. Watching the players made me want to get back into the gym or go back to my Yoga class. There was an inner athleticism in me that I had as a youth. I played softball, ran track, cheered, and was on the drill team. But dealing with my weight issues made it hard for me to be consistent. One month, I'm motivated, but as soon as I didn't see results, I would get discouraged. Witnessing my son on the field and observing his growth and inner strength gave me a sense of pride.

"Players, hold your ball in your right hand and balance on your left foot." Rocko led the drill. The players began adjusting from their usual stance.

"Lean forward and touch the ground with your left hand. Players, you will do five reps and then make a quick cut after the fifth rep. Every five reps you will switch hands."

Rocko stood on his left foot, holding the football in his right hand for five reps to demonstrate his expectation.

"Take off your helmets. Put the helmets beside you." He gave them 2 minutes to get their helmets off. If their heads were as big as King's, and they needed assistance, Coach L would help them. Coach Rocko surveyed the players who were struggling with their helmets, and Coach L was already on it as he went to help a few of them.

"Let's go, let's go. Everyone should be ready by now," he shouted and began counting, "1-2-3-4-and 5. Switch. 1-2-3-4-5 and switch. Get your balance together. Everyone should be on your right foot and holddddddddd." He held no punches. He walked around each player to ensure they were balancing, and it was longer than 5 seconds, but he was testing their level of focus. He loved messing with King, and King loved the extra attention.

"Eh, King, deep breaths, brotha, deep breaths. You got it." He stood directly in front of him.

He instructed them to up the reps from 5 to 10 and then up the intervals to 15. Those kids were beat. One reason why I always wanted to be at the practices and the games is that King had asthma. And even though he was outgrowing it, and his lungs were expanding because of football, my heart raced with palpitations thinking about how many times I damn near lived in the emergency room because of King's asthma flare-ups. So many nights I spent in the ER, wondering if his lungs would collapse because he was coughing up a lung. There were times when the albuterol didn't help, and the doctors had to administer a steroid. Rocko was completely aware of King's asthma, along with many of the other coaches. He really channeled into their breathing and ensured that they were adequately hydrated. If it were too hot during summer practices, the players would practice inside the gym that was air-conditioned. If the news reported Code Red, then they would cancel practice.

"Good work, brothas," he said, clapping. "Clap it up for yourselves." The players began their clapping it up to their own ritual beat. "Y'all came out here with a different energy. Sometimes, it ain't always about hittin' and knockin' a young buck down. It ain't always about touchdowns. Yeah, you wanna win, and you wanna score. But you gotta have focus. You gotta have focus. You must listen and work as a team. There is no 'I' in teamwork. We are building and strengthening the talent that you already have. That's our job. It's your job while you are young to follow directions and listen. It's our job as coaches to develop you and make you better and ready for the next level." He held no punches.

"Bring water. Where's the water? They need water." Rocko signaled to the team mom and water boys. They came running on the field to give both defense and offense water. All the players were sweating, and some were tired but inspired. King was pressed for water because all he drank was water and milk. He didn't desire juice or

Gatorade or anything with a sweet taste. He had been like that since he was a baby. He never liked anything sweet, not even juice, candy, or cake. He was different from most kids when it came to food. "Don't give me nothing sweet," he would reiterate.

Coach Rocko and the offensive coach blew the final whistle. All players knew that practice had ended. They huddled at the 50-yard line, holding their helmets and wiping their sweaty brows. This was the time for the coaches to discuss strategy for the games, identify the strengths and weaknesses of the young athletes, and tasks for individual players. By this time, the players only had food and sleep on their minds and in that order. The players respected their coaches, and their coaches admired them.

I pulled a big bottle of water out of my purse because I knew King would be extremely thirsty and hungry when he got off the field. King began walking toward me, smiling. "Ma Ma. Ma Ma," he chanted. "Maaaaa, you see me out there? I wasn't playing no games."

"I saw you out there, boi. You were doing pretty good. I saw you running your mouth too." King started giggling because he knew I didn't miss a beat when it came to him.

"You know Coach Rocko and Coach L luh me, man. Especially Coach L. He sees something in me."

"That's good, King. As long as you remain focused and keep being ambitious like you are, you'll be fine."

"Thanks, Ma. I'm so hungry. Can we get something to eat?"

"What's the magic word?"

"Pleaseeeeeee, Ma. My stomach growling."

"Here, boy," I handed him a big, bottled water. "You want Popeyes?"

"I sure do." He started walking faster to the car as if he had ants in his pants. King refused to miss a meal, and he was adamant about fried chicken. He had the appetite of a warrior. He placed his helmet, jersey, and equipment into the trunk and hopped in the front seat. "Lock in, son."

"I got you." He buckled up and immediately turned to his favorite radio station, turning the music up. We headed to Popeyes, which was just a few blocks away from the field.

"So, Ma, you don't have a job anymore?" King pondered, yet his question was serious.

"Son, it's not that I don't have a job. It's that I made a choice to work for myself. I have my own business that I'm kicking off," I responded.

"So, you a boss now? You gonna be rich soon." He got so excited.

"Hopefully, soon. Hopefully, by the time you get in middle school. I gotta figure out a lot of things on the business end. So, you're gonna see me heavy on my laptop. Mommy is gonna be going to meetings, the library, and writing grants and proposals."

"What's a proposal?"

"Pretty much it's a typed document that describes the mission and services that I offer, as well as answer the questions of the funder. My organization will help youth and communities in different ways, and some companies and agencies fund and donate to causes that I plan to serve."

"So, you gonna be working with them bad kids again like when I was a youngin?" he laughed.

"You got a point." I pulled into the drive-through. "Hold up, King. Let me place our order."

"You know what to get, right?"

"Naw, I don't know. I'm only your mama. I know you.

"Excuse me, can I please order a three-piece meal, dark. Can I order two wings and a biscuit with a strawberry soda?"

"What side would you like with your meal?" the woman spoke over the intercom with a heavy accent.

"I want french fries as my side. Thank you."

"Is that all?" She was blunt.

"Yes, that's all." I completed my order and pulled ahead. There were two cars ahead of me.

"But back to you, King. I plan to be working with at-risk youth. As you would say, bad kids. Really trying to help them to do better and want better. I'll create programs for music, dance, creative writing, and mentoring. My goal is to show them that there is a light at the end of the tunnel."

"That's good. So you can make money doing that. Like, we gon' be good, right?" He was concerned.

"We will always be good. Plus, son, I'll have time to spend with you and time to come up to the school to check you when you act up."

"Oh Lord. I'm doing better, though." He was convincing.

"Boy, I get a call at least once a week from the teacher or the dean. It stresses me out. Why you can't just go to school and learn? That's what I did when I was your age."

He looked away. The cars were moving. I drove to the pickup counter to get our food, immediately handing King his chicken box.

"Thank you."

"You welcome. So, you not gonna respond, huh?"

He started demolishing his chicken thigh within seconds. "You right. It's those kids and teachers. The teachers get on my nerves. They don't know how to talk to students."

"Your job is to learn. Don't go back and forth with them. You do your part and go to school. If you have issues with a teacher or staff, let me handle them."

"OK," he said, lowering his voice.

"I love you. I just want you to be great. Better than me."

"I gotchu, Ma." He was focused on the fries now.

"The goal for us is to go all the way to top. I got your back from the beginning. I will never leave you or abandon you. At the end of the day, my goal is to create a better future and more opportunities for you and us."

"It's always been us, Ma. I mean, I know we got Kenya, but I'm not sure how long that's gonna last."

"*Excuse* me? *Really?*"

"I like him. He cool. It's just I will never trust another man since my father left us."

Tears welled up in my eyes.

"That's understandable, King. Well, my heart is still guarded. I dig him, but I can't be no fool again. My heart won't take it anyway."

"Just be careful, Ma." He ripped into the skin of the chicken wing. "Yea, we all we got."

I placed my right hand on top of his head, gently rubbing his waves. King was nearing his teenage years, yet he was an old soul. He spoke in a tone that only the ancestors and I understood. I could tell he was excited about our future, but he remembered the heartache. And I vowed he wouldn't see darkness in the season. We would welcome all light and heart to center. I would take risks and secure him tightly. I couldn't afford to lose the joy in his eyes.

# Chapter 8

*Paper Planes*

*"I picked up King from preschool, ordered carryout, and sat on my couch at the edge of my seat waiting for the results of the election, with a new friend of mine, Kenya."*
~Excerpt from *Free*, a novel

There was a complexity to Kenya that was beyond complicated. One angle of him appeared to be very stable, reliable, kind, and anchored. Yet, he was showing signs of being wild, impulsive, aggressive, and sometimes uncontrollable. I paid attention but not to the details.

Kenya began complaining that I was more engrossed in starting a business and less focused on him. It was hard to balance being a mom, starting my very first business, and being a good girlfriend. I loved my son more than anything in the world, and I vowed that we would never go back to poverty and struggling as hard as I did. The hustle was real for me, and Kenya didn't understand that I was taking baby steps to launch my own empire. LOVE was important to me, but not as much as being prosperous and wealthy. In my mind, LOVE was a verb that men defined as an adjective. LOVE crushed me to the point of almost no recovery. And although I had a soft spot in my heart for Kenya, subconsciously, I was guarded. He said I was becoming "boring and that we needed to go out more, party, and have a good time," and he was actually right.

It was a crisp fall night, filled with a cloudless, midnight-blue sky. We would go to a club downtown where Kenya's homies would meet us. These were guys that he grew up with, ones that he trusted. They spoke the same language, and at some point, they got money like "duffle bag boys." Kenya didn't trust too many people, but if he was bringing me amongst men, that meant he wasn't gonna put me in harm's way because there was a deep respect and code in their world.

Adorned with 20 inches of wavy Brazilian hair, silver doorknockers, fitted jean jeggings, a vintage off-the-shoulder shirt, and cropped, black leather coat, in my mind, I was fly than a muthafucka, and as long as he was happy with how I looked, we were good.

"Come on, baby." He walked ahead of me, taking my right hand in his left palm.

"I got on heels, boy."

"Yea, but you walking slow as usual." He was pressed to get into the club, which was a block away.

"I told you my homies waiting on me. They left our names at the door, so we don't gotta stand in line. You got your license?"

"Yea it's in my bra."

"Cool. Mine is in my pocket, so we guchi," he smiled. Kenya had a dark blue polo shirt, black jeans, a fresh pair of Prada sneakers, and wore his black Armani shades. During the week, he looked dusty, but he was the type of brotha that cleaned up well. He stood 5-11, but with his shoes, he was 6 feet tall. Kenya walked up on security like he *was* security.

"Excuse me, we on the guest list," he spoke to the lady holding the guest list who stood right next to a security guard.

"What's your name?" The hostess thought she was cute.

"My name is Kenya Jackson, and her name is Dream Angelou."

The hostess began scrolling down her list.

"Let me see your IDs," the security guard said.

We both pulled out our IDs for him to verify. The host put checks by our names.

"They good," she said feistily

"Hold your arms out," the security waned Kenya, patting down his pockets, pants, and ankles.

"Go in."

Kenya took a few steps up near the entrance waiting on me. I already knew what to do. My hands immediately went out so that I could be waned. Little did they know that I kept everything in my bra, especially my money and my ID. The guard nodded and cued me to go in.

"Come on, baby, they pressed like shit." Kenya grabbed my hand again. He was very overprotective of me. You could hear Young Jeezy booming through the narrow walls, and the whole club was jumping. It was packed, and the violet lights were electrifying. He walked straight to the bar.

"Eh, excuse me. Can I get blue Amsterdam on the rocks? Whatchu want, boo?"

"An apple martini, thank you."

"You don't have to thank me. We good. I just want you to have a good time. I want us to have a good time. Don't be thinking about no work shit. You know King wit' his grandma, so he good. Let's just party, and when we get home, we can color." He grabbed me by my waist, wrapping his arms around me and pulling me close to his chest so that he could peck me twice on my lips.

Kenya knew the art of affection, but I fell short in that area. It was like I was so hesitant to give kisses and hugs. Ever since I was a li'l girl, I was leery of men based on the stories that I heard from family members and my friends who had issues with men straight violating them. In my subconscious, I thought giving a man affection was doing way too much, and it was a barrier that was difficult to get over. It was no shade to Kenya. I was just not affectionate, and it was hard showing it, even though in my mind, I was vulnerable.

The bartender was quick and handed me the drinks while Kenya paid for them.

"All right, let's head to the VIP. We got a table. The big homie got us one."

"Oh yeah?"

"Man, I'm not gonna take you to no bootleg shit. We real niggas, baby."

"I know, babe." I smiled as we walked toward the VIP. All I saw was dudes that favored Kenya, with hats to the back, chains on, and bottles. It was apparent they were his boys.

"Ehhhhhh, nigga. What up? Glad you came through." His friend Frank gave him a big brotherly hug. Next to Frank was a young petite chocolate woman who smiled at me.

"Is this the golden girl I've been hearing about?"

"Yea, Frank, that's my Dream!" Kenya cheesed from ear to ear.

"She's beautiful, man." Frank hugged me like he knew me my whole life.

"Man, he always talks about you wherever and whenever. You're his pride and joy." Frank made it plain.

"Yea, she is."

"So, this must be Reagan." Kenya pointed toward Frank's significant other.

"Yea, this is my Reagan." He put his arm around her like a typical hood dude.

Reagan was poised and cute, but you could tell Frank had her groomed.

"How are you? Nice to finally meet you, Kenya and Dream. Your hair is really cute," she said, beginning small talk as we stood face-to-face.

"Thanks, girl. I try."

"Y'all go ahead and talk while me and my boi catch up." Kenya gave orders as he and Frank walked toward some seats in VIP and grabbed a bottle.

"You guys been here long?"

"We got here about 15 minutes ago, so not too long. This is a nice club. Not too big and not too small," Reagan said, looking around.

"Yea, it's cute."

"Are you from this area?"

"No, I'm from Cali originally. I just went to college out here and ended up staying."

"Really? California is beautiful. What made you come here?"

"Yea, it is, but Black people are moving and shaking out here."

"I guess they are," Reagan responded. "But you got Hollywood and all the stars out there."

"Yea, but Hollywood isn't for me. I'm too revolutionary."

"I get it. Yea, it's about politics and business out here. Do you have kids?" Reagan had her questions lined up. You could hear T.I.'s "Live Your Life" come through the speakers. All you could see is everyone put their hands in the air, rocking from the right two steps and then to the left with the crazy two-step.

"Yea, I have a son, and Kenya has a daughter, and you?"

"I have a daughter too. My one and only."

My mind began drifting from our conversation and into the music. I sipped my martini and vibed to the sounds of the deejay. I looked back at Kenya, who was with his boys as they kept filling up their glasses with vodka.

"Eh, baby! Dream," he called my name.

"Yes?" I turned around.

"Come here, baby. Come chill with me." I began walking toward him. Frank signaled to Reagan to come to the VIP table as well. Kenya grabbed my hand immediately, holding his drink in the other hand. He began his two-step, intertwining his fingers in mine while holding my right hand in the air. We began partying as the deejay mixed T.I. with a little 50 Cent, and then when Lil Wayne came on, it was like the energy transformed the club into the "Ninth Ward."

"Yea, my nigga!" Kenya and all his boys began congregating, and the two-step got harder as soon as "Duffle Bag Boy" began echoing throughout the speakers. All you saw were Prada and Nike boots jamming in unison. Their bottles of Moët were raised higher, they swayed harder, and they flashed the stacks of rubber band hundreds that came out of nowhere into the air. They were in a cypher, and all you could hear was dem say, *"If I don't do nothing Imma ball/I'm counting' all day like the clock on the wall/now go and get your money little duffle bag boy/said go and get your money little duffle bag boy."*

I felt like I was around local celebrities.

"Eh, boo, we real niggas. We Uptown's finest. Best believe these are my men. We ain't rocking like nuffin', we ain't going for nuffin'," Kenya's D.C. accent thickened up.

As the club became more lit, you saw scantily clad women who worked in the club as hostesses walking around damn near naked with bottles and lit confetti tops. They were uniformed in black and barely had their nipples covered. They came to entice the men in VIP to buy more bottles—it was a strategy. And I watched how Kenya's men shadily groped the girls as they passed by saying slick nothings in their ear. Frank had the most money, it appeared, and he was buying bottle after bottle. Reagan was in the cut, clocking his moves all night long. I started sipping a few glasses of champagne, and the more I drank, the more I began dancing to my jams as if I were in college partying with my girls all over again. Kenya was throwing back glasses of vodka, and he was getting louder and louder.

"Ehhhhhh, baaaaaaby." His words became elongated and slightly slurred. "This is my big homie, Quante. This my nigga for life. Like for real!" Kenya got emotional.

"Hi, how you doing? It's nice to meet you." Quante extended a handshake.

"I'm good." I stayed cute and observant.

"This boy is crazy about you. He always talking about you, so you must be a good one."

"I *am* a good one." We all laughed. Quante had a foreign accent. Yet, he had the look of a Yankie. He was short, medium build, had cornrows, a D.C. hat on, and some True Religion jeans with a fresh button-down. He had a nice smile, but I could tell in his eyes that he wasn't nothing to play with.

"He from Trinidad, fa' real, but he been in the States since he was a kid. He an Uptown nigga fa' life!"

"And you know this!" Quante shouted as he sipped. One of the club hostesses started making her way toward us as if she knew we had money.

"Y'all want anything?" she tried to be cute. I looked her up and down like, if you make the wrong move, bitch, I'm going back to the ol' me.

"Yea, bring us another bottle of dat white," Quante handed her a bill. Kenya got close to her from behind and tried to give her a funky roll on the low. She smiled back. I felt my blood pressure going through the roof.

"What the fuck are you doing? See, man!"

"Yo, chill, Ken. You see shorty right here," Quante tapped his shoulder to get his attention.

"Man, I ain't doing nothing wrong. I'm dancing and cooling. She just mad 'cause she want a nigga in her face." His whole disposition changed.

"I want a nigga in my face? You was pressed for me to come here, nigga! I could've stayed home."

"Man, shorty, go somewhere!" he raised his voice.

Quante got in between us. The hostess left as soon as she sensed the tension. He was twisted fa' real and had me all the way fucked up.

"Y'all chill. We came here to have a good time. Man, do better. And, sis, just fall back; don't trip." He was the voice of reason.

"Fuck her, I ain't trippin'." Kenya began slightly stumbling toward Frank. Quante moved the liquor bottles away from Kenya as if to say he knew where the issue lay.

I stayed in my position. My feelings were hurt, but then my jam came on abruptly, banging like heck throughout the club. The strobe lights switched from orange and bright red to violet and electric blue. The night was cranking up a notch. All you heard was the beat drop from M.I.A., the Sri Lankan princess.

*"I fly like paper/get high like planes/if you catch me at the border I got visas in my name/if you come around here/I make 'em all day/,"* then the beat and her voice dropped harder.

Kenya, Frank, Quante, and some more of their boys ran to the dance floor and took over. Women ran right behind them and began dancing with them. Reagan walked over to me and was like, "They doing too much, ain't they?" as she folded her arms and sucked her teeth.

"Yea, my nigga is doing too much. This shit is crazy." Kenya was dancing with a girl as if I weren't even in the building—partying away. They did have the club jumping. Part of me didn't know if I should have felt disrespected or what. "Paper Planes" was our song. We even had our own dance. I put him on to new music, and he was just gonna dance with bitches in the middle of the dance floor.

"I don't know, Reagan, but I'ma grab one of these champagne bottles and crank up since they doing them."

"Pour me a cup, girl." Reagan was feeling some type of way too.

"You got it." I popped the bottle and poured her a full cup.

I kept the rest of the bottle to myself and began dancing to the mix of "Swagga Like Us" wit' M.I.A., T.I., Jay-Z, Kanye, and Lil Wayne.

*"No one on the corner have swagger like us/Swagger like us, swagger swagger like us . . ."* Reagan and I began dancing and singing together. *"Swagger like us, swagger, swagger like us,"* we chanted.

Kenya and Frank noticed that we got in our zones and tried to walk over to us. Reagan and I paid them no attention.

"What's up wit'chu, man?" Kenya got loud in my face.

"Ain't nuffin'." I turned away from him. He grabbed my face.

"No, for real, why you be trippin' off of nothin'?"

"You need that much attention? Do you see me in any of these niggas' faces?"

"You better not get in any of these niggas' faces. I will break your face *and* that nigga's face."

"You ain't breaking nuffin'. You doing the same shit. C'mon. Anyway," I kept dancing. He grabbed my arm, but I pulled away from him.

"Don't make me get with you in here." He became more aggressive. He reeked of vodka.

"Go somewhere, go party with dem girls. I'm good."

"Oh, you good?" he walked all up in my face.

"Man, get out of my face. You blowing me."

"I'm not going anywhere."

Frank saw what he was doing and intervened.

"Bruh, you good? Chill, man. You got that liquor in you. You letting that liquor get to you. You got a good shorty."

"She jealous, man."

"You gotta respect her."

Kenya started stumbling more. His eyes were red. He didn't look as fresh as he did coming in. His face turned a dark mahogany, like he had drunk a gallon of liquor.

"I'm ready to leave."

"We ain't leaving yet. Fuck you talking about?" He was belligerent. I started gulping the champagne in the bottle. My goal was to get drunk enough to ignore his dumb ass.

"You OK?" Reagan asked.

"I'm OK. He had too much to drink," I made an excuse, but I was embarrassed because Kenya was loud, and people started paying attention. She observed the drama.

"Kenya, I'm leaving in 15 minutes."

"You can go. You boring anyway." He went looking for more liquor, but Quante hid most of it. Quante was a hawk and watched everything. You could tell that he was the one who could check Ken if he got out of line.

The DJ began spinning a li'l Kanye, and I was mellowing out and prepared in my mind to go. I shook the bottle of champagne and realized that I damn near had a whole bottle to myself, and there were maybe only a few sips left.

Kenya walked up on me from behind.

"So, you just gonna leave me? I mean, I'm good, but we came together." He was bipolar.

I rolled my eyes. He was having too many moods for me.

"Whatchu gonna do?"

"I'm leaving soon."

"Go ahead then." He popped me on my ass.

Then all of sudden, "Thug Passion" came on by 2Pac, and the DJ had the nerve to mix it with Go-Go Band Backyard's rendition. The whole club went up. Kenya got himself back on the dance floor with all his homies.

All you heard was, "Yeaaaaaaa, My Nigga! Crank! Crank dis shit!"

*"You got me dripping wet/From the way you make me sweat/Give me some of your Thug Passion baby/Ooooowoooooowooo,"* the crowd sang.

The music got louder, you could hear the bass and congas rip through the speakers, and the imitation of the locals "beating their feet," as they called it. Go-Go had a way of taking you back to Africa or making you rep your hood. It was D.C. culture, and you had to respect it and feel it one way or another. We all partied, but in the back of my mind, I wondered if this was the behavior that I would have to deal with in the long run from Kenya. It was like I saw two sides to him, and I wasn't feeling it. There was not a sip left in my bottle, and all the bottles in VIP were completely emptied.

The club started dying down. The DJ began playing reggae, which transitioned the energy. Kenya and his boys all looked like they were stumbling back to VIP.

"It was nice meeting you, Reagan."

"It was nice meeting you too, Dream. We gotta get together soon."

"Yes, we do."

"You ready to go, huh?" Kenya was drunk as hell.

"Yea, are you?"

"Yea, we can roll out." He looked like a kid who tried to stay up all night and was fighting being sleepy.

"All right, y'all, I love y'all!" He gave all his men hugs and daps.

"I'm outta here. But I'ma see y'all around the way."

"All right, Ken. Nice meeting you, Dream," said Frank.

Quante was like our bodyguard. He escorted us out, making sure that Kenya didn't fall. The brisk air hitting us felt so good. As we walked down the street, the liquor definitely crept up on me. But I was focused enough to get us home in one piece. The corns on my feet were hurting. If it were summer, I wouldn't have any problem walking down the street without my shoes. When we got to the car, Kenya was damn near asleep. Quante really knew him and made sure that he got in the car without a problem—like a big brother.

"All right, slim, you good?"

"Yea, I'm good." Kenya got in the front passenger seat and reclined his seat all the way back and passed out.

"All right, Dream, y'all get home safe. He gon' sleep like a baby. He drunk as shit."

"Yea, y'all set me up, leaving me with him. I'm not babying him. He get on my nerves."

"You love 'im, though. I can see it in your eyes." We both laughed.

"OK, see you and thank you." I put on my seat belt, rolled the windows down, and slowly put my foot on the gas. We were about 20 minutes away from the house.

Ken was knocked out, and I was so irritated with how he carried me at the club that I wanted to jolt him and wake his drunken ass up, but I chose to let him sleep.

As I rode through the empty downtown streets to my suburban community, I turned on the radio to the Magic station so that the grown and sexy music could radiate through the speakers. Anita Baker was soulfully singing, "Sweet Love," and I sang right along with her. From Anita, to Jeffrey Osborne, and then Chaka Khan, the "quiet storm" session had me in a peaceful zone.

I pulled up in front of my house, turned the car off, and attempted to wake up Kenya.

"Wake up, boy, wake up. Wake up, Kenya," I jolted him.

"Okay, man." He shrugged his shoulders and proceeded to go back to sleep.

I kept his door open, hoping that the fresh air would wake him up and went inside the house. My corns were burning, and so was the bottom of my feet. My bed was calling my name. There was no time to put on pajamas. I took off my heels and my jeggings and hopped in my bed, wearing my shirt and panties.

"Baby, baby, where you at?" Kenya stumbled through the door.

"I'm in bed. Close the front door, boy."

"I'ma get me some water and wake the fuck up."

"What, boy?"

"What time is it?"

"It's three in the morning. I'm going to sleep."

"Well, take your ass to sleep," he yelled from the kitchen. "I'm going back outside."

"This neighborhood is quiet. Why you gotta wake the neighbors up?"

"Man, I'ma tell the homies to pull up. I'm about to be up. I ain't ready to go to sleep." He was amped.

"Well, I'm going to sleep. Close and lock the door when you leave."

"I ain't going far, baby," he assured.

My nature was that I was an early bird. I went to sleep early and woke up early. Kenya went to sleep late and woke up late. I was day, and he was literally night. I wasted no time and curled up in a fetal position, snoring for hours in the comfort of my bed. Saliva ran down the corner of both sides of my mouth.

I woke up around seven in the morning to use the bathroom and realized that Kenya was not in the house. I walked around the house and checked each room to make sure that I didn't assume wrong. I opened the door and found him outside of my house, pacing back and forth as if his whole world were crumbling. He appeared different, way more different than when he was drunk. His eyes were wide open, and he was touching his head and patting his arms and body as if he were having a breakdown.

"Kenya, what's wrong, dude?"

"Dream, oh my gosh, oh my gosh. Help me, Dream! Help me, Dream!"

I grabbed the blanket that was on the couch and wrapped it around my waist. Clearly, I had no idea what was going on.

"What's wrong? What happened while I was asleep?"

"They tryin'a kill me. They tryin'a get me," he said, panicking.

"Who?" I said, looking around.

"Them."

"Who is them, Kenya? What's wrong with you?"

"They wanna see me die. They want me gone. They trying now to kill me," Kenya screamed. I was so nervous that my neighbors were gonna come out. And hell, I was also looking for the people that he was talking about. I didn't need no one trying to come into my house and kill my son or me.

"What's going on? Did someone say they were gonna kill you?"

"No, I jus' know." He raised his shirt to show all the bullet marks and wounds from when he was shot years ago.

"Is it those same people, Kenya? Is it the people who shot you before? Are they after you?"

"No, baby!" he said, sobbing like a child.

"Come into the house, Ken. Come in the house, baby." I was shaken as I took his hand and tried to lead him back in.

"Come on, I got you. I'm not gonna let anyone harm you, Ken. I got you. Trust me, love." I held his hand and watched both of our backs just in case a crazy tried to run up.

"Come in and come talk to me. I'm gonna get you a glass of water." He sat down, and his face resembled Frankenstein, like he was in a trance. He was not himself.

"Baby, can you get me some milk?"

"Yes." I poured him some milk in a glass and handed it to him. He drank the glass down like he was dehydrated.

"Some more." He was thirsty. I filled his glass and handed it to him. He sipped the milk down and became calm this time.

"I was smoking." He stared at the wall.

"Smoking what?"

"I was smoking a stick."

"Whatttttt? What are you talking about?" I got more worried. I hadn't even begun to understand what he was talking about.

"Look!" He pulled out what appeared to be a wet Newport. "I was smoking this." He looked as if he wanted me to take it away from him. I grabbed the cigarette and observed how wet the Newport was. The texture of it was different, and it had a strange aroma that hit my nose.

"This cigarette stank! It ain't no weed in this cigarette. What the hell?"

"Naw, that ain't weed, Dream. That's some demonic shit. I ain't have no business smoking it. Sometimes, I smoke it to think and reflect, and other times, I get like how I just got."

I listened, and I was lost. "So, that cigarette has a drug in it? What kinda drug 'cause you are bugging?"

"It's a drug, sweetheart. A real drug. My drug of choice. It keep a nigga dick hard and make me crazy in one breath. Sometimes, I feel like smoking because it keep me closer to the heavens, but I also see hell."

The last thing I needed was to love someone who was drug addicted. Damn, where did I go wrong? How did I miss this during the intake? I thought I knew everything I needed to know about Kenya, but I was drawing blanks. I was lost. I needed to meditate. It was over my head.

"Demons, we all got 'em, Dream," he whispered as he adjusted his body to lie down.

"Yea, we got demons. Next time tell me about yours. Anything else you need to let me know?" I sat at the marble island table, stunned.

"Love me for who I am, just love me," he said and closed his eyes.

"Love Boat. It's the Boat that got me fucked up," he whispered some more.

"Angel Dust?"

"Yea, that's what y'all call it in Cali? That's what I smoke."

I flicked the Newport in the trash can, hoping that he would never have an episode like that again. I was embarrassed and didn't know the first person to talk to about this. I began Googling "Love Boat" and the side effects. My plate was too full.

I held back my tears. My head was spinning like a paper plane. It hurt my heart to see Kenya like this. He went from my protector to me protecting him. His demons were beginning to look like they were too big for me.

This was definitely not in the position description.

# Chapter 9

*Chocolate in a Venti Cup*

My mind was racing through the aroma of a Grande Cinnamon Dolce Latte and the smell of old white men that gave off the scent of broken-up Marlboro Lights.

I had $500 and a dream—No investors or bank loans, no drug money, and no sugar daddy. My vision was colossal, surpassing my 503 FICO score and my demographics. Everyone in the coffee shop had a laptop, whether dingy, brand-new, or like mine, with a few missing keys. You knew that everyone was there to do business or was being consulted on business.

My goal was to research the process of obtaining my Employer Identification Number (EIN) as well as understanding the process of getting my business license. Working for the Men of Valor provided me with lead ways on taking my very first step toward legitimately putting my business on the map. I put my headphones on, played my classic Mary J Blige mix, and zoned into my element.

As I began researching the local small business website for the city, the link led me straight to the IRS website. Lord knows that I didn't want any run-ins with the IRS, but the EIN number was necessary for any entrepreneur, big or small. The EIN application was standard, which was perfect for me because I was crafting in my mind the type of services that I would offer and whether I wanted to establish my company as a limited liability company or nonprofit organization.

There was a great need for nonprofit and community-based work in urban areas. Youth violence was on the rise, and the hoods needed more havens and safe passageways for young people. It was in my heart to design programs that were creative, innovative, yet raw and empowering for youth and young adult populations. Deep down, there were so many brown girls and boys who grew up like me in the hood while being raised by a working-class family—dreaming of becoming great. I met so many like me when I was working for the Men of Valor. These brown girls and boys had so many trauma-filled stories of abuse, abandonment, and neglect.

Once, a female youth confided in me that when her mom passed away that her dad couldn't even step up to the plate to raise her because he had a crazy crack addiction, which put her in the custody of her aunt. While living at her aunt's house, her uncles would take turns sexually abusing her while the aunt was gone to work or running errands. She would explain that there were so many horror stories of victimization that occurred in her aunt's basement that when she got her weight up, she began fighting off her uncles. She eventually told her aunt that she was being sexually abused and raped by her uncles, and the aunt swept it under the rug. As a result, she spent her entire teen and young adult life fighting everyone who she came across because the pain was unreal, and she could no longer suppress it.

Every time she would see me, she would have a story to tell me, and I would embrace her, strengthen her, and show her ways on how she could escape the abuse and devilish environment by applying to a college and going away to it. She had a 3.0 GPA, and I would help her to apply to her top five postsecondary institutions, as well as assist her in applying for scholarships. She pressed hard, weathered the storms at 17, and would later become accepted into a good college that offered her campus housing. Her future was brighter, and she had the opportunity to flee from her demons.

While I had never been molested, sexually abused, or raped, those horror stories that the youth would tell me in confidence always had me at the edge of my seat, yearning to start an organization that would be a place of refuge, peace, and a fortress for the needy and hurting people of the community

I began filling out the online application, and with excitement, typing the name of my first business, "Passion for Change!" I added the demographical information and began writing out my mission on paper. I could visualize the mission, but the words had to be meaningful.

I wrote, "*Passion for Change mission aims to empower, transform, and assist at-risk youth and individuals in overcoming their fears, discover their gifts, and manifest their destiny.*"

I added, "*We serve as a change agent for the community!*"

In my mind, my organization would change lives, change perspectives, change hearts, and offer a synergy of passion for the youth and communities.

I looked in my bag and pulled out my glasses that I never wore and glanced at the screen for a second look to ensure that what I was typing in the application made sense.

The next tab read, "Description of Services." There were so many services that Passion for Change could offer. Concepts began flowing through my mind that I quickly jotted down. *"Passion for Change will offer creative and performing arts programs for youth, mentoring, tutoring, college preparation, violence intervention, and career training."* There were so many things that needed to be met in the community, but I stuck to what I knew since I knew that I would be working as the first employee until I secured my first grant.

The next tab read, "Position Title."

*"CEO/Founder/Executive Director."* My spirit leaped because I was actually manifesting something that was on the inside of me into the real world. Working for many organizations over the years now made sense to me. I put in all that work so that I could officially become a "BOSS." Typing those words sent chills and flutters throughout my body. My mama would say, "If you can see it, baby, then you will believe it." The vision was on paper for the very first time.

There were additional questions, but it carried no real thought, and the answers were simple. Within about 45 minutes of typing, proofing, and reviewing my application, all there was to do was to hit *submit*. With bright eyes and faith, I hit the submit button.

The first task was completed, and next was researching how to obtain a business license. The city had a business licensing agency devoted to guiding and advising aspiring entrepreneurs like me who were first-timers and needed to know what forms to fill out and the costs of the entire licensing process. Applying for the EIN was free, so my budget was still at $500, and I had no problem spending it all until my licensing goal was achieved.

The licensing fee was $250, but there were incorporation, trade name, and all other types of fees that looked like I was gonna end up spending the $500 or pulling money from my savings account to fulfill all the additional required fees.

I clicked on the *contact us* link on their web page and began writing down their address and phone number. Business licensing was about 20 minutes away, but there was more comfort in me calling them first before coming to their office. I began dialing their office number, which rang about eight times, then an automated system came on and gave me several options, including "*press zero*" for the operator. I held briefly, then was connected to a representative.

"Hi, Office of Business Licensing, can I help you?" She had a city-girl undertone.

"Hi, I'm trying to get my business license, and I wanted to know what forms I should submit and what the fees are that I have to pay."

"What type of business are you starting?" She cut straight to the chase.

"A nonprofit."

"Okay, you can go online to our website and click on *online services*. There are a few forms that you will need, like a basic business license application, an application for a certificate of occupancy, a Clean Hands with the Office of Tax and Revenue, and incorporation. It costs $495."

"Oh, wow!"

"You'll need to bring your EIN number from the IRS. Do you have your letter from them?" She was blunt.

"No, not yet. I'm waiting to receive it via email."

"You should get an email soon with your EIN and a mail copy. Whichever comes first, you can come in with that paper, along with the other forms printed and filled out completely to expedite the service."

"Is there an expediting fee too?"

"Yes, it's $100 to expedite, but you will get your license the same day as long as you bring in your paperwork completed and organized. I would suggest that you get a nice-size file folder that is secured with your business documents."

"Thank you. Yes, I'll get one today."

"Also, you might as well come in to fill out your forms because you'll have to go to the Office of Taxes to get a 'Clean Hands' printout that says that you don't owe any taxes and that you're a new business."

"Where's the tax office?" I asked.

"It's right across the street from us. Go to them first. Bring that EIN paper. Are you driving?" The representative began popping gum in my ear. Her real ghetto-ass roots came out.

"Yes, I'm driving." I began walking toward the barista to place an order for a banana chocolate smoothie in a Venti cup. This process began irritating me, and I needed a booster. There was a crazy connection between me and a chocolate smoothie, and if you added banana, drinking it was like an electrolyte high. Chocolate was my muse, my solace, my emotional blanket—it was a way to calm me down, and yet, it was soothing to my soul.

Broken Heart = Chocolate Smoothie

Sad = Chocolate Shake

Anxiety = Hot Chocolate

Menstrual Cycle = Hershey's Chocolate Bar

Working Hard = Banana Chocolate Smoothie in a Venti cup.

Chocolate was my healer.

"If you're driving, you should have someone drop you off or take the train or a cab. Parking is hard to find. There is parking that's underground, but it's expensive." She was making it hard.

"OK, I will most likely just pay for parking."

"OK, but it's expensive," she said convincingly.

"I'm good."

"So, how much do you think I should bring to be safe?" I cut to the chase.

"At least $600 because of the additional taxes. Then you should be good."

"OK, thank you very much for the information. Is there anything else I need to know?"

"That's it, hon!"

"Thanks again for being so informative."

"No problem. You take care, and good luck with everything." She continued to pop her gum like it was the last meal on earth.

"Thank you." We both ended the call.

I checked my account online to see how much I had left in my savings. I needed an extra $150 and $20 for parking, to play it safe. I had another $800 stacked in that account, so I was able to pull from, which was in my favor.

My goal was to use the following day to go to the business licensing office and fill out my forms, as long as my EIN came to my email by the end of the day.

"Venti Banana Chocolate Smoothie," a tall hippyish blonde called for me to get my drink. I took a large sip of my smoothie like it was a meal, when, in fact, it was more like a meal replacement for the time that I spent in Starbucks. I scanned the area and realized that I had spent several hours there, and the same folks were completely glued to their laptops without even a smirk on their face. A realm of focus permeated the atmosphere. It seemed like everyone was "thinking of a masterplan," including me.

I utilized the remainder of my day before picking up King to research local grants and the processes. What all the grants had in common is that I needed a business license and a Clean Hands, just like the representative said on the phone. She wasn't bullshitting, either. The grants checklist read just like the advice that she gave me over the phone. There was so much money in grants, and it was unbelievable because the grants were highly focused on "positive youth development."

Although my eyes needed a rest, the more that I read about the grants and requirements, the more inspired I felt because there was a lane created for someone just like me. I had years of grant and proposal writing under my belt, which meant I wouldn't have to pay someone to write my grants and risk losing money and not being awarded.

I put my headphones back on and switched from my Mary J Blige playlist to Jay-Z. I needed a li'l hood inspiration. I was creating my own brand, and it was in its newborn stages, but I was making progress. While I was leaping for joy on the inside, I moved in silence—not knowing who would be proud of me or silently hating. By the end of the week, I would have my EIN number and my business license. All I needed was a location for programming. I knew a lot of professionals and colleagues in the city, and my network was pretty thorough. I would use it to advance. Research, research, research was my ultimate practice for weeks until I connected with a grant that appeared that I could obtain. All my friends were mostly college friends who were like me, worker bees. While we all made a decent living, none of us were really "winning, winning." We did well for ourselves, but for me, I wanted the cover of the magazine or the newspaper. I wanted to create a movement and a brand. I studied Oprah. I admired her and mirrored myself after her in my mind. It was time for me to create my own lane and my own table to sit at. Oprah did it, and so could I. My dream was activated. This young woman had a smile on her golden chocolate face. Happy wasn't the word. I sipped joy from my Venti cup.

# Chapter 10

*Iridescent Wings*

"King, what you doing?"

"Putting on my shoes. Are you even dressed yet?"

"Yea, smarty-pants, I'm dressed. I'm tryin'a see if you are ready for school. I'm gonna be ready in like 2 minutes."

"I'm dressed, and I'm right by the door putting on my sneakers."

You could hear King getting himself together at a fast pace. He didn't like being late for school.

"I'm coming, Ma."

"All right, I'm grabbing my work bag and purse, and I'm gonna warm up the car."

I had never been so excited about my future. Yet, my anxiety flared up at the very thought of controlling my own destiny. It was as if the stars were in perfect alignment, and the moon was giving balance to my life and the atmosphere. There was no one to tell me where to be, what time to be there, and how to do the work. I was officially in charge of my own destiny, and it was all worth it. It felt so good to throw on my jeans, a casual blouse, some basic sneakers, and my H&M shades. There was no need to pretend that I was bigger than my reality. I was a young Black woman in my early 30s who was creative, innovative, and persistent on so many levels. God was on my side, and so was time.

"I'm ready, Ma." King stood in front of the screen door wearing his uniform, a jacket on, and his book bag.

"OK, did you brush your teeth and grease your face, though?"

"Oops, let me get the cocoa butter." King dashed to the middle closet to put a few dabs of cocoa butter on his face. He was back outside, shining like the sun.

"Oooh, look at your face. OK, you good," I laughed. "Get in the car, kid."

King sat in the backseat, which was like his own apartment with his gadgets, snacks, and belongings.

"I'm gonna go lock up the house. I'll be right back." I locked the front and back door and all of the bedroom windows. Kenya didn't come home, and I had to secure the house. I hopped into the car and began hitting the short pike to King's school. He didn't eat in the house, so I was expecting him to mention it.

"Ma, you know I'm hungry, right?"

"I know you hungry, son. You want McDonald's or 7-Eleven?"

"McDonald's. Can I get two sausage biscuits, a hash brown, and a milk?"

"You got it, kid! You so greedy."

"Ma, you know I like to eat. I'm growing," he laughed as he rubbed his stomach. "Plus, lunch is nasty. So what I eat for breakfast gotta hold me until you pick me up."

"You don't ask me to make your lunch. If you asked me to do that, I would. You gotta remind me, 'K. If you don't say anything, I won't know."

"You be busy all the time, Ma."

"Well, I have more time on my hands since I don't have a job." I giggled softly because King would come with a billion questions.

"Whatchu mean you don't have a job?" he was serious.

"Well, King," I laughed more as I swerved into the McDonald's drive-thru, "I don't work for anyone. I work for myself now. I quit my job to start my own business."

"So, where are you gonna get money from then?" He was concerned.

"I'm gonna write what you call grants and proposals so that I can get money."

"Isn't that what you were doing before?"

"You remember? You have a keen memory. I was writing for other organizations, and they were getting rich. Now, it's time for me to write for my own company and make myself rich."

"So, you think you gonna be a millionaire by the time I get to high school?" He held no punches.

"The goal is to become one by then. But at the end of the day, I just want to become my own boss."

I pulled up and placed our order.

"Are you gonna have a big, big building?" King's imagination began running wild.

"You mean an office?"

"No, a *building*," he insisted.

"I'm looking for an office right now. Maybe an office for me and someone who would assist me. I don't need nothing big right now. I just gotta get started." I drove to the second window to pick up our food, handed King his food, and placed my Mocha Frappe with no whip in my cup holder. Then I headed toward the pike and took a shortcut into the city. There was a crisp silence in the air as King began inhaling his food. He had a love affair with food, and everyone who loved him understood how serious he was about his food. He wasn't a quiet child unless he was eating or sick. His news channel questions abruptly stopped as he ate his food.

King was onto something. While my thoughts were on my immediate needs, his mind was futuristic, and he often saw me in a radiant light. He believed in me more than anyone in the world, and I owed it to him to do better and be better.

Office space in the city would cost more than my rent, and I knew that I couldn't afford it. However, I had built relationships with influential people in the community while working with the Men of Valor, as well as forging a strong network with my colleagues that attended Bison University with me. Once I dropped King off at school, I would hit up a few highly resourceful people.

The streets were free of traffic, which was rare, and it was also a blessing. We were about 10 minutes away from his school.

"Ma, can you turn that up? That's my jam!" King was done eating his food.

"Make sure you put all your trash in that bag. Don't leave anything back there." King was messy.

"I'm not, Mom. I got you," he replied. "But for real, Ma, can you turn it up?"

"You don't even know this song, boy. This a grown folks' rap song." I turned up the volume and started laughing.

King ignored me and started bobbing his head to "Shawty" by Plies and T Pain. It had a cute ring to it. The beat was bumping, and the lyrics were catchy.

*"Even though I'm not your man, you not my girl, I'ma call you my shawtyyyyyyy."* My son was singing like he had the lead.

"OK, li'l man, you got it." I started snapping my fingers, and King was singing in key.

*"'Cause' I can't stand to see you treated bad, I beat his ass for my shawtyyyyyyyyyyyy."* He was so serious.

King had a voice on him. The performing arts charter school that he attended really did him justice. The school cultivated so many students' lives and creative energy that it gave the students that attended SOAR an advantage over the children in the city who attended schools without a specialty. At SOAR, students learned music (instruments), vocals, dance, theater, and visual arts. King wasn't an easy child to teach because he had so much energy. Learning through the arts cultivated him, and to some degree, it was therapeutic.

I pulled up to the front of his school, where the staff greeted the students. King understood the routine.

"All right, Mom, have a good day. Love you." He hugged me from the side and then put on his backpack.

"Bye, baby boy. Love you too, and have a great day at school." I hugged him close and whispered, "God, cover my baby."

King gave Dean Terrance, a male staff member, a high five and walked into the school. There wasn't a greater feeling than to know as a parent that you can go to work knowing that your child is in a safe, loving, and peaceful environment. I could go in grind mode, knowing that the men in the school would maintain order and safety to the highest degree.

As I drove away, I pulled over and parked while still on the campus grounds, gathering my thoughts. Was it gonna be realistic to work my nerves and look for a small office space, or were there community spaces for people like me, budding entrepreneurs who were going to give back? I grabbed my phone and began googling community centers and recreation centers that were nearby. I recalled that the Men of Valor had several community sites that I understood were rent free as long as you gave back to the community. Many were a part of the department of recreation, while others were on public housing grounds. Via email correspondences that I had, I began retrieving emails that had the contacts to a few of the recreation centers where I had the opportunity to do a few workshops and programming while at the Men of Valor. There were a few sistas that managed spaces for community providers and nonprofits. One sista was named Umi Olive, and the other was Mrs. Isis. Both were middle-aged sistas in their 50s who had positive attitudes, were always in good spirits, but you could read were no-nonsense. My approach had to be different for both. Umi, I would go see, and Mrs. Isis, I would call and speak with first. The center that

Umi directed was well kept, pretty safe, and she was well respected. The center was close in proximity to King's school.

On several occasions, Mr. Light and Mr. Fab would have me sit in meetings with Umi to create partnerships as it related to gun violence and prevention. Umi also allowed me to do some programming and workshops as well because her center had enough space to hold the capacity for the youth that we served, and it was a peaceful space and accommodating. Although the center was nice, just a block and a half away was a war zone, and it affected everyone. Yea, it was gonna be key that I had the opportunity to speak with Umi and get her feedback. What I knew for sure is that Umi was from Brooklyn, New York, and she was a no-nonsense Yankee. She had a good heart, she meant what she said, and seemed like she opened her doors to those who really needed help. She was also a caterer, and the meetings that we were in always had delicious appetizers.

I pulled up on the 1400 block of Gail Ln, praying that a parking space was available that would at least give me an hour of free parking. And just as I got closer to the front entrance of the Youth Club Center (YCC), I saw a parking space that could fit my small red Cruiser.

I grabbed my notepad, pen, and purse, and threw on my navy & white blazer. Rocking the air of confidence, I walked into YCC as if there were a place for me.

"Well, hello, young lady. How can I help you?" A staffer who I had previously met greeted me.

"Hello. I would like to know if Umi Olive is available?"

"Do you have an appointment?" The ol' head tried to act professional.

"No, I don't have an appointment, but if she's available, I would like to speak to her."

"What's your name again, young lady?" he picked up the phone.

"Dream. Dream Angelou."

He called Umi to let her know that I was there and if she were available to speak with me. He nodded his head. You could tell she was giving him orders. He hung up the phone. Out of nowhere, Umi appeared from a small office that seemed hidden behind the ol' head. Standing 5 foot 2, honey brown and solid, she wore an all-white linen pants suit tailored to precision.

"Hey, young lady," Umi said, smiling.

"Hi, Ms. Umi. Did I catch you at a good time?"

"Yea, sure. You wanna talk, or you got some money for me?" She held no punches, and we all laughed.

"I don't have any money, but one day I will," I said sincerely. "Can I talk to you for a few minutes?"

"Sure, come on back." She signaled me to follow her back to the office, which was only a few feet away. It was a one-woman office that looked like it could hold three or four people. It was in the cut and was probably a good way for Umi to hear and observe everything in the club from the front end.

"Have a seat. Dream, right?" Surprisingly, she remembered my name.

"Yes, ma'am. Dream Angelou." I gave her the full government.

"So, talk to me." She looked at her gold watch as if to say, "Don't waste my time."

"Thank you so much for allowing me to come and talk to you. First, I want to say that I respect and admire you. While working for the Men of Valor, Mr. Light always spoke highly of you. Not to mention, you are one of the few women of color who is an executive director of your own nonprofit. Just to see a woman in leadership is amazing for me."

"Thank you, thank you." She was so humble.

"I resigned from my position at the Men of Valor to launch my own nonprofit organization."

"Really?" Umi leaned over her desk, while her breasts, which were bigger than mine, sat right on the desk like a baby.

"Yes. I know my family and friends think I'm crazy, but it's right for me. Being my own boss, yet living out my purpose."

"Oh, hon, you aren't crazy. You're doing God's will for your life. Everything else will fall in line. You are young, and you got the brains. Who wants to make someone else rich for the rest of their life? Mr. Light and Mr. Fab are good over there. They have made that organization millions of dollars." She was a sharpshooter. "We gotta position young people like you who can receive the torch when we pass it and carry out the mission."

"Wow! You couldn't have said it any better. My organization is called Passion for Change. We will focus on the youth and equip and empower them for the future. I see so many deterrents and obstacles in their lives, and my organization would like to create innovative and creative programs in the arts, leadership, college preparation, and mentoring to keep them centered," I spoke.

"You're on to something, Dream. Yep, pick one lane and run with it. Don't go in nobody else's lane but your own. Or create your own lane. The issue with the nonprofit world is that everyone is trying to do the same thing and get money and recognition for the work. Just do the work, and God will bless you and keep you. Those are principles. Many don't have those."

"True, true, you are so right, Umi. The lane that I'll create will be different and stand out from the rest because it's based on my experience working with youth and learning how to read their needs."

"Do you have your paperwork intact? You can have great ideas, but how's your paperwork?" she said in her New York accent.

"Yes, I have my business license and my EIN."

"Oh, so you are ready-ready?"

"I'm ready. At Valor, I learned how to recruit, how to do outreach, and how to connect and build with community leaders. I know how to get kids interested in programs that work, and I have relationships with the schools."

"Well, I witnessed your workshops and programming here. The youth were engaged. You and your staff were organized, and you didn't take no BS off nobody. Everyone carried themselves with respect. That's key for me."

"Thank you. We tried. Working with 15 to 20 youth on a daily, with all those personalities and colorful backgrounds, is no joke.

However, I have a template now of what works and what doesn't work with youth programs."

"So, how can I help you?" She was straightforward.

"I'm looking for office space that I can rent in this community since I have a strong connection to the youth in this area. I don't need anything big. Maybe an office the size of this office that's affordable," I expressed.

"So, you need an address? A small-size office that can accommodate you, a desk, a file cabinet, and, of course, a computer and printer. A place that you can hold meetings with power-players, grantors, and bring visitors. What about the youth? Where are they gonna go for programming?"

"I have relationships with the schools, so my goal is to reach out to the deans that I know at two schools to see if the programming can take place at one of the schools in a classroom. It would be easy that way too."

"So, you're talking partnerships. Yea, creating partnerships. You gotta have them." Umi looked down in deep thought. "I have a space on the third floor that I don't use that's next door to my other office. It would be a shared space. It just needs to be cleaned out, and furniture needs to be added. But you could work outta there and build from the ground up. The thing is, if another young entrepreneur comes and needs space, you would have to be willing to share. What do you think?"

"I think that's fantabulous." I smiled like a kid in a candy store. "How much would the rent be?" I was so excited that I was shaking at the offer.

"It wouldn't cost you anything as of now. Look, I believe in paying it forward. Someone helped me. I see something in you, so I'm gonna help you until you get up and running. Then we can talk about how we can help each other. I'm getting old now, and I need to see a young sista like you blazing a trail. You feel me?"

"Oh my goodness, I can't believe it! I can give you something. I *gotta* give you something." I was in tears. I couldn't believe what I was hearing. God must have heard my uttering. There was no place in the world where you could get an office space for free. My hands were shaking.

"Take me to lunch when you got it, kid. When you bring in the big bucks, come holla at me. When you get it, pay it forward like I paid it forward to you. Are you listening? This is *your* season. You think you came in here on your own free will? God sent you here on appointment, and you didn't even know it. I don't even get here this early, and look, I'm here. We're gonna get you up and running. Let's hop on the elevator so you can see the space." Umi was a queen in every sense of the word.

We walked out of her office, and together, we walked toward the elevator. Umi was bowlegged, and she took her time as she walked. She was well put together. We got on the elevator, and she pressed the button to the third floor.

"So, where are you from? You can't be from here. You have an accent."

"I'm from California."

"What part?"

"Santa Monica."

"The beach area?" she seemed surprised.

"Yes, the beach area, but there's a hood too, and that's where I'm from."

"No way. Santa Monica Beach has a hood? Like *Boyz n the Hood?*"

"Yes, pretty much. I grew up with gangstas and drug dealers like the rest of the world. The community that I'm from is in a predominately Black and Latino community."

"Oh, wow, I would have never thought." We began walking down a long hallway and passed a gym, another huge office area, bathrooms, water fountains, and in another cut were a suite and other offices. Umi got her keys out of her pocket, and we walked into a nice-size long room adjacent to hers. It had two large desks and tons of space to put about four more desks and a conference table.

"Let's check it out. I haven't been in here for months. We have had so many classes, workshops, moms, and babies coplay. You name it, we had it in here. Whatchu think? A lot of space, huh?"

"Yes, there is so much space! This is so perfect." I couldn't stop smiling.

"Perfect for you. And I have more desks that I can have my maintenance team to bring in as you need it. But you know you have two desks to start with. Right now, you're in the hustling phase, so you can't afford to have anyone to work for you until you start getting grant money."

"Yes, my next step is to apply for a few mini grants and a summer grant for starters."

"Whose gonna write your grants? Good grant-writers cost thousands of dollars."

"I write grants and proposals. I'm a writer by trade. That's what I also did for Valor and my previous jobs—write."

"Awesome. Did you go to college for that?"

"I graduated from Bison University," I said proudly. "My degree was in communications. My major was journalism."

"Oh, you got it going on, kiddo. You got a head start. You can have this space so that you can solidify your organization, make it official, and focus on knocking out those grants. As I get the grants, I'll give them to you. Plus, I know a few people who are Bison alumna who are responsible for the summer money that's coming out. I got you."

"Ms. Umi, you just don't understand how blessed I feel because of you. I didn't know things were gonna go this smoothly. This is a once-in-a-lifetime blessing. I promise when I get my thousands of dollars, I got you."

"You mean when you get your *millions* of dollars that you got us. Remember, you are now a part of the village. You get blessed and become a blessing to others. That's reciprocity, and it's biblical." Umi gave a word.

"The Bible says, 'Give and it shall be given unto you. Good measure, pressed down, shaken together and running over, will be poured into your lap.' That's Luke, chapter 6." She knew her word.

"Yes, ma'am. 'Give and it shall be given unto you.' I learned that as a little girl." It was as if my mind began to drift as if what I was experiencing wasn't even real. Buzzing in my right ear began as a distraction. Usually, it was a sign that I was becoming anxious.

"I'll talk to maintenance about cleaning up this space. When do you think you'll be ready to move in?"

My thoughts were all over the place.

"In a week. Is that too soon?"

"That's perfect. So, a week from today. That will work. Do you have flyers and business cards?" she began drilling me.

"No, not yet, but I'll work on that this week." I became more anxious.

"Get your business cards and flyers together. You're going to need them after today. You'll hit the ground running next week. So, you have some time. Boy, you remind me of myself as a young tenderoni," Umi reminisced, "with the big boobs, the thick shape, the heels, and pretty brown smile. Yep, just like me. I'm old now, but you inspire me. Wait 'til I tell my husband about you."

Umi locked the office space, and we exited the area together. I couldn't believe that I actually had my own office space, and it was rent free. God was on my side-side!!!

"Next week, I'll get you your own set of keys too."

"Thank you so much for everything." Tears were welling up in my eyes.

We walked down the long hallway. It was as if angels were ushering a fresh newness into the atmosphere. I felt my ancestors, Granny, and dem, making sure that I was good, even from heaven. I was just a li'l Black girl named Dream with a dream. I didn't even have a degree in business. But there was a real "passion for change" that dwelled in my heart. I had a colossal vision that was unexplainable that I hadn't even begun to touch the surface yet.

We got back on the elevator to the lobby. The elevator doors opened, and we walked back to her office and stood face-to-face.

"So, kid, began writing those grants. Get you some office supplies from Staples or Target. They are both down the street. Bring frames and pictures and canvases to decorate your desks. This will be the home of your organization. I welcome you."

"Ms. Umi, I am most grateful for you." I reached to hug her. "God has blessed me. I promise I will do right. You won't have any problems with me."

"I'm confident in you, kid. Let me give you a number to a young lady that has summer money." She wrote her name and number on a Post-it. "Her name is McKenzie, and she's a good sista from Bison University around your age."

"Her name is ringing a bell. I think I may know her."

"You probably do. Give her a call ASAP. She's a resource."

"I sure will."

"OK, Dream, gotta get going, but I'll see you next week around this time."

"Umi, thank you very, very much! Be blessed." I walked out of her office, waving to the ol' head at the front desk.

"You gone?" he asked.

"Yea, I'm gone, but I'll see you next week."

"Oh yeah," he shouted.

"Yea," I winked and walked out of the building. If I were 30 pounds lighter, I would have done cartwheels down the street.

"Yes yes yes. I got my own fucking office space. Yesssssssss!" I screamed and took my keys outta my breast and unlocked the car door and hopped in.

"I can't believe it. I can't believe it. God, thank you. Thank you, Jesus. Like, really thank you, Jesus." I began crying tears of joy. The day was moving so fast, and so were my dreams. I sat in my seat and turned on the air conditioner and cried like a baby for about 3 minutes. I needed that cry. I really needed time to gather my thoughts. I had my own office space, so all I needed to do was make a few phone calls to make connections. Using an old napkin in my glove compartment, I wiped my tears and called McKenzie, letting the phone ring while anticipating it going to voicemail.

"Hellllo." It was the voice of a young lady.

"Hello, may I please speak to Ms. McKenzie?"

"Speaking to her," she responded pleasantly.

"Hi, McKenzie, Umi Olive referred me to you."

"Ms. Umi . . . I love her. She's great."

"My name is Dream Angelou, and I am the founder of Passion for Change. It's a new organization."

"Dream Angelou . . . That sounds familiar. Never heard of your organization, so you must be new-new."

"We're like newborn baby new. I went to Bison University."

"I graduated from the school of communications."

"Me too. My major was journalism. Broadcast journalism." I got excited.

"Dream, did you write for the school paper?"

"I sure did."

"I loved reading your columns," McKenzie said. "You can write, girl. I mean, *really* write, and you had those punch lines too. So how can I help you?"

"I'd like to apply for a summer mini grant. Is it too late?"

"Nope, you're right on time. You have 5 days to turn it in."

"Five days? Oh Lord." My confidence went right out the door.

"Sure, you'll be OK. The grant is only a few pages, and you're a writer; you can get it done in a jiffy."

"You think?"

"What's your email?"

I handed her my business card that had all of my contact information.

"I'm sending it to you now. Read through it and call or email me if you have any questions. Get it in. It's $10K for a 6-week summer program. If you get it in, you'll be awarded. You can write, and that's your advantage!"

"Thank you so much. I'll review it today. I can write, and hopefully, well enough to earn the grant award."

"You got this," McKenzie affirmed.

"Thank you," I replied.

"You're welcome, dear, and the grant is due next Tuesday at 2:00 p.m. sharp. Arrive early to drop it off." McKenzie ended the conversation.

With a long exhale, I rolled down the front windows. I needed air. My life was excelling before my eyes, and what I accomplished in a few hours would take most people a year or two to achieve. My spirit was leaping, my adrenaline was pumping, and I wanted to call my mama, my best friend, Sanaa, and Kenya to give them the great news. I wanted to scream all the way to the heavens so that my ancestors could hear the vibrations of success. Instead, I kept quiet and drove to a cozy sandwich spot in the Brookland part of town because of easy parking. There were no meters, and the atmosphere was low-key.

"My God, my God . . ." I pulled up and parked. "God, all this for me? Is this real? Lord, thank you for favor. Thank you for favorrrrrrr." Tears rolled down my eyes, along with snot.

"Lord Jesus, thank you, thank you, thank you. Lead me, advise, and guide me, God. This is new to me. Please, God, provide me the tools and resources. Never let me go. I need you fa'eva. Thank you, Jesus, for provision. Thank you for your love. Please forgive me, God, for all of my sins. Protect me and King, Lord."

The energy was blessed, the aroma was blessed, and it was an immediate shift. Just 4 years ago, I was a struggling single mother living in the hood with a dream of making a way and perhaps making it out. Like a caterpillar's metamorphosis, my world would change in phases. The snot ran down my face connecting with the saltiness to my lips. Only the Most High could ordain this. My wings were iridescent.

# Chapter 11

## Recess

My dreams were awakened, and there were no days off, for real. It was more like recess, a 15-minute mini break here and there, just enough time for me to reflect and nap.

In my mind, my dreams would lead me to a breakthrough, wealth, access to places that I had never been, a great credit score, a passport, traveling around the world, and a big fucking house— maybe ranch style. My son would be positioned to succeed as a young Black man. He would have a trust fund, a stake in the family business, and more importantly, he would be able to run with the horses and gazelles in the spirit of financial freedom.

Have you ever fallen asleep on your laptop? A sleep so deep that the saliva from your mouth landed on the character and number keys? Well, it seemed like I was going to sleep on my laptop and waking up on it daily. The grind was imperative and lucrative, and I spent my days researching about positive youth development as well as best practices on successful youth programs, locally and nationally. I was typing so much that the keys on my laptop were getting stuck. After days of research, creating an outline for my first Passion for Change grant, all that was left was for me to provide the content.

The weekends were my form of recess. My Saturdays were being spent sleeping in, relaxing, spending time with my kiddo, chilling with Kenya, or hanging with my girlfriends. On Sundays, I looked forward to going to church and a nice Sunday lunch or dinner. My body would more than often send me signals of when a break was needed. On Saturdays, my body chose to go into a deep sleep until being awakened by the aroma of breakfast, King's cartoons, the neighbors blasting their music, or Kenya banging at my door after running the town with his brodies.

*Boom boom boom!* There was an interruption. *Boom boom boom boom!*

The banging on my door woke me up abruptly out of my sleep.

"Eh, Dreammmmmm! Dreammmm!" It was Kenya's voice.

"I'm comingggg!" My voice cracked. I began rubbing both of my eyes, nearly sleepwalking to the door.

"Eh, babyyyyy!" Kenya was loud as shit.

"Hey, you woke me out of my sleep. I was dreaming real good," I said, rubbing the sleep out of my right eye.

"You always sleeping. It's ten in the morning. Wake up, babyyyyyy." He was loud, smelling like Svedka. Standing right by him was Nia. She was smiling from ear to ear.

"I went and scooped Nia from her mother's house. She called me and said she was bored. I know my baby's tired of all dem people in that fucking house. They be showing favoritism," Kenya began to rant.

"Hey, Nia. How are you? Your hair is cute."

"Thank you," she smiled.

"Come in so you can watch cartoons with King. You eat yet?"

"Nooo," she said.

"You want a bowl of cereal? You know King got all these plain boxes of cereal, but I can add some sugar. Is that cool?"

"Yea," Nia smiled and walked in, looking for King. King was sitting on the burgundy carpet watching cartoons on the 60 inch. She tapped King. He looked up and got excited.

"Nia Nia Nia!" King hopped straight up. "Ma, why you didn't tell me that Nia was coming?"

"Your mama didn't know I was bringing Nia, 'heady,'" Kenya responded, rubbing King's big ol' dome. I walked into the kitchen and made Nia a big bowl of plain Cheerios. Nia was into sweets, unlike King, so I made sure that I sprinkled sugar across her bowl.

"Nia, you wanna sit at the table or next to King so you can watch cartoons too?"

"I wanna sit on the carpet."

"Cool." I handed her the bowl of cereal and a few paper towels.

"Y'all good?" Kenya asked the kids.

"Yeaaa," they responded.

"Baby, come talk to me in the room," Kenya said, slapping me on my butt.

"Dang, stop popping me on my butt. I'm tired as hell, and you all banging on the door like it ain't morning time. I'm going back to sleep."

"You think I came here for you to go to sleep on me? Wake your ass up." He pulled my arms close to him and started pecking me on my lips.

"Oooh, boi, your breath smell like vodka. You been drinking all night, huh?"

"You got your nerve. Your breath smelling like sour milk." We both started laughing.

"You woke me up. You was banging at my door all early. I ain't even seen you in days, nigga. You ain't gave me a chance to wash my face and brush my teeth. You appearing outta nowhere like a ghost."

"You been so focused on your new business I thought I'd give you some space. Give you some time to focus on the things you need to write and take care of. I got out of the way and been around my way. You know I been at my grandma's house and with my homies just chillin'."

"Yea, but you ain't checked up on me in 2 days. It's all good, though." I started getting irritated, and I hopped back in bed.

"So, you think I came over here for you to go to sleep?" he started taking off his T-shirt and jeans so that he could get on my doggone nerves. I pulled up the sheet to cover my entire body, including my shoulders. My bed was calling me, but Kenya began taking his shoes and socks off.

"Boy, your feet . . ." We both started laughing. We had inside jokes about each other and giggled at our own inadequacies.

"What? I washed my feet. What, you want me to put my shoes outside?"

"Hell yea. Put 'em outside. That's crazy. Whew!"

"OK OK OK, you got it." Kenya took his New Balances to the porch at the back door so that his shoes could air out. He was shirtless like I liked him. His shoulder blades framed like a pyramid. He walked back to the room like a lion trying to cuff his lioness. We peeked to see that the kids were in their zone, watching cartoons and playing between themselves with empty bowls of cereal on the carpet. I quietly picked up their bowls, emptying the remainder of the milk and leaving the bowls in the sink, then tiptoed back into the room. Kenya grabbed me from behind.

"So, what was you saying again?" He started kissing all over my face. "You know you talk a whole bunch of shit."

"I was saying I wanna get some rest. Let me sleep for an hour or 2; then I'll be up and ready for whatever. Ken, I've been doing all this research and writing this week. It's like my brain needs rest."

"Then chill then. Deal with that on Monday. Give yourself some time to be human. That's all I be saying to you. You always work so hard, and then you don't really get to play. Feel me?"

"Yea, you right. I just don't wanna be fucked up and poor like I was when you met me. I never wanna hit the bottom of life like that ever again."

"And you not, baby girl. God got you, and I got you. If I gotta rob, steal, or hustle, I got us. We good, and it's only up from here." We both hopped on the bed. "You smart and beautiful." He began running his hands through my 22 inches of Indian hair.

"I missed you." He sounded so good that it made me vulnerable.

"I missed you too, Ken." My eyes glazed. With a warm embrace, we hugged each other tightly and began kissing. My adrenaline always started acting haywire when Kenya began feeling on me, even though we had been together for 3 years. It was like every time we became intimate, it felt new. He started kissing all over my neck as he took both of his hands and caressed my nipples. He moved his hands all over my body, becoming in tune to every ripple, every roll, and every imperfection. As he sucked my right breast, it was as if we were both in our happy place. I spread my legs, eager to feel the vibrations of his Isis Pistol.

"Touch me, baby," he said as he took my right hand to stroke his huge penis up and down.

"Yes, baby, I got you." He had my attention, and my intention was to get him completely aroused as I stroked the shaft of his penis up and down, up and down.

"Oooh, baby. Oooh, baby. Oh shit . . . oh, oh." He began leaning his head back. "I wanna put it in."

I wrapped my legs around Kenya's hips while wrapping my arms around his neck. I began gyrating all over him as he began gradually piercing my inner mystery in and out and in and out. His hands were grasping the center of my back as we took turns letting our bodies undergo out-of-body experiences. The lovemaking was second to none. I was sold on the dick, and no one could penetrate my body while connecting me to the soul like Kenya. I closed my eyes as he crowned both of us, beating my insides like a djembe drum. The beat was beautiful, and only we understood it. My eyes were closed. He had my full attention. As we both moaned, it was as if our love language spoke to us unforbidden. Something was electrifying about when we made love. There was peace, healing, and understanding. It made sense.

"Baby, I'm about to come." He began kissing me intensely. "I'm about to come!" The pulsating got real. I began to pull him closer into me until I heard his heart beat against my breast.

"I'm cominggggggg, baby. I'm coming, babyyyyyyyyy!" Kenya released all that was awaiting. Then he lay softly on my breast, opening his eyes to see if my eyes were open, and then he yielded to his peace and closed his eyes.

"Damn, love, that's mine, all the way mine."

"I love you." My guard came down. "I missed you." My defensiveness became vulnerable.

"I missed you too, baby." He took two deep breaths. "Now, we both can get the sleep that we really need."

"Really?" We both busted out laughing.

*Boom boom boom!* Someone knocked hard at my bedroom door.

"Oh, dang, the kids!" Kenya hopped off of me to cover our naked bodies as if we were in the Garden of Eden.

"Ma, what ya doing in there? Can we get a snack?"

"King, yea, you can get a snack. Get one for you and Nia," I yelled at the door.

"What are y'all doing in there?"

"Li'l boy, don't worry about what we doing. Get away from the door, chump!" Kenya tried to affirm his voice.

"I ain't no chump." King got smart. You could hear Nia giggling by the door.

"Eh, Nia, I hear you. Both of ya get away from the damn door and go sit down," Kenya regulated. Next, all you heard were little footsteps running away from the door.

"Go to sleep, baby girl." Kenya knew I was beat. I closed my eyes. He knew that his good loving would have me comatose within 5 minutes.

"OK," I whispered and curled up on my right side in a fetal position.

"I'ma lay with you for a few minutes, and then I'm gonna put some food on the grill for all of us. I'ma even throw some grilled veggies."

"For real, Ken? You gonna sauté them with my special sauce? I love it when you grill the veggies. It's like an aphrodisiac!"

"You know I know I got the Midas touch. I got us. Invite Sanai and her son over so you can really chill and drink y'all wine. You deserve just to chill."

"'K." I felt myself falling asleep. He covered my body, then lay in the bed with me all of 15 minutes.

The grill was calling him. Cooking was his other happy place, and he couldn't resist. He created his special seasonings and barbeque sauces, and no one ever asked what or how. We just knew that we were all in a happy-ass place when Kenya cooked. It could be something as simple as hamburger helper. It didn't matter if he put his foot on the stove, just as long as he put his "foot in the food." He would have the music cranked up real loud, and if he were feeling himself, he would take you from Frankie Beverly and Maze, Chaka Khan, Jodeci, Scarface, Tupac, Devin the Dude, then Michael Jackson, never leaving out Go-Go. Go-Go was the indigenous culture and music of Chocolate City, and he was a native.

"Ma, Ma." King began tapping my shoulder. "Ma, Ma, Ma, Ma!" he tapped louder.

"Yes, yes, son?" I whispered.

"You gonna get up? Can me and Nia go outside and play? Kenya is outside on the grill. He can watch us," he asked.

"Yes, you guys can play outside but don't leave the block." I opened my eyes to see Nia and King standing in front of me.

"We not gonna leave the block," Nia assured me.

"Ma, you gonna get up? It's the afternoon now. It feels good outside. Come outside. Plus, Kenya got chicken wings, hamburgers, and hot dogs already on the grill."

"It smells good too," Nia was convincing.

"I'm gonna get up, y'all. Ma is tired. But I'm getting up. I'm gonna get myself together."

"OK, we going outside." They ran out.

Those all-so-natural juices and berries were on my body. I grabbed the plastic shower cap off my dresser, got in the tub, and took a nice, warm shower. I decided to use my Dr. Bronner's Pure Castile Peppermint Soap, which created a great lather all over my body. Dr. Bonner's liquid soap could be copped from the local organic shops, and it was a form of aromatherapy and cleansing for the body. Aside from my bedroom, the bathroom was one of my favorite places to be because it was quiet, peace and solace were in the room, and there, you could meditate. The peppermint opened up my pores and my nasal passages. The weather was perfect. There was no need for the air conditioner to be turned on or the heat.

As I sat at the edge of the bed with just a towel wrapped around me, I gazed into the mirror and realized that in my natural state, I was absolutely gorgeous. Even with my ghetto pink scarf and wet shower cap, my naturalness was giving "ole so beautiful." All I needed was a cute black fitted tee, some jeggings, and cute low heels.

My dresser drawers had a few everyday pieces, but in my middle drawer is where I strategically placed my cute "to-go" clothes. Kenya had me so dumbfounded that I grabbed my phone off my dresser to see who I had missed calls and text messages from. Surprisingly, no one! I needed some girlfriend company, so I texted Sanai to see if she wanted to come through and bring her son, Amir. I hadn't seen them in a while, and we needed to catch up. Plus, the kids loved Amir and would be happy to see him.

Sanai, what you doing today? I began texting.

Nothing much, girl. How you been? she texted back.

Kenya is grilling. I miss you guys. You wanna come over?

Hell yea, girl. Kenya can cook his ass off. What time?

2 p.m. would be good.

Y'all need anything? Sanai was always so considerate.

We got pretty much everything. You can bring a few beverages for the kids.

Cool. I'll grab some juices and water, but I'll get us a bottle to sip on.

Yes, girl, that's perfect, Sanai.

See you in a few.

'K, see you.

I greased my feet and my elbows. I wasn't concerned about any other area because I had on pants. I threw on my clothes and grabbed a round weave brush to brush my long tresses down on both sides gently, then took my rat tail comb to create a middle part. My hair was my crown.

Kenya walked into the room.

"Hey, sleepyhead, you finally got up."

"Yes, I had the best nap ever, thanks to you." I kissed him on his forehead.

"Come outside and keep me company." He pulled my right hand as I dropped the comb.

The sound of Frankie Beverly and Maze filled the atmosphere. You could smell the zest and soulfulness of what Kenya was preparing on the grill. He was in his element. He already invited the neighbors into our yard, and they brought their 24-case bottles of beer. The kids were happy on their scooters as they led other kids on their scooters up and down the street.

Maze's "Happy Feelings" radiated through our speakers, creating a real funkadelic vibe.

"Y'all know this is my baby." Kenya had a beer in his left hand, and in his right hand, he had a long pitchfork to turn the chicken, a few steaks, hamburgers, and hot dogs over.

"We know Dream is your baby," said Kevin, our next-door neighbor.

"Yep, we have nothing but respect for family, your family . . . family period," added Nate. "When we see the kids outside, we watch everybody's kids, not just our own."

"That's right. That's how it was growing up Uptown. The neighbors were like family. If a neighbor caught you doing some shit you had no business doing, your mama, grandma, or auntie would know about it."

"You right about that," Kevin chimed in.

"I love my family, dawg. Dream, Nia, and heady, this is my family." Ken downed the rest of his beer like it was Kool-Aid. "Have a seat, baby. Did you tell any of your friends to come through?"

"Yea, Sanai is coming with Amir." I sat down in a chair.

"That's what's up. I might have one or two of the homies come through. It's just a nice day to kick it."

"Who wanna go half on some Amsterdam?" Kenya was such an influencer.

"Hell yeah, I'll put up," said Nate.

"I got $7 to add," added Kevin.

"Y'all give me the money, and I can go to the liquor store."

"Eh, baby, can you give them $20 for me?" Kenya asked.

I dug in my bosom, which was more like a safe to me, and pulled out the $20 and gave it to Nate.

"Y'all got a whole 24 case, and y'all finna get some vodka. Kenya, please hurry up and grill the food before it's burnt up." Everyone began laughing.

"You know I cook even better when I'm twisted." He started dancing to the Isley Brothers, "Living for the Love of You." His two-step was mean. Nate and Kevin took off together to the liquor store.

"For real, it don't matter if I'm sober or drunk. My food is good, no matter what."

"I can almost agree. But it tastes better when you're not drunk," I giggled.

Kenya began flipping the meat over. He had a table set aside with his aluminum pans. There were already tables in the yard and chairs. I went into the house to get cleaning spray and a rag to wipe down the tables and chairs since we were all gonna be outside eating and drinking. I kept a plastic purple table coverings under the sink for cookouts or get-togethers that we would have from time to time. Kenya knew how to create an atmosphere. He knew good music and classics from his aunt Tam and from being around old heads as he grew up. They exposed him to good music and practically all the genres. Music connected us.

Nia and King ran in the yard and straight to Kenya. "Can we get some water?"

"Ask Dream." He pointed to me.

"Yea, there's a case of water bottles in the refrigerator. Go ahead."

"Thank you." Nia had manners. Even though the kids were sweating, nothing could keep them from playing.

I began organizing the tables and chairs. "Eh, baby, whatchu know about L.T.D.?"

"I never heard of them."

"What?" he gestured. "You never heard of L.T.D.? You got too. Let me play it for you," he put down his utensils and beer. He had to school me.

He began walking toward me with his old-school swag, putting his hat to the side. The music was beyond familiar. I stood still and listened to the song.

"Oh shit, is that Jeffrey Osborne?" My body immediately started vibing with my own two-step.

"Yea, that's 'Love Ballad,' and Jeffrey is the lead singer in that group."

Kenya grabbed both my hands so that we could dance together. He loved to dance as if no one were looking. And I became like a shy little girl who would follow his lead. The beat alone had me, but Kenya captured me by singing in my ear, *"What a difference a true love made in my life/So nice/So right/Love I never knew that its touch/Could mean/So much."*

I closed my eyes, counted the beat in my head, 1-2-1-2-1-2, nervous like it was an eighth-grade dance. Dancing with Kenya became so intimate, and no man could hold my attention and make me sweat like that. Him holding my hands, aligning our every move, and even twisting me around had me feeling butterflies. What if I stepped on his shoes? What if I was off-beat? What if my tracks were showing? There was an innocence about us dancing together. It was as if he were communicating to me in our love language. We made sense.

"Don't be nervous, baby." We rocked back and forth. "I love you, boo. We just jamming. It's just us. This like some real G shit." He even closed his eyes.

"Like a nigga like me ain't even supposed to be alive. God got me here for a reason, Dream. We moving in a direction where we will most likely spend the rest of our lives together. We might as well get used to this."

"Yea, you right, Ken. I'm new to this. Even though what we have has been going on for years now, I just be wondering, like, is this forever, God?"

He began singing the lead, "*What we have is much more than they could see. What we have is much more than they could see. What we have is much more than they could see.*" The music faded, and we opened our eyes. We heard footsteps.

"Well, look at y'all. Ain't y'all cute." It was Sanai and Amir. Kenya and I both grinned.

"Hey, Sanai." Kenya hugged her and gave Amir a pound.

"Y'all all in love and shit. Priceless," said Sanai.

"Yea, this is love, girl." My head was spinning.

"I see the look in your eyes." Sanai was hilarious.

"There you go, Sanai. Are y'all hungry? The food is almost done." Kenya winged her in with food.

"Thank you. Yes, we are. But we didn't come empty-handed. We have juices and a case of soda. Amir, go put everything in the fridge." Sanai had a Southern accent. She was from Ocala, Florida, and you could hear it all in her voice.

"Wait a minute, nephew, give me a hug. I missed you, and you getting tall." I hugged Amir. He was like a son to me. He was just a year older than King, and he was a great kid. He was well behaved, always had manners, was considerate, and just an overall good kid. King was rough around the edges, but they balanced each other.

"Where's King?" Sanai asked.

"He's down the street playing with Nia and the neighbors' kids. Nephew, when you come back out, walk down the street. You'll see them. I definitely hear them."

"Wow, I hear them too," Sanai laughed.

"Come over here, Nai Nai," I affectionately called her. We sat down at the table.

"You got the cute li'l purple table cover. That's my favorite color."

"The tables needed covers. They were dusty, girl."

"Baby, the hot dogs and hamburgers are ready. I'm gonna cover the buns and put some ketchup and mustard out here for the kids. The plates are over here."

"Thanks, babe."

Nate and Kevin came back with a big bag of liquor. They pulled out a gallon of Amsterdam. Ken's eyes were wide open, like it was Thanksgiving.

"*That's* what I'm talking about."

"We got ice and cups." Kevin put the bottles, bag of ice, and cups on another table.

"Holy shit! Look at that bottle," Sanai peeped. "Yea, Kenya ain't gonna be no good."

"Hell, I wouldn't be neither."

Kenya stood between both tables.

"Fellas, this is Dream's best friend, Sanai. She is more like a sister. She's family," he introduced her. "Her son is the 'Rico Suave' young brotha who's walking down the street. That's like our son son, you dig."

"Hey, Sanai," they were all googly-eyed.

Sanai was a pretty young thang. She was mixed with Jamaican, Irish, German, and basically, she was the United Nations. She was a brunette, though. She was raised by her white father, who reminded you of a Michael McDonald. He only dated and married Black women. All his children were by Black women, and if you heard his voice or tasted his food, you would assume he was Black until you saw him.

I met Sanai freshmen year in college at Bison University, and we were best friends ever since. We partied together, studied, rebelled, traveled, and thugged it out together. When she had her son, I was right behind her a year later, delivering my own.

We were like Salt-N-Pepa, night and day, orange juice and pomegranate juice, but our friendship was and will always be authentic.

"Yea, them two thicker than thieves," Kenya announced. "Y'all enjoy ya'selves 'cause we finna be filling our cups up with this white stuff."

"Oh boy." I glanced at Kenya's full cup of vodka.

"We ain't tripping off of them. I got us our own bottles. We can have wine or tequila. Lemme know I was prepared." Sanai was just getting us started.

"Let's do the tequila, girl. On the rocks, though."

"Cool. I got a bag of ice too."

"Let me go get a small cooler. We might as well put the juices, soda, water, and ice in it, and whatever else someone might bring."

"Let me help you." Sanai walked with me into the house. I pulled the cooler that was right next to the back door. I rarely used it because it was small.

Sanai opened it up and began putting ice into it. I took about half of a case of waters and juices and threw them in the chest. Sanai filled two glasses up with ice, tequila, and cranberry chaser. Then she rolled the chest through the back door.

"That's what we need. You got ice in there?" Kevin asked.

"Yea, there's ice in there," Sanai responded. "But y'all fishes got your own bag. 'Cause y'all drinking, drinking."

"Sweetheart, we ain't fishes. We *sharks*," Kenya interjected.

"Whatever." Sanai placed the cooler near our table, yet close enough for the kids to get to it. Then we sat down.

"So, what's been going on with you? I miss you so much."

"Girl, just working—working my butt off. I'm gearing up to apply for the assistant manager position at my job. It's the salary I need."

"You deserve it. You been on that job for years. They need you, and they like you. You blend in as well."

She laughed out loud. "Girl, they don't know what nationality I am . . . if I'm mixed, Spanish, from an island, or India."

"Yea, you really don't know looking at you until you open your mouth." We busted out in laughter.

"You a Black girl when you talk. There's no getting around it."

"You never lied. It's just a lot of responsibility. Getting Amir back and forth to school, working 10 hours a day . . . I'm pooped. I'm so glad you invited us over. Plus, Amir has been dying to play with King."

"Look at them." We spotted all the kids playing together on the sidewalk.

"They are growing up before our eyes."

"Yea, they almost in middle school, girl," Sanai reminded me.

"Let's drink to raising these boys." She handed me a glass.

"Yes, it's long overdue."

"So, what's been up with you, Dream? You always got exciting stuff popping off in your life."

"More like wild stuff."

"Talk to me."

"So, I work for myself now."

"What? You quit your job?"

"Yes, I quit my job a few months ago, and I started my business. I finally did it, Nai Nai!"

"Shut up! So you work for yourself? You ain't got a boss. This is your dream, girl. You fulfilling it."

"It's scary. And guess what?" I whispered.

"What, girl?"

I leaned into the table. "I got my own office. My very own office!"

"Girl, so you must be getting money."

"Nope, not a cent."

"How'd you get an office then?"

"I got an office from an elder named Umi. You know, the lady I talked about who was low-key mentoring me and giving me the business about the business world out here. I met with her a few days ago, and she blessed me with an office suite in her building. It's so perfect, Sanai."

"Is she charging you?"

"No, she's really paying it forward. It's divine. God blessed her with her own business, and now, she's positioning a sista like me to follow my dreams."

"Wow, so are you gonna have a soft launch? Or grand opening?"

"No, right now, my focus is writing grants so that I can bring in revenue. I need to write the grants and pray that I'm awarded. It seems like the stars are aligning themselves. My first grant that I'm working on now is being managed by a Bison grad who we went to school with."

"You are so blessed, Dream, so blessed." She poured more tequila in both of our glasses.

"Yes, God got me. This drink is starting to get me too!" We fell out.
"You too?"

The kids started coming into the yard. It wasn't just the three musketeers, now. Two other kids who lived down the street were with them.

"Hey, Mom, can we eat? I brought my friends too." King was direct.

"Come follow me, kids. Line up so I can make you a plate. King, please grab the bags of chips on the table."

Each kid got a hamburger and a hot dog, a bag of chips, and a drink. We didn't eat pork. It was either beef or chicken. I took the chicken wings off the grill because they were ready. I put them in another pan and covered them with aluminum. Sanai came to help put the condiments on their plates.

"Hey, kids, you can sit at the table in the front. All of you can fit there. Please make sure you put your plates in the trash once you're done. Don't forget to get a napkin."

"OK," they shouted in unison. They were rushing to eat.

"There're extra hamburgers and hot dogs too, so you can come back for seconds."

The music genre changed from the '70s and '80s to rap music. From Tupac to Gucci Mane, Kenya and the neighbors were sipping down cup after cup. Ken's best friend, Saul, had arrived and joined them as well with a bottle of vodka. Ken got louder and louder.

It was more girl talk with Sanai once we got the kids settled down to eat at the table.

"So, back to you, honey. Are you scared, Dream?"

"No, I'm not scared. I always wanted to be an entrepreneur. This is Dream's dream, feel me? I dreamed of days like this."

"Yea, I know, but it's surreal. I'm like living through you."

"Yea, it's surreal, but it's real too. I have this great responsibility to God, myself, my kid, and my community to do the right thing. I can't drop the ball. I have to succeed."

"What y'all talking about?" Kenya walked over, being loud with a drink in his hand.

"She's talking about her new business. My girl has her own business. You should be proud of her."

"I am proud of her. I love her." He started slightly slurring. "That's my boo."

"He's drunk. Ughh!" I felt like Ken was gonna turn it up a notch.

"Look at that bottle, girl. It's halfway gone, and that's a gallon," she pointed.

"That nigga drank all of that," Kevin snitched.

"We *all* was drinking," Nate said. "We can't put that on that man. We all drunk, for real."

Ken started walking directly toward me.

"We grown-ass men! We drinking and enjoying ourselves. What the fuck are y'all drinking?" He got louder.

"We sipping tequila, and we are cool as a fan." I looked him dead in the eye. "You need some water. You don't need to drink anymore because you're starting to get loud. You ain't even walking straight."

"Don't worry about me. Worry about yourself. Worry about being boring. Yea, you smart and all but you boring as fuck!"

"What he say?" Sanai had that look on her face like, "Nigga, you got one more wrong word to say."

"Now, I'm boring. Then why are you with me?" I was offended.

"No, really, save me the disappointment, nigga." I hurried up and drank all my liquor.

"Yea, you need some more. He trippin'." Sanai was observing everything.

"Bitch, I don't have to be with you." Kenya got louder to the point that now, the kids started looking. Sanai didn't want the kids to be exposed to his rants, so she told them to go play. She sensed that things were going bad.

"Who you calling a bitch? You not finna disrespect me in my own house. You are drunk and crazy at this point. Kevin, get your friend."

The neighbors were just as drunk as Ken but had more common sense than him. They started walking toward him to attempt to calm him down.

"You acting like a snob-ass bitch. You all up your own ass about this business. Yea, you started a business, but how you gonna pay the bills? You ain't gonna have no money for a while. You gonna need a nigga like me to help you. You need to take your head out of the clouds and get a corporate job. Fuck that business!"

"What? How dare you! I don't need you to do a muthafuckin' thing for me. I've always been independent. I never asked much from you but for your support and sometimes your opinion. But I don't need your opinion. Look at you! You let that liquor fuck up the remainder of the evening. You got the kids looking at your stupid ass. You ain't setting no example." I went in.

"Whatever. Like I said, you boring as shit. That's why you can't keep a man because you up your own ass. You think the world revolves around you. The only thing you give a fuck about is your son. That's about it."

"Excuse me," Sanai was furious. "Can you guys get your friend? He's not gonna keep talking to my friend like this. She don't deserve that. Don't just stand there—do something."

"Come on, man." Saul walked over and began trying to coerce him to leave the yard. "You doing too much and for nothing. Come go with me, cuz."

"Naw, I don't need to go with you. I need to put my steaks on the grill and cook the rest of the food. She ain't even feed these kids." He was steadily stumbling and totally clueless.

"She did feed her kid, my kid, your kid, and the kids down the street," Sanai raised her voice. "Ken, you gotta go. What you're doing is not right."

Kevin started talking to Ken, convincing him to leave the yard, but he refused to put his cup down.

"You are a bipolar, manic-ass nigga, you know that!" I yelled at him. "You act like you doing me a favor. You ain't doing me no favor!" I clapped back.

"Bitch, please. Like I said, no nigga wanna be with a bitch who is up her ass. You don't have any balance. It's work work work, or you sleep. You boring."

"Say what you want. This shit gonna pay off one day."

"Well, why we waiting, sweetheart? Just remember, you was like 'Jenny from the Block' when I met you. A couple of niggas hit you, and I still messed with you and cleaned you up. Don't forget that!"

"Boy, bye. I worked for everything I have. No one gave me anything. Yea, you moved me, but you didn't give me the money to move into this house. Where's your contribution, Ken? Where your money? Always talking but never activating." The tequila was warming up to my brain. My nerves were bad. He had fucked up my moment. He embarrassed me—totally embarrassed me.

"Come on, Dream, let's go in the house. Let his mad ass be mad. You ain't got time for this." Sanai grabbed her wine and tequila bottles.

"Keep playing, kids! We'll come get you when we ready," Sanai yelled out to the children.

"Come on, girl. This is crazy."

"Yea, he's wild. Like everything was all good. We were minding our business." My mind drifted.

"You be dealing with stuff like this all the time?"

"No, he's normally cool until he drinks. I've never dealt with an alcoholic. I'm seeing he's a different person when he drinks."

"Yea, he's night and day."

"Don't deal with that disrespect. You better than that." We both sat on my black leather love seat.

"I'm not gonna deal with it. No man has ever . . ." My voice began to crack.

"Yea, 'cause I know you. But I see he all cock diesel and strong. You would have to hit his head with a bottle, 'cause he could knock you out with one punch."

"Yea, he could. I'm learning to walk away."

"But this shouldn't be on the regular."

"It's not. If it gets too much, I guess I'm gonna have to walk away."

"You better."

Deep down, I was starting to feel like a foolish dreamer. Maybe Kenya was right. Maybe the business would become a flute. Maybe I was up my own ass. I was kind of self-absorbed. Maybe I was boring, and it turned off all the other men that seemed intimidated by my intelligence. Maybe me being too focused was too much. Perhaps Kenya and I didn't need to be together. He was dysfunctional. He had a drinking problem, yet told the drunken truth. But then again, I wasn't gonna be too many more bitches.

"Your phone is going off, D. It's on the table. Here." She handed me the phone.

I reviewed my text messages and missed calls. My whole mood changed.

"What? What now? You smiling that quick? Is that Kenya already calling to apologize?"

"Roca."

"Whose that?"

"It ain't Kenya."

"Well, damn. What's his name again?"

"His name is Roca."

# Chapter 12

*Time*

Hey, you.

Hey, Roca.

I miss talking to you, Dream. How you been? Roca was on my line.

I've been good, just in grind mode, I texted back.

You always in grind mode . . . always hustling and working too hard. Roca already knew.

How you been, tho?

There was something about Roca that was intriguing, but it was like we both were in a situation. He was with his baby mama, Fatima, and they had a son together, and I was bunned up with Kenya's irritating ass. The deck of cards that I always got never seemed fair or even close to fair. Me choosing men was like wanting to purchase a pair of shoes where the only pair in my size would be the shoe on display that other customers had the opportunity to try on—go figure my luck.

Are you busy today? You wanna get some breakfast or lunch? he texted.

Lunch would be cool. I'm in the office supply store, grabbing a few things for my office and working on a grant.

I was geeked to drop King off so that I could be in an office supply store by my lonesome, being a nerd among nerds.

I walked in Staples and grabbed a shopping cart.

Oh yeah. You back with Men of Valor or you doing your own thing?

I'm doing my own thing like for real, for real! I texted back.

There was a brief silence. Being in Staples was like entrepreneurial heaven. With a budget of $250, my goal was to get what I absolutely needed for the office.

I walked straight to the pens and pencils section and grabbed three packs of black pens, one box of sharpened #2 pencils, a box of Wite-Out, a box of paper clips, and a stapler.

Roca texted back. We definitely gotta go to lunch. You gotta catch me up on life, and I gotta catch you up on my life.

Yea, you got that right, I texted while looking at a wall decal that was calling my name. It read "*Destined for Greatness*," and it went straight in my basket. There was a mini dry erase board for goals and reminders. It went in my cart as well.

Love, I should be free around 1 p.m. You in the city? It was just 8:45 a.m., and I had time to bring the supplies to the office and wrap up my grant.

Yea, I'm in the city. 1 p.m. is good. You wanna meet at Chipotle, your favorite place?

We sure can. We can meet at the one by the zoo. It's in the cut, and the food seems fresh.

OK, love, can't wait to see you. You could smell his emotion. Can't wait to see you too! I texted back.

Whew, chile, who knew where that lunch date would go? But anything would beat being cussed out and disrespected by Kenya. I couldn't let no one, not my boyfriend, kid, family, friend, or stranger get in my way.

I perused around the store, which seemed pretty empty. Next, I went to aisle 3 to get file folders, hanging folders, packs of paper, sanitizers, sharpies, sticky tabs, a calculator, desk organizers, and a few desk racks. What I really wanted was a fresh plant with violets or sunflowers. There was an artificial violet plant that would keep my desk perfect company. More importantly, I needed my own printer. There was a nice-size Canon printer for $89.99 that came with the ink, which was a steal. I placed three packs of copy paper in my cart as well.

Umi had six desks and file cabinets, which were awesome and took a load off me. What else was missing? I walked down aisle 5 and 6 to ensure that I had what I needed.

I tossed a 4-pack of Scotch Tape, a pack of highlighters, one weighted desktop dispenser, a 3-tier desk shelf, a universal mesh organizer, a black mesh small trash can, and loose-leaf paper. Was $250 gonna cover all the shit that I had tossed in my cart out of emotion and excitement? I wasn't sure. But there were only two other people in the store with me, so if I had to put a few things back, I didn't look too crazy.

In the middle of an open display area, there was a black-on-black leather Bugatti briefcase that was calling my name, along with a black leather Soho High-Back. They were a perfect match, but they would cost me well over $200. They would become a part of my business wish list. And one day, when I made real money, I would come back for more. Instead, I settled for a $6 pack of Clorox disinfecting wipes and walked my happy-go-lucky to check out. My cart was full.

"How you doing?" the young male cashier greeted me with a nice smile. His name tag read Hector. He was Latino, but he was giving Puerto Rican or Dominican. He was brown with loose, black curls.

"I'm good."

He started ringing my items up, and he was at $109 in no time. When he got to the mesh items, the total increased quickly to $230. He had four more items to scan.

"The total is $263.07. Are you paying with cash or credit? Oh, do you have a Reward Card?"

"Hector, can I enter my number on the keypad?" I asked.

"Yes, you can. You must have read my name tag, right?"

"Of course. I'm entering it now."

The cashier entered a few keys and provided a new total.

"With your rewards discount points, your new total is $258.35."

"Yes, I needed that discount because I came here with a budget of $250, and I did good." I pulled my debit card out of my bra, as usual. Luckily, there wasn't any sweat on the card.

"Yea, you did do good." Hector handed me my receipt and began bagging all my supplies. He placed all six bags in the cart and made room for my printer.

"Thank you very much. You have a great day." I pushed the cart out of the store smiling from ear to ear. I was so excited knowing that all I had to do was drive four blocks up, and I would land right at my new office. As soon as I popped the trunk and looked up, I noticed Kiana walking toward me. We both locked eyes. She was looking fly as usual. Her hair was given about 20 inches of silky flat ironed hair with a part in the middle. She wore a pair of jeans, sneakers, and a nice, long-sleeved blouse.

"Hey, Dream." She seemed happy to see me.

"Hey, Kiana, how you been?" We stood right next to each other.

"I'm good. We miss you at MOV." She sounded sincere.

"Y'all don't miss me."

"Mr. Light and Mr. Fab dearly miss you. All they do is talk about you. And Mr. Raymond just asked about you too."

"For real, I miss all of them too. I learned so much from them. I have nothing but respect and love for them."

"They gotta lot of respect for you too. I've been around for 5 years, and I never saw them ever let a young woman like yourself rise to the top."

"Really?"

"Yea, not even Queenie. And Queenie been around for more than 10 years," she spilled tea.

"Wow, I didn't know that. I didn't come to step on anyone's toes. God put me there for a season, and it was a great experience," I said with respect.

"Are you working on your own thing?" Kiana wanted her own tea.

"Well, yea. I have my own organization now," I said with pride.

"Your own that quick? You haven't even been gone for a year."

"Yea, but I've researched it well. It was in my heart. It was time for me to move to the next level."

"So, you have your papers and business license?" she pried.

"Yes, all of that," I sassed. "As a matter of fact, I'm headed to my office now. It's just up the street."

"This is my neighborhood, girl. I live a block away. Where's your office located?"

"My office is gonna be on Gail Ln."

"Where, at the rec?"

"Yep, in the rec on the third floor. I have my own office, and it even came with desks. That's why you see me with all these supplies." I began putting the bags into my trunk.

"You need help?" Kiana offered her assistance.

"No, thank you." There were only a few bags left to place in my trunk, and there was room in the backseat for the printer.

"Are you gonna hire staff?"

"Right now, I can't afford to hire myself, but I know probably soon, maybe within the next 3 months, I'll need an assistant because I won't be able to handle the programming responsibility on my own."

"You gotta card?"

"No, not yet, but I will by the end of the week."

"Take my number down. I could use some part-time work." She was adamant.

"Really? You locked in at MOV."

"I'm not locked in. I could use some extra hours. I wanna make money too and go on trips. Out of respect for them, if you hired me, I would let them know. I have nothing to hide."

"Sounds like a plan. Plus, you have an advantage. You're a great assistant to Mr. Light, you get the job done, and you have bomb energy." I grabbed a pen and piece of paper out of the glove compartment and wrote her number down.

"Thanks. It's good seeing you and call me. I can come anytime and see the space. I'm so proud of you." She hugged me, and I gave her a sisterly hug back.

"Thank you so much. I'm gonna call you soon." I hopped in my car and drove off. It was as if the stars were in perfect alignment. God knew that I would need a good, strong assistant for my business. Someone who could get the job done and was trustworthy. If Kiana could administratively run the hell out of MOV, she could do the same thing for Passion for Change.

In a swift 3 minutes, I was already on Gail Ln., searching for a parking space. There was a small 2-hour free parking space located in the middle of the block, and it had my name on it. I pulled up and paralleled parked right into that space and popped my trunk. Carrying the six bags and my laptop bag was no problem, but that printer would have to stay until I felt like carrying it up. One of the front doors of the center were automated, so I walked in and was greeted, surprisingly, by Umi.

"Hey, kiddo, let me help you." Umi was right on time. She took two bags out of my hand.

"Thank you so much, Umi. You didn't have to."

"You needed help, child. Plus, I was waiting for you anyhow so that I can give you the key to get into the office. I got a copy of the key made for you and maintenance. So we're good." She pressed the elevator button for the third floor. We hopped on and went straight up to my floor.

"You got what you need?" Umi had such a strong accent.

The elevator doors opened, and we walked swiftly to the office.

"I made sure I got pretty much a starter kit of supplies."

Umi laughed. "Never heard anyone say a starter kit of supplies. So, basically, you got what you needed?" She took one of the keys out of her right pants pocket and opened the door. I walked right behind her and placed the items on the oak conference table in the center of the office. The room appeared to be freshly vacuumed and organized. It had a total of six desks and a conference table with six chairs.

"I had my maintenance crew move the conference table from the other office room that we have and made sure that desks and chairs were in here. That's the least that I could do." Umi was generous.

"Wow! Thank you so much. You have really gone beyond for me. I'm just grateful for you and your staff." I looked all around and was mesmerized.

"I put a leather high chair at the desk. I thought of you. Welcome to being your own boss, hon." Umi handed me the key. "I gotta few meetings to go to, and I gotta get my eyebrows and lashes done. I'm outta here. Here's my number." She handed me her card, then started walking toward the office door. "Oh, and get those business cards," she asserted. Then Umi was gone.

"Yes, ma'am." I paused at that moment. Shit was really surreal for me. My future was in my own hands, and I couldn't afford to fuck up. My son was banking on me. Hell, *I* was banking on me. It was like the thoughts of my mind and imagination were manifesting at a frequency that was above me.

I claimed my desk immediately. It was the second desk on the left-hand side of the room. It was informal, but the desk was in perfect condition. It was cherry oak, and that's where the leather black swivel high chair was pushed in. It looked identical to the one in the office store. I pulled my phone out of my bra and went to click on the R&B Pandora station. As soon as SWV's classic song "Right Here" came on, I was in a zone. I took out the Clorox wipes and began thoroughly wiping down each desk. The desks were pretty dusty, and you could tell they hadn't been occupied for a while. I went a few doors down to wash my hands. The bathroom was spotless. It had eight stalls and four sinks. The third floor was pretty quiet. There was no traffic. You could tell only Umi and special events were allowed on that floor.

I took everything out of the bag to set up my desk. I placed my artificial violet at the right corner, the desk calendar was in the center, and the desk organizer, shelves, and the desktop dispenser were perfectly placed on my desk. I put my pens, sticky notes, and Sharpie Notes on the dispenser and set the black mesh trash can beside my desk.

I ensured that the other two desks on my side of the room had desk organizers, pens and pencils, sticky notes, and a Sharpie inside the desk drawer. In addition, I set up file folders on the first three desks in the room and envisioned my own staff at those two other desks. The remaining supplies would be stored inside the file cabinet in the far-left corner of the room. Lastly, my decal, which was too powerful, had to go up in the center of the left wall. Hopefully, Umi didn't mind, 'cause eventually, there would be some beautiful canvases going up just as soon as I could afford it.

If only some incense were burning, the atmosphere would really be amazing. It was showtime, and I had a grant to knock out. I took my laptop out and placed it on my desk as I sat comfortably in my leather chair. For a few minutes, I closed my eyes, leaned my head back, and gave thanks to the creator, the Most High, for guiding my path. Then I took some deep breaths.

I cracked open the mini grant file and the outline that I had already created, which would make the writing process smooth. McKenzie was right. The grant was actually more feasible than I thought.

I began typing the cover page, "Passion for Change Summer Mini-Grant Proposal." I played with the fonts, wanting them to be simple yet bold with color. The second page was the Applicant Profile, which was a standard one-pager requesting the organization's name, project title, duration of the grant, description of the grant, proposed budget, and programmatic contact information. It took me no more than 5 minutes to complete it and insert my electronic signature.

The mini grant consisted of six areas where I had to craft the mission, vision, and response to questions very carefully regarding history, past performance and experience, success and impact, program design, schedule, and budget.

The mission focused on utilizing the creative and performing arts to build innovative youth and adult programs, catapulting healing, building safe communities, and lifelong success.

The vision needed depth. The vision had to be laser sharp, authentic, and tangible. At the end of the day, Passion for Change could not become a gimmick. It had to come to life in the realest way. The words rolled through the keyboards descriptively. "Our vision is to be a service to the community and impact the lives and the communities where we live through self-worth, self-value, and knowledge of self. Our vision is to become a platform of public service that promotes maximizing one's full potential."
The words kept flowing, and best believe, spell check and the thesaurus were on deck. Although I was entering my first year of business, my story and contribution to the community were enmeshed in the work with the youth and working in the trenches with MOV, as well as the wealth of community organizing that lay in my experience working on the campaign trail with President Hope. As a young Black woman, I was unafraid to go into any neighborhood. It was as if God put a shield on my life, and "no weapons formed against me, prospered."

There! I meditated about success and impact. Didn't really understand how a girl from the hood like myself could bring hope, but the labor to do this type of work was calling me. My experience spoke to preparing youth rising out of the ashes of the ghetto and making their way to 4-year universities and colleges. The impact spoke to me creating safe havens in public housing projects where most were too scared to come to the "basement." I literally took old, tarnished centers and cleaned them, nurtured them, and gave them life so that the youth in the same community could come to a unique place to do their homework, study, graduate, get mentoring, life coaching—the guidance was endless, and the impact was real.

I had buried in my heart that if Harriet, Madam C. J., Mary McLeod Bethune, Angela Davis, and Assata could create impact, love, and future, then I could follow suit. This was the picture that I painted throughout my grant . . . that the work had been done, and thus, I was no stranger to the work. This time, I had an EIN and a business license to go with a résumé.

Butterflies fluttered in my stomach when I meditated on the grant question on program design and schedule. My programs had to be nontraditional and out of the box. I continued to type. My target population would be inclusive of youth ages 14 to 21 who came from all communities in the district. The design would focus on youth creating their own newsletter. The first 2 hours of the day would be slated for creative writing and the fundamentals of journalism. From 12:00 to 12:30 p.m., the students would break for lunch. Upon returning, they would engage in their life skills and leadership courses. I reflected on incorporating a 10:00 a.m.–3:00 p.m. schedule, Monday through Friday, and the last 15 minutes would be used to have a wrap-up session, where we would use it to debrief.

Having an engaging, fun, and impactful summer was attainable, and my goal was to make sure that the words in my grant proposal came alive. McKenzie made it clear that the budget for the 6 weeks was $10,000. My goal was to fill in the line items for salary, supplies, equipment, and refreshments. The budget was in Excel, and it was pretty simple. You entered the numbers and the totals populated. Off the top, $8,000 would go to salary, and my goal would be to hire one other staff. Most likely, the other staff person would be from the Men of Valor. There was no doubt about it that MOV made men and women both thorough and extraordinary. I itemized $1,000 for supplies, $600 for two Dell laptops, and $400 for refreshments. All teens loved snacks, food, and pizza. Fridays would be identified as a day where we provided lunch, and it was a strong incentive for attendance too.

My fingers were typing at more than 60 words per minute, and it felt so good to respond effectively and concisely to all the questions in the grant. I was completely sold on my own grant, and the words just made sense as if to say, "This gon' work." Yea, it sounded good on paper, but if I were awarded, I would have to set the tone with this grant so that I could demonstrate who we are as an organization and what we came to do.

I intended to write my conclusion in my notebook so that I could strengthen it before typing it. I took a few minutes to close my eyes and meditate on language, expression, and affirming the right message. My editing and proofreading process would come after. The printer was in my car, and I didn't have the patience to get it and set it up. My plans were to email the grant proposal to myself before meeting with Roca. All that needed to be done was to print it off in the morning and submit it to McKenzie by 11:00 a.m., instead of waiting until the last minute. The universe was making my dreams so fluid and seamless. It was hard to believe that in a few days, I would write the first grant for my own company—Yea, hard to digest.

Leaning back in my chair with my eyes closed and head to the sky, pen in my right hand, I made sure I saved my document at least three times so that there were no errors or deletions. Immediately, I emailed it to myself 'cause I couldn't lose out on my blessing and then closed out my documents and placed my laptop in its tote. I grabbed my BCBG bag, my laptop, and a bottle of ginger I had been saving. I was truly thirsty and ready to eat. My office looked like a real office, and no one could take that moment away from me. After gathering my items, I locked up the office and hopped on the elevator, all geeked 'cause I could really sit down and talk to Roca.

Where you at? I texted Roca as I sat in my car.

I'm headed to you. You done yet? he texted back.

Yea, I'm done. I'm about 10 minutes away, I texted him.

OK, luv, we gon' get there around the same time, he responded.

'K, see you in a bit.

I adjusted my seat, rolled down my front windows halfway to feel the breeze, and turned on the radio. The vibrations were cool, my spirit was in a blessed state of mind, and the frequency was a silhouette of what was to come. As I navigated through the Heights into the Woodley Park community, I had flashbacks of years prior pushing King in a stroller, kinda sad, pretty weary, very teary, and just feeling unfortunate. It was as if the glimpse were a reminder of how God repaired my life.

 As I pulled up in front of Chipotle and parked, I watched Roca's tall kingly frame walk in. From the outside looking in, Chipotle seemed pretty packed. Guess 'cause it was lunchtime. Roca appeared to be standing off to the side, waiting for me.

"Hey, boi." I tapped him on his right shoulder.

"Hey, baby," he smiled, showing the mini gap in his mouth.

"Hey, it's so good to see you." We embraced each other like we were kindred spirits.

"You just don't know how good it feels to see you," he said, rubbing my face gently.

"Yes, seeing you is a breath of fresh air."

"You know what you want to eat?" Roca asked.

"Yea."

"Go ahead and order." He grabbed my hand so that the server could take my order.

"Hi, can I take your order?"

"Yes, can I get a chicken bowl with pinto beans, grilled veggies, tomatoes, the verde salsa, sour cream, cheese, and light on the guacamole?"

"Sure, would you like a beverage?" she asked politely.

"Yes, can I have that Izze Grapefruit drink?"

"You sure can," she responded and moved my bowl to the cashier.

"What about you, sir? Can I take your order?" She smiled from ear to ear as she took Roca's order. He was fine and all, but dang, her cheesing was a giveaway.

"Can I get a steak and chicken bowl with extra steak? Give me some black beans, cheese, sour cream, corn, salsa, and a li'l bit of hot sauce." He sounded all country.

"And your drink, sir?"

"Please give me what she has," he said, rubbing his fingers through my long tresses.

"Would you like me to put the orders together?"

"Yes." He pulled out his debit card and paid for the food. "Eh, Dream, get us some forks and napkins and find us somewhere to sit. I got the food."

"Cool." I started walking around. There was a quaint window seat in the cut with our names on it. I placed the forks and napkins in the middle of the table and sat down.

He was right behind me with a tray. He sat down and placed our bowls and drinks on the table.

"This is a good spot for us to eat and talk without people being all up in our business."

"Yea, you be wanting to be all inconspicuous. All in the cut," I read him.

"That's the best way to be." We both grabbed our forks and dived into our food.

"So, what's up with you?" I cut to the chase. "Where you been hiding? Whatchu been doing?"

"Dream, I've been grinding real hard. Since we both left MOV, I went on to work as a building maintenance technician for the government. Then I needed more money, so I started working for my dad's towing company."

"That's right. Your dad does have his own towing company."

"Yea, he has one of the top towing companies in the city. His tow company been around for 25 years. I'm towing every chance I get. I don't need a lot of sleep, as long as I'm breaded up. I got my daughters and my son to provide for."

"Yea, I get it." My veggies tasted so good in the guacamole. The bowl was giving me life.

"How's King doing with his badass?" he started eating his food.

"My son ain't bad."

"That li'l nigga is busy, but that's my li'l man." We both laughed.

"Yea, he's off the chain. It's in his DNA. That's King. He doing good, though. He's in sports, so that's really helping him with discipline and focus. He was in soccer, but he's taking football real seriously."

"Yea, football is good for him. You always been a good mom."

"Thank you. Appreciate that."

"So, you still with that nigga?"

"Stop being a hater." I wiped the sour cream from the corner of my mouth with a napkin.

"I've never been a hater, sweetheart. Just inquiring."

"We still together. What else am I supposed to do? You ain't available." I got smart.

"Yea, I'm still with Fatima for my son's sake for real. I can't trust her, though. She been doing wild shit. Stuff that is questionable."

"For real? I thought she was your ride or die."

"Yea, me too. But I'm patient, and I see her ways. She be entertaining other niggas like I don't know. She been fucking this nigga at your ole alma mater," said Roca.

"Dang. You are like a really good dude. Like every woman's fantasy. You're tall, chocolate, handsome, have a beautiful smile, charismatic, positive, intelligent, and just a dope brotha." I started sipping my Izzy.

"You think? I appreciate it. It's like I'm working, taking care of our son, allowing her to go to Bison University, and she is unappreciative. She don't understand that I could be hoeing and having plenty of women."

"So, what's stopping you?" I asked bluntly.

"Our son. I love our son. I love family. That's how I was raised. I was raised by men, my grandfather and my father. They came from Trinidad, and they had principles and instilled them in my brothers and me." He kept eating meticulously.

"It's amazing that men raised you. Most niggas are raised by their mom or grandma. Most boys are abandoned when they're little—

most of 'em, like my son. I appreciate you being there for your son. Family is worth saving."

"I don't know if it's worth saving," he said, sounding torn. We stared into each other's eyes for a brief moment.

"If you don't save your family and relationship, what the fuck are you gonna do?"

"I'ma do me. I'ma be single. I'm gonna live life by my own rules." He was adamant.

"Being single ain't all that. These broads nasty. All you gonna do is catch something. They ain't loyal."

"Yea, but I just wanna be free. I can't keep letting my baby mamas dictate my future. It's about my future and my kids. Women change, and I see it with my own eyes. That's why I always really wanted to get to know you, but you was in a situation, and I was in a situation."

"Yea, it seems like that's how my life be. I can never really get what I want. End up settling for a little bit of love. Just a little," I said, staring out the window.

"You happy wit' him?"

"Not lately. He was just disrespecting me yesterday in front of my best friend and the kids. He kept emphasizing that I was stuck-up and boring." Sadness came over me.

"What? Why would he disrespect you? You're full of life. You ain't boring at all. I see you as adventurous. You are so beautiful. You are perfect for a nigga like me."

"Well, he says I'm full of myself. He paints me as a snobby female. He's not being supportive of starting my own business. I think he thinks I'm gonna be depending on him until I get revenue. Roca, I've been grinding day and night to make my dreams come alive, and it's like now that I'm being proactive and demonstrating progress, he's not supportive."

"Dat's crazy. He doesn't make sense. Do you know how many men wish they had a girlfriend or a wife who started her own business? You moving full speed ahead. Tell me more about your business. Last time I checked, you were running the hell outta MOV. You talked about stepping out on your own," he reflected. "You move fast. What's the name of your organization?"

"Passion for Change. It's a nonprofit that focuses on positive youth development and creating programs for the youth that are innovative and electrifying. I'm incorporating the arts, life skills, life coaching, and work readiness into my program, for starters," I explained.

"*That's* what's up. Where's your office?" Roca asked.

"It's in the same community center where MOV used to have me run those after-school tutoring programs."

"For real, Dream? In the same building? That building is big as hell!"

"Yea, an older sista named Umi, who has shown me love from the beginning, put me on. She was always lobbying for me. It was as if God sent her."

"What floor is your office on?" Roca was interested.

"It's on the third floor. It's a nice-size suite. It has six desks and a conference table. It's furnished, painted, and overall, just really nice."

"You are blessed! Is it a lot of money to rent?"

"Naw." I leaned in and whispered because white people were paying too close attention to us. "It's free, dude. It's free! Can you believe it?"

"What? Yea, you *blessed*. Everything in that area costs thousands of dollars to rent. You got time now to really set up your nonprofit."

"Yea, so that's why I'm going so hard. I can't afford to play. My destiny is in my hands. I got a grant I need to submit in the morning for the summer. It's only for 6 weeks, but it pays $10,000. That will get me together. If I get that grant, it'll open doors for me."

"You already know. That's so good, Dream. I'm so proud of you, baby girl. You are so ambitious and so pretty. Sometimes, I wish I would have met you before I met Fatima. You are so ideal for me." He held both of my hands.

Roca was so doggone fine. His eyes reminded me of Tupac. They were bright, crystal clear, and adorned with poignant, long eyelashes. It was like I was uncomfortable when his eyes connected with mine. His brown skin just radiated in special ways that I couldn't but wonder about it.

"So, are you gonna have some staff?"

"Yea, eventually I'm gonna have to. But to start with, I can't afford to hire anyone. I'm gonna be working for myself for a minute," I added. "But if I get this grant, I'm gonna bring on Lee from the MOV who used to work with my program and a lot of the other programs. He would be good. And if I could afford a part-time assistant, I would bring Kiana."

"Oh, so you just gonna bring the young staff from the MOV to your company. You real slick." We both giggled.

"Well, I need to know who I'm hiring. I would bring you on as well. You're reliable, on point, precise, and supportive. So, yea, you on my radar too. Hopefully, in 6 months, I can have a few part-timers, at least."

"Baby girl, the world is yours." He started caressing my hair. "But as for me, I think I wanna go in the military. The navy. I wanna be in the navy."

Roca surprised me. "For real? Damn, I would never get that from you. I just can't get into our men fighting the white man's wars. This country stay bullying other countries, and next thing you know, we at war. We been in the Middle East for how many years?"

"Yea, but I need a future, I need stability, I need guidance and discipline, and I'll get it by enrolling in the military. I could see the world, Dream. If I'm out here in these inner-city streets, a nigga might kill me, or I might kill him. There's too much hatred. I need to get away. Once I establish myself, there'll be some consistent income for my children and me." He spoke from the heart.

"I just don't want you going away and not coming back alive. Like I need you to stay alive and reach your full potential and destiny. You have so much to live for. You're amazing in my eyes. Maybe go to Atlanta or somewhere where you can thrive as a Black man in America."

"Dream, I'm really considering it. My kids would be the only reason why I won't enlist. I've talked to recruiters, and I'm healthy and ready."

"Boy, oh, boy. Okay. If you wanna do it, I support you," I said, but I wasn't feeling the military, and he knew it by my facial expression.

"This is what's best for me. I need support to be better as a man."

"Okay, then I support you. If it makes you happy, then do it. I'm gonna be your friend, no matter what," I expressed strongly.

"Thank you." He put all of our food on a tray and moved the tray to the side.

"Either way, I'm gonna let you know what I'm gonna do. I think about you a lot. I really wanna get to know you. I know you got someone, and I do too, but if it's in the deck of cards, hopefully, we'll see what the future looks like. I like you, Dream." He kissed me on my bottom lip. It was like one of those romantic kisses on the big screen. I closed my eyes, and my badass wanted more, so I kissed him back. Then we pulled back at the same time.

"Dang, you nasty, boy."

"I just wanted to see how them lips taste wit' all that red lipstick."

"Really?" We laughed and giggled like we were seniors in high school.

"You gonna get in trouble messing with me."

"Naw, you gonna get in something you ain't gonna want to come out of, fa' real." Roca rubbed his hand across my right cheek.

"So, you like me, huh? I like you too. What we gonna do?" I wasn't for certain.

"Time," Roca admonished. "Time, Dream. I learned to be patient in life. It's all about timing in what we do and what we aspire or desire to do. If we wait, time will reveal who and what we'll be to each other."

"You think? Kenya crazy, though."

"Yea, and I got heart, and I ain't scared of him."

"Fatima don't seem like she bow out gracefully, either," I chimed.

"Her actions will terminate her position. She's on her way out. But you loyal. I can see it in your eyes."

"Yea, I'm too loyal. But if Kenya keep wilding out and being a bamma, then I'm outta this bitch! Solomon already broke me. I can't take another broken heart. Plus, we ain't got kids, so I can escape the madness without ties."

"It ain't gonna be easy with him. He know what he got. Just understand who you are. You are beautiful, smart, awesome, and now you a boss," he reminded me. "Don't let no man take that away from you. That's why I say time. I would never wanna break your heart. So, I will wait until I know I can present myself to you in the most authentic way. If anything, I'm gonna protect your heart!"

Roca picked up the tray and walked a few feet to empty our food into the trash can, placing the tray for collection. Then he walked me out to the front of my car.

We embraced and just hugged each other like we were homies, lovers, and friends.

"You smell so damn good." I sniffed up and down his neck.

"Yea, I'm big on colognes and oils."

"Oooh, you just let me go before I get myself in trouble!"

"I don't mind getting in trouble with you. When we gonna get together again? I hope soon."

"Whenever. I work for myself, so I can always arrange my day. Maybe we can go to a happy hour or a lounge? Your choice."

"Look out for my phone call and text. I'm really tryin'a spend some time with you. Remember what I said," he reminded me.

"Time," I said softly.

"Time is everything." We began drifting and walking away. The universe was beautiful. He kissed me on my forehead.

"Dream, time is on our side."

# Chapter 13

"Mama, we gonna have a real big house soon, huh?" We pulled up in front of King's school on a bright Tuesday morning.

"Why you say that, King?"

"It just seem like you been focused, Ma, like you not letting nothing get in your way. I just see you every day with a smile on your face taking me to school, going to your new office, picking me up, and us going home."

"Yea, son, you always paid attention. You are far beyond your years."

"What does 'far beyond your years' mean?" he asked.

"It means you are so wise. Like you been here before. Even though you're young, you speak as if you're a grown man."

King began laughing as we were less than a mile away from his school.

"It just seems like we gonna be rich soon."

"I'm trying, son, to be focused—really focused. It's not easy, but each day, I think of you, and I think of us. I want you to have access to the whole entire world."

"What about millions? Do you think you'll have a million by the time I make it to the eighth grade?" He was so serious.

"Wow," I leaned to give him a kiss on the forehead. "I think I'll have a million by that time. I have a few years to get it together, right?"

"Yea, you gotta go hard, Ma." He sounded like his coaches.

"Really, King? Are you my coach now?"

"Yea, I'm your coach. I want you to win, Ma. I don't want you to fail. And I heard Kenya the other day. He was wrong. You are not a snob, Mom. You doing good. I remember when we lived on Clay Street. That was thuggin', and that was the struggle."

"You remember that? As far as Kenya is concern, we not listening to him. He will see that your mom is cut from a different cloth. I don't give up or give in."

"I know you don't, Mom. I don't like him talking to you like that, though." King was sincere.

I was at the stoplight right by his school, just realizing that my son was paying attention to everything, including the good, bad, and the struggle. My baby boy didn't miss a beat.

"You right, son. He has no business disrespecting me. Ma is not gonna continue to tolerate the disrespect, either. Your own father wasn't even disrespectful."

"He wasn't?" King asked.

"Nope. He betrayed and abandoned us. He may have cussed me out once, and that was it. If I made your dad mad, he would just leave. But he never verbally disrespected us."

I made a left into the school campus. There were several cars in front of us—parents dropping off their kids too.

"Well, that's good about my dad. But, yea, Ma, living on Clay Street wasn't that long ago, Ma. I remember playing with the mice, hearing the gunshots, seeing the crackheads, and watching Jeremy and them sell drugs."

"You have a good memory, son, but we ain't ever going back there. As long as I have breath in my body, we gonna push through, and we gonna be good. I promise you, son, I got us."

"I believe you, Ma." King put his backpack on and took a sip of his bottled water. He kissed me on my cheek and opened the passenger door.

"Love you, Ma. See you after school."

"Love you, King; see you later." I was feeling slightly emotional. I drove in a U-turn so that I get off the school campus and back on the road. The water in my eyes welled up. My baby caught onto what was going on. He was getting older, wiser, and protective. I was all that he had, and he reminded me in a single moment that he witnessed the disrespect of his mother, and it affected him.

Yea, Kenya was cool on the one hand, but he was getting out of hand, and to be honest, I had never dealt with his type ever. He was loving yet impulsive. He was caring yet disrespectful. He appeared protective yet insulting. Kenya and I would have to converse about our relationship and how imperative it was for me to be respected. Without respect, our relationship would fall off into a dark abyss that would end before it really could progress.

"My God," I drove slowly, shaking off my tears. I was 7 minutes away from printing my proposals and submitting them to McKenzie.

In my mind, McKenzie said 2:00 p.m. was the final submission time, but waiting for that deadline wasn't gonna work for me.

"Dear God, thank you for waking me up today. Thank you for waking up my son today. God, I just wanna thank you for giving me another chance to get my life right. I wanna thank you for loving me and not giving up on me," I started praying. "I know I'm hardheaded. I know I don't always listen to you. Please forgive me, Lord. Please help me to do better. Reveal to me where I should go, who I should talk to, who I need to be around, and who needs to be removed. Guide me, Lord, in this thing called life. Please, Lord, I need to hear from you."

My prayer became deeper.

"Lord, you delivered me from depression, suicidal thoughts, abandonment, poverty, and the spirit of not feeling like I was good enough. You established me in the realest way. God, please let me know if this is the route that I need to go. Being an entrepreneur, is this what I'm supposed to be doing? Jesus, it is the desire of my heart, but is it what *you* want me to do, Lord? I need to hear from you and no one else. 'Cause people have an opinion and will have an opinion, but only you, God, know my beginning and my end."

I pulled up right in front of FedEx Kinko's, placing my car in park and closing my eyes in reverence.

"You knew me in my mother's womb. You know me more than anyone in this world. Please, speak to my soul, speak to my spirit, and move me. I don't wanna mess this destination up. No detours. No more years being wasted looking for love. No more years loving people who don't love me back. Jesus, please let me know the way that I should go. Guide me with your eternal light. Lord, please grant me favor with this organizational entity and more entities so that I can be awarded more grants and proposals. I pray I got this one." I lifted my head.

"I know you got me, God. In Jesus' name, Amen."

Praying and faith were all that a sista had. It was my navigation, blueprint, and my spiritual weapon. God more often than not answered my prayers, and if He didn't, I understood in my spirit that it wasn't for me. I grabbed my work bag and locked the doors, then walked into Kinko's.

"Hey, lady, haven't seen you in a while."

"Yonas, I've been busy, bra."

"Yea, you have too because you normally in here typing away, creating flyers and doing your thang. You still working with the youth?"

"Yes, but I'm on my own terms. I started my own nonprofit," I said proudly.

"Holy shit! Really? That's so awesome. You always had the aura of a businesswoman, so it makes sense to me. What you working on today?" Yonas was one of the coolest Ethiopian brothas I knew. He printed résumés, flyers, marketing collateral, laminated, and helped design my portfolio. There was so much more, and he always was supportive, never really charging me the full price.

"I need to print a grant that I just wrote. I'm gonna need two copies for the organization that's reviewing the grant as well as a copy for myself. Two nice black folders will do too."

"You have it on your USB, or you have it on email?" he asked.

"It's on my email. Should I get on one of those computers?"

"It's pretty busy. Since you're on a deadline, you can go into your email on my desktop and open the file so that I can print it out. Is it in color?"

"Thanks so much. I appreciate you. Nope, I'm not that sophisticated. It's in black and white." I placed my work bag on the workstation that was adjacent to me. Then I started logging in to my email on his desktop. My poor laptop moved so slow, and, of course, his desktop moved at a fast gigabyte. There were a few off-brand emails, and then there was the email with the grant. I opened the file and scrolled through it and inserted the page numbers at the bottom center. There were eight pages in total.

"Is that the document?" Yonas asked.

"Yes, this is it."

"Oh, it's a small file. You need two copies?"

"Yes."

He clicked the mouse and was at the printer in a jiffy. Within a couple of minutes, he brought two copies of the grant to me. I carefully went through each page of the grant to make sure that it flowed, was in sequence, and ready for submission.

"Here are two nice black folders. They're about $3 apiece. What you think?"

"Yes, they are nice."

Yonas rang up the folders and the cost of printing quickly. "Sis, give me $8; you good. You doing stuff as always, and I'm supporting you."

"I appreciate you. You know I'm coming to you for all my business needs. Your work is always dope." I pulled a $10 out of the right side of my bra and handed it to him.

"Keep the change, Yonas. You always got me. You think if I send you the content and concept, you can do my business cards? Nothing too elaborate. Just something nice and simple. Plus, I'm low budget right now until I start grossing revenue."

"I got you. The funds will come. When you need it by?"

"By the end of the week."

"I'll have them done in 48 hours. Just email me the copy."

With joy in my heart, I carefully placed each copy of the grant in the black folders. I held both folders for dear life.

"I'ma send you the copy this evening. Thanks so much again for everything."

"You got it, sis." He gave me a thumbs-up.

I grabbed my bag and put it on my right shoulder and held the folders with my left hand. So much joy was in my heart. No one would understand this joy unexplainable.

I placed my work bag in the backseat, and my folders were in the front seat riding shotgun. Together, my grants and dreams headed to McKenzie. I glided like an eagle down the short four blocks it took to get to her office. Parking spaces were scarce. However, there was a small parking space in front of her building where you had to pay to park. I squeezed in and found one quarter and a dime in my cup holder and placed it in the meter. At this point, even time wasn't gonna stop me. The meter only gave me 11 minutes, and in my heart, 11 minutes was all I needed to get up three flights of stairs and into the grants office. I wore jeans, a graphic tee, a denim blazer, and MK sneakers. By the time I got to the second flight of stairs, I was breathing. I needed to go to Yoga before the day was out. My center was calling me, and after all of this, so was my peace.

As soon as I walked into the grants office, I saw McKenzie sitting at the receptionist's desk. She appeared like she was ready for folks like me, who would be out of breath, all over the place, and nervous as hell to submit their grant proposals.

"Oh, look at you, Bison. You early." McKenzie was all loud. Her coworkers stood near, signifying.

"Yea, girl. I thought it would be in my best interest to submit early, 'cause it's competitive."

"Well, you're being strategic and smart. We like that. Are those for me?" She pointed at the folders. She was aggressive.

"Yes, they are." I graciously handed her the folders.

"Told you, you could do this in a couple of days. You're a writer by trade. You were influential when we were in school. You probably thought you were just writing. But you were putting words together that were inspirational, informative, and all-around, most of us wanted to hear what you had to say."

"Really? That's so inspiring to get that feedback. You are right. I just be writing, and it flows. It makes sense to me, and it's therapeutic for me to release my writings into the universe."

"Well, Queen, you're on your way. I personally look forward to reading your grant. You'll know in a week if you're awarded. We gotta roll out this grant for the summer, and summer is right around the corner. You'll be notified real soon." McKenzie time-stamped both proposals.

"Thanks again." We shook hands.

"You got this. We'll be in touch." She was coded.

My heart was beating fast. My nerves were going crazy with excitement as I moved down the three flights of stairs, out the front door of the building, and back to my car. It was like so much was manifesting at a faster pace than expected.

No ticket was on my car, and the meter had 1 minute left. My cell phone began ringing as soon as I opened my car door. I pulled it out of my back pocket to see who it was, and, of course, it had to be Kenya. As my cell continued to ring, my thoughts started racing. Was Kenya even worth talking to? Was he gonna be humble or say some wild shit that would throw my amazing morning off?

But I needed to talk to him. We needed to have a conversation about respect, and there was no letting up.

"Hey," the shade was thick.

"Hey, baby." He sounded calm.

"Really, baby?"

"No matter what, you're still my baby. We gonna go through shit, but you are my baby, no matter what."

"So?" My attitude was in full throttle.

"Whatchu mean, so? Seriously. The shit that I did the other day, I didn't mean it. I was drunk as fuck. I was trippin'." He became even calmer. "I support your dreams, Dream. Like I really support who you are and what you're gonna do."

"How can I believe you after what you said? It's like when you drink, you become a monster. You act wild and uncontrollable. It's embarrassing as hell to have the one that I love and care about cuss me out in front of my best friend, the neighbors, and my son—the kids. Come on, that can't happen." My emotions took over.

"You can't disrespect me. You can't disrespect who I am. I worked too hard to get to this place. I gotta li'l peace, nigga, and you ain't gonna take it away."

"I'm not gonna disrespect you. I was raised by all women. I love women. I love you. Like I said, the liquor got to me, and I tripped. That won't happen again. Please, listen to me, baby. I don't wanna be beefing with you. You make a nigga better. You have a big heart, and you loyal. Never had a woman like you." He became sentimental. "You know all I dealt with was hoodrats— confrontational women. Women who just wanted sex, money, and drugs, and that's it. You're intelligent, college-educated, pretty, and sexy. You're responsible. I apologize, baby."

"You used to disrespecting the women that you be with. Those words rolled off your tongue like water. It wasn't nothing. It was too natural to hear and watch you go off on me. Then you said I be up my own ass and that I'm a snob. Do you *really* think that? Is *that* how you feel?"

"On the real, Dream, you can be a li'l snobby. It's not a bad thing, but sometimes you are so gung ho about your goals that you forget about the li'l people. It's like you get in a zone and don't come out until you finished. I never had a woman like that."

"Well, thanks for being honest." I pulled a piece of bubble gum out of my work bag and popped it in my mouth. "Yes, I'm laser sharp, Ken. Like all I got is my dreams. Ain't nobody giving me shit out here. I have to work hard and fight for my spot. I'm not trying to offend you, nor am I trying to be mean. But I am in a zone. If I win, you win; we win. And if you win, we win, and I win. That's my philosophy. When I was working for MOV, and even at the college, I was helping other folks win. Now, for the first time, I have the opportunity to create my own enterprise, and if it's done right, just imagine where we can go as a unit."

"You right, baby. I want you to win. Just give me a hug, a kiss, a nice rub. A funky roll," he burst into laughter.

"A funky roll, though? Why you gotta play so much? OK, just say you need a hug. Say you need some love. Don't cuss me out and then be like you need a hug. 'Cause the bitch in me ain't gonna hug or love anyone who is deemed as a problem. Plus, my son observed how you treated me and felt some type of way."

"For real? Damn, li'l man didn't need to see that. Did Nia see it too?"

"*All* the kids saw it, Kenya. The *whole block*. It was a bad look for us."

"I'm gonna apologize to King. That's my li'l man. Dang. I dropped the ball. My daughter didn't need to see that neither."

"No, none of the kids needed to see that. Your daughter is gonna seek a boyfriend or man one day that will be just like you. Think about *that*."

"Yea, you right. I gotta get some things in order."

"Correct. Let's not go down this road anymore."

"We not. We gotta show ourselves and others that we can be positive, and even when we have differences, we can talk it out like this face-to-face."

"It's about communication. Black men and women need to communicate effectively and positively, that's all."

"Yea, we'll start here. We'll promise to talk it out and figure things out together. Where you at now?"

"I just dropped off my first grant." I was cheezing from ear to ear.

"Oh yeah? That's what you were working on last week, right?"

"Yep."

"You finished that in days. You write fast as hell. But then again, you wrote fast on all your other jobs."

"Yep. If writing is half the battle, then I have a chance at winning. The grants are the resources. That's what will feed the organization and give me a jump start to the work that I do."

"You're right. So when can we get a bite to eat or hang out? You free for the rest of the day? I just wanna see you. Maybe we can meet up in an hour. I'm Uptown at my grandma house."

"Bet, I can come get you. I guess we can chill before I pick up King."

"Let's go eat some of your favorite Mexican food. Celebrate you starting your business. Drink a margarita or two."

"Sounds good, but you don't need no margarita. You need nothing but water." We both started laughing.

"Come on and come get me. I'm out here with Saul, chillin'. Waiting on you."

"All right, I'm on my way." He hung up.

Kenya had a way with words. And when he was sober, he was the coolest, calmest, nicest man. He knew how to make my heart happy, yet he knew how to make my heart mad. We had been together for a couple of years, and things were still kinda new. It was like we were still learning parts to each other that took a lot of vulnerability for me. We had barely scratched the corner of the surface. We were so opposite, but it was like we made sense when things were aligned. He knew how to reach me. He was in tune with my favorite food, my favorite colors, the places that I like to go to. He knew how to find my happy place, and that's what really had me more forgiving. Although my nature held grudges forever, it was hard to stay mad at him.

I drove from the Heights toward Bison University and hit the avenue to get near his grandma's house which was about 15 minutes away from McKenzie's office. Kenya was raised in the Totten. It was a nice middle-class community sorta like mine growing up. It represented the duality of Black America. You had working-class families led by female matriarchs. Most of Kenya's childhood friends were born and raised in the Totten. As a matter, the way that Kenya explained, there were three and four generations of families residing in the Totten. They included politicians, teachers, postal workers, laborers, veterans, and a host of students living in the community because of the three neighboring colleges.

The community was on a hillside, with tons of greenery, vegetation, and if you didn't pay attention at night, you could hit a deer or two. It was a nice all-around community, so it was hard for me to digest how there were gangstas, thugs, drug dealers, crackheads, and dope fiends now. As a matter of fact, his mother's family and father's family lived within a block of each other.

Being raised on the beachside of sunny Southern California, most people wouldn't think that there would be crackheads, dope fiends, gangs, hippies, and a whole apartment complex at the corner of my block for mentally challenged individuals. It was like you saw the beach 3 miles away from my childhood house, but on any given day, you would find "Alvin, the neighborhood bum," passed out from drinking his life away. Then there was "Miracle," a woman who was a loud alcoholic who loved me as a kid, but she couldn't let that bottle go. My community was filled with a duality as well. You had working-class folk, and then you had welfare mamas, who had got caught up in being fly girls who would either be dreamers or a dream deferred falling in love with hustlers, making babies.

My mama was an '80s fly girl who fell in love with my father, who was an athlete. The way that my momma tells it is that the problem was that she built him up when my father didn't have shit, and when he started looking like something, he became arrogant, and then a womanizer. She also said that when she had me and my father started going to college, he would fake like the women were his study partners. In real life, he was messing with them too.

My mother was cut from a different cloth. Her grandmother and uncles raised her in a middle-class family full of entrepreneurs and college-educated professionals. My father was born in poverty. My grandmother Mary was a single mother raising five kids on her own. She had the heart of a lion and was a nurse by trade but without the credentials. During the evenings and weekends, she recycled plastic and beer cans and put them in her white pickup truck. She wasn't no slouch, but she had four beautiful sons, and their father was in and out of their lives. When you have no guidance as a young Black man or no blueprint, you can run off with the wolves and never return. I understood the Black middle class. We were different. We had secrets that grandma and auntie and uncle and them would never share or exhale at Thanksgiving dinner. We stuck together and would bail one other out if we had to. There were too many women running these households. You could tell. There were too many young Black men being emotional like women and being lost in the shuffle with no navigator for real on manhood. Perhaps Kenya was one of them.

I pulled up on Kenya to see him chilling in front of his grandma's house with his best friend, Saul. They had been friends since their mothers carried them in the womb. They were glued to the hip. Saul seemed like he would carry Ken's deepest dark secrets to the grave, and Kenya would kill for Saul. Saul to Ken was like my Sanai.

"What's up, Dream?" Saul greeted me.

"What's up, Saul? How you been?"

"Chilling. Staying out of the way." Saul never really said too much. He was neutral.

"Baby, baby. I missed my baby." Kenya was loud as a mug.

"Why are you so loud?"

"'Cause I miss you, sweetheart." He leaned into the car to kiss me.

"You don't miss me. Come on, boi. You get on my nerves."

He hopped in the car like he couldn't wait, smiling.

"OK, playboy, I'll see you later. I'm with my baby. I gotta take her to get some Mexican food. She deserves it. She works hard. I owe her."

"All right, I'ma see you," said Saul. "Y'all have a good time."

We waved and sped off.

"You got some new hair," Kenya started caressing my hair. "You look like a Dominican mommy."

"Boy, stop. This hair is old. I just washed it. When I get my money up, I'ma get the hair I want."

"I know you are. You look good in dem jeans. That lipstick look good too." He rubbed my bottom lip.

"Why you look so good? You been around a nigga, ain't you. You ain't just gon' to drop off no grant."

I held my composure, but Lord knew I wanted to bust out in laughter. Roca was on a sista's mind.

"No, I had to get this grant out of the way. If I get it, I'm on. That means it's gonna open the floodgates for me." I turned left at the light.

"How so?"

"Because if I win this grant and really produce, then I can apply for more grants with this organization. This means I'm creating a track record. The goal is to be tried, tracked, and proven."

"How much is the grant for?"

"Dang, you all nosy. Did you write the grant for me?" I sassed.

"No, I didn't write the grant, smart-ass, but I'm your man, and I'm curious."

"It's for $10,000."

"That's a nice start."

"Yea, it's for 6 weeks."

"Six weeks? Hell, yeah, that's big money. Are you gonna be doing what you did at the MOV?"

"Pretty much, and that's why it's a no-brainer. This grant will really put me on, Kenya." I glanced at him as we drove to ORELA, our Mexican joint.

"I missed you." His eyes were clear.

"I missed you too." My eyes told it all.

"I gotta do better, don't I?"

"Yea, you do. We can't be going through unnecessary stuff. If you can't handle your liquor, then you need to chill, 'cause you had me thinking."

"Thinking about what?" He knew.

"Thinking about if it's worth it. Are you and I gonna work?"

"Why would you say that? Yes, we *are* gonna work. People go through things. We are gonna go through things. You know that, Dream. We're only human."

"Yes, I know that we're human, but my mama didn't raise a fool." I pulled up to OLERA and parked. We stared into each other's eyes with full attention. Then we hopped out of the car. Kenya walked on the outside of me, and together, we walked into the restaurant with raw energy.

"Hola, welcome to OLERA. My name is Javier, may I seat you?"

"Yes, you can, Javier," Ken said sarcastically as if he couldn't wait to get with me.

"Follow me." Javier provided us an intimate window seat, then handed us menus.

"I'll give you a few minutes to look at the menu, and then I'll be back to take your order."

"OK, thank you," I smiled.

"Now, back to you, Ms. Smarty-Pants. Whatchu mean, 'Mama didn't raise no fool'?"

"She didn't. You know all the shit I went through with Solomon. I can't do it again. I don't have the energy or the heart for another heartbreak. Naw, I can't handle it."

"I'm not gonna break your heart, Dream. I love you too much to hurt you. You're the best woman that I ever had. I just have issues. I have my demons just like everyone else. I'm sure you have your demons too. But we gotta work through it. Don't give up on a nigga."

"I'm not giving up on you. I want us to get to the point where we are focused on building and not destroying. As Black men and women, we gotta be forward-thinking. We spend too much time arguing, beefing, and going against each other. I wanna be in a relationship where it's peaceful, beautiful, honorable, and authentic."

"You have a son, and I have a daughter. Wouldn't it be great if they grow up with us as a family?" he proposed. "It would be great for them to see a stable and warm, loving environment. We gotta start from somewhere. We need to start from here and move up. Things will get rocky, but I promise I'm gonna get better. Believe in me," Kenya said with sincerity.

"What would you like to eat?" Javier came back around to take our order.

"Whatever my lady wants." Kenya was charming.

"I would like two chicken tacos with beans and salad, no rice."

"Anything else?"

"Yes, is it too early to order a margarita?"

"No, señorita. We have strawberry, peach, mango, and Cadillac."

"Can I have a mango margarita with sugar on the rim? Thank you."

"Amigo, can I have two steak tacos with beans and rice?" Kenya asked.

"Yes, sir. Anything to drink?"

"Let me get a Cadillac margarita. Nothing on the rim and a shot of Jose Cuervo."

"Here we go." I was hoping this boy didn't get too drunk and turn the joint out.

"I got this. Thank you, amigo."

"Okay, my friends, I'm gonna put your order in." Javier walked off.

"You think I can't handle my liquor or something?"

"Every time you drink, you cut up. There's nothing wrong with you sipping. You just be maxing out."

"Not all the time. I'ma keep it cool. I just wanna be with you and have a good time. I missed you. You be working so hard, or I be on a job, or we got the kids . . . It feels nice to get out with you."

"Okay, we can sip and be merry."

"You know it's about to be my birthday next week. What we gonna do?"

"What do you wanna do?"

"I wanna have a get-together. Invite my homies out and have fun."

"What about bowling, happy hour, or karaoke?" I suggested.

"Karaoke sound good, for real. You know me and my homies act a fool. The bar is already there, and we can have it during happy hour. My birthday falls on a Saturday, so that would be perfect."

"That does sound like fun. How many people you think about inviting?"

"Maybe about 10 or 15. My close friends, a few of my cousins, and that's cool. I just wanna have a good time."

"Cool. I'll check and see if Fridays have karaoke, and if we can reserve some tables. If so, I'll reserve it for you. All you gotta do is invite your friends."

Javier brought the margaritas over for us.

"I wanna make a toast to my boo thang—my everythang. I wanna toast to you being your own boss. I also wanna toast to our love getting better." He had me gushing.

"Thank you, baby, I appreciate you." I couldn't stop smiling. Couldn't even be mad at him.

"I also wanna say, Dream, I want us to have a little one. What about having our own baby? What about us getting married?"

"Oh my, a baby? Really? Are you even *ready* for a baby? I don't know if I'm ready. Like we just getting settled. I'm just getting outta the hood. I don't even know if *I* could handle it." Reality kicked in.

"We can handle it. I would love for you to have my son."

"Lord, how do you know I'm gonna have a son?"

"'Cause you had King. You just look like you produce sons. Look at your strong body, girl. You gonna have my son."

"I don't know. Maybe 6 months down the line or next year we can think about it. Let's see how you act. Plus, it seem like every time we get into it, you go MIA. I don't know where the hell you be at. But I do know every time there's an issue between the two of us, you roll out. You never tell me where you going. You just leave for a few days." My tone changed like a li'l girl.

"You right. I be rolling out 'cause you be blowing me. It's like I fuck up, and you be going the fuck off. You don't just go to your room or chill out. You act like a nigga too." We both busted out in laughter.

"What type of woman do you think I am? I'm not a 'yes-woman.' I'm a *responsible* woman. The energy that you give me you are gonna get back. If you go off, I'ma go off. If you max out, I'm gonna max out. If you are cool, calm, and collected, then that's what you're gonna get from me. But you wild, so you turn me into a wild lioness."

"Well, I just want you to be cute and chill. Know that I love you. I don't mean no harm. I gotta learn how to communicate better and deal with you head-on. I don't be going nowhere but Uptown or over at my cousin's house. When I leave, I go Uptown and hang with my men or chill in front of my grandma's house. I just be getting more fucked up, for real. I don't be doing nothing."

"Yea, I don't know what you be doing. But about this baby business, if you can be on good behavior for the next 6 months to a year, then you can have my baby," I giggled.

"*Your* baby?"

"Yea, *my* baby. I don't want no boy. I want a girl."

"I have a daughter already. I need a son in my life. I need a man-child to raise."

"I'm raising a son, and I need balance in *my* life. I need a li'l me. Wouldn't that be cute?"

"I'm gonna name my son King."

"Is you drunk? My *son* is named King. You forgot?" We both damn near sipped our margarita down past the halfway mark.

"Yea, dang, it is. These tequila shots messing with me. What about Chosen? I like that name. It gotta a nice ring."

"Chosen is nice. What about Legendary for a boy? And Dynasty for a girl?"

"Only you would come up those ole Janet Jackson-ass *Poetic Justice* baby names. Yea, Justice. I like that. It could be a boy or girl name."

"Justice all right. Chosen sound better. But I'm banking on a beautiful, chocolate baby girl."

Javier brought our food out. You could see the steam rising from the fresh food.

"I like all of dem names. You gonna give me a baby. Well, since you all independent, we gonna go half on a baby," Kenya insisted.

"Yep, give me 6 months of love on top, and you gonna take care of the baby. I wanna make the money. I wanna grind for real. I wasn't really thinking about no baby, but since I am my own boss, then in 6 months, we both should have a bankroll sufficient to take care of all of our children, plus an addition."

"Yea, we gonna be good. 'Cause I hustle, and ain't none of us gonna go without," he said firmly.

"That's what I love about you. We never been without. You always made sure we're good and protected. You are consistent in that area."

"I'm a man, baby. I'm a cold-blooded man. As long as I have breath in my body, you will always have. King and Nia will always have. We will never go hungry, and I put that on everything."

There was a silence in the air. I took my phone out of my bra and began googling Fridays that have Karaoke night on the same day as Kenya's birthday.

"Whatchu on the phone for?"

"I'm googling Karaoke night nearby."

"Oh." He caught himself before he jumped to any conclusion. "You see any near us?"

"There are two. There's one like a mile from our house. Then there's one 15 minutes away."

"Let's do one 15 minutes away." He got excited.

I called immediately and asked to speak to reservations.

"Hi, how are you doing? I would like to know if there are tables that I can reserve for March 30th? That's Karaoke night, right?"

"How many tables?" the young representative asked.

"Three tables for a birthday party. Will it hold at least 10 people?"

"Yes, the tables can seat 9 to 12 people."

"Okay. Can I reserve three tables? How much is it?"

"What's your name? It's $50 down. What's your email? I'll send you the email to confirm and pay." She was short and detailed.

"My name is Dream Angelou. My email is Dream Angelou at rocket.com. You can send everything there."

"Awesome. I just sent you the link to reserve. Click on the link, and you can confirm everything and make a payment as well. Make your payment within 72 hours."

I opened up my browser to check my email to make sure her email was there, and it was.

"Got the email. Thank you for your assistance. I'll make the payment by tomorrow," I said.

"You're welcome. You'll receive a reservation number upon paying. Thank you. We look forward to seeing you on the 30th."

"What she say, baby?"

"She sent me this email." I showed him my phone.

"You move so quick. *That's* what's up. We gonna have a ball. Can't wait to call my homies tonight and tell 'em to be there." He kissed me several times on my cheek.

"Give me some suga." Kenya pecked me on the lips, and I, of course, gave him the juicy kisses he'd been waiting on.

"That's what I'm talking about. When our love is like this, it means so much to me. I hate when we beefing. What we have is different, Dream. We're gonna be an example of Black love, and watch . . . We're going to have haters. But what means the world to me is to see you smile and us happy."

"I just can't afford another broken heart. I can't afford to waste another 5 years recovering from a broken heart. It's all about a forward movement. We gotta push through our insecurities, our differences, and balance each other out," I reflected.

There was a brief silence in the air. We basked in how good the food was. Our margarita glasses were empty, and so were Kenya's shots of tequila. It felt good to be around each other with clarity. I truly loved Kenya. Roca seemed perfect for me in hindsight, but I knew Kenya when I didn't have shit.

As he would more than often remind me, "Dream, I met you when you were 'Jenny from the block.'" Which translated to "I knew you when you were Black Girl Lost."

Roca wasn't familiar with that girl. He wasn't familiar with the girl who didn't have a car, who didn't have money, who was utterly abandoned, and a lot of times didn't have food or not enough to make a meal and had to thug it out and sleep on the floor until my father flew into town and bought me a bed out of guilt.

Kenya met me at a vulnerable point. He saved me from the brokenness and believed in me and rallied for me to get the fuck out of the hood and elevate to a better environment and living conditions for King and me.

I owed him an opportunity to prove to me that he could be the man that I was searching for in my subconscious. He fucked with me despite my flaws and found something beautiful out of the concrete. He was my Tupac. He was my Chicago, and I was his Justice. We were both the soil and the dirt. Yet, the water of life, if it flowed in patience and forgiveness, would one day grow us to become roses. In my heart, I committed to being more patient with Kenya in the hope that we'd grow happy, peaceful, prosperous, and even thoughts of having another baby would be absolutely bountiful.

Our lives were like a seesaw at the playground. We faced each other with so many raw emotions. As we bounced up and down and up and down and then up in the air—the balance was the realness that we needed. But the laughter, the quiet giggles were childlike. We needed the laughter. Certainly, we needed the laughter in this lifetime.

# Chapter 14

*Epic Dreams*

I had saliva running from the corners of my mouth, a chapped bottom lip, and stank breath, yet, I lay in a fetal position, snoring in the comfort of my bed. My red, black, and silver pillow was adorned with 20 inches of straight Indian hair, slayed in all my imperfections. What would come to me in my dreams I would never even fathom because my spirit was content with a new business, an amazing son, and a lover that I looked forward to loving. But my subconscious was unresolved, and my soul needed to make amends for my own self-inflicted tragedies.

The vision came, and my spirit went viral. There were several beautiful brown children in several hues of chocolate from toffee, Snickers, mahogany, and reddish brown. They were dressed in all white, playing together in the grass, yet, they waved to me, and I waved back. I studied their slanted eyes and beautiful smiles. The moment was breathtaking. I had seen their souls before. On good days, I would suppress them. On weary days, I would communicate with them, asking for their forgiveness.

It was vivid. There was an older child who was a teen. She was tall, slim, with a toffee complexion. Adorned with dimples and gorgeous wild, curly hair, I knew her in the spirit realm. I started walking toward her, but there was an energy stopping us. We were footsteps away from each other. Our vibes were so kinesthetic. She had a journal where she sat Indian style in the grass and wrote, wrote, and wrote. She was a young scribe with freedom fighter facial expressions. She would often look up, and I stared into her eyes for confirmation. Her vibrations were transparent, but what she penned was coded.

Just footsteps away from me was a young girl and a young boy who stood next to the oldest child. They appeared to be preteens. They looked like twins, as if they had the same father. They were a reddish brown. The brother had on a white linen shirt accompanied by white linen shorts. He wore the cutest white brim hat. He was dancing in the grass. He was silly. The little girl had on a white mini linen dress that was slightly off the shoulders. Her red complexion and long wavy braids reminded me of Pocahontas. She was serious and serene as she watched over her brother. She was the mature one. I walked toward both of them, and they were ecstatic. There again was an energy that was too profuse that I couldn't get to them the way that my spirit wanted to get to them. I just wanted to hold their hands, putting my right hand in the palm of the boy and putting my left hand in the palm of his sister. They were so close to perfect. He played so hard, and his innocent giggles let me know that he was just fine. However, she confiscated my attention as if there were words that needed to be said, but neither of us could speak freely. There was a divine connection between us. Baby girl stood poised. I felt her, understood her, and I walked near her to let her know that I loved her.

There was a little stunna who was playing with a football and basketball in the field. He was all over the place. He was flipping through the grass, running until he got tired—He had on white jean shorts and a white tee. He had three long cornrows. He was a li'l chunky, but so handsome. I paid attention to his laughter. He couldn't have been more than 5. He kept running in circles. He was having such a good time that I didn't want to disturb him. He was so yummy. He was the color of a Snicker's bar. He waved to me over and over again, and I waved back. I leaped across the field just to hug him, but there was a paralyzing feeling that perplexed me, causing me to pause—I wouldn't be able to get to him. He was mine once upon a time, and I never had the chance to love him without boundaries. Observing his laughter brought on complexities, and the tears welled up in my eyes. This barrier, I perpetuated, and the intensity was real.

There was nothing surreal about these children, for I knew them all, and they came to visit me. They had questions for me, and I had so many questions for them. All I could do was read their body language, posture, and actions and connect the dots.

There was a baby girl who was wrapped in a white swaddling blanket in a flat land. She had a white bow in her hair. She was a radiant mahogany. Her hair was curly and jet black. She had freckles and a dimple in her right cheek. She was an infant, but she was angelic. Her eyes were wide open as she observed every movement and sound around her. The energy that she generated was so serene. She was Holy Ghost amazing. I smelled a lavender aroma that gave off soothing and calming vibes. I was able to walk directly to her, but what hurt was that the energy would not allow me to grace my fingers through her hair or hold her close to my breast. She cracked a smile just to let me know that she was a remnant of me. She was brand new in the realist way!

They were the core of me—the most innocent, awesomeness, godly, and pure, perfect parts of me. They were my magical bronze Picassos, and I was attached to the innermost part of them. They knew my soul before. They were a part of my past that was heavily deeply rooted in both love and uncertainty. They once swam in my womb, ate what I ate, drank what I drank, and heard the words that I spoke as we time traveled. They dwelled with me in horizons unseen. When they came into my life, I was weak, weary, worried, or just in a place where I felt that I would be stuck to raise a child on my own—again.

I loved King dearly, but I hated, I mean I absolutely hated that I had to raise him alone. Not having his father to partake in coparenting damn near killed my soul. The level of abandonment pierced my heart. Those 270 days of carrying King were spent in a depressed state, where the nights were concaved blues enmeshed in brokenness.

I was convicted with every baby I carried, whether miscarriage or abortion. I connected with every soul in the most naked way. I fed them, talked to them, rubbed my stomach, all while crying in the dark, 'cause I knew that I couldn't bring them into this fucked-up world, or they decided they didn't want any part of the trauma!

I heard a doctor once say that the "baby that isn't strong enough to be here in the world will miscarry. A woman who isn't strong enough for the baby will abort." And if the baby is beyond strong and willing, it will arrive through the energy of grace and mercy to become her "ancestors' wildest dream."

I had experienced all three, but what haunted me in my dreams are the babies that I wasn't strong enough to have. Subconsciously, I knew the fathers would not be strong enough to raise their children. Subconsciously, I was terrified of being stuck with the full responsibility of being both mother and father, knowing that being a father was impossible for a woman. Subconsciously, I suppressed my anointing and purpose and was led by my emotions, consequently, forfeiting my maternal instincts. There was no doubt in my mind that I wanted my babies, and my babies wanted me, but like Jill Scott sang, *the baby coming even if the daddy ain't ready.*

Flashbacks of carrying King was like a 9-month jail sentence in solitary confinement. I just couldn't believe the level of misery, the level of betrayal, and how lonely I was. His father despised me for having him, and as a result, he would jump ship, not return for years, and forsake both of us. King would still arrive against the odds, and he was born with bronze radiant skin, wooly hair, and red eyes—he was my Messiah!

The deeper the dream, the louder the snore.

"Why the fuck did these niggas choose me to fuck over? What? I wasn't pretty enough to have their baby? I wasn't light enough to have their baby? I wasn't small enough to have their baby? I wasn't wealthy enough to have their baby? There was no understanding. I was the coolest, most creative, loyal, and loving woman any dude could meet. I wasn't perfect, but you could trust me. You could trust that if I said I loved you that I actually did." I screamed at my subconscious.

God never condemned me. He loved me despite my sins and iniquity. Those lessons, though, the creator saw fit that I would learn from 'em. Consciously, I wanted that Clair Huxtable life. A life where my husband, fiancé, or life partner would accept all of our children, name them, love them, and speak greatness over their lives. Dreaming of acceptance. Dreaming of a sea of brown babies where we would collectively laugh, play, learn, and grow. My heart was hardened, but seeing my beautiful babies in a dream was so clear to me that I was forgiven for my sins.

My babies meant everything to me, yet, I had mental scars, and I just didn't want to repeat the cycle of rejection and abandonment over and over again.

The oldest went and picked up the infant clothed in white, gathered the 5-year-old on the field and her two siblings who were playing. The children faced me in unison and mouthed, "Umi, mama, mami." Tears rolled down my cheeks as I stood blowing kisses to them, waving, all while yearning to hug and hold each one of my babies. I tried to walk as close as I could to them, but the spirit caused me to freeze. There was a divide. I was in a different world, and they resided with God in a paradise realm.

"I love you," I yelled. "I miss you!" I yelled louder, hoping they could hear me.
The children gathered around the baby girl, building a standard against anyone and anything—they were protectors. They held hands as if they were singing "Ring around the Rosie."

I yelled, "I love you all. I love you so much! Please, forgive me! Please, forgive me!" My tears roared and fell like a lioness who had lost her cubs. "I love you so much! I miss you dearly! Stick together, y'all. Please, stick together!" Tears rolled down my cheeks. I felt like I was losing my breath. My womb began cramping again. I started grabbing my stomach as if I were experiencing major labor contractions. Each of them started waving at me. The youngest boy yelled back, "Luh you!" The oldest one wrote in giant letters in her journal, "I LOVE YOU, MOM!" My Pocahontas baby girl blew me a kiss. My second oldest boy welded up with tears. They were a unified front.

My dream was ending, but I felt like the energy was so strong that I just wanted to take them with me. I wanted my babies to forgive me. I just wanted to take them all on this ride that I was on. I didn't want to leave them. I never did.

As the dream faded, they were watching me and thinking of me as much as I thought about them. I gave them empowerment names, praying that maybe they would come back to me in the near future when love from both sides was overflowing. They reminded me that I was still their Umi. And they . . . They be my stars. The love was never lost. The love is forever.

# Chapter 15

*You Got Me*

*"If you were worried 'bout where*

*I been or who I saw or*

*What club I went to with my homies*

*Baby, don't worry, you know that you got me,"* I sang in my Soprano
2 voice while grasping the mic with my right hand as I sang a cover.
They didn't even know I owned the stage.

*"Somebody told me that this planet was small*

*We use to live in the same building on the same floor*

*And never met before...."* I broke down Erykah Badu's melody and
began rhyming the Black thoughts part. Kenya had no clue, but I was
a spoken-word artist in my past life, and rocking the mic was natural.
Didn't need the words on the karaoke machine to recite my jam that
came out in 1998. I had nothing but admiration for Erykah Badu and
The Roots. It took me back to when Sanai and I were sophomores at
Bison University. Kenya had no clue about me, for real. Quiet as
kept, he and his friends were mesmerized. I wasn't your typical girl
from the hood.

I broke into a melody.

*"If you were worried 'bout where*
*I been or who I saw or*
*What club I went to with my homies*
*Baby, don't worry, you know that you got me."* Hip-hop was me, and
so was spoken word. I was in my real artistic zone. Kenya was
shocked and didn't even realize there was another side to me.
Before I could walk off the mini stage, Ken grabbed me and hugged
me and kissed me all over my face. His friends and the crowd began
clapping and whistling.

"You did that, sis," a brotha yelled from the side of the bar.

"You rocked the hella outta that," a sista gave me a high five outta
nowhere.

"Thank y'all so much!" My smile was radiant.

"Baby, baby, I did not know you could rock the mic like that! I
mean, you would mention how you wrote poetry, and you were good
back in the day, but you surprised me tonight."

"I told you I could get down," I giggled. "Happy birthday, Kenya." I
kissed him. He wrapped his hands around my waist and kissed me
back.

"Thank you, baby. Come take a walk over here to say hello to my
friends. They at the tables over here." He grasped my left hand with
his right hand, walking me over to the tables that I reserved.

"Hey, everyone, this is my baby right here. This is Dream. This
karaoke night was all her doing. This is my heart!" Kenya sounded
adamant.

"Hi, nice to meet you. I'm Big Fats. I'm his sandbox friend. You rocked the hell outta that Roots joint. You must be a professional." Big Fats stood about 6 feet tall with a light caramel complexion. He was chunky, but he seemed charismatic.

"Yes, a few years ago, I was heavy on the poetry circuit. Performing at all of the spoken-word nightclubs throughout the city and even some in California."

"Oh yeah?" Fats was impressed.

"My baby a star for real. She got two published books. You can get 'em in the bookstores or online," Kenya boasted.

"You got a star. She seem like a good girl. Don't run her away."

"That's my baby. She a keeper. I'm not letting her go."

"Oh, I'm not going anywhere. I'ma stick around for a while," I said sarcastically.

"What's up? We met a few times around da way," one of Ken's homeboys extended his hand to shake mine. He was tall and brown skinned. He cracked a smile, but he seemed like he was there to spectate more than to show Kenya love.

"Babe, that's the homie, Tre. That's another one of my sandbox friends."

"Oh, OK. Nice to meet y'all." I was laid-back, peeping everyone.

"Have a seat right here and get comfortable. You want some wine or champagne?" he gestured.

"Yes, love, you already know. Let's do a few glasses of champagne."

"Place the order and get me a few shots of tequila. Ouch, ouch, it's my birthday!"

Everyone started laughing.

"My nigga!" A loud, tall, brown, and cut-up dude came out of the cut and gave Kenya a bear hug. "It's a real nigga birthdayyyyy!" It was Wayne, and he was amplified.

Kenya bear-hugged him back. Wayne, I believe, was a real and sincere friend to Kenya. Wayne had been to the house to visit Ken. We had been out a few times, and I had met Wayne's mom, who was a local prominent youth advocate. Wayne was also in the military and hadn't been back in the country for too long.

"Man, I'm glad you showed. I know you be working and shit, so I wasn't sure you were gonna make it," said Kenya.

"Hey, Dream, it's good to see you."

"Good to see you too, Wayne."

"Let's order some shots, fool. Eh, bartender!" Wayne was aggressive and got straight to the point.

A petite, light-skinned girl in a black cocktail dress with curly hair pranced over to Wayne.

"What would you like to order?"

"Let me get six shots of tequila and two Blue Motorcycles."

"Dream, you wanna order your drinks now since he got her attention?" Kenya asked.

"Can I get two glasses of champagne? Preferably Moët."

"Got it." The bartender heard my voice, even though I was a few feet away.

"Here's my card." Wayne beat her to the punch. "Yea, you can keep the tab open."

Wayne walked closer to the tables. "What's up, Big Fats and Tre?" He acknowledged them. They were all from the same hood.

"What's up, Wayne? You din got all cut up and shid," Big Fats responded.

"Yea, man, I be in the gym getting it in," he said shrewdly.

The bartender placed all the shots and drinks in front of Kenya. Wayne and Kenya were drinkers, and I could tell the energy of his birthday was gonna go from 0 to 100 real quick.

"Let's take a shot, y'all." Kenya started handing everyone a shot, including me. "I just wanna say I feel blessed to be alive. I thank God for giving me another year to get my life in order. Thank y'all for coming out to celebrate with me. Drink up."

Kenya had the hugest smile on his face.

"All right, let's get this karaoke show on the road. Come on, Wayne, let's go sign up. Fats and Tre, what, y'all too grand to sign up? My baby already showed us how to do it."

"Come on, cuz." Wayne went with him to sign up. They stood near the host, cheezing like little kids.

Some of Kenya's other friends started coming in, including a few females that I would occasionally hear him about, but I never paid attention to.

"Coming to the stage are two brothas from another muva. Celebrating his birthday, we have Kenya and Wayne. Brothas betta bring it!" The host brought the energy.

The strobe lights were fluorescent purple and an electric blue. Wayne and Ken stood in the middle of the stage with their heads down like they were really a music group back in the day. The host handed them mics, the beat dropped, and the song was nostalgic. The crowd started swaying like they were at a concert. "Can You Stand The Rain" by New Edition was a classic song in '88, and it was as if they were taking us back to our childhood.

Kenya stood in the middle of the stage looking real handsome, with his Armani purple sweater on, Armani jeans, and, of course, he had the shades to match. He cleaned up really good.

" *'Cause I need somebody who will stand by me*
*Through the good times and bad times*
*She will always, always be right there,*" Kenya sounded smooth as baby lotion. He captured my attention. "Can You Stand The Rain" was an epic jam.

Together, he and Wayne began their own two-step routine as if they had rehearsed it back in the day for a middle school talent show.

"*Sunny days, everybody love them*
*Tell me, baby, can you stand the rain?*
*Storms will come*
*This we know for sure*
*Can you stand the rain?"*

They had the whole Friday's crowd two-stepping. Women started goosing, so I had to hurry up and move toward the front and claim my man.

"*But I need somebody who will stand by me*
*When it's tough, she won't run*
*She will always be right there for me (meeeeeee),*" Wayne and Kenya harmonized.

Kenya and Wayne got on their knees well-coordinated like they were really New Edition. They closed their eyes and concluded the song. The crowd went wild. They exited the stage sweating like they had performed a set.

"Y'all betta sangggggg!" Some older women who appeared to be in their late 40s were waving at them.

"Go 'head, Kenya!" I heard a woman's voice from behind me. It was Nia's mom, Taja, and I didn't understand why she was even at the birthday party. Clearly, she had an invite, and as bad as Kenya talked about her being an irresponsible parent, I didn't have a clue about why she was there. My smile turned into a frown, and I needed answers.

"Hey, Dream, how you?" Taja made herself known. *Like was she the girlfriend or was I the girlfriend?* I began thinking in my mind. I was thrown off.

"How are you?" I cracked a fake smile.

"How you doing, Dream?" Taja's friend, Kia, a big, thick, tall girl, made herself known—looking like security.

"Eh, playboyyyyyy," Kenya's friend, Van, who was from the Bay Area, came outta nowhere.

"Playboyyyyyy! My man 50 grand! I'm glad you came out." Kenya gave Van brotherly love.

"Nigga, I see you all on stage being a real player. What's up, Wayne?" said Van.

"What's good?" Wayne was focused on his Blue Motorcycle, which were left at the table.

"Happy Birthday, Ken." Taja made herself known.

"What's up, Taja?" Kenya was nonchalant.

"Hey, Big Kia!" Kenya gave Kia some dap.

"What's up, Ken? I see you dawg lookin' real clean."

"It's my mofo birthday, ouch ouch ouch!" Kenya gently pulled up the top of his sweater.

"Babe, you good?" He kissed me on my cheek. "This my baby!" He made it known who he was with, and Taja was not feeling that.

"Come on, Taja, let's go sign up for karaoke. Ain't this what we here for?" Kia tried to change the atmosphere. They both went to sign up.

"Come on, y'all, let's go back to the table and chill. They gotta enough singing for me. I need my liquor," said Kenya.

"We'll be back! Until then, I'm drinking my drank. We ain't got time to babysit," added Wayne.

"What you drinking?" Van asked Ken.

"Tequila all night. Get me that Jose."

"Oh shit, you know this fool ain't gonna be no good. How many shots you already had?"

"Man, I had a few shots and some champagne."

"OK, I got you on two shots. We gotta watch you!" Van didn't bite his tongue.

"Don't nobody gotta babysit me." Kenya was not convincing.

"Nawwww, cuzzz, we all know you," Big Fats interjected.

Even I knew if he had too much to drink, it was gonna be a problem. I was just crossing my fingers and saying my prayers that we were gonna have a great night and that he really had a good time.

"Here you go, playboy." Van gave Ken two shots, and he had two shots. "To a real nigga." Van gave him a toast and saluted.

There was too much testosterone, and the estrogen was funny. I didn't invite any of my homegirls when I should have at least told Sanai to come with me. I was tripping, but I had no clue Taja and her friend were gonna be there, and I didn't want any problems. Well, they didn't want no problem because Kenya would act a fool if anyone fucked with me.

The electric blue lights transformed into a myriad of colors giving a unique vibe.

"Coming to the stage, we have Taja and Kia! You know you gonna have to show out because the brothas who came before you put on a show." The host pumped them up and handed them the mic.

"Oh, we got this!" Kia was aggressive.

"So, what are you gonna sing tonight for us, ladies?"

"'Right Here,' by SWV," Taja announced.

"Okay, we just living up the '80s and '90s tonight. The stage is yours." He stepped to the side and proceeded to play the song.

"*Lately, there seems to be some insecurities*

*About the way I feel, where I wanna be*

*But you know, it's with you*

*No one can do the things you do to me*," Kia had a set'a lungs on her, and she could really sing. It was as if her voice came outta nowhere.

"*Never to be mistaken, long as it's love we're making*

*There's gonna be some rain, gonna beat the pain*

*But as long as I know, boy, time will show*

*Our love will grow, and I know*," she closed her eyes.

"Hey, Kia, you betta sing!" Kenya blurted out.

"Yo, Kia can sing fa' real." Van took a quick shot of Jose.

*"Love will be right here*
*Be right here, right here*
*Be right here*
*No fear, have no fear*
*No tears, love is here,"* Taja joined her. Taja clearly didn't have a pair or even half a lung, but it didn't matter because Kia dominated the stage, and on the mic, she was a natural. Then Ryan, the boyfriend of Kenya's cousin, Keema, showed up without her, but even still, Ryan was always pretty cool and laid-back. He gave everyone dap.

"Ken, happy birthday, dawg! How you feel?" Ryan asked.

"I feel good, man. I feel blessed. I got my baby here and my closest homies. It's a good feeling, you know."

"That's what's up. What you drinking on?"

"Shit, he drinking everything." Wayne was a li'l wasted. "We din had about six shots of tequila. Plus dem Blue Motorcycles is gonna have us in here singing all night." We all bust up in laughter because Wayne was a big nigga, and he was leaning.

"Man, them shots wasn't nothing. I drink half a gallon of that and still be standing."

"Yea, I'm hip. Well, I'ma order a few shots myself. What's up, Dream? You all quiet. What you sippin'?"

"I'm chilling. I've been sippin' on champagne. I'm the designated driver, so I can't get too drunk."

"I hear you. I'ma go to the bar and grab my shots and sit here with you."

"Cool."

Kia and Taja were wrapping up their SWV karaoke segment when two other women came to the table with gift bags for Kenya.

"What's up, y'all? I didn't think you two were coming." He got all excited.

"Happy birthday, brother." They both gave him a group hug.

"We was coming. You know we couldn't miss your birthday," said the brown-skinned woman. She was about 5-9 and looked like she was about 45 years old. They both were well put together, but they were suspect. I could tell that one of them had relations with him, so I sipped and observed them.

"Dream, these are my homies, Jamir and May."

"Hey," my eyes locked in with theirs.

"Hi," May, who was the older lady, spoke.

"Nice to finally meet you," Jamir came off pleasant but short.

"We got you those boots you wanted." Jamir handed him a gift bag that May was holding.

"Y'all looked out for real. Appreciate it." He looked inside the bag and placed it beside Ryan.

May and Jamir stood in the back where Big Fats and Tre were standing.

"Don't worry about that shit. It ain't about nothing," Ryan whispered in my ear.

"Whatever. I'm watching all these bitches." I downed my fourth glass of champagne.

"You want a shot of tequila?" Ryan read my mind.

"Yea, I need one 'cause it's a whole lotta questionable stuff going on."

"But then again, what the hell is Taja doing here? Did he invite her?"

"My point exactly. Why is she here, and why is she here, and why is she here?" I started getting irritated.

"Stay the classy woman you are. I'm sure they jealous. He loves you, girl."

Kenya walked to the back and conversed with May, Jamir, and his other homies. Kia, Taja, and Van started walking toward our tables.

"Everyone gotta drank but us," said Taja.

"The bar right there, Taja, go get one."

"Shut up, Ryan. Where your six-figure wife anyway?"

"She home where she need to be. Sike, she didn't feel like coming out."

"You want something to drink, Taja? What about you, Kia?"

"Get me an apple martini." Kia was simple.

"Yea, Van, get me a Cadillac margarita with a shot of Jose," Taja requested.

Kenya walked over, and May and Jamir walked out of Friday's.

"What's up, everyone? Everyone good? Taja, I see you brought your big head ass out." Everyone busted out in laughter.

"Shut up, boy, you said I could come, right?"

"Yea, you was pressing my mans, Van, out, so, yea. Plus, I wanted to see big Kia."

"How you been, bruh?" Kia walked closer to him.

"I've been good. I'm working, trying to raise my daughter, be a lover and not a fighter."

"Oh yeah," Kia responded. "That's a good look on ya."

"I'm tryin'a grow old, make this money, and be a provider. I'm not asking for too much."

"Speaking of which, where my daughter at now?" he asked Taja.

"She at home. She good. My mother is there. Don't play with me, boy." Taja caught an attitude.

"I'm just checking." He brushed her off.

"Wayne, come on, bro, let's hit the stage again." He started feeling the liquor because he was loud.

Wayne was wrapping a girl up at the bar.

"Okay, okay, it's your birthday. Whatchu wanna sing next?"

He whispered in Wayne's ear like he wanted it to be a surprise.

"Gotcha. We gonna rock the shit outta it. Van, come up with us."

"Hell naw. Y'all got it. I ain't no singer. I'm good guarding your drinks." We all giggled 'cause the more tequila they had, the louder they got.

They hit the stage again. This time, they were twisted, so who knew the outcome.

"Coming back to the stage again is the birthday boy Kenya and his brother Wayne!"

The stage lights changed to an electric blue, giving it a real R&B feel.

"Who do they think they are?" Ryan asked.

"They are actually good."

"Oh yeah? Well, let's see."

The beat dropped, and if you didn't recognize the intro, then you missed the early '90s, and shame on you.

"*So you're having my baby*

*And it means so much to me*

*There's nothing more precious*

*Than to raise a family*

*If there's any doubt in your mind*

*You can count on me*

*I'll never let you down*

*Lady, believe in me,"* Kenya sang from his heart and signaled me to come close to the stage.

"Whatchu looking at? Girl, if you don't go up there . . ." Ryan was like an old uncle.

"Okay, I'm going." I began walking close to the stage.

*"You and I*

*Will never fall apart*

*You and I*

*We knew right from the start, baby, baby*

*For days*

*We fell so far in love*

*Now our baby is born, healthy and strong*

*Now our dreams are reality,"* Kenya sang directly into my eyes. For once, I became a believer.

"Honey, he must love you," an old head said to me, who sat at a table near the stage with a platinum blonde close crop. "He got a voice too. If you can't see that, chileeeeee . . ."

I stood there in front of the stage, smiling from ear to ear.

Wayne came in on the chorus.

*"Forever my lady*

*It's like a dream*

*I'm holding you close*
*You're keeping me warm*
*If this is ecstasy*
*Forever my lady*
*I say just what I mean*
*Forever and ever*
*I pray is what I see."*

Wayne and Ken did a mean two-step and swayed back and forth like they were the fifth and sixth members of Jodeci. All they were missing were the curly high-top fades and jean overalls.

"Look at these niggas here." Van stood near me. "They really think they Jodeci."

"Look at Ken. He got a li'l voice on him. He crushing on you, Dream." Ryan stood beside me.

I smiled. I was in a happy place. They had the whole crowd singing with them in unison. Although they were drunk, the melody was still on point.

*"And I saw we made it from the start*
*The day*
*We fell so far in love*
*Now our baby is born*
*So healthy and strong*
*Now my dreams are reality."* Kenya grabbed my hand to let me know that this was for real.

*"Yeahhhh*
*Forever my lady*
*Ah yea, baby*

*Forever my lady*

*I say just what I mean*

*Forever and ever*

*I pray is what I see,*" Wayne sang and ended with a cool falsetto.

"Well, got damn!" The host came on the stage. "We got Jodeci right here in the DMV."

"Yeaaaaaa!" the crowd shouted.

"They need to be singing karaoke every Friday night!" The host tried to be funny. "For real, happy birthday to you, bro, and many, many more." He gave Kenya dap.

Kenya stepped off the stage and gave me the warmest hug, running his fingers through my hair. He held me for a minute.

"I love you, Dream. I really do. Thank you for making this one of my best birthdays ever."

"You welcome, Ken. I wanted you to enjoy yourself, and you did. You rocked the hell outta that Jodeci. You really touched me, baby boy. Love you too!" I held his hands, looked him eye to eye, and kissed his forehead.

Taja was standing with her hands folded, feeling some type of way. I'm sure she was plotting.

It was our moment, and nothing even mattered at all.

# Chapter 16

## Double Lines

I felt nauseated. I ran to the bathroom, lifted the toilet seat, and began throwing up chunks of yellow. I got on my knees and had the worst feeling in the world while placing my head over the toilet, making sure that I didn't mess up the floor. I put my fingers in my mouth and two fingers down my throat. The nausea hit me erratically, and more yellow stuff shot out of my throat and into the toilet, splattering everywhere. The vomit smelled different than a hangover, and even though I had one too many glasses of champagne, drinking bubbly always made my stomach feel good and not terrible. I kept my fingers down my throat until I gagged, and my stomach felt empty.

My phone began ringing, but I was so sick I couldn't get to it. The bathroom felt like it was spinning outta control, and I didn't know what to do.

"Babe, you don't hear the phone ringing?" Kenya yelled.

"Babe, grab the phone and come here. It's an emergency!" I felt so weak.

"What the hell is going on? You din threw up everywhere. What's wrong, baby girl?" He looked perturbed.

"I don't know." I lifted my head slightly and looked at him. "I woke up feeling really nauseated, and I knew I was gonna throw up, so I ran to the bathroom, so I didn't throw up on you."

"Oh, hell naw. Did you have too much to drink? Did you mix drinks, Miss Smarty-Pants?"

"No. All I did was drink champagne, and I had two shots of tequila. I was feeling fine. I just feel weak. Can you grab me a glass of water?"

"Yea, baby. What you think is wrong? What did you eat?"

"I had some light appetizers. No seafood. I had some wings and bruschetta, and that's it. It's something else." My phone began ringing again. Kenya looked at the Caller ID.

"Oh smack, it's Grandma Coco. She calling about King. You wanna talk to her?"

"Oh shit, yea. Hand me the phone." Kenya handed me the cell phone and went to the kitchen to get me some water.

"Hey, Coco." I sounded terrible.

"Hey, Dream, I know y'all partied hard last night. You have fun?"

"Yea, we had fun." My voice was low.

"You sound beat. King can stay home for the day and hang out with Grandma."

"Yes, that would be perfect. Plus, he hasn't missed too many school days. Is he asleep?"

"Yes, he's asleep, child. When he wake up, I'm gonna make him a big ole breakfast. I miss my baby. You know we like to hang tight, okay?"

"Thanks so much, Coco. I could use some rest." My stomach began slightly cramping.

"I know you do, love. Take off for the day. Chill. Everyone needs a day off, and you deserve it. I got King. I'll bring him to your house this evening. Plus, I have a car and train set that I bought him that we gonna work on to set up." She was excited.

"Oh, that's dope. Thank you, Coco."

"Dream, get you some rest. Call us later." Coco hung up the phone. She was from the old school, and she had the last word. Before I could even say bye, she hung up. I sat up with my back against the bathtub. I used the porcelain tub to balance me out. I felt like I wanted to throw up again, but it would hurt 'cause there was nothing left in my belly.

"Here, boo." Kenya handed me a tall glass of ice water and sat right next to me. He touched the top of my forehead to see if I had a fever. "You not hot. What you think is wrong?"

"I don't know." I began drinking the water. Kenya kept looking at me.

"What?" I responded. "This water taste so good. I could use some more."

"You pregnant?" he blurted.

"I don't know." I started tearing up. "I don't know. I haven't felt nauseated like this since . . ."

"Since when? Since you was pregnant with King?" Kenya was being sarcastic.

"Yea, since King." Tears began welling in my eyes. "How'd you know? What, you psychic?" I giggled and cried.

"I can tell. You don't ever throw up. And you didn't eat or drink enough to make you throw up. You gonna take a pregnancy test today."

"I need to. Can you help me up, baby?" I held the glass of water in my right hand. He grabbed my left hand and pulled me up, then walked me to the bed.

"Get in the bed, baby. I'm gonna put a small trash can by your side just in case you gotta throw up again. Just rest yourself. I'm right here. I'ma get you some more water. You drank that like a fish," he said, walking to the refrigerator.

"Thank you, baby. You think I'm pregnant?" I raised my voice so that he could hear me.

"Yeah, buddy." I heard the refrigerator close.

"For real? Oh Lord."

"Whatchu mean? It'll make us stronger."

"Right, but what if I get these grants and blow up? Am I gonna be able to handle everything?"

"I got the baby, and I got us. You run the ball. Don't you got a pregnancy test somewhere around here? Your medicine cabinet is like a pharmacy." He laughed and handed me another glass of water.

"No. Can you go to the store and get a pregnancy test?"

"Yeah, man, let me get my shoes and jacket. I'll go get my baby a test. You scared, huh?"

"I don't know how to feel other than nauseated."

"I got you, baby. Use the trash can if you need it. I come back soon."

"OK." I leaned over toward the trash can and started spitting up yellow and some gray matter. My mind started racing. What if I was preggo? Was I ready for two kids? And sometimes three if Nia stayed at the house for a while. How would it be carrying for 9 months all over again? Maybe it was just a really bad hangover or stomach virus that was attacking me. As I lay on my side, I grabbed my cell phone from off the nightstand. There were no missed calls, but there were a few email notifications. I opened my email, and the first message in the inbox was from McKenzie. My nerves were jumping out of my heart, but I had to open her email.

It read,

*Greetings, Dream Angelou, we are pleased to announce that your organization, "Passion for Change," is being awarded a Summer Grant with the Northwest Collaborative. We are excited about your proposed services and look forward to witnessing the level of enrichment activities that will be provided to youth ages 14 to 18. The program will kick off in 30 days. Please see your contract attached. Review it in its entirety, then sign and date it, and email it back to me within the next 48 hours. Please call me if you have any questions.*

*Best,*

*McKenzie Graham*

"Yes yes and yes!" I started kicking the bed like a little kid who got the best Christmas present ever. We were far away from winter, but that was the message that I was waiting on. That email alone allowed me to see the power in faith, believing in yourself, and if you invest in your dreams, they *will* manifest. No one knew but stepping out to do my own thing and my own business gave me great anxiety. However, it also gave me great hope that if so many other Black entrepreneurs could do it, so could I. McKenzie provided me with the kick start that I needed to get in the nonprofit realm officially. This grant would set me up in a way that fueled me to write other grants and proposals and win them. Essentially, the summer grant was a seed that I needed to blossom my career as a real business owner. This was my real big break, and there was nothing that would get in my way.

"Thank you, Jesus! Thank you, Lord. God, I know this was all you." I raised my hands in praise. "God, thank you for making provisions for me. I am so blessed. Thank you, Lord!"

"Whatchu thanking the Lord for? You was just throwing up." Kenya walked in while I was praising God in bed.

"Oh, babe, I didn't see you," I said, looking at him.

"Why are you so happy that quick?" He held the plastic bag with the pregnancy test inside of it.

"I'm happy, Ken, 'cause I got the grant! I got the grant!" I started bouncing up in down in the bed.

"Word? For real? The grant you just submitted? You got a response from them people that quick?"

"Yes, that quick. I started checking my emails when you left, and the lady, McKenzie's, was the first one. When I opened it, it was like the biggest blessing ever." I was filled with excitement.

"That's big—real big! I'm so happy for you." He grabbed my face and kissed me on my forehead. "You on now. This is what you needed. Not that you wanna take the pregnancy test now. But I'ma leave in a few with my man, Les."

"What, why are you leaving?" My attitude changed.

"I'm just chilling with the homie. I got a day off, and you got a day off. I ain't seen Les in a while. I'm not leaving at this minute. I'ma be here for a few, but I'm just letting you know I'm gonna get out and get some fresh air. So while I'm here, take the pregnancy test."

"Oh, wow, you gonna set me up to take the test and then roll out on my black ass. Typical."

"Whatcha mean, 'typical'?"

"Ken, I wanted us to just watch movies and chill in the house and be by ourselves, but now, all of a sudden, you wanna be out with your man. It's all good."

"Baby, I'm proud of you. Nothing else will change. Want me to hold your hand and walk you to the bathroom?" He tried to be funny.

"Yes, you can. Take the thing out of the box first."

"I gotchu." He took the pregnancy stick out of the box. "If it's double lines, you pregnant. If it's a single line, you good. But we shall see." He helped me out of bed and walked me to the bathroom.

My heart started racing. I had just read some really good news. Like some excellent news. But the pregnancy test was a curveball. I sat on the toilet, and Kenya handed me the test. I placed the test right below my pee-pee hole. I knew the drill. My urine flowed like I had drunk a gallon of water, but it was the alcohol from the night before on top of the two glasses of water I just drank. I pulled some toilet tissue and placed it on the side of the sink and then laid the test right on the tissue. I wiped myself, flushed the toilet, and pulled up my underwear. Then I washed my hands and quietly looked Kenya in the eyes.

"Well, look at the stick. Those purple lines are coming in. They are coming in." He was eager.

"Boy, you pressed as a mug. I see one line."

"There is another line looking like it's trying to come in."

"It's kinda faint." We both looked at the stick as if it were gonna talk back.

"Yea, it looks kinda faded." Kenya picked up the stick. "Hold up, though. It's starting to come in."

"Let me see." I grabbed the stick from him.

"Dang, you got it, shorty."

There was silence in the air for about a good 20 seconds as the second line came in clear. We looked at each other as if to say with our eyes that a change was gonna come. Didn't know if it was a good change or a bad change, but our lives were getting ready to get real, and the double lines put us on the same team for real. I thought my life had changed with an email, but my life had changed with a quick pregnancy test that spoke in emo. My emotions were screaming inside. Like we talked about having a baby, but that quick . . . That quick, a baby would announce itself with double lines. Did God perhaps give me a double blessing with a double meaning? Two babies being birthed at the same time—a real baby, baby, baby. Growing up, I'd hear the pastor say, "To whom much is given, much is required." God's requirements were for real, and I could not let him down. Kenya pulled me slowly out of the bathroom and into the hallway and wrapped his arms around me with compassion.

"We having a babyyyyyyyyyyyy, baby," he hugged me. "Man, I love you so fucking much! You don't have nothing to worry about. My prayer is that the baby is healthy, and it's a boy."

"I'm really pregnant. Like . . . I'm pregnant." My tears could have watered plants. Kenya began kissing my whole face.

"We in this together, Dream—we in this. I'm not going nowhere. This is official!" Kenya assured me.

"Now, what I want you to do is get comfortable on the couch. I'm gonna bring you a blanket and a pillow so you can get comfortable. I'm gonna turn the TV on so that we can watch a movie. Just chill. I'm gonna make us some breakfast."

"That sounds good, my love."

Kenya went and grabbed the comforter from out of the bedroom, along with two pillows. He wrapped me up like I was a li'l baby, placing the pillow around the circumference of my head. We had a leather sectional that reclined, so the couch was the best place to be in front of a 65-inch TV.

"You good?"

"Yes, thank you."

"Whatchu wanna watch? Find us a movie."

"I wanna watch *Eat Pray Love* and *Baby Boy*." I was happy.

"Baby, for real, though? You got a romance movie and then a hood movie? Yea, you pregnant for real."

"Can we watch *Baby Boy* first?"

"Yes, Yvette, we can watch *Baby Boy*." We giggled.

"Jody, my Jody, Jody a mama's boy." We both giggled.

"I ain't ever been no mama's boy. You being real funny. Now, maybe an auntie or grandma's boy, but not a mama's boy."

"Shut up and fix me some tacos." We both fell out.

"Whatchu got a taste for?"

"Some tacos," I said sarcastically.

"Well, you know that you are the one who knows how to make tacos. That ain't my forte. How about some turkey scrapples, grilled onions, scrambled eggs with cheese, and some toast?"

"That sounds perfect, Ken." I laid on my right side as I flipped through an already recorded *Baby Boy*. "I just hope I don't throw it all up."

"You better not throw it up! I won't season it too much. Maybe just try some toast with a little bit of butter and some scrambled eggs?"

"Yea, let's try the toast first with a glass of ice water. I don't wanna be overzealous. Thanks, my love."

"Bet. You comfortable?"

"Yes. And I'm pressing *play* right now. I got *Baby Boy* on."

"Turn it up then. You know that's my favorite. I swear it remind me so much of us. And the fact that you from Cali, and you still have that West Coast country-ass accent that really got you sounding like Yvette."

"I feel like I'm losing my accent. Like the East Coast has taken over. Their accents are strong in the movie compared to mine."

"See? You hear how you say 'mine'? You be singing your words. East Coast girls don't sing their words."

"Yea, you gotta point."

"Let me get to burning. Just be cute and watch the movie. Put your phone down. No texting and no responding to emails. Let's just vibe like you said."

"'K, baby."

I could watch *Baby Boy* a million times and have the same humor and laughter, but then there were tear-jerking moments as well. Jody was the epitome of so many young Black men that I grew up with, and Yvette . . . Sometimes, I felt like I had a li'l Yvette in me. There was a side to me that was vulnerable, loving, nurturing, and just homegirl-ish. But if you made me mad, forgiveness was *not* in the deck of cards.

All I needed was a cinnamon roll and a bowl of bonbons to go with the movie. There was a level of comfort needed in my spirit because my life would change in 30 days and in 9 months. Didn't really expect to become pregnant, but all the makeup sex that Ken and I were having, a baby was destined to manifest. Was I ready? Not quite. Was I lionhearted? One hundred percent. Raising King was no crystal stair, but so far, this mum was doing pretty damn good. King equipped me with a full set of "mom skills" that would apply to raising a second child. I needed to call one of my good girlfriends or my mama to get some feedback.

"Baby, here you go." He handed me a plate of toast and scrambled eggs. The aroma of the bacon and scrapple smelled so good, but I didn't want to take the risk of throwing up again. I nibbled on the toast.

"Oh, it's on that part when Jody's mom starts schooling him on selling his swap meet dresses. When she's like 'Are you trying to be a salesman or a shyster? You buy from a shyster, you feel like you got took. You buy from a good salesman, and you feel lucky.'"

"Oh yeah, when cuz was tryin'a hustle. I feel him, though. They make it hard for a Black man. If you sell drugs or hustle guns, you going to jail, or a nigga gonna kill you. But who wants to work minimum wage out here? And if your family didn't make enough money to put up for college, then you left to figure this shit out for yourself," Kenya reflected.

"I mean, my grandma raised her kids and their kids off of one salary, and I got nuffin' but respect for her. Mom Dukes was in the streets, and so was my dad. As a kid, he was in and out of jail. As I got older, I wasn't tryin'a hear what my grandma had to say. Women raised me, and the only real man I had a solid relationship with was my godfather. But as I got older, I started getting into shit, and no one could control me."

"What do you really want to do with your life, Ken? Like, when you were a little boy, what were your dreams?"

"Dream, I really don't know. I know I can burn in the kitchen, and I got mean chef skills. I'm good with my hands too. I should have gone away to the military when Wayne and my Dominican homie Bien went to the navy." He started crushing his food.

"Don't live your life in regret." I was watching Ving Rhames's fine naked butt cook breakfast in Jody's mama's kitchen. "You have awesome culinary arts skills. I could see you being a sous-chef or private chef. You are really strong too. How are things going at the job? Will they promote you anytime soon?"

"I'm not getting enough hours, and I'm not making enough money. They got they picks of who they want to promote. It's time for me to do something else. One thing I can say about you is that you always have a plan, and whatever you set your mind to do, you do it. That motivates me."

"What about getting a few certifications under your belt so that you can increase your value and boost your employability? Give me your résumé, Ken so that I can jazz it up."

"Bet. I'll get it to you this week, and you can work your mojo. Look at this nigga, Melvin, with his preachy ass."

"That's what it's all about. Guns and butter, baby. You little dumbass." We both busted out in laughter.

"I love Jody. He like King. He don't want nobody around his mama." I sipped my cold glass of water. "But then again, I get Jody's mama. 'Surprise me, Jody, and leave the nest. Mama gotta have a life too, Jody,'" we giggled together. Kenya rubbed his fingers through my hair.

"Baby, you treat King just like a king, and he got that whole aura about him. He don't like nobody around his mama. Heck, he barely likes me."

"He tolerates you." I rubbed his hand. "He loves you. He just overprotective of me. I'm all he knows and has."

"He got me too!" Kenya became defensive.

"He loves you, but prior to you, you know how it was. It was as if we were growing up together. It was just King and I, and he remembers that. We really didn't have anyone rooting for us."

"We a family now, Yvette."

"Stop playing, boy."

"We are a family now. You about to have my baby, girlll!'" Kenya began emulating Jody's character with a south-central accent. He put his hand on my belly. "How does your stomach feel? You still feel nauseated?"

"I feel a lot better. I really want some ginger ale."

"There's some ginger ale and crackers in the kitchen. I knew that it would soothe your tummy, so I grabbed it when I bought the pregnancy test. When are you going to the doctor?"

"I'm gonna make an appointment between today and tomorrow to get in alignment for the next couple of months. I don't know who I wanna call first, my mama or Sanai."

"You just can't wait to run your mouth. Whatchu think—it's a boy or girl?"

"It's a girl," I said confidently.

"Naw, that's my son in there."

"The way that I threw up this morning, that's a girl. If I keep throwing up and being nauseated, then that's a girl. They say a girl takes everything out of you, including the calcium."

"That's my baby, so it don't even matter." He took our plates and put them in the kitchen. "I'm about to leave in a few minutes, so you'll have plenty of time to call your family and friends."

"Real funny. I may call Sanai, but other than that, I'm gonna chill for a few months before I tell my mama and daddy. Everybody don't need to know. Not everyone is for me. I gotta see my OBGYN and my primary so that I can sync my body."

Someone was knocking really hard at the door.

"Lover, you gonna go get that? Who's banging on the door like that?"

Kenya walked to the door, looked through the peephole, and then opened the door.

"What's up, my nigga?" Les, a good friend of Kenya's, walked his tall, lanky ass through the door, giving Kenya a brotherly handshake. "What's up, Dream? What are you doing home, Ms. Boss Lady? You ain't ever at home."

"Hey, Les, I'm good. Can sis take a day off? Sis needs a break." Kenya brought me a half glass of ginger ale.

"Yea, you right. You are one of the hardest working women that I know. I heard you got your company off the ground." Les sat in the suede high chair in the kitchen.

"Yea, I'm excited. It feels promising."

"I told that nigga, Kenya, he bet not fuck this up. He ain't gonna get any better than you. Women our age ain't thinking about having their own business. They wanna sit at home and have babies."

"What's wrong with having babies?" He irked me. Hell, I had just found out I was pregnant. I was extra sensitive.

"Eh, cuz, don't be talking about babies, 'cause we finna have one." Kenya sat next to me and put on his shoes.

"Oh yeah? Is he for real, Dream?"

"Yea, we got a baby, baby!" We all laughed.

"Congrats. Yea, that mean your black ass gotta come straight home these days and no detours," said Les.

"Man, I got this. I know I gotta change some things, homie."

Kenya's voice cracked as usual when he felt like he had to defend himself.

"As long as you know," Les reiterated.

"Baby girl, I'll be back later. There's still some bacon, scrapple, and toast left, just in case you get hungry. Warm it up. You got your ginger ale and crackers, so you should be good."

"Thank you, baby, I appreciate you."

"Don't forget to go get King later on."

"I'm not. Coco will most likely drop him off to me."

Kenya grabbed his jacket and put on his Washington hat. He had on some basic blue jeans, a gray T-shirt, and some gray NB sneakers. He was smiling and eager to hang out with Les, who lived in VA. He met Les once when he was locked up years before in Rappahannock, Virginia, on a brandishing charge involving a racist white boy. There were no witnesses, no gun found, and no injuries, yet, he was still sentenced. Les was his cell mate. Although Virginia was the Commonwealth and racist toward Blacks, especially Black men, Kenya, for some odd reason, always felt the need to hang out there. He would talk about how he loved the countryside, the scenery, the slow lifestyle, Southern hospitality, and the overall beauty of Virginia. In my mind, I was a liberated Bison University graduate who avoided cities and states that devalued Blacks, and where there was a high possibility that you might be a victim of police brutality or the criminal justice system.

"All right, baby, watch your movies and chill. Make sure you email that lady back about the contract. If you need me, just hit my phone."

He softly grasped my ears like headphones and kissed me on my forehead.

"Gotcha. See you later." I returned the kiss to his forehead.

*Baby Boy* was over, and the next movie in the rotation was *Eat Pray Love*, starring Julia Roberts. There was something about that film that spoke to the essence of a woman's quest for love, peace of mind, and comfort food. The food in the movie never looked so good in my life, and now, my pregnancy hormones had officially kicked in. My phone was calling me, and I needed to check for missed calls, but more importantly, I had to respond via email to McKenzie.

Good morning, McKenzie,

Thank you so much for this award letter. Thank you for the opportunity to serve. My team and I are super excited about the "Passion for Change" Summer Enrichment program and providing an awesome outlet for the youth we propose to serve. This is right on time. I look forward to hearing from you.

All the Best,

Dream

The reality was that I didn't have a team. Lord knows I needed to call Kiana, Cookie, some of the brothas at MOV who needed a side gig or part-time work. It was time to assemble the program. Kiana and a great strong assistant would work until I could bring in some revenue.

The movie was getting good, and I was already at the part where Liz, played by Julia Roberts, had solidified her divorce to Stephen and was onto being a self-satisfying cougar with David. Liz was all over the damn place, but I had a connection to that white woman. I had already lost it all too at one point in my life—now, I was at the gain. My fingers were busy as I multitasked biting on crackers.

GM Kiana, this is Dream. I'm sure you are at work, but I wanted to let you know that I got a summer contract, and if you would like to do some part-time work with my organization, that would be great, I texted.

Within a minute, she texted back.

Hey, Dream, I'm at work. Congrats on your new contract. That is so good. I would love to help you out. How does 2 days a week sound? I can work from home too. She was for certain.

Two days is perfect. I mainly need you to set up my files, help with reports, provide administrative support, and organization. When does the program start? Kiana asked.

In 30 days.

Oh, wow! You not playing. How much are you paying?

How does $16 an hour sound? When revenue kicks in, I can pay you more.

Yes, that's perfect. Are you taking out taxes? Kiana was straight to the point.

Nope. You would be a 1099, like a consultant. I was quick on my toes.

Perfect. Sounds good. Just lemme know when you want me to come in. I get off at 3 p.m., so anytime after that I can walk up to your office since I live a block away.

Let's say in 2 weeks at 4 p.m. That way, I can get a few things in order on my side. Does that work?

Yes, 4 p.m. in 2 weeks at your office. I'm there.

Thanks so much. Kiana. See you soon. We both ended the conversation.

Kiana would be excellent for my team because she kept the front office in order at MOV, so Passion for Change was a no-brainer.

I texted Cookie, my homie, from when I lived Uptown on Clay Street.

Hey, Cookie, I got good news! I waited on her text message. The movie was getting really good. Liz had arrived in Bali. Bali seemed so serene. The houses were so open and beautiful, and there was a sense of oneness.

Hey, Dream. What up?

I got my business off the ground. I got a contract too.

Remember back in the day when I said I would put you on once I got my own business?

Yea, I sure do. We was in front of the 314. I'm so happy for you, D. So, so happy. So when can I start?

I'm putting my team together now. Definitely in a few months. I will most likely need you as an assistant.

That's right up my alley. I'm not working either. You know I can type, organize, clean, take notes, and answer phones. She was straight to the point.

I remember. That's why I called you because you got skills. I'm gonna have a meeting 2 weeks from today around 4:00 p.m. Can you come?

I'll be there. Where is it located?

It's the recreational center on 14th and Gail Ln.

I'm there.

Thanks, Cookie. Can't wait to see you.

Talk to you later, lady. Thanks for thinking of me.

Welcome. We ended that conversation.

There was such a feeling of excitement in my soul. It was as if my name aligned with my destiny. For once, my life was making sense, and the spirit of happiness was all over me. Was it the happiness that Liz was seeking in *Eat Pray Love*? Was it the happiness that Liz exuberated in Bali? Didn't know for sure. Liz had Ketut, her form of a seer and therapist, to guide her in the flesh. Everyone needed a Ketut, a confidant to share life stories with, a shrink, some couch time. I hadn't seen my therapist in about 3 years. God was in my spirit, and He was my guide—never leaving me, never forsaking me, drying all my tears, and loving me unconditionally.

Ketut kept it so gangsta with Liz when he said, "Do not look at the world through your head; look at it through your heart."

My story wasn't practical. Had I used my head instead of my heart with my current move, I'd be in corporate America making tons of money, but no time to spend it and apologetic for taking a sick day or leave for attending a parent-teacher conference. Yea, being an entrepreneur was a better fit. My eyes became low. A nap was inevitable. The vision came, and the future could not wait. The summer was hot and humid, but it didn't stop me from applying for two more fall mentoring and creative arts grants, which were larger grants.

SIX MONTHS LATER . . .

Six months passed, my hips spread, my nose was slightly wider, and I gained about 20 pounds in baby weight. The summer enrichment program was awesome, and we served 30 youth for the entire summer. My team was terrific, and Passion for Change had a heavy buzz in the community. The mission was unfolding.

My mother, father, close family members, and friends were all on board and excited about baby #2. My team was ready and growing. It was Kiana, Cookie, and Eli and Lee from the MOV. I aimed to be an unorthodox nonprofit that brought innovation to the youth and the community. We were not gonna be a typical 9:00 a.m. to 5:00 p.m. stuffy organization. We would be sincere, passionate, positive, brotherly, sisterly, and mission oriented. I gave orders, and it was up to you how you creatively executed them.

King was growing up. He was one stop from middle school, and he was starting to really take football seriously. He was becoming more hotheaded and more difficult to redirect. He wasn't my little "Moo Moo" anymore. He had entered the "growing pains" era where he wanted to ride bikes and terrorize others with the neighborhood boys and play outside. As long as he didn't break a neighbor's window and came in when the streetlights came on, we were good. King felt some type of way that he wasn't gonna be the only child anymore. He didn't seem too thrilled at having a sibling. I understood because I was the only child for quite some time before my brother, Ocean, was born. It was like I wanted to part my lips and say to my mother, "What the fuck you did that for? Why you had to have another kid? What, I wasn't enough?" At least I knew not to say that to my mom, or my whole set of front teeth would be gone, but my actions communicated the same thing. So, no, King wasn't sold on having a sibling, even though his father had five other kids. He was overprotective of his mama. He'd have a few weeks to sleep in my bed before I'd officially kick him out at night. Kenya could be in the bed, and King would find a way in the middle of the night to climb in my bed. Kenya would get under King's skin when he would say, "King, get off your mama's titty, boy." King would respond, "Leave me aloneeeeeeee!" The way that King was tied to my hip, you would have thought that King was breast-fed as a baby, but he became a Similac kid because my breasts would not produce enough milk for his greedy self.

Kenya, on the other hand, was everywhere but focused. He had quit his job as a cook and was on and off taking temp jobs. We had a baby on the way, and it was as if it scared the hell outta him, even though he was pressed to have a baby with me. He was drinking heavier, and he wasn't coming home every night, which became disrespectful. He began hanging with niggas that had just come home that he grew up with, but they weren't guiding him in the right light. It was harder to focus on building anything with him because he wasn't sober long enough.

Then infidelity became an issue.

I was so far along in my pregnancy that I didn't want to upset myself. My goal was to bring our child to term without illness, high blood pressure, or emergencies driven by emotion, so I avoided the drama and suppressed my instincts.

Kenya was sloppy, and there were days that he'd come by just to take a shower, change his clothes, and leave. I would check his cell phone to find out through text messages that he was fucking May, Taja, and a girl named Remy, and whoever else. He used his homeboy Dante, who was May's cousin and Jamir's boyfriend, as a scapegoat to leave home almost daily as if he were going to a real job. He began spending days at a time over at May's house. May was the older woman that hung with his homegirl, Jamir, who came to his birthday party, and it was evident in my gut that the situation was shady back then. It didn't take a rocket scientist to figure out that he was fucking May. May was tall, brown, had a medium build, and the bags under her eyes looked like she had a hard knock life and a mean story. She had to be in her late 40s because we were in our early 30s, and she made 40s look rough. She had her own house, a job, and a lot of kids.

Kenya used to act like she was just his homie, but once he had me pick him up from over at her house, you could tell by the blank stares, dirty thongs on the floor, and giggles that I was being mocked for being so muthafuckin' naïve. Again, I had to keep my heart in place, suppress the hurt and disrespect, and pray that the 2 months that were left of the pregnancy would be healthy despite his foolery.

His text messages also indicated that he was still whoring around with his baby mama, Taja. Never really understood why he would mess with a woman who had issues raising her daughter, Nia, effectively. Nia bounced from house to house, and whatever woman Kenya would bring Nia around, she never forgot. What Kenya didn't know is that Nia would confide in King about the houses he would take her to, and King would low-key hint to me without blowing the cover—he loved his mama no matter what. Taja was a red girl. She was a bus driver, had a car, a Section 8 house, and other children, but there was nothing resilient about her. Maybe she had good pussy, but no emotional stability. She was jealous of me, and she demonstrated it in a text message that she sent to me.

Kenya is fucking that bitch May. He stay over there too. Your baby ain't gonna make it. She wore her emotions on her sleeve as she texted me in the middle of the night.

Bitch, you don't even take care of your kid. Why are you fucking with me? It don't matter what you say. We good over here, you hateful-ass bitch, I texted back and proceeded to block her number. It was hard to sleep. There were remnants of flashbacks of Solomon doing me the same way, and perhaps there was a lesson that I had missed from the first go-round that I'd learn from the second.

Too many nights, I would lock up the house, make sure King was good, turn my body into a fetal position, and shed silent tears. Toward the end of my pregnancy, I would get so fed up that I would tell Kenya to "get the fuck out" since he wanted to be with other women and run the streets. There was a line of disrespect that he crossed, and he knew it, so he left to roam.

Every part of my life was absolutely dope, except that part. I couldn't really talk about the level of hurt that I felt with anyone, but it was enough for me to say to myself, "Once I have this baby, I'm gonna get my body and my face back and get back to me." Solomon abandoned me with King, and even though Kenya called me every day to check up on me, he was neglecting the baby and me for cheap fixes that didn't last. He claimed he craved the "ole Dream," or as he put it, he missed "Jenny from the block," but there was growth here, and he wasn't ready, 'cause he chose not to grow. "Jenny from the block" was a young Black woman finding her way. She struggled; she was searching for love from any place that she could get it. Jenny had nothing and smiled at pebbles. Jenny was needy, unstable, and willing to sacrifice what she had to have a nigga save her. Jenny was abandoned and used prescription drugs and alcohol as a temporary solution for a fixation to anxiety and post-traumatic stress disorder. Jenny was cute but ugly on the inside. She was insecure in every way. I hated Jenny, but most niggas from the hood loved her 'cause they could squeeze her remnants and walk away for good. Jenny was me.

Kenya mentioned over and over that "Jenny" was "fun," but "Dream" was "boring," and "all I cared about was my laptop." What he forgot was the laptop ignited ideas that would generate multiple streams of income, and he misunderstood being "focused" for "boring." My success intimidated Kenya, and it was sad because he was there in the beginning when our reality was just dreams that we'd whisper in each other's ear at night. We'd get excited together over our own ambitions, but when real life began to manifest, he checked out.

As I entered my eighth month of pregnancy, the hurricanes arrived, and they were a Category 3. The winds would blow so hard that my rambler house that we lived in seemed like it was gonna fall to pieces if it blew any harder. The large trees in the yard swayed back and forth, and my prayers were that they were strong enough not to break.

"Mama, you good?" King shouted from his bedroom.

"Yea, I'm good. If the winds get too harsh, we're gonna pack a bag and go to a hotel."

"OK, Mama."

The winds were picking up speed, grasping my attention. Then my cell phone rang.

"Dream! Eh, Dream!" It was a loud country voice on the other end.

"Yea," I said calmly.

"It's Les. I'm calling you because Kenya din got himself locked up." Les's voice was trembling.

"What? How?" I sat up in bed. My nerves were on a 1,000.

"Man, he was over the bitch Taja's house, and they got into it. Man, I don't know why he was even over there."

"What? He's so damn stupid. I don't even know why he would fuck with her. So what happened, Les?"

"He got into it with her. She claim he put his hands on her. She called the police on that man. And they came and locked him up. He had no business over there. He should have been with you. You the one pregnant."

"Oh God. This is too much." The winds began picking up again. "We in the middle of a hurricane, and he got the nerve to get locked up. I'm due in a few weeks. Is he crazy? Was he high? Was he drunk?"

"I don't know, Dream. I just called to tell you the bad news. You a good girl. You don't deserve this. I feel bad, man. Call Central Booking and let me know what they say."

"All right, I'ma call them." I hung up the phone. It felt like my head and heart were on fire. The utter disappointment that I felt couldn't describe my feelings. Why would Kenya put himself in a position to get locked up behind his baby mama? Was it even worth it? Why would he leave me pregnant with uncertainty? He just didn't give a fuck? Jesssssssssssssssus, save me.

I went and got my laptop to research the number to Central Booking. As soon as it populated, I called the number.

Without hesitation, an officer picked up the phone. "Central Booking, Officer Irvin, can I have the inmate number?"

"Hi, I'm looking for my boyfriend. I don't have his inmate number, but he was locked up tonight." It dawned on me that the officer may be my landlord, who was a police officer working downtown.

"What's his name?"

"Kenya Harris. Excuse me, is that you, Mr. Irvin?" My voice quivered.

"Yea, is that you, Dream?" He recognized my voice.

"Yes, Mr. Irvin, unfortunately, it's me. Kenya got locked up tonight."

"Yea, I seen him looking pathetic. Ain't you pregnant?" Mr. Irvin was more like an uncle to me. He wasn't like your typical police. He actually cared.

"Yea, Mr. Irvin, I'm due next month."

"Oh Lord. How's the wind out there? The house OK? You and the li'l boy OK?" He was concerned.

"The house is still intact, but the winds are blowing really fast. Just hoping these trees don't crush this house."

"Let me know if you need to go to a hotel. You're pregnant. You need to be safe."

"Thank you, Mr. Irvin. I will let you know if we need to evacuate."

"Your boy recognized me and made sure he let me know that he was your boyfriend. I looked out for him with a few snacks. He'll be good while he's with me. They holding him, though. He's not coming home." Mr. Irvin held no punches.

"Why are they holding him? For what? I'm pregnant. I *need* him to come home." I became emotional.

"Well, love, Virginia is coming to get him for a probation violation. Whatever time he owes them, he's gonna have to serve it."

"What? Wait. What the fuck? I think he owes them a year. I got a baby on the way, Mr. Irvin. No way this can happen right now."

"Baby girl, you gonna have to be strong. Strong like that young lady I met a few years ago with the son, with dreams in her eyes with fortitude. I got you as far as the house. But you know you good girls like them knuckleheaded-ass boys that don't wanna grow up. This is where they go when they wanna do things their way."

"Oh my God. My Lord," I cried. "What am I gonna do?"

"Baby girl, I'm gonna look out for him. When VA picks him up, I'm gonna let you know. I'm gonna send Todd to you for any work that you need done. If the hurricane gets too bad, I'll send you to a nice hotel for you and the kid for a few days. This ain't the best of news, I know." He tried to comfort me.

"No, it's not fair! What the hell am I supposed to do? The baby is coming regardless. He promised he wouldn't leave me."

"Dream, be strong, OK. You got two kids now depending on you. Two mouths to feed. You gotta get focused now."

"Thank you, and please keep me posted on him."

"You want me to send him a message?"

I took a deep breath. "Tell him I love him. Tell him to call me collect when he gets to VA. Tell him . . ." The tears couldn't stop. "Gotta go, Mr. Irvin." I hung up the phone.

Mr. Irvin was right. I had two mouths to feed. Didn't know how long Kenya was gonna be gone, but he made his bed, and he had to lie in it. As usual, I had to figure shit out on my own. At least, now, the winds began to calm. I rubbed my stomach and listened for guidance from my God. I called on my ancestors. She was on her way.

'

# Chapter 17

## C-Section Dreams

My forearms were wrapped in IV fluids. My leg and arms were taped down, yet my head was lifted up. There was nowhere for me to run. I would face life and death head-on, and only God's grace could save me. The room was bright with lavender and lime-green rays shining through. The oxygen in my nose had the smell of peppermint with a slight crisp of cucumber. I was in a trance, feeling the aroma of motherhood for the second time. I was unafraid but more so mesmerized that I felt so close to death but so close to life in the same divine breath.

Deep down, I awaited my king to hold my right hand in my second coming, but my life is never the way I've predicted it in my mind. I'd swallow the big girl pill, close my eyes, and pray like I never prayed before. I was alone again. No pushing involved, no giving birth in the warm waters being held by her father. Just me. Yet, God's heavenly angels decided to use my womb to usher a woman-child into the world where my mind, body, and soul would speak, "Namaste."

"Shundada, Shundada, Shundada, Shundada, Shundada," I prayed in the spirit repeatedly.

"Shundada, Shundada, Shundada, Shundada."

"Jesus, Jesus, Jesus, oh, be with me, Jesus. Don't leave me, Jesus," I whispered as I held Cookie's right hand tightly.

"Are you okay, Dream? Are you okay?" Cookie saw me drifting away.

"I think so." I was unsure.

"Is my baby here yet? Is she here?" I whispered.

"She's almost here. Just hold my hand. I'm here for you."

"Okay, Cookie."

A sista held my right hand in the absence of my baby's father, and I was blessed. Historically, sistas are reared to be thy keeper in the midst of a crisis and when the avalanche roars. Tears dripped slowly from the edges of my eyes, mimicking the slow drip of IV fluids. As the doctor and surgeon shaved my bikini area, I experienced the buzzing of being pierced again from the left to the right of my lower abdomen. I had already been injected with local anesthesia, and I was as high as a kite as if it were a brisk spring day in April.

"Okay, young lady, you are going to experience us tugging on you. It may feel uncomfortable, but you will feel no pain," the surgeon affirmed.

"How do you feel, Dream?" he asked.

"I feel sick. I feel nauseated like I'm gonna throw up." I leaned forward.

"Give her a bag and adjust it to the side of her. Also, give her some antinausea medicine," the obstetrician spoke swiftly to his nurse.

"Coming right up." She connected a bag to the right side of my shoulder at the bed so that all I had to do was barf in the bag. She provided me with a small cup of water with the antinausea medicine to take before they proceeded with the C-section.

"Okay, Dream, I need you to breathe and relax because your baby is coming," the obstetrician said with his thick Syrian accent.

Cookie looked like she was getting ready to faint at the sight of all the gook, blood, and main ingredients that come with removing a baby from the abdomen.

"She coming, Dream, she coming out! I can see her head full of hair." Cookie was smiling and jumping like it was her baby.

"Here she comes- we are pulling her out as of now!" Doctor Nasir sounded ecstatic. "You will feel one more final tug, young lady. It will be uncomfortable."

"Yuhhhhhhh!" I grunted. I felt strange for a few seconds, and then I heard my daughter cry.

"I hear my baby. I hear my baby. Listen to her." I lifted my head. "That's her." I began crying tears of joy.

"Wahhhhh, Wahhhhh, Wammm, Wammm, Wahh," my baby cried aloud.

It was such a surreal moment. I had done my best. I just wanted to see her.

"Oh my gosh, Dream, she looks just like Kenya," Cookie giggled. "Except she is red and has dimples."

"Wammmmmmmm!" My girl had a set of lungs on her.

"Welp, young lady, it is a beautiful baby girl," said Doctor Nasir.

"Yayyyyy!" Clapped all the doctors, nurses, techs, and Cookie in unison.

"And you won't believe the time," said the nurse. "It is 7:11 p.m. Lucky 7, 11." She wooed us.

I was so amazed. "Really?" I smiled.

I was sealed up in about 17 minutes, about as fast as they opened me up to bring the baby out. It was too fast to be true. Did I have a microwave baby?" This C-section business was getting too good, and I didn't need it to be too good because baby girl would be my last rodeo on the cutting board.

I had a quick flashback while still lying on my back when I gave birth to King, and Dr. Nasir took a lot of my belly fat out and gave me a slight tummy tuck favor without me even asking. I wonder if he could revamp that and make me camera-ready plastic surgery good.

"Eh, Dr. Nasir."

"Yes, Dream?"

"Before you stitch me all up, can you please take a couple of pounds of fat out of my stomach? Better yet, the fat over there that is lying to the side – keep it right over there. You know tummy tuck me like you did when I had King," I laughed.

"I will do you a li'l favor," he smiled and silently showed me using a reflecting mirror the bulging bloody fat that was taken out to the side.

"Thanks," I winked in exhaustion.

The nurse brought the baby to me so we could bond immediately, placing her cheek next to mine. She and I were connected souls from the moment that I felt her squirm in my womb. I knew that she would make me better, so much better. I knew that she would be truly the imitation of my life.

Throughout my 9 months, it was a peaceful ride with her and me. The only time I had a problem with my pregnancy was when I ate the wrong foods. I literally became almost vegetarian during my pregnancy. I could not hold down any poultry, beef, turkey or fish. It was fruit, ice cream, French bread, and Chipotle on a good day. My mornings carrying my baby doll consisted of throwing up and settling with ginger ale and crackers come midday. In my last few months, Kiana would bless me with a warm bow tie from a donut shop and an ice vanilla latte.

Baby girl was the peace and calm. I welcomed her, and she seemed happy to be here.

"We are now cleaning the baby up and getting her weight." The nurse lifted her so that I could see. The baby's cry became softer and softer as her spirit adjusted to LIFE. "Oh my gosh, she is exactly 7 pounds and 11 ounces, born at 7:11p.m. She is your lucky charm, Mom!"

Those who were left in the room began clapping again.

"We need to play those numbers, Dream, when we get home. If you don't play those numbers, I will," Cookie gleamed.

"I'm playing those numbers. Wait 'til I tell my mama and aunties about my lucky star. They are gonna be excited. I think my dad will play those numbers too," I said. "Look at her dimples. Her eyes are wide open, and all that hair…Eh, Cookie, I'm so glad she is not bald. She does look just like her dad but with my lips, hair, and emotion." I sat up to receive my baby.

"Here she is." The nurse handed her to me with her typical swaddling newborn attire and pink and white hat. She looked like a li'l Panda.

"Thank you, thank you," I said in amazement. "Thank you, Dr. Nasir. Thank you to your team. You guys made this a breeze."

"So what are you going to name her?" Cookie asked, and everyone awaited my answer.

"Dynasty. Her name will be Dynasty," I proclaimed. "You know I believe in making a statement with how I name my children. And for me, at this time in my life, I want to restore confidence, prosperity, love, and a legacy that no man or woman will be able to destroy."

"Wow, well, Dream, you have always had unique names," said Dr. Nasir.

"I knew you were gonna name your baby something far, far out. I just knew it," said Cookie. "I love it, though. It suits her. Just look at her eyes. She's so amazing."

I cuddled little Dynasty in my arms. Our eyes locked. Our spirits connected. We smiled and winked at each other. She was super-duper dope, and I was a proud mama, My aunties, best friend, son, and godson awaited to see my mini me in my recovery room. But the person that needed to see Dynasty was her father.

"Hold up, Dream, your phone is ringing. You want me to answer it?" asked Cookie.

"Yes, please intercept all calls. Folks should know I'm having a baby. I'm vibin with my baby girl." I kissed her cheeks and cuddled her on my breasts.

"Dream, you may wanna take this call. It's you know," she smiled. "It's your daddy, Dynasty."

Cookie was so hood and sweet at the same time.

"For real?" I got excited. I looked into Dynasty's eyes and secured her on my bosoms that appeared to be 25-pound pillows. "Your daddy on the phone."

"What's up, baby? How you feel? Is she cute?" Kenya jumped right into the conversation as if I had my baby a week ago and not minutes ago.

"She's beautiful, and she got the nerve to look just like you. I had her about 25 minutes ago. I'm in love with her already."

"Did you push her out or have a C-section?"

"They cut me open, dude. I don't think I have the heart to push my babies out. Plus, I cheated and got a tummy tuck."

"You what?" he screamed through the phone.

'Well, a C-section, the doctor can snatch that baby fat out while you're cut open on the table. Me and Dr. Nasir have an understanding."

"How does your belly feel? How does your body feel?"

"My body is still numb from the anesthesia, but seeing our daughter has me fully awakened. We are here. You know what I'm saying?"

"Mane, I wish I could escape these bars and be there with ya'll." Kenya sounded like he was experiencing a tearjerker.

"I wish you were here too. It's gonna be hard for me, but I think with the right people, I'm gonna be good. Cookie, Sanai, Auntie Nandi, Auntie Maury, Tammy, and the boys are in the recovery room waiting for me. That's good. It's just so hard to know you had my baby and I can't even be there. Does she have hair?"

"Yes! Kenya, she has a lot of hair. She got my hair. She has my lips too. But I don't know where she got her dimples from." I smiled through the phone.

"She will come into her own look. How was the labor? How long you think you gotta be in there? When you getting home?" He began his natural drill session.

"Do you know that I began my labor days ago, and I just didn't know?" When I complained about all that pain and stuff, it was me in labor, I was told by the doctor. Once I got to the hospital, I was already 4 centimeters dilated. I could have pushed. But you know I'm a chicken. Fuck it, just cut me was my attitude," I said.

"That's 'cause you don't know how to sit down. You probably worked all up until today." Kenya knew me all too well.

"I actually worked up until yesterday." My stomach was too tight to laugh. "I guess I be home in 3 days. But I'll need help because I won't be able to drive. Auntie Lela, my great aunt, will be at home to help me."

"That's good 'cause you can't be superwoman, and I'm not there, and you gonna need help. Damn, I wish I could be there, but I can't take back what I have done wrong. I'm sorry, Dream. I am so sorry for what I have done. I should have done right by you. Thank you for having our daughter." The phone was silent.

"But when I get home, you know she gonna be a daddy's girl." He knew I was in my feelings, so he tried to brighten up the conversation. "Hell no, she's a mama's girl already. You have your daddy's girl already."

"What did you name her?"

"I named her Dynasty."

"So, you named her what you said you were gonna name her. Is she gonna have a nickname?"

"Her name is too strong to give her a nickname. Her name is Dynasty, and she's gonna set our Dynasty straight."

The hospital techs began pushing my bed to the recovery room. The dimness of the hallways was quite different from the bright lights that I had just left.

"That's a beautiful name. I can't wait to meet her, my baby girl. I know it's too early in the game. But when you get a chance, can you please bring her to see me in like 3 months? She should have her shots and baby immunizations by then," he asked.

"Yea, Kenya, I hate those jails, maneeee. But I will bring her when I feel like her immune system is up to par."

"You know I have 30 seconds left," he said, the automated inmate system echoed, reminding us.

"You know how this shit go. But I love you and Dynasty, maneeee. I miss you so much. I'm praying for y'all and pray for me."

"I miss you too, Kenya. Call me tomorrow to check up on the baby and me."

"I will, Dream. Love you." The phone disconnected. I felt streams of gray for a few minutes. I had arrived at the recovery room with an entire cheering section of sisterhood and support that meant so much to me. I was with the older women in my family. Those who had seen it, done it, experienced it, or witnessed it. They spoke in codes with their eyes, and we understood. I needed them to be cool, calm, and loving. If they did anything else, I would act the hell up.

"Give me that baby!" they shouted in unison as Auntie Lela grabbed for her. I observed how Auntie Maury and Auntie Nandi sang, kissed, and welcomed Dynasty into the world. King reluctantly walked up to me and said, "Dang. Ma, you look crazy. Are you good?" Sanai and Cookie laughed. "Boy, your mama just had a baby," said Sanai.

"I know, but, Mom, you look all blown up." King stared and touched my hands to feel the swollenness that made him so uncomfortable. He looked at me and realized for once that my superpowers were gone.

"This is what women look like after they have a baby. I won't be ugly for long." I laughed.

"That's my sister?" King rested his head on my shoulder.

"That's your sister. You're gonna have to be her protector and big brother, you know?"

"I know, Mom, I want to make sure you're good," said King.

"He love his mama," Cookie said aloud.

"Yes, he does," Sanai confirmed.

"I love both of my babies." I hugged King and brought his cheek to my cheek. I wanted my son to know that just because I had a baby, we were still a TEAM. And now I have two seeds to look after. I was thoroughly blessed. Yet, I had to be honest with inner self because I was exhausted, happy, overwhelmed, and missing Kenya. He was such a missing piece to the puzzle. Just like Solomon was a missing piece to the puzzle when I had King, so was Kenya. The only difference was that I was in distress when I delivered King because Solomon was a no-show when I gave birth to him. Dynasty's delivery was peaceful. As my family and friends wrapped their hearts around my daughter, I realized deep down that this new chapter in my life would be much different from before.

My life had changed so much from Clay Street to Goode Avenue. My money game was different, and so was my entrepreneurial outlook. My 20s were long gone. I was 30-something with two babies, two baby daddies, a degree, and ambition.

Kenya was locked up, but I didn't quite internalize it because I was free in my heart. I forgave him despite his actions and anticipated his release within a year. My mental health was stabilized, and emotionally, I learned therapeutically to pray, meditate, breathe deeply through my new practice with Yoga. I was a big girl who had put her big girl PANTIES on. It was a forward movement. The blind could see in fluorescence, and the deaf could hear me buzzing as I soared. My Dynasty was a beckoning light showing the beauty of it all – A love so pure.

# Chapter 18
## Cherish the Day

The transporters kindly brought me out of Labor and Delivery to the front of George Washington Carver Hospital. It felt so good to inhale fresh air and experience the light 65-degree winds as I cuddled Dynasty in my lap. She was so beautiful, with a fat panda face, chinky slanted eyes, a full set of jet-black hair, and light brown skin. She laid in my arms in the cutest pink sleeper. My mama always said to pay attention to the color of a baby's ears because that would be a forecast of the complexion that the baby would have. Dynasty's ears were indeed a cocoa brown, so eventually, she'd end up being chocolate like her father. Five days in the hospital felt like several weeks, but after a C-section, you had to be monitored, and your vitals had to be up to par before they would release you. My vitals were out of whack.

On my second day of being in the hospital, I nearly fainted while going to the bathroom. As I went down, I called out, "I'm falling" to a few of my mentees who were visiting me and holding Dynasty. They rushed to get my assigned nurses, and the nurses responded immediately, hitting my face with ammonia. I recall that ammonia being so strong that I woke up in about 5 seconds, and as tears came out of my eyes in uncertainty, the nurses assured me that I was gonna be OK. My mentees, Chyna and Ayden, were scared as hell because they saw me as a strong woman who had never been weak or vulnerable, and at that moment, they realized I was human.

Cookie pulled up in my silver E350 Class Mercedes-Benz blasting trap music. You could see King in the backseat with eagerness in his eyes looking for his mama. Cookie put the car in park, and the porter assisted her with securing the car seat, which I never figured out how to secure with King.

"Hey, Dream, you look like you ready to come home!"

"Yes, I am, girl. Thanks so much for coming, Cookie."

"You know I got you."

King hopped out of the car. "Ma, thank God you coming home. You OK?"

"I'm good, baby boy. I missed you, King."

"I missed you too, Mama." He kissed me on the cheek. I know King missed me, and I missed him dearly. We were in the struggle together, and we were inseparable. With Dynasty, it was magical.

I handed Cookie my baby girl so that she could secure and lock her in the car seat. The porters assisted me with getting in the backseat so that I could be next to the baby. Just stepping up made me realize how sore my body was and how beat up my stomach felt with the incision.

"Lord have mercy. Thank you guys so much," I said as I sat down uncomfortably.

"You got it!" They closed my door and waved.

King sat in the front seat and put his seat belt on. Cookie took off. All I could do is give thanks to God for keeping me through the process and protecting me and mine continuously each day and every minute. Cookie took the scenic route to my house. I cracked the window and just vibed out to what was on the radio. My eyes time traveled as I glimpsed at Dynasty as she slept quietly. The car was quiet, but the humps and bumps in the city streets gave my stomach a run for my money. The pain was real, but the blessing was surreal, and I caressed my lower abdomen, channeling positive energy.

Finally, we were home.

"Dynasty, you home!" Cookie was loud and excited. Dynasty didn't open her eyes, not once.

King grabbed the stuff in the trunk and the diaper bag. I told him, "Here's the key. Go open up the house for us."

"OK." He was cool as a fan and seemed like he had matured and grown up this past week.

He got the baby's belongings and bags that Cookie had brought for the baby from the trunk.

Cookie took the baby out of the car seat and held her like it was her baby. I pushed down on the top of the car window so that I could get a good grip as I pushed myself up, gently closed the door, and took baby steps to my front door.

King opened the front door for me with the silliest smile on his face as if to say, "Welcome home."

The house looked relatively clean and in the condition that we left it in. It felt so good to be home with both of my babies. I sat on my black leather sofa, turning the TV on and reclining myself. The TV would be watching me eventually.

"King, can you look in the diaper bag and hand me my cell phone?"

"Okay, Ma." He put the diaper bag on the table as we went through fresh newborn diapers, baby wipes, newborn outfits, and extras.

"I found it. Here you go! Ma, who you gonna call, though? You just had a baby." King handed me the phone and was such an old soul.

"Dang, can I see who called me? You know I'm important," I giggled.

As soon as I opened the phone, I had several missed calls and a few congratulation text messages from my family members, my brother, Ocean, my father, and my mommy. There was a missed call from Rappahannock, which let me know that Ken had called. Cookie was just smiling, walking around with Dynasty and talking to her—the connection between the two was authentic. Cookie was the first person other than the doctor and nurses to see the baby.

"Chile, all I need is this bay window in my house." She handed the baby to me. "I would be smoking my green, drinking my 1738, and watching my neighbors."

"You so nosy. I hardly ever be in that window unless I'm looking for King when he's outside."

"Gurlaaaa, it's so peaceful you don't even know what you missing. It's quiet, and you don't hear no sirens or gunshots."

"Thank God it's peaceful and quiet on this side. There's nothing but senior citizens who focus on rising early and keeping their lawns manicured. I'm literally just recalling when to set out the trash."

"Yea, this is a far walk from Uptown."

"Ma, can I play the game out here in a few minutes?" King asked.

"Yea, just as soon as Ma changes Dynasty and gets her settled. We'll be in the room, and you got the front, son."

"So, what's the plan? What you need me to do?" Cookie asked.

"To be honest, Cookie, I need you to take King to school every day and pick him up for me and bring him home. I need you to run a few errands for me from day to day and grab groceries for us. Kinda like a personal assistant. I have cash to pay you, but I can't really do anything until my body gets strong." I carried Dynasty to the room and placed her on a changing pad on my bed to change her diaper. She was gradually waking up. Although I had her nursery fully set up in her own room, I was overprotective, and her bassinet would be next to my bed. Then I laid her on my bosom.

"I got you. That's no problem."

"And take the car. I can't drive. I'll give you gas money. Just don't get it booted or towed. I got tickets, chile," I said, making it plain.

"I got you. I'm gonna have my dude wash and clean out your car. Your car needs a wash. You need me to go to the store for you before I head out?"

"No, I think I'm good for the evening. Worst-case scenario, I'll order some carryout for King. I'm on soft foods 'cause of the C-section. I'll eat some soup and yogurt if I get hungry. My aunt Lela will be here in the morning from Oklahoma to get me together. She's an herbalist, and I need that ancestral touch."

"Okay, kiddo, and, baby girl, I'm gone. King, I'm gonna pick you up in the a.m. to take you to school."

"Okay," King replied, playing on his game system. He had snacks that Cookie got him prior from 7-Eleven, and he didn't have a care in the world.

"See y'all in the a.m.," Cookie said, then left.

The atmosphere felt so different. Being a mom of two was so unique but powerful. There was a peace that the household had. In my mind, I would learn how to multitask to raise two kids, a boy and a girl who were 7 years apart. Kinda like my brother, Ocean, and I. We were 7 years apart as well. Learning how to balance and raise two beautiful Black children, again on my own, would be the challenge, but God never forsook me—never did and never will.

"King," I yelled from the room, "come here for a second."

He ran to my room with his controller in his hand.

"Yea, Ma?"

"I'm gonna order you chicken wings and french fries from the carryout and an ice tea for me. I have a few $20 bills at the very bottom of my diaper bag under the baby's clothes. Take $20 to pay the Chinese man when he comes and keep the change and put it in your piggy bank. Mommy is in a li'l pain from having the baby, so I'll need you to help your baby sister and me."

"I got you, Mom. You need me to get you something now?" He was concerned.

"Just bring me a Gatorade, a few bottled waters, and a yogurt to the room and place it on my nightstand. Lock the front and back door."

He went into the fridge and brought me what I asked for and more, most likely so I wouldn't keep asking him to do stuff. He was smart.

"Aunt Lela will be here in the morning to visit us and assist us too. Cookie will be taking you to school and picking you up until I'm strong enough to drive."

"I be glad when you can get back to driving and being yourself," King said sarcastically.

"Me too. I will soon, son. Just be patient. Thank you, son."

I called the carryout and placed the order. As long as King had his food, I could gently fall asleep on my back, placing the comforter across my breasts. Dynasty lay comfortably across my breasts that were about 25 pounds and most likely felt like pillows to her. It was our first night together on Goode Avenue. Every 2 hours, I would wake up to breast-feed the baby. She latched onto my breast pretty well, and it was saving me tons of money, strengthening her immune system, and eventually slimming me down. The sleep felt so good, and the rest was well needed.

The morning had risen, and I placed Dynasty in her bassinet with her blankie on top of her. My goal was to wash up, brush my teeth, and at least place my hair in a wild bun and put a hoody and leggings on. My body was sore, but I had a C-section with King, so the sensations were familiar. I walked around the house and checked each room. King was already dressed and in the kitchen, eating a bowl of cereal, watching the news.

"Look at my li'l man. You already dressed and eating breakfast."

"Yea, Mom, I'm a big boy. I didn't want to wake you up, so I got myself together. You said to help you, right?"

"I sure did. Wow, you *are* growing up. Thank you, baby boy."

Someone knocked on the door.

"I'll get it."

"It's Aunt Lela and Uncle Marvin!" King rushed to check the peephole and opened the door.

"Well well well. Look at you! You got so big. I haven't seen you since you were a toddler. You got taller and so handsome," Aunt Lela began, hugging him and giving him tons of kisses.

"Hey, King, you helping your mama?" Uncle Marvin walked right in after King.

"Of course, I'm helping her!" We all laughed.

"Well, hello, my dear." Aunt Lela walked toward me with a gentle hug. Her eyes were filled with wisdom and love. She had a connection to my grandma, my granny, and my big mama that no one had. She was indeed the matriarch of the family at 80 years old. She looked great and gracious.

"Hi, Aunt Lela and Uncle Marvin. Thank you guys for coming." We all stood in the living room.

The baby's cries echoed.

"Is that Dynasty?"

"Yes, lemme go get her so you can see her." I moved swiftly to pick her up from the bassinet. She held no punches when it came to her crying.

"Yes, baby, Mommy got you. Stop crying, Mommy's baby. I got you." I placed her on my shoulder and walked toward Aunt Lela and Uncle Marvin.

"Look at her. My my my," Aunt Lela spoke with amazement.

Dynasty opened her eyes as soon as she heard Aunt Lela's voice.

"You wanna hold her, Auntie?" I gestured for her to take Dynasty.

"Yes, lemme hold this precious baby." She picked her up, cradling her body in both of her arms.

"Looking just like your mama. She does favor her daddy, though. Hey, precious. Hey, precious. We love you. Welcome!" Aunt Lela began singing to the baby.

"She is beautiful. Look at my great-niece. What a mighty and powerful name, Dynasty." Uncle Marvin stared into her eyes, affirming greatness.

"Mom, I'm gone to school. Cookie is outside." King went dashing toward the door.

"Love you. See you when you get back. Tell Cookie I said thank you."

"All right, Ma."

"See you, man." Uncle Marvin gave King a high five.

"Who is that? One of your friends or your employee picking him up?" Uncle Marvin asked.

"That's one of my good friends, but she is also doing some side work for me, like picking King up and dropping him off and running errands for me until I get stronger."

"That's good. Let me know if you need me to pick up King too. I could pick him up and bring him to you. Let me know if you need anything else. I'm here."

"Thank you so much, Uncle Marvin. I'll keep you in mind."

"Is she a crybaby like how you were when you were a baby?" Aunt Lela asked as she sat on the sofa with her.

"Lol. This is her first time crying. She seems pretty calm, and that's because she knows I'm right there."

"She's gonna be spoiled rotten, just like you were, but you were a crybaby. *Whewwwww*, you just wouldn't stop crying. I called your mama and told her I would come for a few days to help you."

"I didn't know she was a crybaby, Lela."

"Realllllllly?"

"She was, but she grew up to be strong, didn't she?"

"Dream is my baby. Yea, she strong, and I'm so proud of her."

"Aw, Uncle." I gave him a side hug. "Thank you for always coming through and being here since I arrived to go to Bison University."

"That's what your grandma and great-grandma would want me to do. Well, ladies, and li'l one, I'm gonna head back home. Call me if you need me. I know your aunt Nandi will be by to visit."

"OK, see you, Marvin. Talk to you tomorrow," said Aunt Lela as she held the baby.

"See you later, Uncle." I walked him to the door, then closed and locked it.

"Aunt Lela, would you like a bottled water or some tea?"

"No, baby, I got bottled water in my bag. I have diabetes, so I try to keep water on me."

"You hungry?"

"Not right now."

"Okay, I'm gonna eat a bowl of Raisin Bran with some soy milk. They have me on soft foods for the next few days because of the C-section."

"Oh yeah. Make sure you eat according to the diet that they prescribe and drink plenty of fluids. Are you breast-feeding?"

"Yes, I am."

"That's wonderful. That'll get that weight off of you fast. So definitely hydrate because you need nutrients, and so does the baby. You know I brought you a bag of herbal goodies."

"I knew you would. Thank you so much."

"Yes, we gonna get you together. After you eat cereal, I want you to come up with a grocery list of the stuff that you need, and I'm gonna go to the grocery store and get you some stuff. Plus, I'm gonna get some greens and corn bread for you to eat and a few cases of water."

"Yes. Your famous greens . . . that's what I need in my life. I plan on cooking it this evening for dinner. You are gonna love them, honey, and it'll feel good for your stomach. So tell me something, how do you feel?"

"To be honest, I feel exhausted. But I'm so happy she is here. I know it's gonna be a li'l hard raising two kids vs. one, but I can do it."

"Sure, you can. And take your time. The healing process takes time. Eat a lot of fiber and fruits and vegetables, drink your water and sometimes green tea, and you'll strengthen yourself. Those herbs are gonna help as well. So, have you heard from Kenya?"

"Yea, we spoke a few times. He called to check up on the baby and me, and it was a good feeling to hear from him. He called me right after I had the baby as well." I drank the milk out of the cereal bowl and washed my hands. A composition book and a pen were on the table. I began jotting down things that we needed from the store.

"Do you miss him? How are you processing him being away?"

"I miss him so much. I wish he were here. But I know that he cares, like really cares about the baby, and it gives me peace. We promised to talk at least every other day, and I'm gonna start writing to him next week."

"That's awesome. Moral support is support, and that's imperative." She was quiet, but her eyes were wide open. She was nosy. "You talk to your mama today?"

"Not today, but I'm gonna call her. The remote control is right next to you if you wanna watch TV." Old people always watched the stories, *Jeopardy*, and the news around the clock.

"Oh, honey, I might glance at it, but I have my witness books." Aunt Lela was a Jehovah's Witness. Every opportunity that she got, she would share those Watchtower books. She wasn't imposing, but if she got a moment, she was gonna share a good word, and best believe, she was gonna leave a few of *The Messenger* books on my coffee table or dresser.

"Here's the list, Aunt Lela. I'm gonna nurse the baby now." My mama instincts kicked in.

"Oh good." She handed the baby to me. I plopped next to auntie, adjusted my bra, and placed the baby blanket on my left shoulder and pulled my right breast to begin breast-feeding Dynasty. She latched on like a pro.

"How far is the store from here?"

"It's 3 minutes from here in a car. You can go up Goode Avenue all the way to Pike Avenue and make a right. Drive three blocks, and the supermarket is on the left side."

"That's really close. Well, let me use the restroom, then I'll be on my way. I have my cell phone, so I'll call you if I need you."

"Sure." Dynasty and I locked eyes. Breast-feeding was spiritual on so many levels. It was as if she were communicating with me. She made the cutest sounds as she was fed.

"Love you, princess. Love you, my pretty baby." I rubbed her tiny fingers. Her right dimple was strong, just like her daddy's.

My cell phone began ringing loud from the coffee table.

"Hey, baby girl!" It was my stepdad, Major.

"Hey, Major, whatcha doing?" I held the phone to my left ear and burped the baby with my right hand.

"Thinking about you. Your mom and I wish we were there with you. Our money is funny, but give us a few months." He was sincere.

"I know you guys would be here. I have support, though. Aunt Lela is here, helping out. Uncle Marvin, Sanai, and Cookie are supportive as well."

"Yea, that's good, baby girl. So how's our new princess, Dynasty, doing? Take a picture of her and send it to our cell phones."

"I just finished feeding her. She's so cute and peaceful. She doesn't cry much. She literally just stares deeply at you, eats, and sleeps."

"Is she sleeping through the night?"

"Kinda. Every 2 hours, I wake her up, or she wakes me up to feed her."

"Are you breast-feeding her?" My mom entered the conversation on speakerphone.

"Hey, Mommy. Yep. Can you believe it?"

"That is so good, Dream, because King would not take that titty, and you spent so much money on milk. How does your C-section cut feel?" My mom was always concerned.

"My body is beat, Mommy. My stomach is really sore. It's uncomfortable when I'm sitting up."

"That was a major surgery, girl. Take your time and try to sleep when the baby sleeps. Don't be quick to go back to work. Take all the help you can get until we can get there to help you. Where is Lela?"

"She's at the store."

"I talked to her, and she can't wait to make you some greens and corn bread. You need some fresh greens in your system anyway."

"Yea, I can't wait to eat them because they have had me on liquids and soft foods. I'm starting to get an appetite now."

"Keep eating the soft foods and get some fruit and veggies into your body. And lots of water too. How's the baby?"

"She good. I just sent a few photos of her to your phone. She is such a joy. She is so peaceful."

"How's King? Is he jealous of her?"

"King seems like he grew up in a week. He's been helping me. He seems a li'l distant with Dynasty. He probably thinking to himself, is this baby gonna take my place?"

"Yea, you were the same way. You did not want any parts of Ocean. When I had him, you wouldn't even come visit him. I spoiled you rotten, and you always wanted to be the only child. Ocean grew on you, though. Plus, he was cute. You couldn't help but love him. Well, King will learn to love Dynasty in due time."

"Yea, I think so too, Ma."

"Well, I'm gonna check on you tomorrow. We love you and take care of them babies. Rest, baby girl."

"Thank you, guys. Love you. Talk to you tomorrow."

Dynasty fell asleep. I placed her back in her bassinet, which was portable, and pushed it to the living room where I put a pink cotton teddy bear blanket on her. Wherever I went, my baby would go too. Aunt Lela was now at the door. You could hear her fidgeting with the doorknob. I opened the door, and she had bags of groceries. I thought about helping her, but she reminded me that lifting anything other than Dynasty would not work because of my incision. Two by two, she brought the groceries in the house.

"You just sit down. Close your eyes and take a few deep breaths. You don't need to pick anything up. I'm gonna take my time and put the frozen foods up. I got us a rotisserie chicken already cooked and some potato salad as well as a fresh avocado salad."

"Thank you so much, Aunt Lela. I appreciate you. I'm tired boots. I'm gonna lie down and watch you work." We laughed in unison.

"Precious, take a nap. Now, if that angel of yours wakes up, then you wake up—otherwise, nap. I'm gonna make sure your lunch is ready.

I'll prepare some fresh greens and corn bread for this evening. I'm gonna straighten up a little too and organize the house and your room some more. By that time, King should be home from school, and anything I need done, he'll help."

"Okay." I nodded off.

She didn't miss a beat. I loved how Aunt Lela was cool, calm, real, wise, and intuitive. You could just sit with her and learn so much about life and history. There was nothing that she did not know about my mom's side of the family. She was the historian. She remembered everyone's date of birth, how they lived their lives, the secret children out of wedlock, and then some. Her mother and my great-grandma were sisters, and she was raised with my grandma and great-uncles, but she really was my grandmother's first cousin and my second. In my family, if you are an elder, you get promoted to an aunt or uncle. It just makes sense.

Aunt Lela never had any children, and she never expressed why. She was married once to an abusive alcoholic who would later die. No one cared for him, and eventually, she would have the heart to leave him. If auntie dated, we never knew about it. She was nice looking for a senior and in really good shape. She studied the science of herbs and understood anatomy as if she were a wellness doctor. She would give you some goldenseal, echinacea, Tei-Fu, dandelion—you name it, she had the Nature Sunshine healing kit. What stood out to me the most was that if you became ill, she would be there like a nurse—never leaving your side. She took care of my uncles and my great-grandma until they transitioned. Perhaps it was her way of paying for a nice area in eternity.

Even when I was rebellious as a teenager, she would pick me up from summer school. Then we'd get a bite to eat and just talk about life. She had a pretty tight hold on me, and she wouldn't dare leave me outta her sight. She had me reading from *The Watchtower* every chance she could get. Some of the stuff made sense, while the other information seemed outta my realm and outta touch with reality. However, if you were grown and had a chance to kick it with Aunt Lela on a good day, you could drink a glass of red wine with her. She didn't mine sipping.

The aroma of garlic, onions, and fresh herbs permeated my home, reminding me of when I'd go to my granny's house and break bread with her over a plate of collard greens and hot water corn bread. Granny and I shared so much over hearty, soulful meals. Those were times that could not be replaced.

You could hear Cookie and King making their way through the front door.

"Shhhhhh," demanded Aunt Lela. "They're asleep, and they need to stay asleep. Dream is tired. She needs rest."

"Yea, she does," Cookie responded. "I'm sorry. Let me introduce myself. I'm Cookie. I'm Dream's friend slash assistant." She extended her hand.

"Hi, I'm Aunt Lela. I'm the great-aunt. Nice to meet you, Cookie. Thanks for bringing King home. I appreciate that. We gotta get her back stronger. My niece will need to have that whole work, life, and motherhood balance."

"You cooking greens?" Cookie worked her way to the kitchen.

"Yes, mixed greens. Got some collard, kale, and turnip. Cookie, I'll put some greens to the side for you if you like. I'm gonna make enough where we can freeze them. You eat greens, King?"

"Yes, I do, Aunt Lela, but do you have chicken?"

"A baked rotisserie chicken."

"Can't wait to eat that. I'm hungry!" King rubbed his stomach.

"Boy, you ain't no hungry. I just got you some hot Cheetos and a bottled water. You good. Don't get on their nerves, you hear?" Cookie was giving King the run down.

"That's what I'm talking about. Well, King, we are gonna have chicken, greens, corn bread, and salad for dinner. Does that sound good to you?"

"Yep!" He ran to his room and took off his book bag, then proceeded back to the kitchen.

"Do you think Dream needs anything?"

"I went to the grocery store earlier. She provided me with a list, and I got those things. She should be OK for now. Are you gonna take King to school in the morning?"

"Yes, I'll be here at 8:00 a.m. Be ready, man. OK, my boyfriend is outside waiting for me. But I'll see you tomorrow."

"See you," Aunt Lela responded.

"So, King, there are a few things I need you to do to help me. Put the rest of the groceries up. Make up your bed, clean up your room, and make up your mama's bed."

"OK, Aunt Lela," King responded.

"Thank you, sir. I'm gonna put this corn bread in the oven and make the salad now."

The aroma of fresh greens permeated my senses. My stomach growling was more important than sleep. Being on a soft diet was good because the baby fat was melting away; however, my body needed food and nutrients. My eyes were open. I yawned, stretching my arms out in a warrior 2 pose.

"Oh, the big baby is up," Aunt Lela observed. "The li'l baby is still asleep."

"She still asleep?"

"Yes, that's why I said nap when she naps."

"That's a good thing. Dem greens smell so good." I stood up and walked to the kitchen.

"I got us a big rotisserie chicken. The greens are about done, the corn bread is in the oven, and I added some tomato, onion, and cucumbers to the salad."

"Can't wait to eat." I went into the refrigerator and grabbed a Gatorade and a banana off the table to nibble on.

"How your body feel?"

"My stomach feels so tight where they cut me. I feel sore as a mug, but I'm in good spirits. I know the drill. This will eventually pass. Can't wait to get my body back."

"You'll get it back. The herb package that I brought you is on your dresser. Take the multivitamin with your food daily. It's best to take it in the a.m. For your mental health and metabolism, take the B Super Complex twice a day. Take the dandelion midday. It will relieve the water weight. There is some chamomile tea. Drink a cup of it in the evening before bedtime to relax and relieve anxiety."

Auntie did not play any games when it came to health!

"That's the plan. Thank you so much, Auntie. I so appreciate you. Where's King?"

"He on cleaning duty. Got him cleaning his room and making the beds up."

"Really? You are good 'cause he is lazy."

"I figured that, but he needs to get busy. He needs to be tasked, and he is certainly getting older."

"Hey, King! How was school?" I snuck up on him while he was making up my bed.

"Hey, Ma." He gave me a big hug. "School was good. I didn't get on red today. I was on yellow."

I held my stomach to keep from laughing.

"I'll take yellow any day of the week. Anything but red. But the day you get on green, we can go shopping, and that's my word."

"For real, Ma? You should have said something." He tried his hardest to lay out the comforter evenly.

"Yep. Get on green, son, and you will make life easier for your teachers, yourself, and less stress on your mama."

"Bet." He straightened up my room.

"The baby is crying," Aunt Lela yelled.

"OK, give me a second. I gotta pee first and wash my hands. Mommy's coming, baby."

The crying stopped. I walked into the kitchen, and Aunt Lela was showing King how to hold the baby. It was the cutest moment, but I was terrified.

"Lord Jesus, please don't drop my baby."

"She's showing me how to hold my baby sister," King said.

"I see. Just make sure you softly place your arm under her body, using both of your arms. It's like securing your football on the field, except that's a human being." We stood next to him for security, but he was doing a great job.

"She's pretty, Ma. How she get so light, though? You aren't light, and her daddy is black."

Aunt Lela began cracking up.

"You were born light too, and your daddy is as black as Kenya, and I'm brown. Some babies are born light, and over months or years, their real complexion comes out."

"Oh, OK. So, she'll probably be brown like you and me?"

"Most likely chocolate."

"Dinner is ready!"

"Here, take my sister." King handed her to me and ran to the sink to wash his hands. His appetite was never an issue.

"We know who's hungry. The greens are on the stove. The rest of the food is on the table. Dig in. Dream, you want me to hold the baby while you eat?"

"Sure. Gonna get a bowl of greens and that corn bread and a few slices of chicken. King, the pot is hot, so I'll get you a bowl of greens. You can put the sides on your plate."

The food gave a real Down South feel. Felt like Granny's house. The greens had a lot of fresh garlic in it, but it was succulent and nicely seasoned. The corn bread was baked to a tee, and with a tad bit of margarine, my temptations were elevating. On any given day, I could eat a pan of corn bread, a basket of yeast rolls, or monkey bread . . . You name it.

"Is it good?" Aunt Lela sat on the couch holding Dynasty as she watched the news.

"Yes, ma'am, it's delicious."

"This chicken tastes so good." All you could see were wings on King's plate. He loved chicken like he loved me.

After cleaning my plate, Aunt Lela and I switched places so that she could get her grub on, and I could breast-feed the baby.

"Hey, poo-poo. Hey, lovey, Mama's baby." I began feeding her.

"I thought I was your baby, Mama." King held no punches.

"You are my *big* baby, and she's my baby, baby."

"OK, Just checking."

"He's a trip, ain't he, Dream?"

"Yes, he is."

"Tomorrow afternoon, Marvin is going to pick me to take me to the airport. Do you need me to take you anywhere before I go? Do you have any errands you need to run?"

"Yes, I need to go to the bank and cut checks for my workers. I gotta pay them because they're running the operation while I'm on maternity leave. And maybe we could stop at Starbucks so I could get a Venti Mocha Frappuccino."

"Certainly. Let's leave after your friend picks King up."

"That works." I burped the baby and rocked her. Eventually, once everyone got their bellies on full, we sat together watching everything from *Jeopardy* to *Family Feud*. We had a wonderful time trying to guess the letters and solve the phrases. Aunt Lela was a breath of fresh air. After funning for a few hours, I made sure that King and I took our showers, and I put down Dynasty in her tub. Auntie said that she would get herself together once we were in bed and rested. Dynasty was like her dad, a night owl. Her eyes were slanted yet bright, and you could tell she was feeling the vibes because she was calm as lavender.

King was tucked nicely in his bed. I attempted to put Dynasty in her bassinet so that I could stretch my legs out and become comfortable in my postpartum body. It felt better sleeping on my side. The lights were dim, and I got my life knowing my babies were fed and sleeping well. Dawn would come before we knew it. On average, baby girl would wake up every 2 to 3 hours to be breast-fed. If I got 5 hours of sleep, I was lucky. For me, it was about being proactive, so I woke up at 6:00 a.m. so that I had time to get myself cleaned up, fully dressed, provide King support, and make sure that he had breakfast and a lunch to take to school. Mommy duty was real.

"You dressed already." Aunt Lela beat me to the punch and was reading her Bible in the room.
"Yes, I wanted to pace myself and get used to the process of getting us ready for school and eventually work."
"That's smart."
King was already getting himself ready for school. I put a bowl of Cheerios and 2% milk on the table and packed a Lunchable with an extra bag of chips by his bowl.
Then I got Dynasty together, packing up her diaper bag with two outfits, a sleeper, baby wipes, diapers, and placed her in the car seat in the living room.
"Ma, is this for me?" King asked, sitting at the table.
"Yes, that's your breakfast. Put your lunch in your book bag."
"OK, thank you." He took colossal bites of the Cheerios, then downed the milk as if he knew Cookie was coming in the house.
"Good morning." Cookie smiled from ear to ear as she entered.
"Hey, Cookie, where Miles at?"
"I dropped him off at school before I got here. I see you got yourself together. Where are you going?"
"I gotta run a few errands. Aunt Lela is gonna take me to a few places before she catches her flight today."
"She leaving already?"
"Yea, she is. She was such a help for me."
"I bet she was."
"I'm ready." King put his bowl in the sink and walked toward the door.
"Precious, give me a hug before you leave. I won't see you for a while. Cookie, lemme give you the Tupperware bowl of greens that I promised you." She handed it to her.
"Yes! Thank you. I can't wait to eat these for lunch. You ready, King?"
"I'm ready. Bye, Mom."
"See you later, King. Have a good day. Thanks, Cookie."

I gathered the diaper bag, along with my wallet, full names and payment amounts for the staff, and notes to myself. Dynasty was sound asleep, dressed in a pink baby sleeper, a pink baby hat, and a jean jacket. Aunt Lela pulled her suitcase to the living room, along with a small tote. She picked up the car seat with the baby in it, and I gathered her purse, locking the front door. We took our time securing the car seat, and I sat right next to Destiny. Our first stop was a drive-through Starbucks that was nearby. Going to Starbucks was such an energy booster for me.

Just inhaling fresh air and seeing people walk the streets dressed in their business uniforms gave me a sense of reality. I ordered a Venti Frapp without the whipped cream, a string cheese, and a pack of almonds. Aunt Lela ordered a tall coffee. All Aunt Lela wanted was the radio to be turned to smooth jazz and guidance on how to get to the bank. She was simple to please. We cruised throughout the city, taking the scenic route. She was able to see the gentrification and developments, as well as the progress of the toughest neighborhoods being transformed by businesses and charter schools. She was impressed to see how progressive Blacks were in town. She was able to drive past my office building and was thoroughly amazed.

Auntie secured a parking space in front of the bank. She watched the baby while I went to handle my business. I pulled out my payment notes and reviewed them. My entire staff was 1099s, and they were paid as consultants—with no taxes taken out. Umi put me on how to pay staff without the complications of taking taxes out. It would be their responsibility at the end of the year to pay Uncle Sam, and it was my duty to create an organized tracking system of payroll, expenses, and revenue. My workers were paid once a month on the 15th. There was Kiana, my assistant, who worked part-time; Aki, who was a full-time assistant but led day-to-day operations, tracked progress, researched, and assisted with grant writing, and he was the go-to for the staff when they had issues and concerns. Then you had Lee, who was the lead on outreach and mentoring; Tammy, who was the female lead in mentoring; Maaz, who was a male mentor; and Cain, who was a mentor and assisted Lee. Kiana and I had previously worked with Aki, Lee, and Cain at MOV, and Aki and Lee worked with me directly on several projects. Their work ethic was superb. Cain knew everyone and was a social butterfly who was well connected and was a strong person to mobilize outreach. However, you'd have to watch him closely. Tammy was in her mid-40s, who was referred to me by another sista that I knew from working in education. Tammy was energetic, she had her own car, and she was a go-getter. However, Aki would later put me onto her shady ways. My staff wasn't perfect, but the majority were Black men that I hired, and they all had rough stories on how they went from tragedy to triumph. They were rough around the edges, but they were thorough, coachable, reliable, committed to Passion for Change, and dedicated to progress.

While the summer contract for 6 weeks was for $10,000, my year-round mentoring and tutoring contract would pay out $12,000 to $20,000 a month depending on how many hours my staff would work combined. While witnessing thousands of dollars in my account at a minimum, $10,000 went to payroll. As an organization, it was our goal to max out on our hours collectively so that we could all eat and eat well.

I submitted the full names and salary amounts for each staff member. Although there was a small fee for cashier's checks, it was professional and a good source of tracking for bookkeeping purposes. Aki would pick up the checks the following day and forward the pink payment slips to Kiana for filing purposes. Altogether, payroll was $10,500. The expenses were $500, leaving me a payout of $5,500 for myself, of which $1,200 would go to my landlord for rent. I took about $1,000 in cash to have on hand and to give Cookie some money for helping me. I placed the cashier's checks in envelopes and stashed them in Dynasty's diaper bag like everything else.

We would run a few errands, including placing my rent in my landlord's drop box, taking Aunt Lela to get a few things for her trip from CVS, and grabbing lunch from Panda. Dynasty was up for most of the ride. She was observant, and her eyes were adjusting to the sunlight. You could tell that she was digging being outdoors. I breast-fed her during the ride and changed her on her changing pad. Multitasking was in me. Aunt Lela and I had a really good time together. We reminisced, we bonded, we laughed, and I took notes on how to heal my body. Minutes after we got home, Uncle Marvin was already outside. Old people were never late and didn't believe in wasting time.

The screen was unlocked. He announced himself and walked right in.

"It's Uncle Marvin. Where's my baby?"

"She's right here, Uncle Marvin." I held her as I walked around in the living room.

"She's up too. Look at those pretty dark brown eyes. She's alert." He smiled, gushing over her.

"You ready, Lela?"

"Yes, I am." She had her purse and small carry-on in her hand.

"I'll grab your suitcase and put it in the trunk. Do you have anything else?"

"You can put my carry-on in the trunk." She handed it to him. "Well, honey, I had a great time with you. Take your herbs. Take good care of yourself. I love you. Let me give Dynasty some suga." She kissed her on her forehead and reached out to hug me. She looked into my eyes and said aloud, "I'm proud of you!"

"Thank you." I held back my tears. She walked to the car, and Uncle Marvin drove her off to the airport. I was home alone, and the tears began to roll profusely down my cheeks. I used my sleeves to wipe them, but the waterfalls wouldn't stop. I sat on the couch holding my newborn in my right hand, and uncertainty in my left. My big kid was off to school, but I was home alone and somewhat scared because, for once, there was no one around. I was feeling postpartum, wishing Kenya was here to comfort me, and imagining how things would be better if he were there. I also wished my mama and stepdad would fly in. My close comrades were at work, hustling. I'd have to pace myself because my body felt different from when I gave birth to King. I was able to bounce back swiftly after a C-section with King. Yet, with Dynasty, it was as if I were moving slowly and in more pain.

Within 2 weeks, I was at the hair salon with King getting my hair done, taking walks in the neighborhood, and feeling healthy. However, my whole anatomy felt delicate with baby #2.

All I could do was nurse, watch TV, do a few things around the house, and get on my laptop. A few days would follow after Aunt Lela had left, and Aki was scheduled to come to my house to debrief me on the business. While watching TV, my stomach began leaking blood. The blood would not stop even with a warm compress, so I called Aki and asked him to hurry and pick us up because it was a medical emergency. I called my obstetrician to let him know that I was leaking from my C-section area, and he told me to immediately meet him at Labor and Delivery because that was a sign of infection. I grabbed Dynasty's diaper bag and put her back in the car seat and ensured that the stroller was by the door. Then I placed my wallet and keys in the diaper bag. Within a few minutes, Aki was at my house.

"What's wrong, Dream?"

"Grab the baby and put her in the car along with the diaper bag. I'm bleeding a lot from my C-section area, and it won't stop. My doctor said to bring me straight to Labor and Delivery," I said, giving him immediate orders. "At the bottom of the bag are all of your checks in envelopes. Make sure everyone is paid and signs off on the check-received list. I don't know what's going on, so hold this shit down."

"I got you, boss. Don't panic and breathe." He sped off, driving as quickly as he could, maneuvering through downtown traffic. My hospital was near Georgetown, and we were about 15 minutes away. I could feel blood gushing through my clothes, but there was nothing that I could do.

"I'm texting you my friends, Cookie's and Sanai's, numbers. If I have to stay, please communicate with them because most likely, they'll have to get my kids."

"I got you, boss." Aki was on the front line, and I needed him.

We pulled up in front of the hospital, and he parked and placed his emergency blinkers on. He informed the guy working in parking that it was a medical emergency. He grabbed the car seat and placed Dynasty inside the stroller, locking her in. We rushed past the information desk and took the elevator to Labor and Delivery.

"How can I help you?" a nurse greeted us.

"I'm supposed to meet my obstetrician here. I just had my baby here a few days ago, and I'm leaking blood from my C-section," I said, trembling.

"Is your name Dream Angelou?"

"Yes, ma'am." Aki stood next to me with the baby in the stroller.

"Please follow me to the back to your room. There's a gown all ready for you. Please put it on. I know you have the baby. Are you gonna stay with her."

"I'm her staff member. I'm gonna wait until the doctor comes and reach out to her support system."

"Fine. That will work."

"Thank you very much."

There was a bathroom in the room. I literally was right back where I started as if I were delivering another baby. I went into the bathroom and changed into the gown, placing my clothes into a plastic bag. The blood continued to ease out of my stomach. I used toilet tissue to wipe what I could, then put the plastic bag with my clothes in the closet area. I took a few deep breaths and lay on the hospital bed, adjusting it so that I could sit up.

Aki was a devout Muslim who was well disciplined and held his composure. Dynasty fell fast asleep.

Dr. Nasir walked in, wearing his full uniform and gloves.

"Dream, what happened, dear? Were you lifting anything heavy?"

"No. I've been in pain since I left the hospital and very uncomfortable. I have only held the baby."

"Let me see what is going on here."

He had a nurse to help him who brought in what looked like a mobile station of instruments and medicine. He placed my feet in stirrups, then looked under my gown with a light and began checking the incision.

"You're clotting. Your C-section burst open. This is not good."

"Oh Lord."

"Expect to be here for a few days. I need to get these blood clots out of you so that they don't travel to your lungs." He injected me with Novocain.

Tears ran through the corners of my eyes.

"Aki, can you get in touch with Cookie and Sanai and let them know that I'm here and that it's a medical emergency. Ask Lee to come get Dynasty and to coordinate with Sanai on bringing the baby to her. Have Cookie bring King to Sanai as well. Hold the fort down with Kiana. Let the staff know what's going on. Pray for me." I stared at the ceiling and began to feel Dr. Nasir open my stomach back up.

"Inshallah. Inshallah. My prayers are with you, sis. Allah has you, and we got you. It is my duty to keep things intact. I will make those phone calls and make sure your children are safe," he assured me and left.

"Dr. Nasir, will there be a nurse to help with my baby? She's asleep now, but she'll need to be changed and fed. Someone will be here later on to get her."

"Yes, there will be a nurse to help, but we gotta get these clots outta you." The nurse opened up my stomach so that Dr. Nasir could begin suctioning out all of the clots. I felt pressure and there was a lot of blood. He placed the clots in a biohazard can. For about 30 minutes, he meticulously took every clot that he could find out of my womb. I could hear the sounds of suction, pulling, and pressure. My spirit was in a trance, but the pain was limited. I was near death again; yet, I was willing to fight—my babies needed me more.

Once Dr. Nasir suctioned out all the clots that he could see, he and the nurse began washing out the womb thoroughly and then equipping me with rounds of antibiotics on both IVs and a blood thinner.

"Young lady, you are fortunate that you recognized what was going on with your body. This could have gone really bad."

"I'm glad that I came too. But I thought when you sealed up my incision after the C-section that I was sewn up 100 percent. What happened?"

"Your incision was closed well with invisible stitches. I don't know what caused the clotting and hemorrhaging. Only 4 percent of women have postpartum hemorrhaging. My goal now is to get you well. We will have you on antibiotics via IV for the next few days. And if the infection is gone and your vitals are good, we'll release you."

"My stomach feels open."

"I had to leave the incision open so that it can heal naturally from the inside out, and the drainage will be taken care of through wound care. Twice a week once you are discharged home, you will come to me for wound care so that I can clean out your wound because you will not be able to do it."

"Oh my God! What is *really* going on? Come on, are you serious?"

"Yes, the healing will be a process. You will get through this. You won't be able to drive for a few months or pick up anything but your purse and your baby. The goal is to get your body to heal so you can live a normal life. Sometimes this happens. Don't get down," he said with his Syrian accent.

Lee came and got Dynasty and took her to Sanai. I was weak and exhausted. It was as if I had surgery all over again with limited numbing. I explained to Lee that I needed him to work with Aki to ensure the fundamentals of business were flowing even with my hospitalization. Dynasty and Lee were born on the same day. They were Libras, so they had a real connection. Lee was like the big brother that I never had, and I was like the big sister that he had lost years ago to a drug overdose. He had my back too.

I called Sanai as soon as the doctor said I could and explained to her what was going on and how much I needed her to take care of the kids for a few days. Luckily, I had gone to the hospital on a Friday, and the hospital was down the street from Sanai's job, where she worked as an assistant manager for a prestigious credit union. Sanai had Lee bring Dynasty straight to her and proceeded to coordinate with Cookie to get King. No matter where I was in life, Sanai, was right there. We had 15 years of sisterhood, and we were each other's ride or die. Her concern was that I got well and that I paced myself at healing because she knew that it was hard for me to sit down. For this season, I had no choice but to sit down.

My last two calls before being stabilized in a recovery room were to contact my mom and stepdad and my uncle Marvin and aunt Nandi. Upon picking up the phone first, Aunt Nandi heard in my voice a cry for help.
Her swift response was, "Say no more. I'm on my way to you now!" Although Aunt Nandi was an in-law, in my eyes, she was blood. She was indeed an elder that I could count on from my college journey to adulthood to motherhood. She was loving and transparent. She was very close to my maternal grandma, and once my grandma passed away my freshman year of college, Aunt Nandi really stepped up and stood in the gap. Whatever phase of my life that I was in, Aunt Nandi was there, never judging and, most of all, demonstrating unconditional love.
"Baby, I know you are making your calls, but I need you to use the arm that the IV is *not* in because we need the medicine to get into your body. When you use your right arm, you are slowing up the process," my assigned nurse came in to check up on me. She was a sista. "You'll be on IV fluids today. Tomorrow, I might can get you some Jell-O, broth, or frozen yogurt."
"I'm sorry. I'll use my left hand. I gotta call my mama. Thank you. I appreciate you," I responded.

Using my left hand, I called my mommy.

"Mommy," my voice quivered. She knew in the first second something was wrong.

"I'm at a funeral with your stepdad. His cousin B passed away."

"Wow, OK."

"What's wrong?"

"I'm in the hospital, Mommy." I started crying.

"What? Who got the baby and King?"

"Sanai. My stomach was leaking blood this morning. My staff member, Aki, rushed me to the hospital because my doctor said I needed to meet him at the Labor and Delivery. He found blood clots everywhere," I cried profusely.

"What? Oh my God! I never liked him anyway. He wasn't good when you had King, and now he damn near killed you. God got you, though! Lord Jesus, baby, I wish I was there. Did he get the clots out?"

"Yea, so he says. I'm in a room now, and they got me hooked up to IVs. They're giving me antibiotics and blood thinners and are saying I gotta go to wound care."

"What?" she screamed through the phone. "Wound care? That sounds like a lawsuit. Malpractice. He fucked you up! He didn't sew you up right. Jesus, Jesus, heal and protect my baby and grandbabies. Who's there with you?"

"Lee and Aki were here, but they've gone to help with getting the kids to Sanai and handling company business. Aunt Nandi is on her way."

"Thank you, Jesus! Send angels her way, Lord. Major, talk to Dream; she's in the hospital."

"Hey, baby girl, what's wrong?"

"My C-section was leaking with blood-forming clots. It was really scary, Major. They seem to have gotten the clots out. I'm in the hospital now on all types of antibiotics to fight the infection."

"Baby girl, baby girl, I am so sorry. If I get some money, I will at least send your mama to be out there with you. Seems to me that that obstetrician didn't do a good job sewing you up. That's ridiculous that you delivered my grandbaby and had to come right back."

"This is too much," I continued to sob. "My incision is opened. I'll be going to wound care a few times a week."

"You need wound care so that you don't get another infection. Don't miss that for nothing. Who's gonna help you with the kids?"

"Sanai will have them for a few days. My friend Cookie is helping as well. I'm gonna talk to Aunt Nandi as well when she gets here."

"Yea, Aunt Nandi and Sanai are thorough, so I'm glad they are there. Just hold on, baby girl. You ain't gonna stay down for long. What the devil meant for evil, God is gonna mean for good. You stand on that word. Keep affirming to yourself that God got you 'cause He does! You not cut from the same cloth as everyone else. You know that, right?"

"I just don't know, Major. This is a setback. I'm overwhelmed." The snot and tears saturated my face. There was no tissue. I took a portion of the sheet to wipe my face.

"A setback for a mighty comeback. Watch how bold, how strong, how amazing you become. You are my golden child. You are my golden child," he repeated. "God has never failed you, Dream— remember that. They need us back at the funeral, but we're gonna call you as soon as we come from the burial, OK?"

"OK." The emotional and physical pain were both tormenting me.

"Dream, I have never seen you fail in the face of adversity. God got you. You won't fail now."

As much as I felt sorry for myself, there was a divine connection that I had to the Most High, where, in the darkest hour, I found favor in His sight. I never needed Him so much in my life.

"You'll bounce back stronger than before." Major dropped that word and hung up the phone.

God entrusted me with a prince and princess, and for once, I had to fight like our lives depended on it. The sounds of the IV drippings and blood pressure machines rocked me to sleep. I was breathing.

# Chapter 19

*Good Stock*

"Ms. Dream, does that hurt?" The wound care specialist slowly but surely opened up my incision. I closed my eyes tightly. I couldn't bear the sight of my stomach being wide open or the pressure of the instruments that they were using to look into the whole area of where my C-section took place.

"It's irritating, and I feel the pressure."

"Yes, I understand. I will do my best to try to make you comfortable. I'm going to irrigate the inside of your incision, utilizing an instrument to clean the womb thoroughly and assess if there was anything foreign left in your womb."

My eyes couldn't be any tighter. "OK." My stomach was wide open, and I lay on the wound care bed like a veteran. My stomach was itchy, slightly burning after the irrigation, yet there was a feeling of relief that I was on the road to recovery.

"How long will it take for my stomach to heal and close?"

"Several months. The goal is to observe your stomach, and the incision will close on its own. Right now, your stomach looks like a mouth." He held up his right hand and postured it, imitating a puppet's mouth. I wanted to laugh and cry at the same time, but I just listened instead.

"You want a closed healthy mouth without any sign of infection, so that is why the process of healing should be slow and steady. When you come twice a week, we will irrigate, clean, use necessary antiseptics, and dress the wound," he assured me.

"Several months? I have children to take care of, including a newborn! I have a business that I'm running. This is a blow." My eyes watered up.

"You cannot drive, ma'am. We gotta put you back together. Those clots could have been fatal. Now that you are doing much better, you are in a good place to heal. All you have to do is keep your wound clean in between the days that you don't see us. Do you have someone at home to help you to clean your wound?"

"My Aunt Nandi can help me or a friend of mine."

"Good. So, no baths until your stomach is fully closed and healed. You can take showers but make it quick and make sure your wound is covered. I will give you packs of medical wound dressings and adhesive tape to take home with you. If you run out, you can go to a CVS store."

"That adhesive tape hurts when you take it off. Your stomach is extremely sensitive too. So, take your time removing the tape," he said as he began dressing the wound.

"Also, I found a few staples inside your incision. Your obstetrician could have done a better job."

"Are you serious? What the hell was Dr. Nasir doing down there? He butchered me. He really fucked me up! My first C-section did not go like this." My nerves were elevated.

"Young lady, your focus must be on healing. You are here now. Take your time and know that as long as you are committed to doing your wound care sessions, your stomach will heal, and in months, you will be back to business," he said, smiling.

"Yea, I better because this ain't right."

"You are free to go. I'm all done. See you in 2 days." He had a great bedside manner, even though I was snappy.

"Thank you very much. See you in a few." I pulled up my black leggings over my bulging gut, tossed my gown, and then put on my bra, V-neck, and hoodie. Just getting up to walk was difficult because of the reality that no one really knows how much you utilize your stomach muscles until you have a stomach injury. I wore socks with flats or sliders during this process because bending over to tie my shoes was an issue as well. I couldn't wear jeans, only leggings. I could barely brush my hair into a bun or ponytail 'cause again, I was using my stomach muscles. No Mac lipstick, no weave, no fly clothes on, no jewelry, no weave—it was just me in raw form.

Things were different. I relinquished my "Ms. Independent" attitude and humbled myself, welcoming the support of my uncle Marvin and aunt Nandi. The kids and I needed to stay with them on my journey to healing and wellness. I could not do things on my own, and they were right there for me. Uncle Marvin waited patiently for me outside. He watched the baby while I was at wound care. King was at school. I took my time walking to the car, unlike my usual racing self.

"Hey, y'all." I opened the car door. Dynasty was sitting in her car seat, bright-eyed with curly black hair smiling in a cute yellow sleeper.

"That wasn't too long. How you feel?" Uncle Marvin asked.

"It was uncomfortable, but not a lot of pain. They really irrigated the area. The wound feels clean but itchy."

"Yea, that itchiness means you are healing. Did the doctor or nurse provide an update?"

"He said I would not be able to drive for months." My voice cracked. "He said driving requires the usage of my stomach muscles and that I need to wait 9 months before I can drive. That ain't happening."

"Niece, 9 months is a long time. Well, we pray that you heal sooner than that so you can get back to your life and running your business." He began driving back toward his home, which was about 30 minutes away in a nice upper-northwest section of town.

"Unc, this is so hard and such an inconvenience. I can't be depending on you to take me to wound care or to take King to school. You have a life too."

"We're family, and you need us to be right by your side until you get stronger. Plus, I love the kiddos being around, and Dynasty is a cutie pie. She is just quiet and cool. Surprisingly, she rarely cries. She is a joy to be around. And King is a li'l man with a burst of energy. We love y'all." Uncle Marvin was sincere.

"I appreciate you and Aunt Nandi. Thank you very much for everything. I swear when I get rich, I got y'all." He laughed, and I tried too, but it pained my stomach too much.

"You gonna be the one to do something, Dream. There is something special about you. Ever since you touched down at Bison University, it was like we knew you were gonna be great. This is just a little obstacle."

"You're right. I need to be hopeful that this too shall pass." I looked back and started playing with Dynasty. Her hands were so soft, and her smile became wider and wider. She was so content and peaceful, which made life smoother on my end.

While at their house, I took the time to pump as many bottles of breast milk as I could, just in case we were out at appointments, and Unc had to feed her. But she didn't seem hungry. She was simply observing her surroundings.

We arrived at Uncle Marvin and Aunt Nandi's house Uptown. They had a beautiful white three-level home, where the front lawn was perfectly manicured. You could hear the birds chirping and the chimes that swung on the front porch. The neighborhood was filled with entrepreneurs, doctors, and professionals, and most were upper-middle class or wealthy. Uncle Marvin retired from the airlines, and Aunt Nandi was a retired educator. In their 20s and 30s, they were revolutionaries who were in the field fighting for the rights of Blacks and making a mark in the community. They were also college graduates who were educated and empowering. They both had one child each before their marriage, but any couple that could stay married for more than 3 decades, I saluted.

Together, they were a symbol of Black excellence, and I admired them. Uncle Marvin carried the car seat with Dynasty into their house to prevent me from lifting. Aunt Nandi greeted us with a warm smile at the front door.

"Well, hello, darlings." She hugged me softly and went to take Dynasty out of the car seat to hold her. She truly had the ambiance of an elder.

"Look, I washed my hands," she said, showing her clean hands. "I know how you are about your baby."

"Auntie, you good." I walked in and sat on her African-designed love seat. She sat right across from me, holding the baby. Uncle Marvin walked right past us and went down into his basement, which was his man cave. He sat in a tall red chair that was draped in football paraphernalia, and right behind his chair was a full bar containing beer, whiskey, Cognac, wine, and spirits. Uncle Marvin had to have him a fresh cold beer as he watched his shows on TV.

"What did the doctor say?" Aunt Nandi cut to the chase.

"He says I have 9 months before I can drive." My emotions started festering.

"Yea, your body needs to heal. You were cut open twice within a few weeks, and it was serious. Your wound has to heal. We got you, though, Dream. We got the kids too. Take some time and stay here until your body is strong and well." She made full eye contact. "Thank you for allowing me and the kids to stay here, but I can't wait 9 months. I'm gonna continue to go to wound care, but I may need your help to show me how to clean my wound because I don't know how to."

"You got ants in your pants, but let your body heal, please. Let me see your stomach." Aunt Nandi was indeed a medicine woman. She probably was a doctor in her past life. She studied and understood anatomy and infused natural herbs and created concoctions that promoted healing. She was about 4 foot 11, curvy, light-skinned with freckles, with coolie Native American hair that reached the middle of her back. She didn't have that privilege attitude of most light-skinned Blacks. Instead, she carried herself in the spirit of Angela Davis. I stood up, struggling to take the tape off the dressing and opened up my wound, closing my eyes.

"Lord Jesus, what did they do to my baby?" She held the baby on her right shoulder, stepping back and leaning slightly to the side. "It look like a mouth," she motioned her hands and made a mouth. "Do it look like *Little Shop of Horrors*? Do it look crazy?"

"Oh boy, yes, it look like *Little Shop of Horrors*. What they are probably gonna do, Dream, is have it heal from the inside. What you do is take some warm water and gently clean the wound, add some Neosporin to it, and then dress the wound. Did they give you dressing and surgical tape?"

"Yes, I have boxes of the dressing gauze and two rolls of tape. It's so embarrassing because sometimes when I change the dressing during the day, it smells horribly. I use some peroxide and cotton balls. How long will it take to close up?"

"The peroxide is good with warm water. The smell is because it's a raw wound, and you're perspiring. I have some Neosporin for you to apply after you clean the wound. I'll add a few healing herbs that you can use afterward, and then you can dress up the wound. Time is a healer, and God hears your cries." The baby began getting fussy. I went to the bathroom to tape up my wound and to wash my hands. Dynasty gave off the vibes that she needed to be fed and changed. Aunt Nandi handed her to me. I placed a burping cloth on my shoulder and a soft blanket and began breast-feeding her. She needed her mommy. My son needed his mommy. God-willing, I was gonna heal. Dynasty latched on really good as I sat introspectively. There was no doggone way that I would stay in auntie's house for more than 3 months, let alone 6 or 9 months. That wasn't me. I didn't want anyone feeling sorry for me—not even me.

Auntie Nandi made it real comfortable for us. The baby and I were in the guest room, which was covered in earth colors and gave off Native American vibrations. King was in another guest room where he was coolin'. Most of his days were spent in school. Uncle Marvin would fix him breakfast in the morning, take him to school, and pick him up for me. During the day, I would spend bonding with the baby, nursing, getting used to motherhood, and gradually getting back on my laptop to check on my staff. With Aki and Kiana taking the lead and Lee running the outreach and field component, Passion for Change was making progress, which gave me a sense of hope.

"You heard from Kenya?" auntie asked from the kitchen.
"No, I haven't talked to him. Normally, when you don't hear from an inmate, they may be on lockdown."
"Let's pray they are not on lockdown," she said as she handed me a long yellow notepad, a pen, and an envelope with some stamps.
"You have a lot on your mind. Put it on paper. Take your time and write to him. There is so much you need to say. He misses you, and you miss him. Write him a letter and put it in the mailbox that's at the corner." She was adamant. My emotions were triggered. I nodded in silence.
Aunt Nandi knew how to get under the surface and bring up what needed to be addressed. Writing was therapeutic for me, and there was so much that I needed to say. Kenya had nothing but time to read my thoughts. I took Dynasty into the bedroom and rocked her to sleep. Although I needed the rest, what auntie said was real game that needed to be soaked up. My cell phone began vibrating.
"Hey, baby!" It was Kenya.
"Oh my God! I miss you so much. What took you so long to call me?"
"Baby, these crackers had us on lockdown. We couldn't call out or see visitors. I was writing to you, though. This was my first day out, and you were the first person that I called."
"Ken, it's been so hard. I was hospitalized. My stomach busted open." My anxiety rose.

"What? What happened? Don't tell me that. Are you OK? Where's the baby?" He was hysterical.

"I was watching the baby and TV, and I noticed my stomach was dripping blood. It would not stop. I was scared out of my mind. My body hasn't felt the same since I fainted. And when I came home, I was uncomfortable and in pain. I called the doctor, and he said to come back to Labor and Delivery. Then I called Aki to come get us and rush us to the hospital." You could feel his painful silence.

"Baby, I wish I was there with you and Dynasty. I'm supposed to be there protecting you, and I'm in this hellhole. Did they have to operate on you?"

"No, Dr. Nasir took the clots out of my stomach and drained the blood. I think he jacked up my C-section. He didn't stitch me up properly."

"He probably didn't. These doctors don't care about Black women and their health. You got a lawsuit on your hands. So, did they have to staple or sew your stomach back up?"

"No, my stomach is open now, Ken. It looks like a mouth wide open. It's so nasty to look at. It's hard to keep it clean too. The specialist said it gotta heal from the inside out. Me and the kids are staying at Uncle Marvin and Aunt Nandi's house until I get well. I can't drive, they say, for 9 months."

"Thank God you are there. I feel a lot better knowing that you and the kids are with auntie and unc. No doubt they gonna have your back. You gotta keep your wound clean. I know all about wound cleaning from when I was shot up. You can do it. You gotta let your body heal gradually. You gonna bounce back, champion."

"It's so hard." I began bawling. "It's like I'm handicapped. I can't even take King to school. I can't go to work. It's like I'm just existing."

"Dream, don't think like that. I was shot twice, multiple times, and I'm still here. You can't give up. Let your body heal, and you'll be back in no time. Who has the Benz?"

"The Benz is at the house. Sometimes I have Cookie use it to run errands for me."

"Be careful about letting Cookie use your car. She lives in the Toga, and that's the ghetto. I don't want anyone stealing or ransacking your car. How's daddy's baby?"

"She's getting big. She's such a joy. She's so cute. She look like a Panda."

"You have 1 minute," the automated jail system announced.

"Damn. I hate this place. This is what I need you to do . . . Focus on healing, taking care of the baby and King. Pace yourself. You're gonna get back. This is gonna make you stronger. Write me every day, and I'm gonna write you every day. I'll try to call you every other day. Also, please, baby, go online and add money to the phone, and when you get a chance, add money to the books. The government paying you on time?"
"I got you, Ken. Pray for us, and I'll pray for you. Aunt Nandi gave me a notepad and a pen today, an envelope and stamps," I smiled. "I'ma write you tonight. Call me tomorrow, okay? I'll add more money to the phone. I love you." The octaves of my voice went up. "Love you too, Dream, and kiss the baby." The automated jailhouse system disconnected the vibrations.

Nine months could not have come any faster. As Dynasty slept, the yellow notepad paper was saturated with five pages of ink, real expressions, and saltwater tears.
I never needed Kenya so much in my life, and he never needed me so much in his life. While incarcerated, he was maturing, growing up, and came with a wise perspective that he never displayed when he was on the street. I was committed to writing him through the week. It was indeed a form of therapy for me. He continuously called, if not daily, every other day just to hear his daughter babble and to flow into deep conversations about the pursuit of happiness and dreams, as well as what life would look like for us once he came home. In my heart of hearts, I did not want to raise my babies alone. It was tough raising King on my own, but with two children, I needed the support and unconditional love, which required a unified front.

My support team was thorough and airtight. However, one of my weaknesses was that I put too much trust in those I considered my comrades and friends. If I loved you, I would break bread with you. Those vibrations weren't always on the same frequency. Uncle Marvin and Cookie rotated the responsibilities of taking King to school and picking him up while I focused on attending my wound care appointments and becoming truly well. While Uncle Marvin is blood, Cookie was an Uptown girl from Clay Street, where we both experienced the struggle and promised each other that whoever succeeded first, she would put the other one on. This was a "girl code" that we abided by.

One brisk morning, King awaited Cookie to pick him up to take him to school. After eagerly waiting by the front door minutes . . . and more minutes, Cookie never showed up. In one sense, I was worried because Cookie had my pretty girl Benz, but my son would miss school, and he had perfect attendance. Cookie was usually reliable, but this time, her movement was peculiar.

"Hey, Cookie, where you at? King is late for school."
"D, I'm so, so sorry." Cookie sounded like she had been weeping.
"What's going on? What's wrong?"
"Dream, Z took the car last night and never came back." She sounded like the biggest idiot of the year.
"What the fuck are you talking about, girl? You let a nigga take my car? Are you crazy? What were you thinking? He didn't come back with my shit?" I stood up pacing. King knew by my body language and my mouth that there was a B.I.G. problem. He kept looking.
"Ma, where's the car?"
"I'll tell you later, King, give me a second."
"No, D, he left last night to fill up your gas tank, he said."
"Bitch, what? Dummy, you couldn't see that if he was gonna fill up the gas tank that he had a mission to accomplish? Now, where's my car? Where do you think my car is?"
"He took your car to some female's house about 7 minutes away from here . . . some lady named Shirley that he used to mess with when I met him. He's at her house."
"How you know?"

"'Cause, I called his phone a million times, and he didn't answer. I had one of my homegirls drive past there, and sure enough, your car was sitting out front."

"What's the address?"

"You want the address for real?"

"You think I'm gonna let some cheating-ass, no-good nigga run off with my car? He got me all the way fucked up. He better be glad Kenya is locked up 'cause he would make that nigga disappear."

"Dream, I'm so sorry, so sorry. I didn't think he would do no shit like this to me. I'm so embarrassed . . . so embarrassed. Will you be able to get someone to take King to school?"

"King is gonna miss school today 'cause of you! But what I need is the address and location of where this female lives so that I can go get my car. Text it to me. I'm gonna have one of my staff members bring me to wherever he at and get my shit."

"Dream, you can't drive. Didn't your doctor say that?"

"Look, I can't trust you to do something as simple as take my son to school and pick him up for a few dollars and make sure my car is good. You let this nigga work you. So, it doesn't matter if I can drive. I'm driving my shit today 'cause I'm all that I have at this point. Text me the goddamn address and meet me over there in 45 minutes."

"I'm texting you the address now. I'll get a ride over there. Be careful, Dream. I'm very sorry."

"Naw, that nigga better be careful. I know goons too. Don't take advantage of me like that," I said and hung up the phone. I immediately called my staff member Lee to tell him what was going on. Lee was extremely pissed off that Cookie would allow a man to get over on her like that, but he was more upset that Z had the audacity to take my car as if it were his and not bring it back. Lee was concerned about the kids and me, and he knew that I was at my weakest, so he vowed to check up on me more until Kenya came home. Lee was in the field, and he wasn't too far from us. Lee was an OG from the heart, but he was humble, laid-back, and cool. Although he caught a murder beef years prior to me meeting him, he had the heart of a lion and a protective soul. He said that he was gonna pick up Cain, one of the other male staff members, for backup—just in case things popped off.

"King, watched the baby while I throw on some clothes real quick. We gotta go get my car. Lee is gonna take us. Cookie's dumb ass let

her boyfriend take my car last night, and he never brought it back."
It was hard to control my emotions.
"What? Are you for real? How he gonna take your car? That's crazy.
If Ken was here . . ." King shook his head.
"If Ken was here, this would have never happened. Watch your
sister."
I went into the bathroom and wiped myself down, secured my
wound with a new dressing and tape, then pulled my jeggings over
my stomach. I put on a pair of sneakers and a black leather coat. Lee
pulled up in a jiffy with Junkyard Go-Go Band blasting and Cain in
the front seat. King and I loaded the back with the car seat and baby.
Lee remembered that the baby was with us and turned the music
down.
"Where we going?" Lee was straight up.
"We're going to Twenty-first Street NE right off of Benny Road."
"Oh, you going up in the hood," said Cain. "Boss, who is this nigga
that got your car?"
"It ain't my nigga. It's Cookie's boyfriend. She let him fill up my
tank with gas, and the rest is history."
"Don't tell me that, Ms. Dream. He got some good gas in that nice
Mercedes-Benz and went to the next broad house."
"That's *exactly* what he did," Lee added. "But what he don't know is
that I will tear a nigga up behind Boss Lady. Dream, you like my
sister."
As we drove closer to Twenty-first Street NE, it was as if we all felt
a connection. The ride became silent. King knew my capabilities and
how ratchet I could be and fell back to see what the end result would
be.
"Ms. Dream, we have a client that lives right over here. If I'm not
mistaken, he lives right over here on this very block." Lee pulled up
as soon as he saw Cookie and her friend standing outside, looking
lost.
"Oh, really? Yea, my mentee live over here. The one I told you his
mama and stepdad seem like they could care less about this boy."
"Wow! I hope you're documenting your visits in your case notes."
"I sure am."
"King, stay here with your sister. Keep her some company. We'll be
right back."
"OK, Mom."

Lee, Cain, and I hopped out of Lee's car like we were the police. Cookie was shaking, looking like a chicken with her head cut off. She had never seen me with other men.

"Dream, that's the apartment right there," she pointed. "You see that window? That window is Shirley's bedroom window. He probably is in there."

"ZZZZZZZZZZZZZZZZZ!" I yelled toward the window, which was on the second floor of a duplex. "I know you hear me. It's Dream. Drop my keys down so I can take my car. Give me my damn keys!" I screamed. Lee and Cain stood right beside me.

"Man, fuck that shit. Call the police, Dream. The police ain't gonna play with this nigga. They will get your keys ASAP. He playing games." You could see the blinds open up from Shirley's bedroom. One of them was lurking at the window.

"There he go right there," Cookie whispered. She was indeed shaky.

"911 Emergency, how can I help you?"

"Hi, I'm calling because a friend of a friend stole my Mercedes-Benz. I'm at the location of where my car is, and I need my keys. The guy won't give them to me."

"Excuse me, what is your name and the location?" Even the emergency operator was confused.

"My name is Dream Angelou. I am at 999 Benny Road. My friend allowed her boyfriend to take my car last night, and he has refused to return it. I'm at the location of where my car is. I need my keys."

"Is the registration in the vehicle to prove that is your vehicle? Do you have your license on you?"

"Yes. I do."

"Do you feel safe?"

"Not really, but I am not alone."

"I'm dispatching an officer now to you who is already in the area. Stand by."

"Thank you very much." I glanced over at Lee's car to make eye contact with King. I gave him the thumbs-up, and he gave me the thumbs-up back to let me know that they were good.

"Are they on their way?" Lee started smoking a cigarette.

"Yea, they're their way."

"That's good because you don't got time to be dealing with no clown shit. You can tell your friend ain't focused, and this nigga probably do this all the time to women, but he's gonna learn today."

The police car arrived with two Black male officers. I pulled my license outta my wallet. They began walking toward us.

"Who is Dream Angelou?"

"I am, sir."

"Let me see your license." I handed it to him. "So, what's going on now?"

"Mr. Officer, I just had a baby. I have two kids, and I let my friend, who is standing over there, have my car so that she could help my son get back and forth to school and assist me because I had a bad C-section. She let her boyfriend take my car last night to fill it up with gas, and he never returned."

"Whoa, this is a bit too much."

Cookie walked over and stood next to Cain.

"Which car is yours?"

"It's the silver Mercedes-Benz. The E Class."

"Oh, that makes sense. So, he's refusing to give the car back to you?"

"Yea, Officer. I brought her over here so that she can get her keys and take her and her kids back to the house. This is ridiculous."

"And who are you?" The officer was connecting the dots.

"We are her employees. We work for Ms. Angelou. We got her back too," Lee was serious.

"So, all you need is your keys? Is this building locked?"

"Yes, it is, Officer." Cookie made her way closer.

"And you are?"

"I'm Cookie. I'm Dream's friend. That's my boyfriend who took her car and never brought it back. This is a female house that he's at."

"Whoa. This is a mess. Well, you gave her car to him, and you see the results? Ms. Lady, I hope that you learn from all of this," said the officer. Lee and Cain shook their heads in disgust.

"Eh, Cookie, what's his name, and what's the female's name?"

"His name is Z, and her name is Shirley. That's her apartment on the second floor. You can see them peeping down at us."

"Z, this is the police. Throw Dream Angelou's keys down out of the window or bring the keys down to us." One officer stood under the window, while the other officer went to the front door and banged on it. You could see a woman about 45 staring out of the window.

"That's that bitch!" Cookie was in her feelings.

"Oh, I know her. That's Ms. Shirley. I told you, Ms. Dream. That is our client's mother. So don't tell me the tall, light brown dude with the glasses is the nigga who got your keys?"

"What? Cain, are you for real?" asked Lee.

"Yea. that's them," Cookie confirmed.

"This whole situation is getting more and more wild by the second," the officer standing by the door responded.

"I just want my keys!" I folded my arms in disbelief at all of the unnecessary drama.

"Z! This is MPD Police! You have the car keys to a silver Mercedes-Benz. Drop the keys out of the window. If you do not, we will have to come in and arrest you. This is your last opportunity!" We all stood waiting. By this time, the neighbors were looking out the window, like "Nigga, drop the keys." He looked out the window like a deer caught in the headlights, opened the window, and dropped the keys. The officer put on his gloves and picked up the keys out of the dirt and walked over to me. He tested the keys out and unlocked the car.

"Dream, can you please do me a favor and grab your registration from your vehicle. It's protocol."

"Yes, sir." I was so relieved. I walked over to the glove compartment and found my registration. My car had never been so cleaned and detailed. It was as if Z thought he was gonna have my car for days or weeks. I handed the officer my registration, and he compared it to my license, then gave them back to me.

"I don't know what's really going on here. But here are your keys. You should get a spare made too. Better yet, don't give anyone your keys because people are sheisty out here. You can't take no chances," he said, handing me my keys.

"Thank you, Officer. We sure do appreciate this," Lee responded.

"Thank you very much, Officers!" I said.

"Yes, this was a blessing 'cause that fool could have done anything to your car," Cain added.

"I'm sorry, D." Cookie looked pathetic.

"I hope you learned, Cookie. He ain't right." I jumped in the car and started it and made sure that it was running and okay. Lee and Cain inspected the vehicle for me.

"This car is clean as a mug." Cain walked around it.

"I'ma bring the baby and lock her in. King can sit back there with her." Lee had common sense.

"Ma, you good? You got the key?" King couldn't wait to come talk to me.

"Yea, the police officer got the key for us. That was a blessing, so mama didn't have to catch no case." We both laughed. "I need you to sit in the backseat with your sister. Is she up?"

"She was up for a minute. I was talking to her and playing with her."

"Make sure you get the diaper bag and put it in the backseat. There are a few bottles that I pumped. If she gets hungry, feed her."

"OK, Ma, I got you."

Lee had locked the car seat in the middle so that I could see her from my rear. King sat right next to her like a big brother.

"Ms. Dream, y'all should be good now. But I know you ain't supposed to be driving. Please take your time going over these raggedy streets and the bumps. You don't want to end up back at the hospital, so drive slow. And then if you need something, call me. Don't call on no one you can't trust. I got you."

"Thank you so much, Lee and Cain, for everything. Follow me closely to the Pike. I'm a li'l scared. Can't afford any stomach injuries."

"I'll be right behind you." Lee hopped in his car and blasted Chuck Brown. The whole hood could hear him.

"Mom, are you scared of driving?" King knew me all too well.

"Yea, a li'l, but I'm gonna take my time and pray us all the way there."

"Does this mean we'll be able to move back home, and you can take me to school?" King began with the questions.

"Most likely. Let's see how comfortable I feel, King."

"Okay, Ma."

It was the most awkward feeling driving. My stomach was open, and I could feel the muscles vibrating the more that I stepped on the gas. I prayed all the way home, and it was a silent prayer. The bumps and potholes were inevitable, but I was in the slow lane and driving at about 25 mph. If I were in a healthy condition, it would have taken me about 20 minutes to get home, but in my condition, it took me about 40 minutes. When I noticed that Lee was not behind me, that is when my "superpowers" ignited. It was just us now.

As soon as I pulled up, I noticed that the grass needed to be mowed and the trash needed to be set at the curb. My house seemed abandoned. I walked toward the front door and noticed how full the mailbox was. There were tons of letters from Kenya. King brought the baby in for me, and it was as if he knew we would have to stick together like we never did before. I walked around the house and checked the rooms, which were still secured and clean. Upon looking in the refrigerator, I found a few items that expired that I immediately trashed. While standing over the kitchen sink, I began washing my hands with soap and warm water, reflecting on how far I had come and how much I needed to go. My prayer to God was that He would supernaturally heal my body and equip me with the power to drive and the ability to use strength to take care of my kids. God had mercy and granted me that . . . and more.

From that day on, I would explain to Uncle Marvin and Aunt Nandi that I was most grateful for their hospitality, but I was moving back home. They may have been concerned, but Uncle Marvin knew the good stock that I was made of, and if I were my great-grandma and big mama's legacy, then I would push through the odds. They gave me their blessings but still checked on me throughout the week. I would build my stamina so that I could take King to school in the morning, and Aki or one of my supports would pick him up for me and bring him home. I would get up at the crack of dawn, say my prayers, pace myself, eat something light, prepare King's breakfast and sometimes lunch, pack the baby up while she was asleep, and take him off to school. Dynasty would sit quietly in her stroller as I continued with wound care for another 2 months, and by the fifth and sixth month, I could see the results of my stomach healing and closing.

SIX MONTHS LATER . . .

I pulled out my right breast as I sat in a high-back leather executive chair at the Passion for Change mahogany conference table. It felt so good and surreal to be back in the office. I began nursing Dynasty as I prepared to meet with my staff and Umi. Dynasty was chunky with chinky eyes, fat cheeks, a left dimple, chocolate skin, and a head full of dark brown curly hair. She looked just like Kenya, with a few of my attributes. She was a happy baby who would become fussy when she was hungry or needed to be changed. She babbled, crawled, and was attempting to stand. Breast-feeding was healing my body, gradually slimming me down to a size 12 with a small FUPA, and my face was starting to give asymmetric. Nursing was strengthening Dynasty's immune system and saving me money from having to buy cans of Similac every month. She ate organic baby foods, and when I had time, I blended fruits for her to eat.

"Look at the baby!" Kiana walked into the office, smiling. I put my boob back in and sat her on my lap as she sat in the cutest lavender outfit with a lavender headband.

"She got so big, Dream. I see you still breast-feeding her. She eating cereal?"

"She is eating cereal, mashed potatoes, yams, carrots, and applesauce. As you can see, the baby don't miss no meals."

"She is so chocolate and cute. Are those diamonds in her ear?" Kiana smiled.

"Yes, honey. I got her ears pierced, and she didn't even cry."

"Go 'head, Dynasty. I'm gonna go wash my hands so I can hold her."

"Oh, look at you all slim and back." Tammy, a.k.a. Tammy Fay, was one of my lead female mentors who earned the most money out of all my staff. She had about 10 to 12 clients, and she was clever in how she maximized her time with them. Tammy was in her mid-40s, a single mother, yet, she had two other side jobs working with the disabled. She was a true definition of a hustler. Her hair was always done, her lashes were dramatic, and she stayed fly even though she was only about 4 foot 11.

"Hey, Tammy. How are you? Yes, I'm back. It feels good. How's mentoring going?"

"You know I'm getting all the referrals. I have mostly girls and a few boys. My mentees love me. They always hungry. Every time I pick them up, they act like they're starving. So, I take them to

McDonald's or Subway. Some of the mentees are mild mannered, and then you have the ones who are off the chain."

"Don't keep feeding them because we don't get reimbursed for food. You can get a box of snacks and give them that. But they get stipends and checks, so they can feed themselves. Don't fall for it, Tammy. Make sure your case notes are on point and on time. I'll send out an email to the staff that case notes are due on the 25th. It will give Aki and Kiana enough time to edit them."

Kiana walked back in and got the baby and held her as we all met.

"Okay, if you say so. So, how your stomach feel? Are you healed up? I see you driving."

"Yes, I'm healed up and back on the road. But I'm not gonna move too fast. I'm still postpartum."

"We been holding the fort down for you, Boss Lady. Things are pretty good. Aki keeps us on our toes. He don't play about our grammar, reports, or notes. He's a stickler and a perfectionist. Kiana, you know, is big on attendance and inputting our case notes."

"I am because you guys be all over the place. I know how Dream is, and y'all ain't gonna jam me in with her." Kiana was playing with Dynasty.

"Well, Aki is cool. Lee, you know, mentors his clients in between selling his oils on Benny Road. Maaz just wanna be a fly nigga. He ain't doing nothing. He barely seeing his clients. And Cain won't leave me alone."

"Shut up, girl! Lord, your mouth!" Kiana was shaking her head.

"KiKi, you know I'm telling the truth." Tammy had a mouth from the South.

"So, Maaz ain't doing nothing? And what's up with Cain?"

"Maaz just think his good looks gonna get him to the top. He lazy. He ain't maxing out on his hours. Cain is crushing on me hard. He giving me half of his check. Taking me out to lunch, paying for stuff, and buying me flowers."

"Lord Jesus, *what* is going on with my organization? Well, I will be tracking Maaz to see what's good. You and Cain need to stop before this becomes a fatal attraction. I don't got time for that. Stop taking his money, Tammy! It will not be a good look when you decide to let him know that you really don't like him." My facial expression gave business.

"Here we go. Oprah is back. Okay, li'l Oprah!" We all began laughing. "I'm glad you are back, though, sis. I have clients to see you. You still need me?"

"No, I think we're good, Tammy. I'll connect with you in a few days. Thanks for everything. Remember, snacks only for the youth."

"You got it, Boss Lady," she said sarcastically. "See you soon." Tammy left.

"Kiana, do you have any updates for me? How are things going on your end?"

"Everything is good. The meetings at the agency are pretty boring, as usual. I need you to tell the staff to tighten up on their case notes. It's as simple as spell check. The staff gets lazy because they know Aki and I are gonna edit what they email us. They also need to sign in and sign out consistently. They're responsible for their own time. Please communicate that to them, and we need office supplies." She was bouncing Dynasty on her lap.

"I'm on it. Email me a list of what supplies are needed and an estimate of the cost, and I'll give you petty cash for it. My goal is to be in the office about 3 days a week to help troubleshoot and begin working on new grants and ways to expand. On those days, I'll allow Dynasty to do drop-in day care with my friend, Chantelle P. Time for my baby to be around other babies," Dream said.

"For the most part, things have been on track. Are we gonna be paid on time this month? The staff wants to know," Kiana said.

Dream replied, "As long as they turn in their case notes, the notes are accurate and uploaded, and the invoice is submitted on time. They ding us on case notes, accuracy, and delay. I'll have Aki crack the whip on them. Any staff member get in the way of my money, they won't be able to work—simple as that."

"Got it. Where's Dynasty's toys or her teething ring? She just drooling all over her bib."

"Oh, let me get her teething cookies. That should suffice." I looked in the diaper bag and handed her a few wrapped teething cookies and a teething toy.

"Come with me, so Umi can see her before we meet. Can you watch her for me for a few minutes while we meet?"

"Of course. This my chocolate baby." Ki stayed cuddling her.

"Look who I have gracing my office. Dream gotta baby. Look at her, Dream. She's beautiful," Kiana brought her closer.

"Look at those Asiatic eyes and that coco skin. She looks like you and her father."

"You think so?"

"Yea, she's a nice combo of the two of you." Umi's accent was so Brooklyn. "Have a seat."

Kiana took Dynasty back to the office.

"How you feel? You look good. You look strong."

"I feel stronger. It feels good to be back."

"Most days, you can telework and come in a few days a week to make your presence known. Your staff has been doing good in your absence. I haven't had a problem out of them."

"Whew. That is so good to hear. That gives me relief, knowing that business was being run smoothly, and the staff was on point."

"We need to partner on some grants together. We need to get the money that is out there without selling our souls. I'm gonna send you a few to look at so you can give me some feedback."

"Awesome. Umi, we're on the same frequency. I received a few invitations to bid from the government, and I'll take some time to go through them thoroughly. Then we can sit down and follow up."

"Listen, I'm not gonna be in this building for long. I wanna set you up and set myself up so that you are strong financially. Parks and

Rec are gonna take over this building, and I plan to put you in a position that you have at least 6 to 9 more months here, and then you can get your own office space. So be thinking of an office space where you can thrive, and the rent is decent."

"Gotcha. I'm listening, Umi. Yea, this time is critical. I need to write at least four to five grants so that we're good for a few years."

"Yep, bring the baby in here. You the CEO and get busy on that laptop. I did it with my two kids, and you can do it with your two kids. I have never seen you fold. When does the baby's father come home?"

"He'll be home in 2 months." I was cheezing.

"Look at you. Get on some birth control when he comes home. Lord, you gonna be fertile, and his body and mind are gonna be stronger than ever. Yea, but when he comes home, put his ass to work with the kids so you can do what you need to do."

"You're right, and I am. Can't wait 'til he comes home. That'll help me a lot, so I can be freed up."

"Exactly! You are building an empire. You're like one of my daughters, and I'm gonna see to it that you become a millionaire. Look at Chase. He has multiple cleaning contracts that Councilmember Small got him, and he's making big bucks. Just stay in your lane and keep your nose clean. The programs for youth are in your lane. The arts are in your lane. You gotta figure what else you can do to monetize on it."

"I appreciate you, Umi, so much just for rocking with me and taking the time to show me the ropes."

"You got it, Dream. Check your email today. I'm gonna send you a few other grants. Just email me back and let me know which ones you want to be a part of, and I can subcontract you off the break."

"I'll read them all and get back with you."

"Take care of you and those babies. Hydrate too. You breast-feeding?"

"Yes, I am."

"That's what'll keep you and the baby healthy. That's how you slimmed down. Breast-feeding is a miracle. You have big breasts like me, so you've got milk." We laughed together. "OK, baby girl, go get your baby. Tell the big boy, King, that Umi said hi. Let's circle back soon."

"Thank you, Umi. Love you." I got up and hugged her. She patted her hands on my shoulders like a true queen.

Umi was my angel on earth. She had my back in a way that was authentic, and only God knew why. Whenever I came up, she would be the first that I would bless with stacks. She deserved it in the realest way. She was a motivator, encourager, and mentor. People like that came once in a lifetime.

Things were going well at the office. We were making money, and the reserves I would let increase and accrue interest straight to my business banking account. Kenya wouldn't believe that ole "Jenny from the block" was sitting on close to $50,000 in the bank and chilling.

There was no greater feeling to know that Kenya was en route to freedom, and in 2 months, he would be released. We grew so much and spent these months truly learning about each other and bonding through letters and phone conversations. He was a different man, and I knew that together, we were gonna be a power couple. Just to see him hold his baby for the first time would bring me to euphoria. We would be a real family, and I anticipated how great life would be. He gave me his word that we would be on lock, and in almost every conversation, he mentioned marriage. Being married was a bit much for me because most marriages that I saw went to shreds, except my mama's marriage to Major, and that was dysfunctional as hell. I forgave Kenya for cheating, but in the back of my mind, I wasn't sure that he was gonna come out and be faithful. Niggas go to jail all the time and swear that they will be so faithful, and yet, their penises are tried by fire, failing monogamy every time. Kenya was sold on us getting married over the summer, but I was guarded with trust issues. And if we got married, it would have to be at the justice of the peace simply because he didn't have no money, and I wasn't spending mine. Kenya and I were better off being common-law lovers who loved eternally. That was my relationship goal. He was sappy, but I was content with what we had.

A few weeks before Kenya came home, Roca appeared out of nowhere, wanting to meet up and chill. Dynasty was with Ms. P, and I was free. I hadn't heard from him in a few years, and so much had transpired during that time. He had an infant around the same age as Dynasty, and he was done with his baby mama, Fatima. He moved onto a red girl named France. He didn't say much about her, and I didn't ask. In the back in my mind, I wanted to know why he wanted to see me after all this time. We kicked it and chilled around his way on the South Side.

"So, what's up with you? You din had a baby on me now with that wild nigga?"

"You had a baby on me with some girl. It ain't even Fatima."

"You was so pressed to be with Kenya. Where he at anyway?"

"He been locked up. He comes home in a month. It's good timing that you reach out to me now. I had complications with my pregnancy and all. It took me some months to get back to myself."

"For real? You ain't called me. I would have been there to support you."

"Well, I'm OK, now."

"You miss me?" He was so arrogant.

"Naw, I don't miss someone who has been gone out of my life and just appears. But I am happy to see you. You look good."

"You look good as well, Dream. You been on my mind. If you would have stuck around and not been so impatient, we could have had our own baby. We could have been together."

"I felt like I was pursuing you, and you weren't really that into me. I got tired of tryin'a make you recognize that I was official. Kenya showed me that he was into me. You look good. The females be on you. You fly as hell. You hustling now?"

"I'm getting money. That's all that matters."

"That's cool. I see you with the big office. How's business?"

"Business is good. I have about six staff now. God has really showed me favor. I feel blessed."

"You are blessed. Look at how far you came from MOV 'til now."

"So much has changed." My mind drifted.

He kissed me on my lips, and I kissed him back. He began sucking on my bottom lip. He wanted more. But I had a whole nigga on the way, so I had to stay focused. Roca was a nice distraction. Hadn't even gotten myself back to 100 percent, and here he was, enticing me.

"I gotta go get King, Roca."

"Damn, I forgot about ole King. I know he got big as a mug. Yea, he about to be in middle school. So when am I gonna see you again?"

"You got my number, just hit me. I live in the same place, and you know where I work. You know how to find me. Pull up." I hugged him, not knowing if we'd talk again. Or if it would be years before we'd see each other once more. Roca was beautiful and too perfect. He was tall, dark, and handsome with the charisma of King Solomon. I would have easily had 10 babies by him, but he was still distracted by whatever "secret life of bees" that he was into. We had undeniable chemistry, but I couldn't be with a man who didn't demonstrate that he was into me a 100 grand. I didn't have Roca's heart. Maybe as Badu put it, "Next lifetime."

Kenya's heart laid safely in my palm. As the shackles came off his feet, I envisioned him black, built like a stallion, real Ghanaian features, a crooked smile, and grams spinning. Perhaps he really did change his life for the better and for his children. Maybe he'd come home and square up and leave the streets alone. Perhaps marriage wasn't a bad idea, after all. What I knew for sure is that I did a bid with him and never folded. Kenya was on his way home, and I had to roll the dice on him. Black Love was all that I ever wanted. The kind you'd see in *Ebony* and *Essence* magazines, and you'd cut out the photos of beautiful Black couples and tag 'em to your vision board. The Ossie Davis and Ruby Dee type of love. "Never leave me" type of love. And if we found favor in God's eyes, then it was real love.

# Chapter 20

*Homecoming*

The nightmare was over. I don't know if he was selling me a dream, but the dream seemed real. There was nothing more amazing than seeing him come out of his prison orange jumpsuit looking warrior strong! With Dynasty on my hip, together, we rushed to embrace one another. With my eyes closed, we had the longest embrace ever. Our group hug felt like it could have entered into the Guinness World Records, 'cause it was lengthy, it was invigorating, it was renewed, and it was what we ever wanted.

Ten months seemed like I had lost 3 years of my life. Not quite a year, but it felt like years of obstacle courses that my stamina and agility were too weak to overcome. Touching Kenya's hands assured me that our protector was home.

"Thank you, God! Thank you, God, for my freedom! I got my family back. Look at baby phat-phat. She look just like me, man." He smiled from ear to ear with his right dimple piercing. He took Dynasty straight outta my hands like I knew he would. It was as if he was saying to me, "I got her, D; you can rest now." As he held his baby girl in his arms, she giggled and smiled, and they connected in their own love language. Instantly, she knew that was her daddy, and the immediate eye connection was heartfelt. Dynasty didn't cry. There was no fussing. It was all infinite love that ignites the foundation of love that Black girls absolutely need and replenishes their fathers with agape. I took my phone and snapped a photo for the archives.

"Look at her eyes. They slanted just like mine. She chocolate now. She was red when you had her. She got your lips, though. But my whole face . . . She is beautiful. My God, thank you for blessing me. All that hair . . . Why you put that white girl headband on her? She need plaits. She got hair. Daddy gonna take my phat-phat to the braiders." He stood her up on his lap.

"Just let her hair be free. She a baby."

"Here we go," Kenya said. "You want my baby looking like Angela Davis?" He was cuddling and kissing her on her cheeks.

"Why not look like Angela? Anyway, Ken, I got you a fresh outfit in this bag. You can't be walking out in your prison fit. You gotta come outta that shit ASAP. You take a shower?"

"That's my baby. Yea, I took a shower and gotta haircut for you. I was woofing. After they call me to give me my release and probation papers, I'm gonna go change."

"That works. You look good. Real good." I started batting my eyes at him.

"I tried to keep myself up while I was in here. That's why the money that you was putting on my books was so important. I wanted to keep up my hygiene and get strong. I've been lifting too." He showed off his guns.

"I see. I'm so freaking happy you home. You just don't know."

"Where's King?"

"He at school."

"Nia is at school then too."

"I can't wait to see my big girl. I know she misses me so much. I gotta stay out of prison and far away from incarceration for my girls. I got a big baby and a baby phat. Look at daddy baby thighs. What you feeding her?"

"Baby food. Some blended and some organic. She's still breast-fed, but I'm trying to wean her off."

"Wait 'til I make her my food. We gonna eat fried chicken, cake, ice cream, and good stuff. You not gonna wanna hang with Mommy." Kenya was having his own conversation with Dynasty.

"Kenya Harris, Kenya Harris," an officer called him up to the front. He handed her to me. The officer gave him some papers to sign. You could tell that he was being read the terms and conditions of his release. Kenya had a frown on his face. He took the papers from the officer and walked off.

"Baby, hand me that bag so that I can change into some civilized clothes."

"Here you go."

This—Was this gonna really really work? It was the life that I wanted. Just my babies, lovers, success, prosperity, and happiness. Real love and joy that could not be taken away from me. Maybe we needed the time away from each other to get ourselves right. Perhaps God saw fit that Kenya was removed from my life so that he could soberly see my value, and I could recognize my worth.

"How I look?" He walked out clean as a whistle. He wore a coral V-neck, some blue True Religion jeans, and some fresh NB sneakers. With his haircut, he looked like a new man.

"You look good, babe." I kissed him on his forehead.

"Let's go! Let's get outta here. I don't wanna see these people ever again. They can kiss my ass, sea bass." We held hands walking out of the prison doors and straight to the car.

"I'ma put pretty baby Dynasty in her car seat and lock her in. Is she gonna cry?"

"She should be okay. As long as you look back at her and give her some attention, she'll be content."

"Yes! She ain't a crybaby. She can really go with Daddy." He buckled her up and kissed her on the cheek.

I immediately played "All I Need" by Mary J Blige and Method Man to set the tone. He reclined his seat and put his left hand on my right thigh.

"You wore this cute skirt for me? You don't even wear skirts. You look good. What type of hair you got? Brazilian?"

"Yea, I wore this skirt for you. This is Indian hair. I got it from Snob Hair."

"You got money too. I can tell. You too quiet. You gained a few pounds."

"Dang, yes. I gained a li'l baby weight. I mean, I did just have a baby."

"I'm teasing you. You look good. We look good. It feels so good to be home. Fresh air . . ." He cracked the window.

"You wanna grab a bite to eat?"

"I'm doing whatever you like." He began finessing his fingers through my hair.

"We can go to Friday's near the highway 'cause we can't be in the Commonwealth for too long. They don't like Black people."

"Yea, for real, they don't. So, let's hurry up."

"Whatchu gotta taste for? Some buffalo wings and mozzarella sticks?"

"Mainly some appetizers."

"Nothing major? I need a drink too. A glass of wine."

"Damn, what, you nervous or something?"

"Yea, I'm nervous as hell. I ain't seen you. I'm so excited. I just wanna hop on you and kiss you all over. It's been so hard for me. It seem like you wasn't ever gonna come home. It's like a sigh of relief. But I gotta squeeze your hands and scratch your neck so that I know you here for real." I got teary-eyed.

"I'm here, baby. I ain't going nowhere. Phat-Phat, I'm not going nowhere, I promise. Baby, I need my phone on, baby. They gave me my phone and belongings."

"Your phone is on. I paid the bill." I swerved real smooth in my big body silver Benz. I bossed up while he was gone.

"Oh, you got money? Lemme find out my soon-to-be wife got breaded up while I was gone." He checked the phone out to see if I really turned it on. Then he started dialing.

"You was serious, huh? I'm calling Grandma. Gotta call Grams." He put the phone on speakerphone.

"Helloooo," she sounded firm.

"Grandma, it's me. I'm home, Grandma!" He sounded like a happy kid.

"Kenya?" she responded. "You home? That's good. Now, stay out, ya hear?"

His grandma was nothing to play with. She told you exactly how she felt, and you better had believed her the first time. She told me to leave him alone when she first met me, and I didn't believe her. I guess she had a point, but I was hardheaded and curious, and I wanted to see how long this love could go.

"Yes, Grandma, I'm gonna stay out this time. I miss you so much. I'ma come see you first thing tomorrow."

"No! You need to go see Nia first. That baby needs you. Her mama is as dumb as a doorknob. She ain't no type of mother. Your daughter needs you now. And when you get yourself situated, you need to take custody of her. Her mama is running the streets and don't know how to be a mother."

Kenya bowed his head.

"I'ma get my daughter, Grandma. I just got released a few minutes ago. I was just letting you know that I'm home since you raised me. I love you, Grandma." Kenya tried to wrap up his convo, taking her off of speakerphone, shaking his head, and making the conversation private. You could tell his grandma was telling him some real shit. "I'ma be staying with Dream. That's where I'll be. I don't need to be nowhere near distractions. This is my time to be a man and stand on my own two feet."

I pulled up in the restaurant parking lot and parked near the entrance. It was midday, so it wasn't too crowded. Kenya carried Dynasty into Friday's like she was a baby doll, and we were seated immediately. "Can we get a booster chair for her?" I asked the greeter.

"Yes, you sure can." He placed two menus on the table along with a coloring sheet for Dynasty. I had to watch her closely to make sure she didn't put the crayons in her mouth and that she would scribble on the paper.

"OK, Grandma, we'll talk tomorrow in detail. I love you." He hung up and put his phone on the table.

"Grandma sure do know how to kill a nigga's vibe, Dynasty. Look at my baby in a high chair. Dream, I missed almost her first year. But I'ma be here for your first birthday, baby. Daddy ain't missing that."

"You wanna order appetizers? We can share them."

"Yea, we can get something light. To be honest, baby, my stomach bubbling. I don't need anything heavy."

"You gotta lot on your mind, huh? What did your grandma say?"

"She was coming down on me about Nia. I know I need to get her, but I just got home. I wrote out what I'm gonna do. I gonna bond with my baby. Get our relationship strong, so we can get married. I'ma gonna get on a career path and start working. I wanna get my CDL or have a job making money in the labor or construction field. I like to use my hands. I gotta be able to help you. You helped me. That's what my family don't understand. I'm moving on with my life with you. They may not understand what type of woman you are, but they *will* respect you."

"Hi, can I take your order?"

"Yes, can we get the sampler with buffalo wings, mozzarella sticks, and potato wedges?"

"And for the child?"

"Yes. Can you get her a side of mashed potatoes, a bowl of fruit, and an apple juice box?"

"Certainly. Any beverages?"

"May I have water, please. Get my baby a glass of wine. I can see it in her eyes that she need a glass of wine. I'm staying away from the liquor."

"What? That's good. Yep, stick with the water. Sir, can I have a glass of Pinot Grigio?"

"I'll put in your order and will be back shortly."

"Thank you."

"Kenya, my anxiety is a li'l elevated. I'm happy, excited, and overwhelmed."

"I got you. I got us."

"What's your family issue with me? I ain't ever done nothing to them."

"They just wanna control me. They can't control you. You are your own woman. They don't like it. You not like my baby mama asking and begging for shit. You're self-made. You started from the bottom and look at you now. It's simple as that."

"That's crazy. I took the baby to see your grandma a few times."

"Yea, Keema told me that her and Ryan watched Dynasty a few times."

"Yea, they did, and the baby seemed like she took to them, but you know I don't trust nobody with my baby."

"Yea, I know you were overprotective with King. You act like you were molested or something. I don't know why you act so paranoid when it comes to kids."

The waiter brought out our food and wine. I placed the plastic bib around Dynasty's neck and gave her sips of apple juice, which put a huge smile on her face.

"My baby like sweets. Yeaaaaa, that's right. I'ma feed her some mashed potatoes. Go ahead and eat." Kenya was excited to feed her.

"But back to what you were saying. I am paranoid. Working with youth over the years and hearing their stories of sexual abuse and neglect scares the hell outta me. My job is to protect the kids."

Kenya and the baby were having a field day bonding over food. I began sipping my wine and dipping my potato skins in sour cream while eating only the flats.

"I know you gonna make sure the kids good. That gave me peace while I was locked up." He began eating a few buffalo wings.

"I gotta call Nia as soon as we get King from school. They should be out around the same time. My big baby need me. She gonna be lit when she hear my voice."

"Yea, she is. She is the true definition of a daddy's girl."

"Why you didn't get her when I was locked up? I've been meaning to ask you that." He took Dynasty out of the booster seat and onto his lap.

"Nia's mama is a mess. You know she said she hope my baby die a month before you went in—she gotta lot of shit with her. I can't do it. While you were gone, I was healing and getting my body strong again."

"Ah, nawwww! She is a sick bitch for saying that out of her mouth. She's jealous and envious. She didn't wanna be with me, and now, she's mad because I have moved on to something better. I know you don't like drama, so I respect that. Yea, her mama ain't tryin'a work with nobody. She don't want a nigga to live. I'm back."

"Dynasty, you ain't paid Mama no mind since you seen your daddy. Dangggggg." I played with her li'l fingers. She kept giggling and bouncing on her dad's lap.

"You ready? Take a to-go box for the rest of the food. I'm sure King would want the wings."

"Good idea. Yep, nice afterschool snack." I pulled a few twenty-dollar bills outta my bra and left a tip for the waiter. I sipped the rest of my wine, and then we headed to the car. In no time, we were on the highway headed to Good Avenue. The sunlight never felt so good. Dynasty was fed and content and fell fast asleep. I played all our classic jams on rotation from Jeezy, TI, Plies, to Rihanna. Kenya managed to call his closest homeboys to let them all know that he was home and that they needed to pull up on him. They were super excited that he was home. Kenya was always the life of the party.

He called his favorite cousin, Keema. They were raised together like brother and sister along with his other cousin Desiree. Desiree and Keema had him by 5 to 6 years in age. When he was a youngin, his cousins looked after him, but when he became a young adult, he became their protector. Keema was a brown-skinned fly girl with a big butt who drove a Mercedes and had a lot of niggas. Although she didn't have a degree, she managed to climb up the career ladder where she made good money and was an only child who had one kid. Desiree was a red girl. She seemed humble and college educated and was in the military. She was the only child too. She was in NC for her college education and would later on move back to the city.

Keema, Desiree, and Kenya's mother were sisters; however, his grandma raised everybody under one roof and under one income. "Cuzzo, I'm home!" We were close to the house.

"Hey, Kenya, that's good. When you gonna come see me?"

"When I get some wheels. I'll be at Dream's house with baby Dynasty. You gotta car, cuz. Come see me."

"Y'all live far from here."

"If you can go to Ryan's grandma's house, you can come see me, cuz."

"I'll see. You call Grandma?"

"Yes, she was the first person I called. We talked."

"You call your mother?" she began drilling him.

"Nope. I'ma call her, though. Is her number still the same?"

"Probably not. I'll text you her number. You call Nia? You need to call Nia. She been going through since you been gone. It's been hard for her. Between me and grandma, we try to get her, but Taja be trippin'."

"Grandma told me. I'm hip. As soon as I get myself together, I'm gonna get custody and shut shit down. I'll let the courts handle her. I'm not fucking with her ever again."

"All right, well, I'm still at work. I'ma text you when I get off. Welcome home, cuz."

"Thanks, cuz." They hung up, and we pulled up in front of the house. He carried his phat-phat right into the house and placed her into her crib, setting the tone of fatherhood. I followed right behind them with the diaper bag and my purse because I knew she needed to be changed. The diaper bag wasn't as heavy as it used to be because she was older, and all we needed were diapers, wipes, a few juice bottles, teething cookies, and a toy or two. If she wanted breast milk, she would become fussy and pull at my breasts. Her teeth were coming in, and they were sharp. The goal was to get her off the booby by the time she was 1.

We walked in the room in pure silence, sitting face-to-face on the bed, as if there were a thousand words to say between the two of us, but it just didn't come out that way.

He pulled my hands close to his. "Dream, I know I made a lot of mistakes, and I apologize for all my wrongs. I should have been there in that delivery room. I should have been there when your C-section busted. I should have been there, but I wasn't. But I'm here now."

"I forgive you. Let's move forward and make it count. The past is in the past, and we can't get it back." My words were heartfelt.

"We gonna make it count. We gonna do what they think we can't do. I got you. You hear me? I got us. And you got me." He pulled me closer to him and began kissing me, rubbing my breasts, massaging my thighs, and becoming passionate. He began kissing me all over, and with every kiss, he was talking to me. My eyes were closed, and my imagination flowed as I reciprocated what I had been missing for a year. As he licked my inner mystery, my moans got louder, and my yearning for him became real. All I could do was take my index finger and trace the waves on his head because they were spinning. With my manicured hands, I began grasping his chocolate shoulder blades, connecting to his energy with the freedom that we had. The moment was right. We were clear. We were balanced, and the lovemaking had amens written all over it. As he penetrated my walls with his huge Isis Pistol, he glided my ass like a gladiator, gyrating me from 90-degree to 180-degree angles. His big black cock was talking to me, and my pussy was talking back. His body was strong, and so was his mind, and with sober dick, I would easily become a victim of pregnancy again. But the lovemaking was worth it. And if he meant what he said, it was definitely worth it. A nigga had my whole body and mind on board with him, and the aroma of oneness was in the atmosphere as he released all the sperm that he had collected over 10 months. I lay on my red sheets in a fetus position, totally surrendered.

We hopped into the shower in the longest silence as we took time lathering our bodies. It was the quietest moment. He kept looking into my eyes with this puppy dog look. The steam from the shower smoked out of the bathroom, and once I felt my body was cleansed, I came out to put myself back together again. Unlike me, Kenya took the longest and hottest shower ever. It was as if he were washing his sins away until he felt pure.

"Baby, that was beautiful. It felt so good to come all inside of you." He took the baby oil gel that was on his hands and rubbed it on my shoulders.

"Really? Why you so nasty?"

"Naw, you nasty. If your daddy knew what his good girl could do in the bed . . ." He shook his head.

"Awee, hell naw. You betta not tell. This is between me and you. You seem like you got lost down there," I fired back.

"I sure did. Couldn't wait to color. Every day I was dreaming of coloring with you. Yes!"

"Ken, we gotta hurry up. We gotta go get King. He get out in like 30 minutes."

"You know I move quick. A nigga still institutionalized like I'm a part of count." We both busted out in laughter.

"Here we go. You ain't gonna be tripping, waking up in hot sweats, talking to yourself, are you?" I put on some high-waisted jeans, a fitted Armani tee, a jean jacket, and a cute wedge. I put a matching jean jacket on Dynasty while she was asleep. The weather would get breezy, and I had a feeling Kenya would have me making pit stops. He was eager to see his people.

"You ready?" He was brushing his waves. "Let me get my baby. You don't need to carry her in no heels."

"I've *been* carrying her. I haven't fell yet."

"I got her." He picked her up and wrapped a blanket on her body. It hadn't even been 24 hours, and he was so mesmerized with his daughter. She was so comfortable in his arms, as if she knew from the jump that he was the other half to her. I jetted to King's school, which was about 40 minutes away during rush-hour traffic. Ms. Lonnie, who worked at the school, was a good friend of the family and had been taking care of King since his nursery days, always held us down. Four out of 5 days a week, I would be late, and those late fees would add up, but Ms. Lonnie would have King in the cut so that the deans wouldn't see him.

This day was special. King would lose it once he saw that Kenya was home. Even though King didn't care for Ken when he would be drunk or disrespectful, they low-key had a bond through food and sports. Not to mention what King was missing in his father, he sought in Kenya. Plus, he could use some help with the trash and being called every 10 minutes to help me around the house or to assist me with Dynasty. King grew up drastically, and Kenya would notice.

We pulled up in front of the school, and Ms. Lonnie was at the end of the breezeway with King. She peeped that Kenya was in the car and began waving. Ms. Lonnie had just had a daughter as well, and her daughter, Maddie, and Dynasty were only a few days apart in age. King began running to the car.

"Kenya, Kenya, is that you?" His hat was nearly falling off his hat. "That's you!" He stood in front of the passenger door in amazement. Kenya came out of the car to give him a grand hug.

"I missed you, boy. I missed you so much. I missed you talking back, getting on my nerves, asking questions, and flipping through the house." We all started laughing.

He rubbed his head like that was his son.

"I missed you too, Kenya. You been gone a long time. My mother needs your help bad. The doctor messed up her stomach. She could barely walk." King began spilling the tea.

"She good now, but she need your help with my baby sister." King did not hesitate to advocate for himself. He hopped in the backseat and took off his backpack.

"Well, champion, I'm home. I'm not going nowhere. I got all of your backs. I promise this time."

"Yes, thank you!" King was banking on it.

"Mommy, I'm hungry." King didn't waste any time telling me he was hungry.

"We got you some appetizers from Fridays."

"Where's it?"

"It's in the house, playboy."

"Yes, but I gotta have a snack." King was off the chain, and Kenya was finna understand that you do not pick up any kid from elementary school without a snack, a bag a chips, or something. School lunch was distributed at noon. Therefore, by 4:00 p.m., children would be hungry again.

"How about we stop by the corner store and get you and Nia a bag of chips?" Kenya smiled, looking like Iron Mike Tyson. He had a crooked smile.

"We going to see Nia? Yes! I haven't seen her in a brick." King was excited.

"Yep. I wanna surprise her. Her grandma most likely picked her up, and she should be on her way home."

"She's gonna be happy to see you!" King affirmed.

"She love me. She always been like that. I always had my baby with me. Baby, pull up at the brown store around my way so I can grab a few snacks for the kids."

"Gotcha!"

King and Ken continued to shoot the breeze. Although they always had a funny relationship, they missed each other. Ken asked him about football, his grades, and the girls. And King, of course, asked him about his experience in prison, and Ken made sure that he described it in a way that King would not wanna venture there. He took King in the store with him to pick out snacks for Nia and him.

Listening to their conversation was beautiful. A Diet Coke and the jams of the radio kept me vibin' positively. It was as if we were here before. Dynasty was Sleeping Beauty. We pulled up in front of Nia's mom's house. I didn't know if Taja was going to cut up or be civil when Kenya knocked on the door, but prayerfully, she would let Nia see her dad.

He knocked a few times loudly until someone came to the door.
"How you doing, Pat?"
"Well, I'll be damn. Look at you. You look good! Nia just got in the house." She stood in the doorway.
"Thanks. You been good, Pat?"
"Yea, I'm good. Taja ain't here. Nia! Nia! Come to the door!"
Nia peeked from out from the kitchen area and saw a glimmer of her dad and leaped.
"Daddy! Daddy! Daddy!" She ran right into his arms, and he hugged her profusely and kept kissing her forehead.
"Daddy, I'm so glad you home. You home for real, right?" Nia needed a confirmation.
"Daddy is home, poo! I'm not going anywhere. I'm home for good. I got out earlier, and I made sure I came straight to you. You miss me?"
"Yes, I miss you so much, Daddy." She had tears in her eyes.
"How's school?"
"It's OK."
"Are you in extracurricular activities?"
"No, but I wanna run track."
"I'ma get you into a sport. You got the build for it. You fast too. Come to the car to say hi to your brother and sister." He grabbed her hand. Nia was his baby, and no one could do or say anything about her. Nia saw King first.
"Hey, King!"
"Hey, Nia."
"Here, your dad got you some snacks." He handed her a bag of chips, juice, and some candy. Her eyes lit up.
"Daddy figured you would like some snacks."

"Thank you." Nia was grateful. "Look at Dynasty. She got big since the last time that I saw her at Grandma's house. She look like you, Dad. More than me."

"You think so? Both of y'all look like me. You are the red version of me, and she is the brown version of me."

"Hey, Nia, poo. How are you?" I waved to her from the driver's seat.

"Hey, Dream!" She was short and waved back. You could tell that Nia always wanted to get close to me, but it was obvious that her mom had influenced her, and she was reluctant about forging a bond with me. I understood that all too well because my biological father had women in and out of his life, and I never was confident that he would marry a woman that could tolerate him for a lifetime. Most likely, in Nia's mind, she was longing that her dad and her mom got back together, like most children do.

They started walking back toward her porch. You could tell that they were having an intimate conversation and that Kenya was drilling her about who was in her house, and who her mom had her around. He would ask her about the men she saw in the house and if she'd recognized any of them. Nia would tell all.

"Listen, Daddy is gonna come get you next weekend. My goal is to get on my feet and bring you with me. Do you wanna live with me?"

"Yes, I wanna live with you!" Her eyes sparkled.

"Well, you're coming to live with me. Give me a few months to get myself together. But until then, I'll get you on the weekends, and on Mondays, I'll take you to school. Just have your clothes packed on Fridays, and I'll come swoop you."

"OK, Daddy." She looked relieved and content. Her daddy brought peace to her life despite the rocky life that her mom had exposed her too. Her daddy was her everything, and no matter where he was in life, he would always make his way to his daughter. He didn't need a girl that was his "ride or die" because Nia filled that position. I never wanted to get in the way of their relationship. I understood the criticalness of a Black father's love for his daughter. He essentially would be the definition of love, and she would seek and quench for the same love even as an adult—until she found it.

"Give me hug, poo. I miss  you, and I love you. My phone is on, so you can call me tonight and call me tomorrow in the morning before you go to school."

"OK, Daddy." She hugged him and began eating her candy.

"I love you, poo! Call me."

"'K, Daddy." Nia was focused on what was in that snack bag.

"All right, Pat. My phone is on. If she needs anything, call me."

"OK, see you, Kenya, and thanks for coming by." Pat was cool.

Kenya walked calmly to the car. Nothing made him happier than to see Nia's face. She was everything to him.

"I got two daughters now, huh?" he smiled.

"Yea, Kenya, it's two of 'em," I smiled back.

"I got a son too!" He laughed and looked back at King. "He just don't know it yet."

"Listen, we have a lot for us to celebrate. You came home, and it's King and my birthday. I figured this Saturday, we'll have a birthday party and a welcome home celebration for you."

"Are you serious?" He smiled.

"Yes, let's invite your friends and family. I'll invite our friends and family. We'll put out the grill, the tent, the moon bounce for King and his friends, and party. It's like your homecoming. You being home is big for you, your kids, your family, and your comrades. And it's especially wonderful for me."

"I love you for that! I'm with it. Let's do it!"

"Let's do it then."

We drove off into the city streets, reminiscing on how we met, jamming to our favorite songs, laughing at how far we came, and reflecting on our future. Our love was so ghetto and organically real. No one understood us but us. The energy was unbreakable.

# Chapter 21

## *The Cookout*

Everything went down in June. And if you were family or a close friend, you knew that summer was my favorite season of the year, and God always showed favor on my life in June. June was a month of balance, new energy, new money, and new beginnings. Summer would knock winter out, shortchange fall, and essentially bypass spring before you could enjoy it. King and I were both born in June, 5 days apart, emotional beings, and yet unapologetic for being in tune with ourselves. And if your spirit wasn't right, you couldn't get close to us. But if we like you or loved you, we would ride with you into eternity. Our loyalty was stamped.

As time went on, I became close with my neighbors on Goode Avenue. While there were plenty of retirees, there were a few young, Black, working-class professionals that I got to know, and we looked out for one another. There was Ms. Nikki and her mother, Ms. Shayla, who lived five houses down from me. Ms. Nikki had two kids like me who were close in age to King, named Riley and Chance. King and Chance became really close friends, and they would play all day.

Ms. Nikki was a few years older than I was. She was a single mom who worked for the same community college that I used to work for when I was a speechwriter. She was a lover of books and good movies. You would find her on her porch, peaceful, minding her own business as she smoked a cigarette. She was sassy in her own way. She was short, curvy, had long, brown hair, and her lipstick stayed popping. Ms. Shayla was her support system and was the grandma in the neighborhood who looked out for everyone's kids. Ms. Shayla had her own mobile party business that did well during the summer months. I would rent her moon bounce to surprise King at the cookout.

Kenya's friend Kevin's grandma lived next door to me, and she was a pastor. Ms. Heart was not your typical pastor. Back in the day, she lived her life and wasn't always a saint, but her goal was to bring the whole neighborhood to Christ. In my mind, her being my neighbor reminded me that Jesus was rooting me, and God had a hedge of protection over my life. She always showed love to King and would pay him odds and ends to help her.

Then you had Nate's brother, Galvin, who lived next door to Ms. Heart with his girlfriend, Mocha. Galvin and Mocha were young, early risers who went to work at the crack of dawn and lived a lifestyle that was suitable for them. You could tell that Galvin was a car connoisseur. He took pride in making sure that his cars were well detailed with a booming system. Didn't know too much about Mocha, other than she had body, a big butt, she was chocolate, and she always spoke. Sometimes you would catch her on a porch with a wine cup, chilling with her friends, but she always waved.

It was a Saturday in mid-June. The weather was 80 degrees and just perfect for a cookout. When King and I celebrated our birthdays, it would be for the entire summer, and it was always lit. But this time, we had a major reason to party, and that was Kenya was home for good, and we could be a family unit and let the past go. Kenya invited his mother, Macy, his closest homeboys, his cousins, Keema and Desiree, and his aunt, Nita. I invited my girlfriends, some of my aunts and uncles, King's friends, his grandma Coco, and his dad. I was an optimist and would test out the blended family thing.

Ms. Shayla and Ms. Nikki came to set up a huge moon bounce in the front of our yard, which let the whole neighborhood know that it was a party. Our three-bedroom rambler house was a one-level flat and cozy, but we had a lot of yard space and could handle the guests. Ms. Shayla was gracious to provide us with cookout and lawn chairs for the yard. Kenya was so excited that he took King with him at 7:00 a.m. to the grocery store to buy all the food and meat for the grill. As soon as he came into the house, he woke me up to straighten up the house and to help him prep while Dynasty was asleep. Kenya was a grill master who owned the grill, and he could cook his ass off. The way that he seasoned food, especially chicken, and created his own exclusive sauces would later turn my body into a pound cake. To top it off, I got a tent set up in the yard along with folding tables, balloons, cake, and party favors from our local superstore. For the first time in my life, I had money to splurge on what made me happy.

I made sure that we were all color coordinated. King, Dynasty, and I had on denim and white, and I bought Kenya a fresh white outfit that had him looking like 50 Cent. While Kenya was incarcerated, he spent much of his time reading, writing, studying, and working out, and it showed. His skin was clear, his waves were spinning, his shoulders and muscles were strong, and I was so proud of the man he was becoming. He even earned his GED while in prison and made sure he showed me his diploma that he placed in his closet along with his important documents and all of our letters corresponding while he was in prison.

Dynasty was trying to walk, but she was lazy at times. King would play with her indoors and used her juice cup to coerce her to walk to him. She would stand, maybe take one step, and plop on the carpet. She was spoiled rotten. King played with his baby sister while Kenya and I set up the outdoor speakers and set up a playlist that consisted of all our favorite songs. He insisted that we played Go-Go, which was the music of the culture of DC, better known as Chocolate City. It was the congas that drew me to the music. It was as if Go-Go instantaneously connected you to the motherland.

As cars pulled up, family and friends began arriving, and we set the tone with "21 Questions," Kenya's anthem by 50 Cent. The music was so loud that the neighbors started to come out and be nosy and witness everything from their front yards. He stood at the front gate of the yard with white shorts, a fresh white V-neck, a fresh pair of New Balances, and a white bucket hat with a white gold blinged-out chain around his neck. He welcomed everyone while holding his baby girl, Dynasty. You couldn't tell him nothing.

The sound of the neighborhood kids and King's friends were the first to arrive, and once King came outside, he was beyond ecstatic to see part of the yard turn kid friendly and festive. Ms. Shayla held down the kids for me naturally, plus her grandson, Chance, had a ball playing with King.

Uncle Marvin and Aunt Nandi arrived along with my aunt Fran and uncle J, who were related to me on my father's side. Although they were in their 60s, they loved a good party, and they were always supportive of me. The rap music that we played may have had a few cuss words, but they understood my generation and just bobbed their heads.

"Hey, baby girl! The yard looks good!" Aunt Nandi came and hugged me.

"Yea, Dream, you fixed up the yard really good." Uncle Marvin hugged me as well.

"Thank you, so glad you guys came. Come check out King over here."

"Whoa, he gotta moon bounce. The kids look like they're having a good ole time."

King came flying out of the moon bounce with just his socks on.

"Hey, Uncle Marvin and Aunt Nandi."

"Hey, you getting big, boy. Happy birthday!" Uncle Marvin gave him a high five.

"This was my first baby. He's growing up." Aunt Nandi began reflecting. "Here's a card. Put it up in your mama's room. You have money in it."

His eyes lit up when you talked about giving money or giving him chicken.

"Thank you!" He ran with the card into the house and placed it on my dresser. Then he came flying out of the house and back into the moon bounce.

"He ain't wasting no time. Where's my baby?" Uncle Marvin asked.

"Her daddy got her."

"That's what I am talking about. Take us to Mr. Kenya." Aunt Nandi was feisty.

We walked over to the area of the grill while he held the baby with one hand and placed turkey hot dogs and hamburgers on for the kids.

"Kenya, this is Aunt Nandi and Uncle Marvin."

"Hey, Unc and Auntie. I'm so glad that I finally get to meet you!" Kenya was ecstatic. "Thank you so much for holding Dream and the kids down while I was on my vacation. It felt good to know that she was safe and with family."

"Yes, we're happy to meet you on these terms. But that's family, and we got her, no matter what," Unc affirmed.

"These are our babies, all of 'em. Now, hand me my baby," Aunt Nandi said, reaching for her.

"Yes, she's getting heavy, plus, I need to get all of this food grilled."
He handed her to Auntie.

"Are you a Washingtonian?"

"Yes, sir, born and raised. I was raised Uptown."

"We live Uptown too."

"Oh yeah? Dream, how far do they stay from my grandma house?"

"They live about 7 minutes away from your grandma."

"Yea, that's real close," Kenya replied.

Aunt Nandi drifted off with Dynasty in her hands, awaiting my other aunt, Maury, to arrive, who was Uncle Marvin's sister.

"It smells good, so, what's on the grill menu?"

"We have about everything. Chicken, wingettes, hamburgers, hot dogs, and fish. We have potato salad, grilled vegetables, baked beans, and you know Dream made sure we had appetizers."

"Yes, I'm gonna stick around so I can have a plate."

"Yea, Unc, have a seat and chill."

"Thanks. I'm gonna bring my case of beer that's in the car. Would you like one?"

"Yea, sure. I'll take one for later. Appreciate it, Unc."

I let them bond because my homegirls started arriving, and I needed to have some girlfriend time to catch up with Desire, who was my friend and hairstylist, Sanai, who was my best friend, and Shae, one of my good friends from Bison University. There was a colleague from the community named Miracle, and she and her fiancé were invited and showed up as well.

The aroma of barbeque and the sounds of Mary J brought in a radiant vibe, giving us permission to be young, Black, and fly. "Be Happy" was a euphoric segue to getting a cookout going.

Sanai began two-stepping through the gate with Amir, and together, we both began dancing together, just like we did at every party that we attended at Bison University. Mary J anything hit the core of our being as a Black woman in America, finding our way, longing for love, being broken along the way, and eventually becoming resilient. But the real shit that meant more was the happiness.

"Yes, girl, you could hear that Mary knocking and booming through the speakers. Yessssssss, that's our jam." We embraced each other in the spirit of sisterhood. And even though we hadn't seen each other in months, we always caught up each other to speed. We were kindred.

"Don't Mary make you wanna just bop?" I began dancing with a mean two-step reminiscent of our freshmen year of college. Mary J spoke in a code that only we understood. "I miss you so much, girl. I miss you so much, Sanai. I'm so glad you came. Nephew! Come here and give me a hug. I missed you guys." I was overjoyed.

"D, you just don't know how much we missed you. We couldn't wait to come."

"Nephew, go ahead and get in the moon bounce. Put your shoes in the house and go play. King will be so happy to see you."

"Yes!" He took off.

"Girl, so I brought two bottles of wine and some tequila to blend some margaritas."

"Girl, thank you so much. Let's go in the house. You can put the bottles on the table. Let's do wine for now, and then later this evening, we can take shots."

"Where's Kenya? That's who I want to see."

"He at the grill talking with Uncle Marvin."

Sanai began walking toward Kenya.

"What's up, Kenya! Glad to see you home," she greeted him.

"Sanai, what's up? Yea, I'm so happy to be home." He began taking the hot dogs and hamburgers off the grill, placing them in pans on a long table.

"I know Dream is so happy you're home. Dynasty, that li'l baby looks just like you. And, Nia, I know she's thrilled that you're home, and even King."

"Sanai, this was it. For real, I learned my lesson, and I'm back for good. My goal is to get a good job so that I can provide for my family and stay out of the way." He put the marinated chicken wings on the grill.

He grabbed me from behind and began kissing my cheeks. All I could do was smile.

"Y'all hear that?"

We looked at him, waiting for an answer.

"Girl, it's easy to love me now. Would you love me if I was down and out? Would you still have love for me?" He began singing "21 Questions," and we all laughed.

"Eh, baby, 50 is spitting some real shit. This song is exactly how I feel. Sanai, I have nothing but love and respect for this girl. She rode the bid with me and held it together despite all of the obstacles she has been facing since I was in. She's strong, and I love that about her." He gave me a big hug.

"Y'all are too cute!" Sanai started pouring glasses of wine. "Would you like a glass of wine, Kenya?"

"Naw, I'm good. I see my homies pulling up now. They got that Jose. A real man drink."

"O Lord. Kenya, be good, please," I said.

His friends, Les, Saul, Frank, and a few others, pulled up in front of the house with bags filled with liquor. Sanai and I looked at each other. We already knew what time it was, so her wine bottles were right on time, and we began greeting the guests and some of my other family members and friends who came to show love.

His homies ran up on him and showed him so much love. From real brotherly handshakes to loud hood expressions, all you could see was Black Boy Joy, and they treated Ken like he was a general who returned home from war. Once Kenya closed the grill, I knew that he was ready to have a good time.

"Look at you, nigga. You fresh to def! Dream got you looking real good. Look at this nigga. His waves are spinning," Les, who was beyond flashy, began signifying.

"Yea, my baby got a nigga back, looking good and feeling good. We ain't wanting for nuffin'," Kenya responded.

"Just happy you home, cuz. Seem like you was gone fa'eva," said his childhood best friend, Saul. "We brought you some Jose and Amsterdam. Welcome home, homie." They had their own personalized handshakes.

"Saul, ouch ouch ouch. A nigga missed you too. Just glad y'all came out to celebrate. Where li'l Saul? You know it's King birthday too?"

"Man, I brought him. Soon as he saw the moon bounce, he ran straight to it. He with King already. You know how the kids do."

"My big homie, Frank." He gave him an embrace.

"Nigga, you made it outta that hellhole. I'm happy to see that we out here free at the same time."

"Eh, Les, Frank was my celly out VA. He showed my baby so much love. He had his girl giving my girl cheddar when the baby was born. He really looked out on some OG shit. You just don't know how much I appreciate that."

"We men. Real men respect real men." I brought a bottle of tequila and cigars and handed him a cigar.

"What? Frank, you always been on some extravagant shit. I'ma light it up."

Frank handed him a lighter, and he began cheefing.

"It feel like a real nigga holiday!" Kenya shouted. They all laughed and kicked it amongst themselves.

Sanai and I started creating plates for the kids so that they could eat. They were eager to play, and most were growing boys, so the food literally disappeared off their plates. I ensured that I got a few plates for Ms. Shayla and Ms. Nikki, who were monitoring the children and the moon bounce. Ms. Shayla didn't drink, but I made sure that I poured a few glasses of wine for Ms. Nikki. My friends, Desire and her stepson, and my other homegirl, Shae, came with more bottles of wine, and we kept the party going. So much joy and laughter filled the atmosphere that all I wanted to do was be present in the moment.

"Well, hello, there," Aunt Maury had Dynasty on her hip with a drumstick.

"Hey, Aunt Maury. I see Dynasty is going from auntie to auntie eating chicken. I don't even give her chicken like that." I kissed the baby on her forehead.

"She sure is tearing up this chicken drum. Can she eat chicken? I figured she could."

"It's her daddy's chicken. You're fine feeding her. Just make sure the pieces are small."

"Yep, they're small. She is such a good baby with her cute chocolate self. All she does is smile and giggle. But she does like to be held. This is a really nice affair. I can't seem to catch up with King to wish him a happy birthday because he and his friends are moving so fast. Boys will be boys."

"Yes, they are."

"Hey, Sanai, how are you and Amir? Is he here?" Aunt Maury knew Sanai because she had been my friend since our freshman year in college.

"Hey, Aunt Maury. Good to see you. Amir is here running with the boys."

"Oh, wow. I'll try to walk around the yard to find him and give him a hug. Well, Dream, enjoy yourself. This is your time to unwind. You have had a tough year, but you look happy and deserve to be. I introduced myself to Dynasty's papa. He's a nice guy."

"Oh, that's so good. Thank you, Aunt Maury."

She walked off with the baby, and I never felt so free. My girlfriends and I sat in the lawn chairs and chatted it up, catching each other up to speed and reminiscing on how bomb our 20s were before adulting. Sanai brought a few more bottles out of the house and kept the vibe going. Kenya signaled me to come over to him. His family had arrived.

"Eh, baby, come say hi to Mom Dukes!" He was loud and had a cup of Jose in his hands.

"Hey, Macy. How are you?"

"I'm good. I'm so happy my son is home, you know what I mean. He's my only child. I see y'all got stuff poppin' over here. Tent's out. My son on the grill. Where da drank at?" His mother reminded you of wild Frankie, the mother of singer Keyshia Cole. She had a raspy voice, blond finger waves, and she was petite, feisty, and a firecracker.

"Would you like some wine? Or you want what your son is drinking?"

"Naw, I don't want no wine. I want what my son's drinking."

"All right, Macy, I'ma get you a cup." Kenya switched the playlist from rap to Go-Go and had everyone dancing to the Godfather of Go-Go, Chuck Brown. Macy made herself at home as she danced in the middle of the yard. She was in her own zone.

"Here, Ma," Kenya handed her a red cup.

"Thank you, son."

"Come say hi to my cousins and aunt." He held my hand as we walked over to them. They had already set themselves up at a table with chairs.

"Look at my nephew! Looking all good!" His aunt Nita was loud too.

"Thanks, Aunt Nita, how you been?"

"I've been good. Glad you home." Aunt Nita stood 6 feet tall. She was a red woman, medium build, with long legs. She was nice looking, but if she got that brandy in her, she would turn obnoxious. According to Kenya, she had the "mouth of the South."

"Hey, Aunt Nita." I was cordial.

"Hey, missy Anne, how you?"

"I'm good."

"I'm sure you are. You have a strong Black man in your bed. Don't have no more babies, hear?" She was fresh.

"Naw, I'm good on the babies."

"What's up, cousins?" Kenya reached down and hugged his cousins, Desiree and Keema. Desiree was Nita's daughter, and they looked alike. Keema and Kenya favored each other with the same complexion and similar features.

"Hey," I spoke to everyone at the table.

"Hey, Dream," said Keema.

"Hey, cuz," said Desiree. "You home now. I'm so glad you home."

"Thanks, cuz. I ain't going back."

"Hey, Ken," responded Keema. "What you sipping on?"

"You know I got some clear in my cup."

"Well, we brought liquor too, if you wanna drink. We also brought crabs."

"You know I don't eat crabs, cuz. I'm allergic."

"Well, you can drink with us. Keke on her way too. She bringing a bottle. Where's Dynasty?"

"She's with my aunt somewhere in the yard."

"Bring her to us when you see her."

"OK, I will."

"Eh, cuz, the food is ready. The table with the food is over there. Go make your plates."

"We will," Desiree responded.

Keema's fiancé walked over and gave Kenya a pound.

"Eh, cuz, welcome home!"

"Hey, Ryan. What up?"

"Everything's good. Y'all gotta nice house and a lot of yard space. I didn't realize that you're about 10 minutes away from my grandma."

"Yep, it's a straight shot."

"You came out strong than a muthafucka!" He checked his temperature and realized that Kenya had size on him.

"Yea, I'm more focused than ever now."

"That's what's up."

"I'll be back in a few. I'm going to go check on the kids." He walked off.

"It's about time that we go sing 'Happy Birthday' to King before it gets dark. I know my aunts and uncles don't like driving when it's dark."

"Yea, let's rally up the kids," said Kenya.

As soon as Kenya saw Aunt Maury holding Dynasty, he immediately raised his hands out, and with a warm smile, she leaped into her daddy's arms.

"You gon' to Papa, hon. Bye-bye, Dynasty," she waved.

"Auntie Maury, can you gather all the other aunts and uncles so we can sing 'Happy Birthday'?"

"I sure can."

Kenya got all of the kids together, and then surprisingly, Grandma Coco and King's father walked in the yard right on time to show support to King. King was overjoyed.

"Hey, Dream," Coco greeted me.

"Hey, Coco. Hey, Solomon. You guys came right on time because we're getting ready to sing 'Happy Birthday' and cut the cake."

"This is nice. You got it real hooked up out here." Coco and Solomon were observant.

"Hey, stinka." King ran up to Coco and hugged her. King and his grandma had their own special bond, and she wasn't gonna miss his birthday or any other holiday for anything in the world.

"Hey, Grandma Coco. Hey, Dad!" King smiled.

"What's up, son? You getting big. Looking fly, son son. Happy birthday, son!"

"Thanks, Dad." He gave his dad a side hug. Solomon rubbed his head. Although Solomon was not the best dad in the world, it felt good when he showed up. For King, seeing his dad affirmed that his dad really loved him, and for me, it gave me a sense of comfort knowing that Solomon had a heart.

"Stinka, Grandma got you some gifts. But there's too many people here, so I'm gonna give the bag to your mom." She handed me the gift bag.

When I looked up, all my friends were standing nearby. Sanai was smiling because she knew all the drama that hatched between Solomon and me, and it was cool that we were being civil. Kenya stood right by me with Dynasty. Kenya's family and friends were to the right of him, and my family was to the left of me. There were at least 40 people in the yard, including my nosy neighbors. You could hear Franky Beverly & Maze in the background.

"Attention, everyone!" All eyes were on me. "Today, we celebrate two birthdays . . . King's birthday and my birthday! Yes, we are the best Cancers that you will ever meet. We are special Cancers too, literally."

Everyone laughed, and most clapped.

"Not only is it a birthday celebration, but it's also a homecoming celebration for Kenya. We are so happy that you are here. Today is a new day. Welcome home, love!" All you could hear were claps and whistling. The smiles were infectious.

"Thank you, baby! Thank y'all for coming out! Now, let's sing 'Happy Birthday' to King and Dream." He kicked it off Stevie Wonder style, and everyone started clapping and bobbing their head. It was one of those moments that was priceless and that I would never forget.

*"Happy birthday, Dream and King. Happy birthday to you!"*
Everyone sang together. King blew out the candles, and together, we closed our eyes and made a wish. I gave King the biggest hug in the world.

"I love you, son. I know you don't eat cake, but your friends do." It was our internal joke because King never liked sweets and never ate his own birthday cake. He didn't like candy, juice, or soda, and you couldn't get him to eat a cupcake. The cake was a large sheet of 50 buttercream yellow cupcakes, making it easy to pull apart. My friend

Shae and Sanai helped pass out the cupcakes to the kids and the adults.

Kenya turned the music up, and all you could hear was all the old-school classics that had my aunts, my friends, Kenya's mom, and even the neighbors up dancing to a li'l Teena Marie, Earth Wind & Fire, The Gap Band, and The S.O.S. Band. It began to turn into an '80s throwback. That "feel good" kinda music. The food was becoming scarce, and looked like everyone ate everything but the hot dogs.

As the evening came upon us, Ms. Shayla packed up the moon bounce, and the kids were content playing catch football in the yard.

"Thank you so much, Ms. Shayla, for everything." I handed her some cash, and she smiled.

"Anytime, baby. The food was good too. This was really nice. Bring me my chairs in the morning."

"I sure will. Thank you."

"Here, Dream. Take phat baby. Me and my mans about to have a crap game in the house. We got money in this."

"O Lord." I took Dynasty. "You missed me? Everyone had you today. I missed you, baby." You could tell she was getting tired. She had no nap. I went and got her a small li'l jacket and blanket to put over her. Then I went and sat down in the yard with everyone.

"Look at her. She's getting tired," my friend Desire peeked at her.

"Yea, this has been too much action for her."

"I know it has."

"Look at Dream with a baby," Shae started gigging. "Y'all are too cute."

"Shut up, Shae. What y'all drinking on?"

"We taking shots!" Sanai was passing out shots to whoever wanted it.

"Just give me one. I don't wanna get too messed up."

My aunts and uncles started walking over. I knew it was about to be their bedtime.

"Hey, y'all, we had fun, but it's time for us to get on the road." Uncle Marvin took the lead.

"We love you guys. And I'll call you in a few days," Aunt Nandi waved.

"Love you too, and thank you," I said.

"Love y'all. We had a good time. Hope to see you soon." Aunt Maury followed behind them.

"OK, kiddo, we're headed up the road. Thank you for the invite and talk to you soon." Uncle J and Aunt Fran were leaving as well.

"Thank you, Uncle J and Aunt Fran."

Coco walked over. "All right, I'm gone. Tell Stinka to call me."

Solomon walked up on me. "Why you got niggas gambling in your house? I went to use the bathroom, and these niggas is gambling. That's not a good look for you and nothing I want my son around," Solomon whispered in my ear. "I'm gone, man." He seemed disappointed.

I held my composure and shrugged my shoulders. When did Solomon start caring about who was in my house—better yet, what was going on in my life? He damn near missed a whole decade of King's life. His best bet was to carry his black ass on and to mind his own business, 'cause no one interrupted Kenya in a crap game, and I'm sure his men were strapped.

"Okay, Sanai," I whispered. "Give me one more shot. The old people are gone. Let's get this party started."

"You got it!" Sanai had her bartending license from when we were in college, and she was a true mixologist.

"Soooo," Desire leaned in, "it looks like homeboy over here kept looking over here, and Kenya's people got mad."

"Whattttt?" Shae looked back.

"You talking about that light-skinned dude over there with Ken's family? Oh, that's Keema's boyfriend. They bet not start no shit. They known to get drunk and kick off a fiasco. Ain't nobody thinking about him."

"Right! Yea, he been eyeing us over here. And so has she. But don't nobody got an interest. He ain't my type." Shae rolled her eyes.

"He definitely not my type." Desire crossed her thighs. "I like 'em tall, dark, and handsome. I ain't neva been into a red nigga."

"Shit, I'm light-skinned, and I don't even like 'em light bright." Sanai was sipping.

"Bring the bottles in the house. It's getting a li'l breezy, and it look like Dynasty is getting sleepy. Let's go in the house."

"That's a good idea." Sanai grabbed everything, and the rest of my friends came into the house. I had a comfortable red leather sectional and a 60-inch flat, so we were chilling like ole times.

"Yea, it feels better in here," said Desire.

"It's nice and peaceful. You got your Martha Stewart going on with the artwork on the walls. You are so creative, girl."

"I try to be. Creating stuff for the house gives me so much peace."

"So, how you feel with your man home?" Shae kicked off the convo.

"It feels so good." I laid Dynasty right beside me, covered up on a pillow. "It's like I feel like I have my family back. We a unit now. It's kinda surreal."

"Yea, he came home all strong. I see him. You fertile as fuck. You'll be pregnant again." Desire was terrible.

"I hope not. We believe in the pull-out method."

"That pull-out shit don't work," Sanai added her two cents. "Yea, give it a year, and you'll be preggo again."

"Y'all are the worst. Well, the pull-out shit works. It's the African rhythm method, and sistas have been using it for centuries. Now, if I get preggers again, then I'm gonna get on some birth control."

"Yea, OK," said Desire.

We giggled.

"How's business? You are such a risk taker." Sanai was inquisitive.

"Business is good. Like really good. Like a bitch is sitting on thousands. It's like I be checking my account to make sure that the money is still there, and that it doesn't disappear. I have a solid team. My assistants are solid, and my mentors and outreach team are really good. We're getting ready to move out of the building that we're in because the government needs the building back to house one of their departments," I said.

"Rent is high in the city. What part of the city are you thinking about going to?" said Sanai.

"Nowhere downtown. Maybe midcity. Anywhere that's safe and affordable. I'm gonna get a realtor to help me. I don't want to spend more than $1,200 a month. I mainly need it for my administrative team and as the headquarters. I have to store files as well."

"That's not bad. There are definitely some office spaces around that rate. You know I know as many salons that I had. You should be good," affirmed Desire.

"How's your financial services job? You know this girl works with the sheikhs and Arabs."

"Whatttttt?" The other girls leaned back for some tea. You could see Ryan peeping through the back door, being nosy and looking at my friends. They ignored him as they should.

"He just gonna keep looking back here," said Shae.

"Ignore him. I'ma tell Kenya about him. He'll check him if it gets outta hand."

"Anyhoo, who cares about that yellow nigga. The job is going good. It's demanding, but it's going good. I have a good salary, and I see myself moving up."

"Yes, you are likeable and have the personality that it takes to climb straight to the top."

"Thank you, and that's my goal."

"Shae, what's up with you?"

"I'm getting my marketing business off the ground. I'm still working in hospitality, but my goal is to have multiple streams of income. I have my son, and I love to travel. She needs coins. Also, let me know how I can market your business."

"Fa' sho'. Send me a few pitches. I'd like to check them out. Every business needs marketing."

"How's the shop?" I asked Desire.

"My clientele is fabulous. But the building that I'm in is not working. The landlord seemed like he rigged the water bill and the electric. And I'm starting to see big giant rats. This is not gonna cut. So, in about a month or so, I'm gonna move."

"Oh no," said Sanai.

"That's messed up. You invested a lot into that shop and made it yours. That's so sad. Her shop looked so good, you guys."

"Wow!" said Shae.

"Those slumlords will get you every time. God is gonna bless you, though," Sanai encouraged.

"Yea, God always bails me out. I'm an optimist. I'm trying to look at the light at the end of the tunnel. I spent a lot of money. Lordy," Desire shook her head. "I'll take another shot, please."

We all giggled. We understood our place being young Black women in America. We understood the challenges and tasks at hand, and my sistas were always motivating and encouraging. There wasn't an ounce of hate in our bodies.

"Mom, can we go to my room and play the game?" King came into the house with an entourage of about seven boys his age. One was Saul's son named after him, and the other was Desire's stepson, li'l Devin.

"Yea, go ahead. Just keep it down. I'm gonna put Dynasty to sleep in her room."

"OK, Ma."

"OK, ladies, I'm gonna put li'l mama to sleep, and then I'll be back to join you."

"Perfect. Y'all wanna roll up a J?" Sanai was a weed smoker.

"I sure do. I brought some green too. We can roll up a couple." Desire was with it.

"I'm gonna stick to the liquor. But I'll hang with you all."

"Okay, let's go outside. See you outside, Dream."

"Yea, give me a few minutes." You could hear the music still booming through the speakers. It was the classic "Before I Let Go," which was the anthem for every cookout. By this time, you could see my neighbors in the yard and Macy dancing by herself. Kenya placed the tiki light torches throughout the yard, giving the yard a real nice golden flare since it was night.

I took Dynasty into her room to wipe her down and change her into her sleepwear. She was sound asleep in her crib. Kenya walked into her room.

"Look at my li'l baby. She is tired boots. I'm gonna make a liquor store run with my homies. I'll be right back."

"OK, Ken." I placed her favorite baby pink bear blankie over her legs and waited a few minutes to make sure she was comfortable and that she was secured. Out of nowhere, I heard a loud commotion. I softly closed the door and came out to see what was going on. I saw Keema and her boyfriend arguing about him being disrespectful and tall-ass Aunt Nita in the middle. Her friend KeKe was standing to the side, and her cousin Desiree was holding her back. All I could think to myself was that Kenya had just left, and I would have to diffuse the situation. By the tone of the argument, you could tell that it was behind Ryan looking at one of my friends. But all you could hear from Keema was, "You are fucking disrespectful. You are so fucking disrespectful!" Their voices got louder, and I intervened.

"Can you guys bring it down?" I asked, standing in front of Keema. "Dynasty is sleeping."

"Fuck you, bitch! You can't tell me how to act in my cousin's house," said Keema as she was being pulled back by Desiree.

In one instance, fireworks started flashing in my mind. I couldn't believe that this bitch Keema had disrespected me in my own house. Kenya's family was known for getting drunk and wreaking havoc. But the lights were flashing in my eyes. And I had forgotten about being a mom, a business owner, and a college graduate in an instant. She triggered the old ole me. She ignited Dreamy from the block. The girl who had to fight her way through high school because of envious-ass bitches like Keema who had it out for me. They could never just ride the wave and stay in their place. Like high school, there always was that one that took you outta character.

"You got me all the way fucked up, Keema. This *ain't* Kenya's house. This is *my* house that *I* pay for. Like I said, Dynasty is sleeping, and y'all are too loud. Go outside!" The flashing lights began.

"Fuck you, bitch!" Keema swung on me.

I immediately stole her back and defended myself. I was never no punk bitch, and she disrespected me, so we went head up. It wasn't nothing. She was in *my* house, and she had to catch *my* hands. However, Kenya's cousins didn't fight fair. Next thing you know, Desiree jumped in, and I was fighting both of them. *How the fuck are these bitches jumping me in my own house?* I thought in my mind as I fought back. The fighting got intense as they pulled on my 22 inches of weave. I lost my balance and fell in front of the doorway. The music became louder and louder. My friends could not hear me struggling to get those evil bitches off of me. Dynasty was sound asleep. The kicking began. Then Aunt Nita began kicking and jumping on me, screaming, "You dirty bitch." Keema echoed her aunt with, "You bitch," as they jumped on me, giving me blow for blow. KeKe threw a few licks. I crawled into a fetal position covering my face from being brutally attacked.

My son heard the commotion and came out to see that I was being jumped and yelled, "Get off my mother! Get off my mother!" He ran and got my friends and my neighbors. As my ears began buzzing, I felt like I was losing strength.

You could hear him scream outside, "They jumping my mother! They jumping my mother in the house! Keema and them, they got my mother." He was panicking.

"What?" You could hear my friends running in from the back door. Shae began trying to pull them off me. Sanai went and grabbed a knife.

"All you could hear was, 'Get off of her! Get off of her!'"


Out of nowhere, my neighbor Kevin flew in, and even though he was a little nigga, he saw Ryan lifting his leg to stomp me out, and he began pulling them off of me.

"Get the fuck off of her! I said, get the fuck off of her! You better not kick her!" Kevin looked Ryan dead in his eyes. He pulled me up off of the ground. I stood up, gathering my bearings. Sanai took a few knives out of the kitchen and started driving those hateful hoes out of my house, locking all the doors. Macy stood in the back of my house near the door in disbelief that her nieces and sister would jump her son's child's mother and girlfriend.

"You good?" Kevin stood in front of me, checking to make sure that I was strong enough to stand.

"Yea." My body had stinging sensations, but it felt numb.

"Someone go call Kenya! Call him now and tell him to come home!"

"Kevin, thank you so much for getting those bitches off of me. I appreciate you."

"I'm going to stab those bitches the fuck up if they come back in here! What they did was wrong! Dead-ass wrong!" Sanai gathered butcher knives outta my kitchen and locked the front and back door. I stood in the center of my house, not understanding how a peaceful person like me welcomed violence. I wasn't a violent person by nature. You would have to drag it outta me. What was a beautiful celebration geared to be a memorable experience ended up being evil. And in my mind, with every blow that they hit me with, it was with malice, rage, jealousy, and envy. It was as if it were all premeditated. You could see the spirit of witches upon them.

"Ma, you good? Why did they do that to you?" King asked. "They wrong. They wrong."

"I'm good, son. Yea, they are rotten. I'm just so glad that you are in tune with me and came out to see what they were doing and called for help. Thank you, son. Thank you, son, for being brave." I hugged him dearly.

"What in the world just happened?" Desire stood checking my face for blood. "So they waited for everyone to leave to do this to you. Those are some low-down dirty hoes."

"Here, Dream, use my phone and call Kenya now!"

I was in a daze and started dialing. Sanai put it on speakerphone.

"Kenya! Kenya! Your cousins jumped me! Come home now! These bitches got me!" My anxiety was high.

"What?" It was hard for Kenya to believe.

"They got her. Keema and Desiree and your aunt and Keema's boyfriend, and some other fat chick jumped her!" Sanai was outraged.

"You telling me that my cousins jumped Dream? I can't believe this shit! I'm on my way, baby! I'm coming now, baby."

"Yea, this is fucked-up. I was trying to get them hoes off of you. They wrong. They are so wrong!" Shae was so mad.

We were all pacing back and forth through the house. There was so much going through my mind that the whole incident seemed surreal. They were cowards, they were disrespectful, and clearly, they were so miserable that they didn't want to see Kenya happy. They attacked me as if we didn't have a connection, and as if Dynasty wasn't their kin. What they didn't know is that Karma was a bad bitch in Red Bottoms, and they would eventually pay for what they did to me in a real way. I was off-limits.

"Oh shit, Kenya is here!" Sanai opened the front door, and we all ran outside. His family nerved up and stood in front of my fence.

He ran up to me. "Dream, you telling me that they jumped you?" He pointed at them.

"Yea, they jumped me. They brought ruckus in the house, Keema and Ryan did. Your aunt called herself trying to break it up. I had just put Dynasty to sleep, and they were so loud that I didn't want them to wake her up. I asked them to be quiet and to go outside. Keema got mad and swung on me, and then we started fighting, and they all jumped in."

"Why your friends didn't jump in?"

"They were outside. The music was loud, and if you were outside, you can't hear what's going on in here. King and his friends saw everything, and it was King who went and got my friends. Shae and Sanai tried to get them off me, but it was Kevin who pulled them off of me and got me off the ground!"

Macy walked over to Kenya. "I can't believe they did that dumb shit knowing how you are."

"Ma, where was you at when they jumped her?"

"I was outside dancing by myself to 'Before I Let Go.'" She put her head down in disappointment.

"Whatttttttttttt? What the fuck?" He screamed at the top of his lungs and walked right up on them—face-to-face. His homeboys knew that he had officially turned into a monster—the very thing that he wanted to bury in the past. No one could stop him now.

"You came to my house and jumped the one I love. You disrespected her means you disrespected me!" He took off his white T-shirt and threw it in the yard. His chest was completely bare. They were babbling and making up lies, but he knew the deal.

"Come here!" he commanded them.

He lined up his cousins and aunt like a game of dominoes and knocked them all down with one solid-ass punch. He kicked his aunt like a dog on the street. He had no remorse. They wailed and cried wolf as if *they* were the victim, and *I* was the adversary.

"Y'all bitches deserve what you get! You better not ever put your hands on Dream again!"

"Fuck you!" Keema cried as she tried to get up.

"That's why I'm gonna call the police on your ass and get you right back in jail," said his aunt, who was hot as fish grease.

"Bitch, fuck you. Call the police. I *want* them to come. And when they come, I'm gonna let them know what y'all did to her. Make sure you tell them that you came to *my* house and jumped *my* girl. Fuck youuuuuuuu, bitch!"

It was like a scene from reality TV, but it was our reality. My friends, King, and his friends, as well as Kenya's homeboys, all stood in the yard watching him release his venom. Ryan walked toward him.

"Eh, Kenya. That nigga was about to stomp Dream out. I caught him as he lifted his leg, and I got her up."

"Who, this nigga right here?" He went straight smack at Ryan.

"Yea, that nigga."

Ken grabbed Ryan by the throat and threw him down on the ground and treated him like a lightweight. He placed his foot on his throat. Ryan pleaded with Ken that he was sorry for what happened. With every molecule in his body, Kenya was milliseconds from snapping his neck.

"You would do that to *my* people? *My* people, nigga? I should kill you! I should muthafuckin' kill you." He kept his foot on his throat for an extra 2 minutes as Ryan pleaded and apologized. Ken had a flash of going back to prison for murder. You could tell that he didn't want to lose his freedom again. He sweated profusely. He spared Ryan, gradually lifting his foot off of his Adam's apple. "Get the fuck outta here and take them with you." He looked down at Ryan. You could see the terror in Ryan's eyes. He got up and jetted to their truck.

Police sirens were loud. It was evident that his aunt called the police on Kenya, which was crazy as hell. Three squad cars expeditiously pulled up in front of my house, and one car was the sheriff. The police jumped out of the car, and I met them at the front of my house.

"Hi, whose house is this?" one of them asked. The officers stood in front of the house. Everyone was in the middle of the street.

"It's my house, Officer," I greeted them.

"So, what happened?"

"They jumped me in my own house," I pointed. "My boyfriend, who is their relative, defended me. They had the nerve to call you guys when *they* jumped *me*."

"No, Officer, my nephew put his hands on us. He just got out of jail and is on parole. Send him back." His aunt Nita was an evil witch in every sense of the word. Keema, Desiree, and Ryan were quiet because they knew what they did was wrong.

"Listen, I'm going to provide you with a report number once you provide me with more details," the officer said to me. We walked off to the side, and he listened as I explained what happened from the beginning. Kenya became unruly as the police talked to him.

"Lock me the fuck up! Lock me the fuck up for defending my family. My baby was in the house when my family jumped my girl.

My family should go to jail for violating *her*!" Kenya stood 6 feet tall, weighed 220 pounds, and was as solid as a rock with both of his forearms stretched out, anticipating being handcuffed. Les, Saul, and Kevin tried to get Kenya to calm down, but he was already at an irate level.

"Sir, calm down. Sir, calm down. We are not trying to lock you up." The sheriff was actually very nonthreatening.

"We don't want a fiasco out here. I understand this is more of a domestic dispute. Everyone needs to leave now!" The sheriff walked over to Keema and Nita. "Listen, you have caused enough trouble. Leave now and do not come back, or we *will* arrest you. Get in your car now, and don't come back!"

Aunt Nita was pissed, but they all got the memo. They got in their car and sped off, looking like the clown asses that they were.

He walked over to Kenya and said, "And so that you don't get yourself in any trouble, someone get him away from here." The police had never been so cool, especially to be white.

I rushed to talk to Kenya after the officer provided me with a report number. "Kenya, come on, come on. Look, you just came home. Your daughters need you. I need you. You cannot go back to jail. I'm gonna have someone take you away from here and come back later. Sanai will stick around. I'll be OK. Let this shit die down, Ken." My eyes watered up. I didn't wanna lose him again.

"I hate my family for this shit! They fucked up something that was supposed to be a celebration. I can't believe them. Watch them lie to my grandma. I'ma tell her the real. My grandma always thinks I'm in the wrong, but I'm in the right this time. Nobody bet not ever put

they hands on you ever again. I'm so sorry, Dream. I'm sorry, baby."
His eyes watered up.

"That's fucked up what they did, man. That's sad," Les added.

"I had her, though. They was not gonna get the best of her," Kevin
assured him.

"Look, Kevin, I need you to take Kenya away from here for a few
hours and bring him back in one piece." I gave Kevin my keys.

"I got you. I promise he'll be back," he responded.

"Thanks, Kev."

"Let me grab a shirt, kiss the baby, and I'm out. You right. I gotta
get away from here before I destroy a nigga."

We all went back into the house. Ken checked on Dynasty as she
was still sound asleep like an angel. I assured King that we would be
okay and got him settled in his room with a few of his friends who
were staying over. The whole neighborhood witnessed what could
have become a bloody riot. The yard was dark, and the tiki lights
were blown out. Mostly everyone was in a state of shock, but they
made sure that I was OK before they left, including my homegirl,
Shae.

"Girl, me and Amir are gonna stay here with you for a while. Just in
case someone else feel like they bold enough to run up," said Sanai.

"Girl, girl, girl . . . I can't believe these bitches. Look at me." Desire
looked at me face-to-face, even though she was as high as a kite and
meant well.

"No scratches, no bruises." Everyone who was in the living room
busted out in laughter. Her mannerisms were hilarious.

"My face look OK, though?"

"Yes, honey. You ain't got no scratches or no bruises. They jumped you and still couldn't do nothing with you."

I cracked a smile.

She touched my hair and took her brush and began brushing my weave. She was my hairstylist too.

"Your weave is still on its tracks. Fuck dem hoes. You still look good. They couldn't do nothing with you. You are intact. POW, honey buns. I'm going take li'l Devin to the house. He scary, so I know he going tell his father about what happened. I'll come back out too, if you need me."

"Thank you, Desire. I gotta process this. I'll call everyone tomorrow. I'm done for the night. Just hoping Kenya comes back home safely."

"I'm gone, boo. I'll be back in a few hours, though. I'm going Uptown. Lock the doors and call me if you need me. I'ma come back with a few hammers, and it's whatever."

"Be safe, Ken." We embraced.

He left with Kevin in my car, and Les and Saul followed him. Sanai helped me to straighten up the house. We noticed a gash in my wall from where I was jumped, which meant the whole wall would have to be replaced. Deep down, I wanted to make them pay for what they did to me. But I was truly confident that the Most High would ensure justice, and no stone would go unturned.

Sanai and I talked all night long and through the wee hours. She forever had my back and was with the business. She did not leave until she had a peace about us—we were family.

I had a final chance to look at myself in the mirror. Despite the enemies' attempt to harm me, Desire was right. I was unscathed. I called home. I just needed to talk to my parents, even though I already knew how they would react. My mother wasn't home, but my stepdad was.

"Hello," I whispered.

"Dream?"

"Yes, is my mom there?"

"No, but what's wrong? I hear it in your voice."

"Major, they jumped me." I started crying. I was in my bedroom talking low because I did not want to wake up the kids.

"Who jumped you?" He was ready.

"Kenya's cousins and aunt. They jumped me in the house at the cookout that I threw today."

"Dream, don't tell me no shit like that. I know that was a cookout for you and King and for that nigga. And his cousins jumped you?"

"Yea. Keema, Kenya's cousin, was acting stupid 'cause her dude was eyeing my friends. She's jealous hearted and started fighting with him. They brought it inside my house, and I asked them to take it outside. Keema got mad and was disrespectful and swung on me. I stole her and started fighting back. That's when her aunt, cousin, and her dude jumped in."

"Don't tell me no shit like that. Don't tell me that! What the fuck is going on out there in the DMV? See, if that was L.A., we would have shot that whole shit up. That would have never went down. They saw you as vulnerable. Did your friends jump in?"

"A few tried, but they couldn't get them off me. My neighbor came and got them off me." I began wiping my tears.

"Hold the fuck up! So, did Kenya do anything?"

"Yea, he was at the liquor store when it jumped off. But when he came back, he knocked them down, and they fell like dominoes. One hit and they were down. He kicked the shit out of his aunt. He was gonna kill Keema's boyfriend. The police came and everything."

"Yea, but that should have never happened. Clearly, they don't respect your man. He better check that shit before I send your brother and some of the Crips out there. You all right? Ain't nothing broken, is it?"

"No. I look like myself. No scratches or bruises." He didn't know that was now our inside joke.

"That's good. They jealous hoes. They weak as fuck. And they better hope that I don't get no money, 'cause I will come out there and get with them. Wait 'til I tell your mama. She's gonna go the fuck off. She might come out there ASAP. Was Sanai there? I know she has your back!"

"Yes, Sanai just left with her son. Yea, she was chasing them hoes out of the house with butcher knives."

"She's solid."

"Yea, Major, but I cannot believe it."

"Where's Kenya at now?"

"I sent him away for some fresh air because the police came, and I didn't want them to take him back."

"Yea, he don't need to go to jail. He needs to stay out so that he can protect his family. It's about his family and no one else. And when I get a chance, I'm gonna talk to him about that."

"Well, Major, I just wanted to let you know what's going on out here. I'm so tired."

"Get some rest, baby girl. The kids safe, right?"

"Yea, they're good."

"Try to sleep that shit off, and we'll call you tomorrow. This ain't sitting well with me, and it's not gonna sit well with your mama. God gonna get them, though. He not gonna play with them. You are God's child. You have always been God's child. He got you."

"Thank you, Major. I'm gonna try to sleep. I'll talk to you and Mommy tomorrow. I love you."

"I love you too. Whew, you got my blood pressure up. Call us tomorrow, baby girl."

"OK, I will. Good night."

"Good night, baby girl."

We hung up. My parents were my original protectors, and they had to be aware of what was going on 3,000 miles away. And they would catch a flight to fuck up anyone who harmed me.


It was hard for me to rest. Kenya came back around 5:00 a.m. When Kevin brought him back, he was slightly drunk and riled up. Somehow, he still had a burst of energy. I noticed that his white clothes had hints of blood on them and that his ear was leaking as he walked into the house.

"Get me a towel, Dream. My ear is cut." He was irritated. I went and got a towel, cotton balls, and peroxide.

"What the hell happened to you? C'mon, Kevin, I told you to bring him back in one piece."

"Your man is wild. He don't listen. Let him tell you what happened."

"So what happened, Ken?"

"I was at a crap game Uptown. I was getting niggas. I was making money. A nigga from your old way on Clay Street was getting heated 'cause I was breaking niggas' pockets. We got into it and started fighting, and he sliced my ear. You know the nigga Beans?"

"Beans? I actually get along with Beans. Beans used to look out for me when I lived Uptown. You know that. What the hell?" I started helping him to clean up his ear.

"Beans think every nigga scared of him. You already know I was enraged when I went up there. I was ready to go for blood 'cause of what my family did to you. At that point, any nigga could have got it. He better be glad I didn't really hurt 'im. I gave him a pass."

"You looked perfectly fine in white earlier and now . . . This is a rough 24 hours." Together, we wiped the blood off his ear.

"Are you gonna need stitches?"

"Naw, I'm a G, sweetheart. I'ma clean it and put some Neosporin on it every day until it heals. It's just flesh."

"All right, y'all. I'm going to the house. I see y'all when I get up. I'm next door, you know." Kevin was our hood angel from that point on.

"All right, cuz, thanks." Kenya laid on my lap, and we reclined the chairs.

"Baby, thank you for giving me a beautiful daughter and having a wonderful celebration. I just hate how it ended. My cousins are jealous. My aunt is miserable. And that nigga, Ryan—I just wanted to kill him for having the audacity even to think he was gonna stomp you out. I won't be dealing with my family for a long time."

"Yea, I tried, but never again will we have a celebration like that."

"I get it. I'm sorry, boo. But I've been thinking about us. It feels like it's us against the world now. But I wanna be with you forever. I wanna get married. Plus, we gotta be married in order for us to be together. The condition of my parole is that we have to be married, or I go back to a halfway house in the Commonwealth. And if the halfway house is full, I go back to jail and serve the rest of my sentence."

"Kenya, us married? Do you think we actually could do marriage? My parents been married for more than 20 years, and it's tough. Things weren't always rosy, but through the fire, they pushed."

"I think we got what it takes if you trust me. I want our family so bad."

"I want us to stay together, and I want us to be a power couple, but we gotta be strong and stick together, no matter what." I was adamant. "We already being tested."

"Yea, that's why we need to be locked in." He pulled me closer to lay on his chest.

"I mean, we could try it, but if I don't like it, there is always divorce," I giggled.

"Really, Dream? Why do you end things before you begin them? Why you already giving up?"

"I don't necessarily think that relationships are made for me. It's always something like infidelity or a nigga leaving me." I shrugged my shoulders.

"Do you want a big wedding?"

"Naw, when I was younger, I did. I just wanna go to the justice of the peace and have a nice honeymoon. Let's take our money and buy property or invest in something. Why should we have a wedding? Clearly, we got haters."

"Well, damn, OK! Whatever you want, I'm with it."

"Yea, I'm simple." My eyes were heavy.

"Marry me, Dream."

"I'll try it out. But you need to get your family. I don't fuck with them. They can't come to the justice of the peace, neither. I don't want no parts of them."

"My mom side is fucked up. But my dad side is cool. I'm gonna start bringing you around them. They're laid-back."

I looked at him crazy and then started dozing off.

"I love you, and I'm sorry. It will never happen again."

"OK. I'm tired, Ken. This was way too much. I need to go to sleep."

"Good night, my love."

"Good night." I closed my eyes.

"Good night, wifey."

They hated us with a passion. Yet, it drew us closer and made us stronger. I would give love a try. Kenya was right. We were locked in.

# Chapter 22

## Heart Chakras

We got married on Friday the 13th. Wasn't sure if I was running into a curse, a blessing, or a divine revelation. I spent 24 hours in a trance from the physical to the metaphysical to the spiritual. It was more than going half on a baby, for the baby had already arrived. I had been a queen without a king for so many years; yet, I learned to build the foundation of my family in a matriarchal society.

Like the profound King Shaka Zulu, warrior leader of the Zulus, my experience was that of his mother, Queen Nandi. A story of abandonment, poverty, humiliation, and mental health challenges that in my weakest hour, I would rise and pull from my inner being and become stronger than they thought. God covered me, protected us, and orchestrated a new path for my life.

On Friday the 13th, I would no longer be a queen alone. My king would show up, promising never to leave me as we merged our souls, creating a matrimony where you'd snap your fingers to "Black Love." That Friday, I would take my rightful place as "his rib," assuming my royal position and smiling while adjusting my crown. We were crazy. Yea, we didn't make any sense. We grew up in 48 hours and discovered a love that would never be replaced.

We shopped for our rings together as we laughed at not really knowing the difference between white gold and silver. As I ate a scoop of coffee ice cream on a sugar cone, you could see the dents of my Red Ruby Woo lipstick that, for most men, were hypnotizing. But if you knew me, I ate ice cream when I was sad, when I was heartbroken, when I was nervous as hell. Ice cream was my comfort. In my mind, I deserved a $50,000 ring, but I was beginning to see that it wasn't about the ring. It was about the vows, and if we were really gonna be about that married life. However, the karat on the white gold princess cut diamond ring was beautiful, and so was the 14K white gold wedding band for Ken.

We paid cash for our rings and agreed that we would have a nice romantic getaway at a beach and stack our money, invest, beach hop, and build our credit. We were in a good place because while he was on vacation, I was building an empire and obtaining lucrative contracts. I had been at the bottom for a long time, and you couldn't pay me to go back. We were like hood stars, money stacks, and diamond rings.

We didn't have a bachelor or bachelorette party. We barely told our parents about us jumping the broom. We were selfish, and for us, it was OK. The day before the wedding, we used the time that the kids were in school to get groomed. Ken spent the day with his barber and getting a fresh linen suit and all the other shenanigans that came with being the groom. And I spent damn near the whole day getting done up by Desire. I dreamed of 32 inches of jet-black Indian hair, but I settled for 24 inches of gorgeous pin curls that cascaded down my back. My lashes were beautiful, and my brown, chinky eyes were ever so clear.

Desire couldn't believe that I was jumping the broom, but she was following my footsteps later that month, and she would be married too. Desire and I had traveled the same path for nearly a decade, being young, free, and full of positive vibrations. Desire was an optimist, and I was a realist. While she was super excited about being married, I wasn't sure if I would be a great wife or if Kenya would be a great husband. We should have pursued marriage counseling, but Kenya was so eager to make it happen captain, that I married him because I loved him with my core, and I was silly enough to move fast. It was like jumping into a pool and not really knowing how to swim, but you trust that your husband is not going to let you drown. Or, in my case, I would doggy-paddle to the side of the pool and get the fuck out.

Kenya would pick up the kids from day care and school while Tammy, who was my staff and who I'd become real close with, took me to look for a wedding dress in some bougie part of Maryland. We went to a few wedding stores, but I wasn't feeling the style of the dresses. I wanted to look and feel beautiful without being dramatic. After spending hours going from wedding boutiques to high-end department stores, we finally ended up at Saks. We had a fifth of tequila, and it seemed like I was good and tipsy by the time we made it to the dressing room. Tammy was top-heavy like me, so she understood the injustice in any dress, let alone a wedding dress that would fit my breasts, accentuate my hips, and tuck my stomach. I started getting emotional and cranky as I had a meltdown in the dressing room.

"Tammy, I'm tired. If the next dress don't fit or look right, then fuck this wedding tomorrow. Hell, I'll wear jeans. I'll wear a business suit."

"Come on, Dream. You gotta look pretty on your wedding day. It's a day that you will always remember. Don't give up. Chill. Lemme pull a few dresses."

"OK, Tammy, but my feet hurt. We haven't even found a pair of shoes. This is too much."

As I sat in the dressing room, I was over it. Thank God I wasn't having a big wedding because I would end up being a runaway bride. My anxiety was too high to deal with the details.

"Here. These are three dresses for you to try on. I'm gonna help you lift up your titties, and we can grab you a Spanx to make sure you look slim and trim."

"All right. I'm gonna try them on."

The first dress was white and cute and fit me like a glove, but it was too hoochie, and it look like it would show every part of my body but my ass. The second dress was a traditional wedding dress, but it had no definition or anything exotic about it. The third dress, however, was more my vibe. It wasn't too long or too short. It was off-white, and it had an off-the-shoulder Cleopatra Egyptian effect. The top portion was adorned with sparkles and stones, the waist was snatched, and the bottom of the dress was flowing. I kept the dress on for a few minutes as I stared at myself in the mirror.

"Hey, whatchu doing in there? Let me see you." Tammy was pressed.

"You like?"

"Yasssss, that's it. You got all that hair for it. You look like a wife. You look so pretty, so pretty." She started batting her Tammy Faye Bakker lashes. "That's you. Now, I found three pair of shoes. Try 'em on. 'Cause the stores are closing in 30 minutes. We been looking for dresses for 4 hours. Make it work." I was getting on her nerves.

"Thanks, Tammy. You know I'm difficult. But I'm telling you now. I want the rhinestone stiletto heels. I'm gawdy. I'm giving the Cleopatra look." I put the heels on, zipping them up. I showed the heel off.

"Oh, you blinging. You showing off. Yep, that's it. Okay, come out of the heels and hand me that dress. I grabbed you some Spanx and a few other things you could use as an undergarment. It's too hot for stockings. Grease your body down. I'll help you in the morning to get you together."

"You are heaven-sent, Tammy. Thank you so much for being here for me. You just don't know. I really appreciate you. Thank you for the shots. I need them now, and I'll need one in the morning 'cause this is too much." I started laughing at my own tiredness.

"You just wanna crunch numbers all day and do business. Well, welcome to wifey status. You gonna have to cook too. All that eat out and shit ain't gonna cut it."

"Look, I clean, and Kenya cooks. We got an agreement. He hustle, I hustle, we hustle. It ain't nothing." I started putting on my jeans, graphic tee, and heels. I had to have a heel on every shoe that I wore. I was short, and it was mandatory. I followed Tammy to the register. She had a collection of items that went along with my wedding dress that were necessities according to her, and she was an expert—I didn't argue. My attitude was ring it up and throw it in the bag. Tammy carried my wedding dress. She had me by 10 years, so she was experienced, and there were things that I could learn from her, even though I was her boss—it didn't matter.

"You good now? Kenya is gonna be the luckiest man in the world."

"You think?"

"I know so."

Tammy was grand at hospitality, and I was going home ever so tipsy after taking a few shots from a local bar with her. Deep down, I was happy about my wedding dress and being confident that Kenya would be proud of the finished product. Tammy was godsent. When she dropped me off, she gave me that look like "It's showtime, Dream." She was right. It was time for me to leave my comfort zone. I knew numbers, research, stats, business, activism, entrepreneurship, and being a writer, but I didn't know love like I had mastered the others.

Kenya had fed the kids and put them to sleep by the time I got home. He was unusually calm, which was weird. As soon as I opened the door, he was walking outside to sit on the porch to smoke a cigarette, which meant that he was just as nervous as me.

"Baby, I missed you. What took you so long?"

"I had to try on a hundred wedding dresses before I found the right one. You know how I am."

"I know, baby. I was missing you. Go put your dress and the bags up and come talk to me."

"OK. I'ma pee too." I hid the dress in the closet and my bags. He was nosy. I wanted him to be surprised and utterly excited. I went to use the bathroom to relieve myself. Lawd, there was so much on my mind. I washed my hands and checked to make sure that my curls were still pinned and that my lashes looked perfect. Then I went and joined Kenya on the porch. The weather felt so good, and I had been drinking, so eventually, I would pass out and go to sleep.

"We got a big day tomorrow. You ready?"

"Whatchu mean, am I ready?" I tried to be funny.

"No, seriously. We locked in forever after tomorrow."

"Yea, I know. It all seems like a dream. Everything moving so fast. I'm trying to digest it all."

"What's real is that we love each other. What's real is that I love you, and you love me. This shit ain't for sale. Just know that. You got my full attention. You got my whole heart, and you gave birth to my whole heart in a human form. You changed my life. I know God brought you into my life to extend it. I should have been dead by now."

"Wow. I believe God brought you into my life to show me what real love, sacrifice, and what a meaningful relationship feels like. What unconditional love is. I pretty much gave up on love until we connected. You made me buy into love, something that I felt was a fairy tale that I would never experience. I'm eternally grateful for you."

He began hugging me as I lay my head on his shoulder.

"You been drinking, huh?" He laughed at me as my eyes lowered.
"You smell it on my breath? Yea, I've been taken shots all day with Tammy. She had that doggone bottle of tequila, and then we went to a bar. I'm done!"

"You could have brought a nigga something to drink."

"In the back of my mind, I figured your boys came through and brought you by something to drink."

"I had a few beers earlier with the homies."

"See, I knew it."

"But I didn't want to get twisted the night before my wedding day and be a crash dummy. I'm trying to do the right thing so that God will bless us."

"Wow! You really *are* serious. You're demonstrating maturity. Welp, I drank for me and you, lover. I love you. I'm tired."

"As long as you're happy, that's what matters to me. Let's go to bed and get some rest. We gotta big day tomorrow. A beautiful day, that is."

"I gotta wake up early to drop the kids off at school and rush back to get dressed."

"Pops, Frank, and Reagan will be here for us."

"OK. Well, Lee will be here for me, and Tammy is gonna help me to get dressed. Sanai will have the kids for our honeymoon." I threw on his wife beater and some evening shorts and put on my bonnet. We got in the bed, and he cuddled me from behind, making sure that I was comfortable. In less than 24 hours, the course of my life would transform. It was déjà vu, something that I foresaw as a kid. I would make Ken and Barbie play together and dream of matching Barbie's cars and matching outfits with matching smiles, and perhaps matching hearts. I had my own personal, real-life Ken doll.

Kenya was up before me, making a light breakfast for the kids and me. The aroma of bacon, eggs, cut-up fruit, and orange juice was all we needed. We were running off of 6 hours of sleep and adrenaline. He had Dynasty in her high chair feeding her fruit and eggs, and he had already awakened King for him to get ready for school. We mutually agreed that we would intimately marry by going to the justice of the peace, have a few witnesses, and then run off to our honeymoon at a beach resort since it was summer, and we both loved the beach. We discussed having a neo-soul-like reception in the near future, but we wouldn't do it until we were ready. Simple was perfectly fine with us.

"Hey, sleepyhead, you up?" He had King at the table eating his breakfast as he gave Dynasty her juice cup.

"Yes, and I'm still sleepy." I walked in the kitchen and hugged King, kissed my phat baby, and gave Ken the longest hug.

"Baby, you got it smelling so good in here. That's what woke me up. Food."

"I knew it would. You ready? You ready? 'Cause I am!" Kenya was hyped. Dynasty was smiling and screaming, "Dada Dada Dada." When he was hyped, she was hyped right along with him.

"So, y'all getting married today while we at school?" King asked with his raspy voice.

"Yea, playboy. While y'all badasses are at school, we gonna be at the altar." We all busted out in laughter.

"Why we can't go? Who's gonna be there?"

"We just doing a two-step, King. We not doing nothing major. We're exchanging vows and our rings. We gonna have a big reception soon where everyone will be there, and y'all kids will participate. Right now, we just sealing the deal," I assured him.

"Basically, y'all just wanna get the marriage thing down."

"Playboy, you smart. You got it. We love y'all. Today, we're solidifying our love."

"I got it. Well, good luck. Who's picking us up?" King was ahead of his years.

"I'm dropping you two off this morning, and we both will pick you up. But you going to Sanai for the weekend so we can have our honeymoon."

"You showing off, Ma?"

"Yea, Mama showing off." I winked at him as I chewed on the rest of my bacon and washed it down with some orange juice. "Get your stuff together because we're leaving shortly."

"I'm almost ready."

"Thanks, son. My li'l mama ain't tripping off of me. She just smiling for Daddy." I picked her up out of her high chair. "Give me kisses, give me kisses." She giggled and embraced me.

"Mama gonna put you on a cute lavender romper with some cute sandals. You gonna be too cute." I placed her on my hip and took her to the room to wipe her down, get her dressed, and put her hair into Afro puffs. She was growing up, and she was saying names and words. She was a happy baby who rarely cried unless something was bothering her. She was a chocolate tone, with smooth skin, chunky thighs, and curly coils of a full head of hair. She had chinky eyes like Kenya and full lips like me. She was such a wonderful combination of us. She went to Ms. P for day care, just like King and my godson, Amir, did. I grabbed her diaper bag, which mainly had toddler snacks, organic juice, and a few bottles of breast milk that I stored in the freezer. I would pump a few days a week and freeze the milk for day care. Although Ms. P had the babies moving at a progressive pace, and they were eating fresh breakfast and lunch every day, I always tried to feed my babies breakfast and pack them a snack. I did it with King, and I would carry on the tradition with Dynasty.

"Come on, King!"

He zoomed out of the kitchen with his book bag on eating the last pieces of bacon and then dapping up Kenya. He was in full uniform, which was purple and black, but he was a cool dude, so he loved to wear a fitted hat to the side. Kenya was on the phone, talking to Saul. He was so geeked about the wedding.

"Love y'all," he waved to the kids.

I got Dynasty settled and locked in her car seat, and King was already in the front seat with his seat belt buckled.

"Everyone good?" I turned on the radio and began zipping through the streets, cutting down shortcuts, and navigating around traffic. Reality hit me like a ton of bricks that I was getting married in a few hours, and my anxiety was elevated. The ride was silent. Everyone was in their own world as the radio played all the jams. I had never been so focused.

"Dang, you got here quick. I wish you would drive this fast every day. Then I wouldn't be late for school." King was such a smart-ass. He gathered his things.

"Boy, shut up and give me a hug. I love you. Have a good day at school, and I'll see you later."

"OK, Mom. Have a good wedding. Love you." He jetted out of my car to be with his friends.

I drove a few miles down from King's school and was at the day care to bring Dynasty in. It was great comfort that the kids went to school near each other, and Nia was about two blocks away from King's school, which was great. I tried walking Dynasty in the day care. She took a few steps, grabbed the rail, and then wanted to be picked up. Ms. P was standing at the front door greeting parents and welcoming babies.

"Give me my baby." Ms. P took her right out of my hands. I handed her the diaper bag.

"Bring her some more diapers. She's running out."

"I sure will. I'll drop off a case next week."

"Where you in a hurry to?"

"Girl, me and Kenya getting married at noon. I'm headed to the justice of the peace."

"Aww, that's so nice. You really have changed that boy. 'Cause back in the day, he was wild. Well, blessings to y'all and see you later on. Y'all going on a honeymoon?"

"Yes, we leaving out tonight. Can't wait."

"You go, girl! So proud of y'all."

"Thank you for everything. See you later. Love you, Dynasty."

I ran off like a crazy bridezilla, jumping in my car and driving like a bat out of hell. I was getting married. I was *really* getting married. How in the hell? I connected my phone to the Bluetooth and began playing all my Mary J Blige songs. There was something about Mary that spoke to every aspect of my life. From "My Life" to "Mary's Joint" to "Share My World" to "I'm in Love," my spirit woman was waking up. There was something about Method Man's voice when "You're All I Need" hit. It spoke volumes to our ghetto love.

As soon as I pulled up to the house, Tammy was waiting on me, and Kenya was in the yard pacing with his cell phone as he let the world know that he was getting married.

"My baby is back. Let's get it. I already took my shower. You got the whole bathroom to beautify yourself. 'Cause you gonna be in there for a long time. I'm hip." He smacked me hard as shit on my ass.

"Hey, girl!" Tammy came into the house. "It's y'all big day. Hey, Kenya!"

"Hey, Tammy. Thank you for helping her last night and being here today. I appreciate it."

"That's my girl. I got her. I know she nervous."

"She nervous. I'm nervous. This is real love, Tammy."

"Yea, I believe it is real. She did that bid for you, waited for you to come home. You came home to her and been about family ever since. Marriage seems right." Tammy sat on the couch with her denim dress on and her cute kitten heels.

"Tammy, I'm in the shower!" I yelled.

"OKKKKKKKK!" she yelled back.

There was nothing like Dr. Bronner's Pure-Castile Peppermint soap lathering my breasts, through my vagina, falling in between the creases of my back rolls, and piercing my healed C-section marks. The warm water felt amazing as it flowed from the top of my shoulder blades, caressing my hips, and cascading the middle of my calves. There were no thoughts, just peace resonating in the atmosphere. All parts were cleansed. I came out of the shower inhaling the steam and drying myself off. The toothbrush and toothpaste swiveled through my wisdom teeth to the top of my crown. My whites were pearly. My curls were misty, but Desire guaranteed that when they dropped, that I would look like Rapunzel. Kenya was getting dressed in King's room. I stepped into the hallway, tiptoeing while smelling the aroma of his cologne scent. He smelled so good.

"You need me?" Tammy was such an auntie.

"Yes, I do." I grabbed the cocoa butter to begin greasing myself.

"Let me get some of that cocoa butter and grease your back shoulders and elbows. Your skin gotta be glowing."

"Yes, help me 'cause I be ashy." I stood straight up.

"Where are your undergarments?"

"They're on the bed." I put on my satin white strapless bra and corset. Tammy began adjusting my corset like a professional.

"Pull them titties up. They heavy, but I gotta button up the corset and adjust it."

"Lord, my titties are an issue." I began cuffing my breasts.

"Baby, are you almost dressed?" Kenya's voice carried from outside the door.

"Ken, I'm getting there."

"I'm dressed. I'm brushing these Grahams for you."

"Okay. I'll be out soon." I looked at Tammy like, "Holy shit, I betta hurry up."

"We gotta be at the courthouse in an hour. Pops is here, and Frank is on his way."

"OK. Gotcha, baby. Tell Pops I said hi, and I'm coming."

You could hear music playing in the background, which meant Kenya caught a whole vibe and was in his element.

"The corset is good. Let's get the dress on you and take out your pin curls." Tammy carefully put the Cleopatra-style dress over my head. It was such a smooth transition, especially since my corset was a good fit. Tammy began taking the pins out of my hair until my hair looked like a complete falsetto. I put my diamonds in my ear and brushed bronzer on my cheekbones. Tammy added some soft gold eye shadow, and I topped it off with a golden peach lipglass. She brushed the bottom of my curls that fell to my waistline. My bride look came alive.

"Yassssss, you look beautiful. Look at you. So, so pretty! He is gonna be pleased. Put those studded-out stilettos on. You look like a Black Indian."

I began spraying perfume all over my body. The sun was shining on my face, and certainly, there was something rare about me at that moment. I placed my French manicured flat feet into the rhinestone-encrusted shoe, and Tammy zipped them on in.

"OK, Black Pocahontas. Let me get a few pictures of you." She began snapping photos.

"Tammy, thank you, sis. Thank you so much." I hugged her.

"You got it. Let's walk you out to the front so that they can see the bride. I gotta go see some of the mentoring clients. But we'll catch up next week after the honeymoon."

She opened my bedroom door as I walked out into the living room area, struggling to walk, but poised in my studded-out bridal shoes. Kenya's pop, Lee, Frank, and his fiancée were in the living room. Kenya stood at the doorway.

"Here comes the bride! Look at how beautiful she is!" Lee said. Everyone stood up, and they began clapping like we were in church.

"Hey, y'all! Thank you for coming at such a last-minute notice. But we are so glad that you were able to make it for this occasion. We are blessed."

"Look at my baby. Look at how amazing you look, Dream. I know I can't kiss you until after the wedding. You are pretty, so pretty in white."

"Look at you in the white linen with your handsome self. My king. I'm ready!"

"Let's go and jump the broom!"

"We gotta get a few pictures of you two out front," said Frank.

"Come on, baby. Let's go out front so they can get the pics." He was so excited as he grabbed my hand. Then we walked gracefully to the front of our walkway that was adorned with a spray of white balloons.

The neighbors were standing outside as they sent us well wishes, clapped, and whistled. We waved and took pictures that captured this once-in-a-lifetime moment. We departed in separate cars so that we didn't break tradition. Ken and his pops rode with Frank and his girlfriend, and I rode with Lee. Lee and Tammy may have been my staff, but it was like we had a deeper connection. They were thorough, had big hearts, and wanted the best for me. Tammy helped me meticulously to get in the car, handing me a platinum, jeweled-out tiny purse that matched my shoes and could only fit Kenya's ring, my identification, and money. Lee turned up the music real loud, playing his classic Go-Go jams as we talked, laughed, and he shared his outlook on marriage. He reflected on being married, understanding commitment, and working through things when they get tough. He expounded that it wasn't about the good times that counted, but it was the hardest and most difficult times that made being married count.

The justice of the peace was about 10 miles from the house, which wasn't far, and with the way that Lee drove, we were there in 12 minutes. We found parking spaces within a few feet of the building. Kenya opened the door like a perfect gentleman, making sure that my white stayed white. He was geeked, high energy, and he couldn't wait.

"Come on, my beautiful baby. Let's do this."

"Let's do this," I echoed his sentiments.

Hand in hand, we walked into the building, went through security, the metal detectors, and were greeted by the civil ceremonies division. While our guests waited in the ceremonial room, we paid a small fee and filled out our licensing documents. The clerk provided us standard information, gave us her blessings, and escorted us to the ceremonial room where our guests were already standing in position.

It was an all-white, quaint, cute room with flowers. We were greeted by a middle-aged Black woman who was our marriage officiant. She gave off wonderful vibes and had a good spirit.

"Look at how beautiful you two look together. Welcome, Dream, and welcome, Kenya, to your very own wedding ceremony. What a beautiful day to choose to say I do."

"Yes, it is!" Kenya shouted like he had a Baptist moment. Everyone started laughing.

"Look at my son. You grew up, son. Dream is the perfect woman for you. Can't believe you getting married, son. If you would have given me some time, I would have dressed more appropriately. But I'm here is all that matters," said Kenya's pops as he stood in his jeans, a navy-blue T-shirt, Timberland boots, and wearing cornrows. He indeed was an OG.

"Thanks, Pops. I wanted you here," Kenya replied.

"It's radiant. The atmosphere is right," the minister began. "Will you please face me?"

We faced her, and immediately, my anxiety shot into the ceiling. It had just got real for me. It was hard to focus, and my feelings were taken away like Calgon.

"We are gathered here today to celebrate one of life's greatest moments, and to cherish the words which shall unite today on Friday, July 13th."

Kenya looked at me as if he wanted to drop an expletive about it being Friday the 13th. But he held his composure, although his hands were shaking.

"Marriage is the promise between two people who love each other, who trust in love, who honor each other, and on this day, you choose to spend the rest of your lives together." The minister nodded her head at us, and we nodded back.

"This ceremony will not create a relationship that does not already exist between you two. This is a symbol of how far you have come all the years that you have been together. It is a symbol of the promises you will make to each other. No matter what challenges you face, you now face them together. The I's are officially removed, and now, it is WE." She commanded everyone's attention. "No matter how much you succeed, you succeed together. When you grow weak, it is growing weak together, and when you continue to grow strong, you grow strong together. And now the vows." She stared into our eyes and connected with our energy.

Kenya had sweat on his brows, embodying nervousness. My feet were stinging, and in my mind, I had asked the question, *What in the hell have I gotten myself into?*


"Face each other. I ask of you both, do you promise to choose each other every day to love each other in word and deed?"

"We do!" Kenya and I said in unison.

"Do you promise to recognize each other as equals and support each other in your goals and wishes for the future?"

"We do."

"Kenya, do you take Dream to be your wife?"

"I do." He looked me dead in my eyes.

"Dream, do you take Kenya to be your husband?"

"I do." My mind drifted . . .

"Groom, do you choose your bride to be your wife, your best friend, and only love? To live together, play together, and laugh together? To work by her side and dream in her arms? To feed her soul and always love her with all your heart?"

"I do. I do." Tears meekly fell down his cheeks.

"Bride, do you choose your groom to be your husband, best friend, and your only love? To live together, play together, and laugh together? To work by his side and dream in his arms? To feed his soul? To always seek out the best in him?"

"I do." Tears welled up in my eyes.

"Please prepare for the exchanging of the rings."

We were hood stars. Kenya pulled my ring out of his pocket, and I pulled his out of my clutch. We held them in the palm of our hands, and the carats were blinging.

"Let's begin with you, Kenya. Take your bride's hand and repeat these vows. I, Kenya, take Dream to be my wife, to have and to hold from this day forward, for better or for worse, for richer, for poorer, in sickness and in health, to love and to cherish from this day forward until death do us part."

He repeated those words like he had rehearsed them all his life.

"Place that beautiful ring on her wedding finger."

Whew, chile, the intensity went up a notch.

"Now, Ms. Dream, repeat these vows. I, Dream, take Kenya to be my husband, to have and to hold from this day forward, for better or for worse, for richer, for poorer, in sickness and in health, to love and to cherish from this day forward until death do us part."

I repeated those words like it was the first time for me at an open mic in front of a crowd of 100 people. I tripped over too many words, and the vows were speaking to my soul in a new language. Kenya was smiling at me with his snaggletooth looking like "Iron Mike."

"Now, Ms. Dream, place that beautiful band on his wedding finger." My hands were shaking.

"Now, as you enter this state of matrimony, you should strive to make real the ideals which give meaning to both this ceremony and the institution of marriage. With full awareness, know that within the circle, you are not only declaring intent before your friends and family, but you speak that intent to a higher power. The promises today strengthen your union forevermore. Do you still seek to enter?"

"Yes, we do!" We were flowing in a gaze.

"With the power invested in me, I now pronounce you Husband and Wife. You may kiss the bride."

Kenya placed both hands on my cheekbones and kissed me like never before. We both were teary-eyed. You could hear our people clapping and rooting for us. We looked up and were surrounded by love and an envelope with our marriage licenses in it. Kenya and I just hugged and rocked back and forth.

"Y'all took a leap of faith. That's all right. Congratulations, y'all!" Lee gave Ken a pound and me a hug.

"Thanks, everyone, for being here. This is a lifer, wifer, my heart. There is no question that I made the right choice, and you are here to witness this. We thank y'all from the bottom of our hearts!" Kenya announced to our circle.

"Man, that was so beautiful. You had me teared up. Nigga, you a G. With a capital G. I got nothing but respect," said Frank.

"You look so pretty, Dream. You look like an angel. I was crying too. That was Black love right there," Reagan said, hugging me.

"Girl, I was so nervous. Thank you."

"It didn't look like it. You two looked like pros."

"Thank you so much!" I waved to the minister. She was gone gracefully like an angel. She winked to let me know that I was in good hands. It was that sister code.

"Come on, baby. The clerks want us to go outside. They have another ceremony coming up. Let's take some pictures out front."

"Yea, it's beautiful outside. Y'all, that was beautiful. I am so proud, so proud, son. You got you a stand-up woman. Now, if I could just get me one." We all walked outside. Kenya was grinning. Our rings looked so good on our chocolate hands. We flossed with our hands, embraced, showing our rings. We smiled as we stood regally like royalty as we gleamed as each person took turns standing next to us. The sun shined on our faces giving us supreme admiration. We had leveled up.

"I am your protector forever. You hear me? Your lover forever. You hear me?" Kenya whispered in my ear.

"Thanks, everyone, for coming out. Lee, we are gonna free you up. Frank, can you take us back to the house to change out of this white and get into our honeymoon attire? Take Pops home for me, please?"

"Yea, I gotcha. Let me pull up the truck for Dream. We can't have the queen walking." Frank was so gangsta.

"Already family. Love y'all. I'm gone. Dream, see you at work in about a week. Y'all live your best lives." Lee gave us his blessings. Frank pulled up in his SUV, and Kenya and I sat together in the back like newlyweds. His dad sat behind us, and Reagan sat up front. We held hands as Kenya cracked inside jokes about us coloring in the sheets and what was gonna pop off. We were so happy, and the energy was bomb. He couldn't wait to call his tribe to let them know he was married. He was already posting to social media pics of our rings, most likely to show the haters. We were home in no time. Frank showed us nothing but love with a few bottles of champagne to kick our honeymoon adventure off.

"Y'all be safe. Stay beautiful, Dream." He had a side conversation with Kenya. "Protect her at all cost and enjoy ya'self."

"Thanks, Reagan. Thanks, Frank. Love y'all." I ran in the house to beat Kenya to the punch and packed up a few rompers, a few cute denim outfits, new sandals, and kitten heels for the beach. I had one scanty piece of lingerie that I was dying to wear, and I was building the confidence to wear it. He'd appreciate it over the weekend.


I sent Sanai, Desire, Kiana, and Shae photos. Sanai was sending me emojis filled with love. That was my best homegirl, more like a sister. Sanai wanted me to have a grandiose wedding because when we were in college, that's what we dreamed. Time and experience were the difference and the reason for the shift. She was mad that she had to work and couldn't attend, but she was happy for me, supported me, and always had my back. She was on board with watching the kids for us as we kicked off our honeymoon weekend. By the time we picked up the kids from school, packed them up, and fed them, we were in beach attire rocking fly hats and designer shades on our way to our beach resort.

The day was long. What seemed like 24 hours felt like 72 hours, but it was so worth it. We were young, free, and the flyest Black couple on the ocean strip. You couldn't tell us nothing. We were ghetto superstars, we were ghetto fabulous, we were a ghetto love prophesy. We jumped the broom like our ancestors did, and we were playing for keeps.

We checked in our room around 9:00 p.m., dropped our luggage in our room, and hit the strip like we were in our 20s. Never had we been so excited before. Even by the ocean, the temperature was 80 degrees, and Kenya couldn't wait to flex his gunz in a white tank top with his jean shorts, sneakers, and black W hat repping D.C. He was one of Uptown's finest. My curls were curling up with the humidity, but I had the cutest pink and white crop top that read "FAMOUS." You couldn't tell me nothing in my distress denim jean booty shorts and my kitten heels. My purple Hello Kitty-inspired shoes and bubblegum lipglass had me looking like a curvy model.

We took a romantic walk along the boardwalk, as tourists took pictures of us as if they knew we were newlyweds or Black celebrities. We laughed and posed for perfect strangers. We snapped so many photos along the strip as we fed each other lamb kabobs, cheese fries, and funnel cakes. We didn't have a care in the world, and the freshly squeezed lemonade was A1.

The bar was calling us. Thank God our resort room was only a few blocks away from the entertainment. You could hear our rap anthems booming from block to block, as the exotic cars and Jeeps with the sunroofs open were on cruise control. We bounced from wet bar to wet bar, taking shots of tequila and popping bottles of champagne. Kenya was loud and rowdy when he was twisted, but we were so fucking happy that we had to make our presence known. We landed at a club that was a few feet away from the beach that was on 1,000. The deejay was spinning all our music, and even though it was multicultural, the music reflected our generation of hip-hop culture.

"What's the special occasion?" the bartender asked because Kenya was super lit and was shaking a bottle of champagne.

"I married the love of my life! I married my baby." He hugged me by my neck and kissed me all on my cheeks. He was officially drunk.

"That's beautiful, homes. Next round on me." The bartender was generous. What he didn't know is that we already had about five shots. I was smart enough to ask for water.

"Yea, man, we got married earlier, and it feels good to be official. No more games, only love and loyalty. This is my baby for life!" The bartender poured our first shot.

"Congratulations, guys. A toast to living the good life. The married life." The bartender was a high-energy cat who was as cool as a fan.

"Yea, to the married life. The good life!" Kenya threw back that shot and took me to the middle of the dance floor.

"Baby, this is us!" He had a mean two-step.

"This is us, Kenya! This is so dope. I am so happy." I started backing my ass on him like the college girl who used to take over the club with Sanai and our other homegirls during the late '90s.

"Oh oh oh, get 'em, mami. Get 'em." Kenya was smacking my ass, letting muthafuckas know who I belonged to.

You could see the stars in the sky. There wasn't a cloud in sight. Then all of a sudden, you hear the classic voice of Ja Rule, featuring Lil Mo & Vita on the classic song "Put It On Me." The club crowd went fucking bananas. The bass dropped, and all you could hear was Kenya emulating Ja Rule's raspy voice rapping, *Where would I be without my baby? The thought alone might break meeeee . . . But every thug needs a laddddddyyyyyyy!* You hear that, Dream? Put it on me. That nigga rule, mannnne!"

Kenya started dancing hard as hell as he took both my hands high in the air, and my hips moved to Lil Mo's part. It was as if the gawds were talking to us. That song spoke to our story; it spoke to what we went through; yet, we washed away all the tears and turmoil in our vows. We danced to all the jams, sweating, laughing, and taking over the club. We had a whole crowd rocking with us, and Kenya announced to the world now, in that instance, that we had tied the knot. Even the deejay was intrigued by us and was on our plane. He then mixed in "4Ever" by Lil Mo and Fabolous, and it was over for me. "4Ever" conveyed every word that I was struggling to say throughout the whole day. The lyrics were fierce ghetto poetry and spoke to every girl from the hood whoever dreamed of being married.

"This is us, Kenya. Listen to this! This is us, babe. Our theme. This our wedding song. This is what I've been tryin'a say all day! This love!" I kissed him all over his face and then ran and grabbed both our full champagne glasses, running back to the middle of the dance floor, and singing the lyrics at the top of my lungs as I grabbed Kenya's hands, raising them to the top of the sky—*"Can You Live With It, Lovin Me For Life/To Have and Hold Forever/Baby, Ride or Die Til Death Do Us Part/Let's Make it Last Forever."* His smile was permanent. I wasn't going anywhere, and he wasn't going nowhere. We were shareholders of both hearts. Our love chakras were perfectly aligned.

# Chapter 23

*Fools Gold*

I pulled up in a pearl-white premium edition of a Cadillac Escalade with light tinted windows, jamming to Kelis's *"You don't have to love me/You don't even have to like me/But you will respect me/You know why? 'Cause I'm a boss/boss, boss, boss, boss."*

Refreshed spirit, new truck, and dressed in all black with a hint of cheetah, the chessboard looked different when the queen made the right moves. My organization, Passion for Change, had moved from Gail Ln to Penn State Avenue into the Hillcrest community of Southeast D.C. We were in an office building owned by a Black dentist, and healthcare providers and practitioners occupied the other offices. We were the only nonprofit organization in the building. We were young Black professionals that brought a different flame to the building because we were serving at-risk teens 5 days a week, and my staff was unafraid, resilient, and willing to go into unchartered waters. What I loved about my team is that they were independent, from the  hood, had a real connection to the community, and offered different elements.

You had Aki, who was my right hand and executive assistant. He was brilliant, well-researched, articulate, and organized. Although he went to prison for a crime he committed when he was a juvenile, he gave so much back to the community that the justice system forgave him and took him off parole. Aki was reliable, dependable, and could run the business without me being present. He was a force to be reckoned with, and the staff respected him. He had a humble spirit and had a way of checking you when you needed it.

Kiana was like a younger sister to me, who understood me in my complexity. As a program assistant, she was learning the details of working directly for a CEO. She was smart, but Aki would call her "Molasses" because she was slow in her approach, but she would get the job done. She was meticulous, detailed, and knew how to take precise notes. Her work was high quality, but more importantly, she knew how to mind her own business and not allow anyone to distract her.

Lee was like a big brother but played the role of a general. He was a foot soldier, unafraid of going into the trenches. Lee was a lead mentor for the organization, and all his youth admired him for being real and tangible. When he mentored, he wanted to get to know the youth, the parents, and the family, and draw that connection. He was from the area, and there wasn't a neighborhood that he hadn't entered. He was the epitome of a Washingtonian. He loved the culture, he rocked Go-Go, and he was genuine. Lee was very overly protective of me, and he could detect a charlatan from a mile away.

Cain was a connector. He worked as a mentor and outreach staff member. He had strong ties to the community and the churches. He was a deacon, he kept a positive attitude, and would go check up on his youth via the bus, by foot, and on a good day, he'd hitch a ride with Lee. When Kenya was in prison, I let Cain mow my yard, wash my car, and help with the maintenance of the business and vehicle. However, Cain ended up being a traitor and a mischief-maker. He had the audacity to steal my mail and register a vehicle in my name. One day while I was checking the mail, I saw that there was a vehicle registration for a car that I didn't own and realized that vehicle was Cain's. Not only did I fire him for stealing my identity, but I also reported what he did to the church that he attended. Then I got the law involved, tracked the vehicle because the title came to my house, sold the car to one of my homeboys who owned a transportation company, and checkmated on that ass. Never understood how you could steal from the person that fed you, but I was learning the art of war and how to recognize vultures.

Tammy was an idea staffer. She was a lead mentor and tutor, and as my contracts evolved, there wasn't a contract that Tammy wasn't a part of. She was like a big sister. She woke up early and positioned herself to win. She had a reliable vehicle, so there wasn't a client that she would turn down. At one point, she mentored about 12 youth and had most of the roster. The other mentors resented her for making all the money, but she had drive, she had hustle, and she always fed her clients, which made her a keeper. She always aligned herself with me and had a good relationship with my executive team. She was a baker who made sure that she dropped me off red velvet and German chocolate cakes to butter me up.

There were two sistas named Christian and Royal that came on board and stood out. They were revolutionary, artistic, educated, and already had their own following as artists. They were organic, a cross between Bahamadia, Queen Latifah, with the uniqueness of an Erykah Badu. Christian and Royal were emcees by trade and were local phenoms.

I met Royal on the spoken-word circuit when I was performing at local ciphers and lounges as a poet. We had healthy vibrations, and we more than often compared notes about artistry, love, goals, and being a Black woman in America. She was a kindred spirit. Royal was ambitious, had a strong personality, and was a deep thinker. Christian had the spirit of an educator and was always the staffer in the group challenging the program, requesting more activities and field trips for the youth, and advocating for gas and mileage for travel. They were fiery, in tune with the earth, and had a great rapport with the community.

I brought my big homie Maaz on the team. Maaz was an OG from Clay Street who knew me when I was a single mother struggling, tryin'a make lemonade with lemon peels and no sugar. He knew Cookie too when she lived around Clay Street. Cookie and I were not the same. Maaz, like Aki and Lee, had done more than a decade in prison, but in my eyes, he was rehabilitated and needed a position where he could make money and give back, so I gave him a chance. He replaced Cain, and his mentees admired him. He was young, fly, and a Muslim. Many of the youngins that he mentored were Muslim or on the verge of converting, so he was a role model for them. He had the full beard before it was popular. You could always see him with a pair of dark designer shades and his waves spinning. He was charismatic, and you could tell the female staff was eyeing him 'cause he was charming and appeared flamboyant. Most of the staff side-eyed him because they thought he was manipulative and used his good looks to get over. But I respected him because he saw how far I came and always supported the growth and never hated.

Lastly, there was my techie, Nadi, who was from West Africa. He was referred to me from a government entity that assisted brothas who had a past, whether it was criminal, substance abuse, or homelessness. Nadi came with a gang of skills. He knew every aspect of the computer, he knew how to research, repair computers, and his knowledge of software was rigorous. His brain moved at the speed of light, and between Aki and me, we needed a Nadi on our team. He was intelligent, attentive, and had a kind spirit. He brought balance.

My Escalade was parked on the corner of Penn State Avenue, and when I pulled up, my staff knew to be in place, especially on days that I had staff meetings. My leadership style was a combination of a democratic free-spirit, but then there was this no-nonsense haughtiness that would rear up in me like a lioness that you did not want to fuck with. During our staff meetings, I usually stood up or sat on the top of the conference table or in the center of a circle. I wanted to know the data, stats, progress, challenges, and how we could be better. Nothing pissed me off more than a staff person who turned in their reports late or whose grammar was unacceptable. If you wanted to get fired, then you would lie on your reports, not meet program goals, or not see your youth at all, which meant you were a liability and had to go.

As a new CEO, I welcomed feedback, but I hadn't arrived at the point where I could accept criticism. Really, there was no room for criticizing me because, in my mind, there wasn't much that I hadn't survived, and my staff were buying houses, buying new cars, boosting their credit scores, and going to the next level because of the opportunities that Passion for Change provided. The men called me "Boss" or "Boss Lady," and the women generally called me by my name. While the women were talented, they questioned, challenged, and were quicker to catch attitudes. I preferred working with men than women. Men had respect, they were laid-back, their attitudes were pretty consistent, and they knew how to read me.

As the organization grew stronger, the animosity grew from other organizations who felt that we did not deserve a seat at the table, and the hatred grew from female-headed agencies simply because they either couldn't be a part of my organization or we didn't compromise our integrity, and there wasn't any kickback. Yea, I had a formula, but it wasn't a formula that I had written down in one of my old run-down journals or scrapbooks. It was in my visualizations, and if I could see it, I knew the exact recipe for success. Many began to resent me for being bold, pretty, curvy, and the fact that I was self-made and well-researched. It was as if the cliché "More Money, More Problems" began to make sense in my playbook. I was a thousand-naire but had millionaire dreams, and by any means, she would get there.

Kenya was paving his own path. He had been hired by a bigwig transportation company called The Xpress that had one of the biggest federal contracts moving veteran families throughout the nation and storing their entire houses on acres of storage. The company was extremely lucrative, and the owner, who was Middle Eastern, had made multimillions in the industry. Kenya knew the power of networking, hard work, and meeting the needs of his very own CEO named Fred. Fred knew that Kenya was rough around the edges, but Kenya's numbers didn't lie, and he had proven that he could move a whole house by himself. He was as strong as an ox, and even though the job was labor-intensive, it required him to count, draft reports, and become accountable for his actions.

Kenya called each day a "hump day," where he had to hump over the hurdles, making it his goal to work his way from being a crew member to eventually having his own crew after about 2 years of showing consistency. While the fall and winter seasons were slow seasons for moving military families, the spring and summer seasons were like Christmas. Once Fred granted Kenya a position as a lead subcontractor, Kenya became responsible for his own truck, storage, and two to three crew members. As a subcontractor, he was generating about $8,000 to $10,000 per month in which about 50 percent was paid out to his workers, and the other half was take-home pay. I was so proud of Kenya, and what aroused me more was that he took pride in wearing his red and white Xpress uniform, sometimes working 12- to 16-hour days, and getting paid every Friday. It was a great balance because when his season was good, my season as a contractor was slow, and when mine was booming, his may have been at a standstill.

Every Friday after his long drives, he would have the kids and me meet him at his job site where all his coworkers would be comparing check stubs on who made the most money and how much liquor they were gonna buy with their money. Most wives and girlfriends with common sense knew to go pick up money from their men before they blew it, and I was one of them. Kenya would give me money for bills and cash for the kids and me. He was pretty generous. He loved being able to provide and hated when it was just me holding the fort down financially, and he couldn't contribute. Working at the Xpress really helped shape his work ethic, and you had to respect it.

When Kenya was focused, he could achieve anything. However, with more money came his arrogance, access to more liquor, pills, angel dust, and infidelity. The more money that he made, the meaner he got. I stopped becoming a priority, and he became invisible.

Kenya would use his job as an excuse for not coming home, and he would be gone for days at a time. After days of being missing, he would more than often come home pissy drunk, aggressive, and confrontational, ready to start an argument so that I could give him a reason to go back to his regular schedule of bullshit. Although he claimed that he was working or hanging with his homies, my intuition told me otherwise. The reality was that I was not ready to deal with the shenanigans. My heart could not take the tea. So, when he would come home, I'd renege on having sex with him, coldly turn my back to him, and give him the silent treatment to communicate that what he was doing was absolutely disrespectful and unacceptable.

The more I refused to accept his blatant disrespect, the more toxic our relationship got. It would go from a simple argument to a blowout where he would call me every bitch in the world and throw objects at me that I had to bob and weave away from. Although Dynasty was young and headed to pre-K, King witnessed the drama, the change in behavior, and on weekends when Nia would come over, she would shake her head as if she already knew her father's capabilities.

Nia was Kenya's ride-or-die daughter. He would take her with him on his great adventures if he was feeling himself, and when he felt like I was a punk-ass pushover, he would leave her at our house for days without ever communicating. King and Nia were entering their preteen stages, and you could no longer protect them from the visuals. They knew the difference between right and wrong, and they had been exposed to too much dysfunction. They needed to see something different, but the more Kenya spent days away, the more I sought comfort in eating fast food, dealing with my hurt. No one could stop Kenya from doing what he wanted to do, and he only feared God on occasions. I began burying myself in my business and my kids, which were my only comfort. Kenya made me feel like getting married to him was a joke that I should have never fallen for. The pressing me out to get married, the rings, the vows, the feeling that he would never cheat again was a complete setup and, thus, only a honeymoon period. The more I pulled away, the more he stayed gone. The fatter I got, the less attractive and the weaker I'd become.

When my friends or his friends came by to visit, they'd witness his level of disrespect. Eventually, he forgave his family and used Keema as a refuge. Keema would hide his secrets out of loyalty. She didn't fuck with me anyway, so the slick shit he was doing behind my back meant nothing to her. I was too embarrassed to tell my friends how he was treating me, but the manner in which he was treating me was starting to wear and tear on me psychologically, so much that I was back at the doctor's office again like I was when Solomon abruptly left.

Kenya's behavior triggered my anxiety so much that my heart raced, putting me in a tachycardia range. My blood sugar was sporadic, dropping, and spiking by the day where I was silently shaking in the kitchen as I tried to feed myself something as simple as a bowl of cereal in the morning. Some days, I wouldn't eat, or I would eat too much sugar, and my body couldn't regulate my blood sugar, making me prediabetic. My primary care doctor became worried about me because my body was out of whack. He was trying to guide me with a nutrition plan, exercising, increasing daily cardio, hydrating, and drinking water. He'd send me to a cardiologist to put me on a heart monitor for 7 days to see if I had cardio issues, but the cardiologist attributed my palpitations and fast heart rate to stress. My business was stressing me out, Kenya was stressing me the fuck out, King even began stressing me out with his bad behavior in school, and things eventually fell apart.

My mind couldn't gather or process what was going on with me. I needed therapy, but I was too lazy to go. My spirit lost its way, and I lacked the motivation to sync my mind and body together. I sought comfort in taking half a bar of Xanax when I simply couldn't handle the stress of life.

Then there was the loss. Loss would send anyone who suffered from anxiety into a goddamn frenzy, but we took a hit when King's grandma, Coco, died from lung cancer. It was like she was diagnosed one day, and then within months, she died. King was traumatized by her loss because they had a special bond, and they were so close. Yet, my spirit grew weary because she was my backbone when it came to helping me with King, and it seemed like every time I'd find someone that I could trust, they would fly away. Solomon was grieving in his own way, and he attempted to spend more time with King, but he had growing up to do, and I simply couldn't count on him.

What made matters worse was that I was utterly devastated by the untimely death of my stepfather, Major. He lost his father one week, and it rocked his world—he couldn't take it. Days later, Major would suffer a brain aneurysm that gave him a massive stroke that sent him into a coma. He would transition, and his death would rock my entire world, sending me into a deep depression for at least a year.

Even Roca slipped up and was gone. His older brother reached out to me on a business tip to inform me that he was serving some time in a penitentiary for being on a high-speed chase with the Park Police because he had contraband in the car. He crashed into another vehicle, injuring the other driver and breaking his own hip. If there were someone I could have talked to, to get my mind out of the clouds, it would have been Roca, but he was on a "vacation" for a few years and couldn't help himself or me.

The loss came like a tsunami, along with the hurt and pain. Kenya added salt to the wound to the point that my heart began to sting. Him being gone for days wasn't an illusion. It was a reality. He turned into a sloppy cheater with no regard for a wife. It was as if he never had one. One day, I got some heart and waited for him to go to sleep and went through his phone, the text messages, and the DMs on social media. The text messages weren't too bad, but the DMs appeared like a lost treasure. He had a white girl out in VA who indicated in her message that she was waiting on him to divorce me. He had another stray that he seemed to be fucking on and off. He had admirers, but one woman stuck out to me. Her name was Demi. Looking at her profile pics, she was fat, black, and ugggggggllllly. There was no way on God's green earth that I'd fathom that Kenya would stoop that low for attention. They had long conversations in his messages. Long conversations that told a story of a budding relationship. He was going to her house, he was around her kids, and her mother was fond of him. He had Nia around her and her kids, which blew my mind. But what might as well put the bullets in the gun was that she bragged on how great his penis was, that they were having unprotected sex, that he was "making her squirt," that she was "feening for more," and that she couldn't wait for him to come back over. The messages were making me sick—so sick that I went into my kitchen and gathered half a dozen butcher knives, stabbing the pillow that he laid on making a circumference around his head.

Why would he do me that way?

Why would he marry me to cheat on me?

Why would he dishonor me?

Why would he hurt me, knowing what nearly destroyed me before?

Why would he leave me alone for days at a time?

Why would he leave me alone to fight a battle with my health that could lead me to a full mental breakdown or even death?

Why would he allow the kids to see his wickedness?

Why the disrespect?

My tears made love to my pillows.

Never would I think that he would trade a queen in for silly pawns that were disposable. Based on the inbox messages on social media, Demi was fucking, sucking, giving him time, liquor, and full access to her money. She was desperate, the type of desperation that I never had and never will. Although Kenya had a fan club, one thing was sure, that Demi, with her ugly ass, was gonna be a problem.

My face was on the ground. I needed my mama. Even Kenya knew I needed my mama, and he called her and told her that I was sick. My mama flew in, and she could look into my eyes and see the same lowliness that she saw when I gave birth to King without his father being there.

It was the same abandonment in my eyes that she saw as I gave birth to King as my life almost withered away. She'd travel 3,000 miles to check on her baby and realized after a few doctors' visits that it was "Matters of the Heart." She knew Kenya was dogging me. She had been there before, and her seeing her firstborn weak as shit didn't sit well with her. But she was a praying mama, and no matter time or space, or drama or bad blood between us, I could call my mama. She didn't stay long, but long enough to leave her vibration and the Holy Spirit. I was grown. No one could tell me what to do and how to do it. I had eloped with the nigga without the proper blessings from my family. I thought I was doing the right thing since we had Dynasty. Yea, I was locked in. I had locked myself into a destructive and messy path. My heart searched for an alternate route, but it was too late—"Fool's Gold" and all. I gave my power away.

# Chapter 24

*Love Recall*

We bonded over food. The dinner table was filled with sweet nothings of fried chicken, macaroni and cheese, fried cabbage, yeast rolls, and lemonade. While there was discord sewn into our relationship, Kenya knew how to bring the children and me together through Sunday dinner. All I had to prepare were yeast rolls and fried cabbage, and Kenya put his foot down frying chicken and baking mac and cheese. The kids loved their daddy's fried chicken, and with the mac and cheese, it seemed like he was creating a wavelength to redemption.

Nia, Dynasty, King, Kenya, and I sat at the table and had one of the best Sunday dinners we could have ever had. It was as if Kenya had been there the whole time, and it seemed like no time had been lost. We hummed as we partook in every bite of our food, the kids laughed and joked, and Kenya and I talked. Even Kenya's friend, Kevin, smelled the aroma and knocked on the back door to see what was smelling so good, and Kenya, of course, gave him a to-go plate.

"Is the food good?" Kenya asked the whole table.

"Yesssss!" the kids responded and giggled.

"This chicken is good." Dynasty was in pre-K and could talk clear for her age.

"You like Daddy's chicken, don't you?" He kissed her on the forehead.

"It's real good," Nia added.

"I see you tearing it up, and King ain't even talking. He's devouring the food."

King nodded.

"What about you, baby? I should have baked you some salmon, but I know you like my macaroni and cheese. How's the food?"

"The food is bomb. Thank you," I replied.

"When you are happy, I am happy." He started digging in his plate.

"I missed you," he said sincerely.

I kept eating. I was prideful, and it was too hard to say that I beyond missed him. I kept eating and listened to what was coming next.

"No, like I *really* missed you. I know I haven't been the husband you need me to be, and I'm wrong. But I'm hoping and praying that we can talk and walk through the storm and make it out. We've been through too much just to throw it all away."

"Yea, but it's gonna take a lot. I'm tired of you saying 'sorry.' I'm tired of the broken promises. I deserve better." I looked him in his eyes. "I can't be a revolving door that you just come through as you please. If you wanted a girlfriend, I could have stayed one. You are struggling with commitment, and it's not fair to me."

"Let me fix this. Just please work with me and let me fix it."

"Please fix it, Jaysus! 'Cause she is getting tired. Don't you want things to get better, Ken?"

"Of course, and it is gonna get better. You can't have the sunshine without the rain, Dream. Yea, I know before you say somethin' smart, we have had enough rain. It's time for some sun." Kenya was so adamant.

The yeast rolls never tasted so good. They were buttery and soft, and I found comfort in being in an uncomfortable spot.

The children were eavesdropping and having their side conversations. They were in middle school, and they both were getting taller, thicker, and had their own added personalities. Nia was sassy as hell, and King was an arrogant piece of work. They were growing up and becoming slightly rebellious in their own way. Kenya was time enough for them. He was the disciplinarian, and if any of our kids jumped out there, he would whoop that ass. The kids knew that, but they understood our marriage was on the rocks, so they would manipulate where they saw cracks.

Dynasty got down from the table as usual and went to play with her chocolate baby dolls. She was a free spirit, and God protected her from the drama. Her slanted bright eyes, chocolate skin, and warm smile were absolutely beautiful. She was our conscience, peace, and balance.

My cell phone began vibrating consecutively, but there were no missed calls or text messages. There was a notification that indicated that I had received a message on my public figure social media page, which was rare. My public figure page was created for admirers, fans, spectators, journalists, and haters who followed my career as a youth advocate, entrepreneur, and writer. I checked the message as I sipped on a glass of lemonade. As I began reading it, my eyes grew like saucers, and my spirit entered into a place of no return. I lifted my eyes to see Kenya intensely staring at me. I was disturbed, and he could sense it by observing my body language.

"What's wrong?" he asked.

I continued to scan the remainder of the message, bracing myself.

"This! *This* is wrong!" I placed the cell phone in front of his eyes so that he could see this message.

"What is that? Who is the message from?"

"The message is from Demi. Demi, the girl you been having an affair with for over a year, according to this message, muthafucka. Demi sent me this message to let me know that you got her pregnant and that y'all have a baby on the fucking way, and that you have been dealing with her for more than a year! Oh no! This bitch said, 'We have a daughter on the way. He did not tell me that he was married at first. I got caught up!' This is the sloppy shit that I'm talking about, nigga!" I got up out of my seat and began beating him on the head with my cell phone because I was infuriated. The kids knew there was gonna be some drama, so they left and went outside.

"Wait, Dream! Wait! That bitch don't want us staying married. She's a thing of the past. I don't even know if that is my baby." He began stuttering as he tried to take the phone out of my hand.

"You betrayed me! You betrayed me! Never would I think you would have done the very thing that I asked you to protect me from. Never would I have thought that you would have done to me what

Solomon did." I kept hitting him upside his head until we made it out of the back door and into the yard.

"Dream, don't let her get to you. She's a stalker!" He grabbed my wrist to keep me from hitting him. "She's a stalker! She doesn't wanna see me happy based on the fact that she knows that I am not gonna leave you! I'm not!" he yelled.

"You married me to break me like this! You just threw the whole fucking marriage away. I can't believe you. You let this bitch get pregnant. You let her have access to me. She knows too much for her to find me on social media. You couldn't even protect me from that nonsense. I hate you!" I was screaming as I attacked him, and then Kevin, who was watching the drama unfold from his yard, hopped into our yard to intervene between us.

"Stop, Dream. Stop!" Kevin had a way of getting my attention.

"No. He got a baby on the way! He got a whole baby on the way! The bitch sent me a message letting me know!" I allowed Kevin to glance at the message.

"Damn! Go talk to my grandma. Go talk to Mother Heart! She can pray for y'all," Kevin tried.

"Prayer? Prayer? We can't even eat dinner without this nigga having some stray contact me about a baby on the way. I would never do that to you, Ken. I would never." Kenya grabbed my wrist to protect himself from being hit again in his face with the cell phone.

"Come on, Dream! Come on! Yes, I cheated, but we don't deal. We don't deal anymore. I'm trying to make things right with you, and she knows that! Wake up. She's miserable, baby! She has nothing going on with her life, and that's why she's sending you messages.

Let's go on *Maury* when the baby is born. Let's get the DNA swab done. But before you judge, please wait for the baby to be born. Don't believe her just yet, Dream. People are gonna do what it takes to hurt you because of me. Come on, Dream!" He tried to be convincing.

"Bullshit! You got a baby on the way. She said in the message the baby would be born in a few months. You couldn't spare me the hurt, huh? You couldn't spare me the humiliation, right? You had to break the very heart that you helped mend. You promised to protect me. You didn't protect me." I began sobbing. I was inconsolable. Kenya wore guilt all over his face. He could say nothing. The tears couldn't stop. The snot dripped on my lips, giving it a salty taste. The thought of him having a child by a woman during our marriage sent me into a panic and an immediate depression.

I left the yard and went straight to Mother Heart for prayer and her wisdom. I walked right into her house and fell on my knees and began whimpering.

"What's wrong, child? What's wrong, Dream?" She was concerned.

"I really gave this marriage my all. But nothing seems to be good enough for him. We were eating dinner, and the same woman he has been having an affair on me with sent a message saying that Kenya got her pregnant, and she's having his baby. What am I supposed to do?" I wept.

"Dream, look at me, baby," She leaned into me, speaking straight into my soul. "You got dem babies to look after, ya hear? You got those beautiful babies to love and protect. They watching him, but they are watching you! God got you no matter what. You gotta do what's best for you! As much as I love Kenya, it's about you." She began hugging me and praying over me. Ms. Heart had a way of getting an open prayer line to God, and He would listen to her. She was an intercessor—an elder who had seen a whole lot and been through enough to know the very essence of God. The whole neighborhood would go to her for prayer. Even Kenya would go get a prayer from her in his own time.

"Thank you, Ms. Heart. Thank you for your prayers." I humbly wiped my tears. "I need to hear from God. My heart is real heavy."

"When you get real quiet, He is gonna speak to you, and you will know it's Him. Go in that house and lie down and get quiet, ya hear? Let Him order your steps. Don't go out there fighting with him. Let it go!"

"Yes, ma'am! Yes, ma'am!" I stood up and took the tissue that she gave me and wiped my tears. I hugged her, then walked back into my house. The prayer definitely took my anger from a 10 to a 6, but there were unresolved issues. Dinner would never be the same, and as a matter of fact, we wouldn't sit down and eat as a family for a very long time after this. Ken had a baby on the way, and he knew that having a baby on me was my "absolute deal breaker." I had to chew on it and digest it one way or the other. The whole situation ate at my soul, and the betrayal broke me into pieces. The tide was too high to make any immediate decisions, so I internalized the pain and silenced him, choosing not to deal with the pain he caused head-on. Demi's message to me was concrete. Kenya didn't have a faithful bone in his body. I wasn't enough for him. She met needs that clearly, I couldn't meet, and the baby was coming with or without my approval. This was some bullshit!

There was no solace at home. The only peace that I found was in my business. And even my empire seemed like it was taking a fall. The city council cut back on mentoring and youth programming contracts because they didn't see real outcomes being met from entities as a whole, which affected my organization wholeheartedly. Not to mention some organizations were making at least a million, if not 2 million, a year off of mentoring and tutoring contracts who lied about their numbers and hardly made contact with their clients, and in the politicians' eyes, it was unjustifiable. However, Passion for Change was doing the work, and we were being thrown bags of nickels that we learned over time those bags we needed for sustainability.

Although we began creating focus groups and developing a pilot around workforce development and performing arts programming, the funding was scarce, which led to me cutting my full-time staff to part-time staff and forced the remaining of my staff to find full-time jobs elsewhere. While we rode the wave of success for a strong 4 years, the fifth year determined the difference between the have and the have-nots. I had to let our office space go on Penn Ave and align myself with an elder sista named Ms. Isis, who saw our potential and proceeded to find us funding in providing holistic programs for public housing. She was Afrocentric and believed that "we have to save ourselves," and that no one could save or heal us but us and the Most High.

For Ms. Isis, we created a series called "Dear Daddy!" that was implemented for youth residing in public housing to use artistry to express their love, compassion, uncertainty, and even disappointment toward their fathers. She believed in us and other small organizations and created a gateway for those she trusted. Ms. Isis was indeed the plug, and she found a magical way to find us a FREE small building that was actually a house in public housing that would equip us to have an office and classroom space. She provided us a segue to the resident council and matriarch named Ms. Niecy, and after proving ourselves and being vetted out, Ms. Niecy would give Ms. Isis the green light to provide us with keys and a lease. In exchange for the in-kind office, we had to provide the community with workforce training, afterschool, and summer programming. The neighborhood, affectionately known as "The Courts," was no stranger to drugs, gun violence, and poverty. We were in the belly of the beast, but I was unafraid and up for the challenge! Ms. Niecy said that "The Courts needed a sista like me with some heart," but what she didn't know was that I was being tried by fire, and I needed "The Courts" to rebuild, rebrand, and to recharge my energy as an entrepreneur and community leader. We needed each other.

My chessboard looked differently for my business. The reality was that I didn't have enough revenue to keep my staff. Kiana went to work for the federal government. There was no love lost, and I fully supported her. Aki leveled up and went to work as a surgical tech for an optometrist. Lee would do seasonal work for me, but he had his own street vending business that he was launching. Tammy went on to work full-time for a group home and security for another company. However, she would come through and do part-time mentoring for the organization. Christian and Royal would go on to pursue their music and artistry careers. I was not a hater, and I was proud that my staff had the opportunity to elevate.

Nothing lasted forever, and I had a small new team now. Surprisingly, Cookie reached out to me and made amends for what she did and apologized for allowing her boyfriend to steal my car. We had a real heart-to-heart, catching each other up to speed. She missed me, and I kinda missed her too. She expressed being interested in working for me as an assistant in The Courts, and it could not have been a better time because I had no staff. Cookie may have been weak with men, but overall, she had administrative skills, she knew how to man an office based on her previous experience, and she wasn't afraid of cleaning, moving furniture, and getting our new office space up to speed. Cookie wasn't afraid to work in the ghetto because she had lived in some of the roughest communities. It was home to her. I was able to coach, mentor her, and sharpen some of her skills. Whatever we didn't know, she would research and figure it out.

I spent day and night bidding and applying for new grants for months until I garnered a big grant to provide an aftercare program that focused a great deal on academics and music. Within 45 days, I had to create a team that was passionate about working with youth who lived in high-risk communities. After posting hiring ads on social media, a long-distance cousin who had been observing me from afar named Abel responded to an ad, and after interviewing him, I hired him on the spot. He reminded me of a hillbilly with his country talk and Southern mannerisms. He was about 6 foot 5, chocolate, had a Colgate smile, and was shaped like a teddy bear. He appeared intimidating, but once you got to know him, you found that he was an emotional being, in tune with his feelings, the environment, and the needs of the youth. His grandfather and my grandfather were brothers. While we were raised in two different worlds, we were kinfolk. Abel was in the lifestyle, and him working for Passion for Change was his first real opportunity outside of working for fast-food chains and hustling. A person's past never mattered to me because most of my staff were rehabilitated and had served time for crimes that they committed when they were young. Therefore, Abel fit the prototype of Passion. He was an asset to the organization for the phase that we were in, and it felt good to be around family.

When things fell apart, the Most High always gave me exactly what I needed to bounce back. While half of my life was a fucking mess, my mama and brother needed me. Major had passed, and my brother and my mom took the biggest loss of their lives. My mom was married 30 years to Major and had given him all of her. She essentially gave up her career and dreams as a hairstylist to help him face his substance abuse demons and his insecurities so that he could achieve his career goals. My mom's career as a star-studded hairstylist never reached its maximum potential because her focus was on being a good wife.

Major transitioned to the ancestral plane, and my brother and my mom had to learn how to pick up the pieces to their destiny. It was their time to find purpose in pain and to create the life that they always wanted. Although my parents looked at me as the "rebellious daughter," there was no doubt in their mind that they knew that I would hustle, take care of my children, take care of myself, and try to achieve my dreams, all in the same breath.

One Thursday, during a workday, I got a surprising call from my brother.

"Hey, big sis!" said Ocean.

"Hey, brother, how are you? How are things?"

"They're not really good. I need a change of scenery. I need to do something with my life outside of California. I need to breathe, sis." Ocean gave off a sense of urgency.

"Yea, I know you struggling with dad's death. It's crazy that he's gone. Life is so hectic. How's Mommy?" I asked.

"Yea, that's the part I need to get away from. I can't help Mommy. I gotta help myself, and Mommy gotta help herself. Daddy was everything to us, and now we gotta spread our wings. Being here isn't cutting it. I wanted to know if I could come out there and stay with you and work with your company if you have any opportunities. I need a break, sis."

"Are you serious? You know I'm going through my own stuff out here, and it's intense. You can come out here, but it's a full house. I got King, Dynasty, Nia, and Kenya. If you wanna work, you would have to hit the pavement soon as you come."

"It don't matter. I gotta leave. I can buy my plane ticket to get there. I can be there next Saturday."

"Okay, you gotta share a room with King and sleep on the couch. If you cool with that, then we good, bro."

"Sis, thank you so much. Thank you so much. I'ma text you my itinerary. You gonna swoop me, right?"

"Yea, I'm gonna come get you. Try to come during the day or in the morning, 'cause I be asleep at night. You know this East Coast shit is a beast, right?"

"I already know I can't come out there playing." We both laughed.

"Nope. Okay, Ocean, I'm gonna see you next week. Can't wait to see you. I know the kids are gonna be happy to see their uncle. I gotchu," I assured him.

"Thanks, sis. I'll text you in a few days."

"Cool. Talk to you later."

"Much love, sis."

"Much love, bro. See you in a few." I hung up the phone.

Lord knows the last thing I needed was another person in my house. Not to mention I was exhausted, and Ocean just didn't understand the pain and agony that I was experiencing with Kenya and the betrayal that came with being married. Ocean would come into a quiet storm that was brewing, and the rainbow was far away. My household was dysfunctional and had fallen apart. But perhaps him coming to the East Coast was a blessing for both of us. I needed a reminder of who I was in my core—the principles, the values, and who I really was—in my essence. I needed real support. And Ocean needed a new start in his life—motivation, encouragement, a career, and a blueprint to success. The universe saw fit that he came and that I could usher him, as a big sister, into the next level of his life. Kenya and I weren't communicating. The relationship was damaged, and I think neither one of us knew if we could recover it, so we just left it alone. Kenya would be gone for days and sometimes a week at a time, and then reappear. The kids and I built an immunity to him coming and going as he pleased, and we subconsciously learned to ride the wave. They were happy when he was home and soaked up his love and attention, but as they all got older, they learned his behavior and knew that he had demons.

Some days, he would come home highly functional after a long day of work, and on other days, he would come home as high as a kite off of a dipper, which was a cigarette dipped in embalming fluid. When he was high, he was out of his fucking mind, and sometimes it was scary to the point where he would pace back and forth looking distorted, or he would become super emotional and sob like a baby. And at other times, he would be ready to go to war. When he had those mental health episodes resulting from his drug use, I would call his alter ego Frankenstein 'cause he'd turn into a monster!

We never knew what personality we were gonna get with Kenya, so the whole family braced ourselves. A few times, I had to call 911 because he appeared half dead. Once, the EMTs had to hit him with ammonia to wake him up because he completely passed out. Another time, the EMTs had to take him to the psychiatric unit for a week because he had a psychotic episode from hitting a dipper. His family enabled his codependency. I didn't fuck with them, and they didn't fuck with me, so it was hard to discuss with them on a real level that he needed help and that he was in a crisis.

The only time I would hear from his family is if he had gotten into a ruckus, or if he self-admitted himself to the hospital because he'd get so high off drugs that it would send him into a panic that would land him in a mental health facility. There were a few times that he would check himself into a recovery house for a week or even 30 days, but his lifestyle and addiction were calling him, and those barriers only Jesus could help him with. While there was a place in my heart that wanted to save him, I myself needed a life raft and needed to be saved.

My health didn't improve. I just learned to live with the symptoms of feeling well on some days and sick on others. I hadn't learned how to regulate my blood sugar. I was prediabetic, but deep down, I was searching for a healing . . . A healing for my soul that would manifest itself physically, mentally, and emotionally. Self-care was calling my name.

Kenya knew that he had sent me to the deep end. One day, he expressed that he wanted to go with me to work and spend the day with me, which was unbelievable. While my first instinct was to tell him no, I welcomed him, not really knowing his intentions. On this particular day, I'd have meetings back-to-back, and the office seemed to be pretty busy. Abel and Cookie were holding the front office down, as usual. While I was in a meeting, Abel began calling upstairs, which meant it was important.

"Dream! You have a visitor. You have a visitor, Dream!" Abel seemed uncertain.

"Come upstairs, Abel!" I sounded agitated because taking care of the front is what he was supposed to do in the first place. His steps were heavy as he came upstairs. I met him at the top of the stairs, and he began whispering in my ear.

"Cuz, some dude named Roca is downstairs to see you. He is real comfortable coming in here. He said that he's an old friend of yours and that he was looking to volunteer."

"Oh shit! He must'a just came home. He was just in for a few years. This is crazy. Why he come here, though?"

"That's my point. Your husband is downstairs. You know Kenya is crazy. Once he heard dude's voice, he came out of the kitchen and sized cuz up. He might be a problem."

"He's not a problem." I crossed my arms and smiled. "He's a good friend. Have him fill out an employment application."

"Cuz, you betta do some damage control. He just came home anyway. What's he gonna do?"

"He can do what none of y'all wanna do. We worked together before at MOV, so I know his work ethic is official. Yea, but give him an app. He's harmless."

"Your husband, though. Mr. Roca seem like he's gonna be a problem, cuz."

"Naw, he ain't." I smiled from ear to ear. "Bring him up in 5 minutes."

I quickly wrapped up the meeting that I had with a monitor for one of our youth programs that we were funded for. I had never been so happy. I mean, I was happy when Ocean came, but Roca was someone who knew how to make me smile. He was always a breath of fresh air.

He walked in, smelling like a bottle of the freshest cologne and looking like an Egyptian gawd. He was tall. It looked like he gained about 30 pounds, so he appeared strong. His skin was soaked in chocolate, and his eyes were soberly clear.

"Hey, you!" He hugged me from the side.

"Hey, Roca! It's so good to see you! I'm so surprised."

"Yea, I wanted to surprise you. You were one of the first people that I wanted to see when I came home. I've only been home for a few days, but I need to get out of this halfway house. I gotta do something constructive. Can I volunteer for your company?" He was so genuine.

"Well, of course. And welcome home. A lot is going on here, but, yea, you gotta catch on fast 'cause I don't have a lot of time to train."

"You know I'm a fast learner. All I did was read and go to the library, work out, and meditate when I was in prison. So, I'm ready. Here's the application too." His smile was so radiant.

"You serious, serious?"

"I made my mistakes. Now I gotta apply the knowledge. I gotta do better. I got kids. They need me. My family needs me. I owe it to them." He was so serious.

"Absolutely. You wanna start on Monday? I don't have any open positions right now, but I have a new grant that will start in about a month or two, and you can get on that contract. It's a contract working with young adults."

"I'm ready for whateva. I'm humble, sweetheart. It doesn't matter. Is that your husband downstairs?"

"Yea, that's my husband. Why?"

"My brother told me you were married, but he look kinda rough."

I giggled. "You know, Kenya. I married him and had a daughter by him."

"Damn! I can't knock you. I gotta family too. I got a fiancée."

"Nice! It's about family, right?" I was quick on my feet. Roca was great with words, and he could sidetrack me real quick, but he would find out that this is a Dream Angelou Production. He would learn that so much has changed and that I wasn't the green, wet-behind-the-ears young woman from prior years. He'd see that life had dealt me a wild hand, and that I was gonna play my whack-ass hand regardless. This diamond was beautiful, but it had sharp edges and a few scratches that made it organically strong.

"It's always about family. Why you didn't answer my calls from jail? There was money on the calls. They weren't collect." He wouldn't let that slide.

"To be honest, my life has been a whirlwind. I have had health scares, and I'm not in the best health. My marriage is rocky. Life,

Roca. Life. I just felt like we didn't have anything in common anymore. Was I supposed to answer the call and boggle you down with my sadness? I actually wrote a long-ass letter to you a few months ago. I just never got it to the mailbox."

"Damn! I thought we were better than that! No problem is too big for me, Dream. Remember, I lost my mom and grandma right before I went to jail. That broke me. Nothing else could break me like that. We're friends. I could have at least listened. But OK, I understand. Well, I'm home, and we can talk. You know, like ol' times." He stood up to leave.

"Thanks, Roca. I'll see you on Monday. Make sure you give Abel a copy of your ID before you leave. So glad you're home." I tried to keep it professional, but it was so hard. There was so much I wanted to say that my eyes conveyed the messages, and he read my body language well.

"Gotcha. See you Monday at what time?"

"Ten a.m. Be here at 10:00. It'll give me some time to train you. You got some business casual clothes? If so, come with it on. If not, a polo and some jeans will work."

"Bet." He walked out of the office.

My mind began racing. I had aged. I was 30 pounds heavier, not as cute as I used to be when we were hanging out, and I hadn't had my hair done in months. My hair was in a bun, and I wore my red prescription field glasses with a pair of old slacks and a button-down. I'm sure he had so many questions, and I was willing to answer them when no one was around. I immediately texted Desire to schedule an appointment to get 22 inches of Indian straight hair installed.

I'd use the weekend to transform into something a li'l better, so that on Monday, Roca wouldn't have to look at a complete slouch. While Kenya never mentioned Roca, his body language told all, and you could tell he was tight-lipped. He probably wanted to know who he was and where he came from, and if I was fucking him. The truth was, I didn't expect Roca to appear. My goal was to carry things respectfully since I was still married, and Roca was engaged. Monday would be the day that I would train Roca, give him a scope of work, tasks for him, and use other days when I had the opportunity to come up for air. The scary thing was that Roca could read me well. And even though I put him in a small corner where he organized my files and got my administrative office back on track, he could see that I was exhausted, and one day, I was nearly feeling so weak, like I wanted to fall apart.

"What's wrong, D?"

"I don't feel well. I'm prediabetic."

"Did you eat?"

"No, not yet." I put my head on my desk.

"You need to eat, D. Come on, man. What's going on with you? Lemme give you some fruit I have in my bag." He handed me an apple and orange. "Eat this. This is good for you. It'll get your levels up. Do people in this office know that you are prediabetic?"

"Yes, they know."

"Then why these muthafuckas ain't bring you fresh fruit? Why they ain't making sure you eat? The fuck is going on here? Yea, you put on a good front, but something ain't right with you. I'm your friend. I'm not gonna allow you to fall out on my watch." Roca handed me a bottle of orange juice.

"Drink this too. Then let's go get a light lunch. Let's go to Mary's around the corner and get some sandwiches and talk at a park. I know there's a park over here."

"Yes, let's go get lunch. I'm hungry anyway. I know I need to eat."

I gathered my purse, and we walked out together and hopped in my car. The whole office was observing our every move. While their heads were probably thinking negative, that was the first time someone had asked me if I had eaten. That was part of the problem. I realized at that moment that everyone was good, but I wasn't, and nobody really cared about *my* health, let alone wanted to understand what was really going on with me.

We grabbed some cold cuts, water, and some more fruit and headed off to one of the beautiful parks that tourists frequent in the community. It was a gem in the hood.

We sat down, eager to converse. There was so much tea brewing . . .

"Baby, what's wrong?"

I burst into tears. "I'm fucked up, Roca! You can see it in my eyes. I married this nigga, and he cold carrying me. Treating me like a piece of shit. You know I thought I was doing the right thing. He was with me, you know, when I didn't have anything. When it was just King and me, and I felt like it was right."

"I can see the pain in your eyes, sweetheart. I knew you were hurting. I just wanted to give you some time for us to sit down. Is he putting his hands on you? Why are you sick? Why aren't you eating?"

"Look, my heart hurt. He gotta a daughter that was just born. A whole daughter by another woman. Like, come on! I know I'm not perfect, but how you have a whole affair on me, though? All I'm doing is grinding, building an empire, tryin'a make sure that I never go back to the ghetto. I'm sick 'cause I'm sick of him. I'm not eating properly. I miss eating meals. I'm not drinking water. I'm smoking fucking Black & Milds, and I'm not exercising. I'm fucked up, Roca! Some days, I feel like I'm gonna die!"

"You are *not* gonna die while I'm here! You are *not* gonna die. I can't believe this nigga is doing this to you. See, if you would have been patient, we could have been married. It could have been us. I got rid of Fatima, and now I'm with a chick named France from Maryland."

"Well, I wasn't trying to wait on you to leave Fatima. I never thought you were gonna leave her, anyway. Y'all had a son together, and I couldn't compete with that. So, I went with Kenya. He was fucking with me, and he was there. But he turned out to be a complete monster. He cheats, he gets high off the dipper, he comes home when he wants to, and has no regard for our relationship. The girl that he had the baby by has messaged me on social media. She even called me to reiterate that she isn't going anywhere, and he continues to fuck with her."

"I know you love him, but when are you gonna get yourself back together? When are you gonna focus on yourself? You know, that pretty brown woman who is royal in every way—where is she? Get into you! Make *yourself* better and take your mind off him!" Roca pointed directly at me.

"I wanna practice Yoga, you know? I went to a few classes years ago, but I wanna practice Yoga and learn the art of meditation. I wanna get my fat ass on the track and walk and jog a few laps. I'm crying inside. I need me back! You are so right!"

"Well, I'm gonna help you. It's more than volunteering to get out of the halfway house. It's more than working for you. I'm gonna be the friend that you need and show you the love that you need to get over this nigga and get back to Dream. While I have breath, I'm not gonna let nothing happen to you. I'm protecting you now!" He raised his shirt to demonstrate that he wasn't playing, and he'd let a whole clip go on his waist and then some.

He hugged me as we sat on the park bench and wiped my tears as they profusely ran down my face. For the first time, I had the biggest cry that had been harboring in my soul for years.


Roca was my angel in a human form. Kinda like the angel that Anita Baker sang about during the '80s. It was as if God sent him to me to distract me from trauma and pain and to be a constant reminder of what it means to seek happiness and to embrace being happy. Mondays would never be the same for me. As a matter of fact, I looked forward to Money Making Mondays. Roca encouraged me to upgrade my wardrobe, to change my look, and to spend more time on myself, even during office hours. He would cover for me and hold the office down as I would take the hard-earned money that I made to go get pedicures, massages, my lashes done, and just take time to myself. Some weekends, I would go get lipstick wasted and run up a tab in the MAC store. Ruby Woo and Candy Yum Yum had never looked so beautiful on me. You could witness the transformation, and not everybody was happy for me, but it didn't even matter.

Every morning, he would bring me a small hot tea with lemon with a few teaspoons of honey. He knew not to make it too sweet because he was rooting for me to come out of the prediabetic range and into a normal blood sugar range. He'd bring me a healthy breakfast, and since lunch was my favorite meal of the day, we would pick days to check out new restaurants in town. He was officially my confidant and BFF, and you could tell some of the staff members were getting jealous that he got so close to me. But any person that was helping me to save my life had my undivided attention. Roca's energy level gave me healing vibrations, and the nights that Kenya didn't come home, he would be on the phone with me to comfort me until dawn. There were so many nights that I would suffer heart palpitations and sleepless nights because I felt so alone, yet Roca found a way to make me laugh and reflect on our conversations.

Kenya was spending hidden time with his baby girl, Sojourn, and Demi, and he didn't think I knew. Demi and her sister were petty. They sent photos to my phone of them together, and they were real comfortable posting pictures on social media. Kenya didn't respect me, and, therefore, neither did Demi or his family respect me. From what I understood, at times, Demi had her own place, but she lost it, and they were living in hotels and sometimes with Keema and even with Macy. Kenya had created a family with her, and as bipolar as it was, I was beginning to accept it. Wasn't sure if the years with him were a complete wash because we had Dynasty, and we had some wonderful times, but perhaps we had outgrown the relationship, and we were now holding on to the history, the moments, and the "forget-me-nots." The love never left between Kenya and me, but the respect did. I demanded separation from him, and although he fought me tooth and nail on formally moving out of the house, he knew that he had to go—the shit was so toxic that if I didn't put my foot down, Kenya would be the death of me. My heart couldn't take it.

The chessboard was different because Kenya had sacrificed his queen for a pawn. What he didn't know was that there was a king in the cut rooting for me, wanting so bad to love me and protect me. Roca and I became so tight that it was as if the stars were aligned on our planets. We were together almost every day of the week outside of work, and he even started upgrading. Aside from working with me on new contracts, he had other side hustles and a power washing company that he kicked off where he saved his money and invested in the things that he desired. He purchased a black-on-black ESV Escalade and fucked everyone up with that move. It was like wherever we went, people would whisper "Secret Service." He began investing in stocks and started seeing residual income. He upgraded his wardrobe, and everything that he wore was designer, from the belts to the watches to the shoes. When you saw us, you would have assumed that we were a power couple and that he was my husband, but he was really my angel. From the White House, to conferences, to fundraisers, to dinner parties, to workshops and special events, Roca was right beside me.

While we created boundaries because of our relationships, we were falling in love. We were the perfect verse, the perfect soundtrack to our own love story. He became my lover, and it was so unintentional. You could see and smell the love, but most counted him out and thought that he was in it for the money, but he was really in it for the love. Roca's father was a multimillionaire. He could have worked for him or worked with a few of his other peers who were on top of the world; he had options.

Roca was absolutely beautiful, and he was truly the poster man for the "beard gang." His beard was full and long, and women near and far tried to lock him down. It was awkward, but we had an unspoken code where we understood that what we had wasn't fair weather. We would confide in each other, we'd share stories, we could fall weak or fall ill and still ride for each other. The lovemaking was phenomenal and more amazing than any level of intimacy that I had ever had in my entire life. Our love wasn't intentional.

The reality was that if I chose happiness, I needed to choose it with or without Roca. He had a whole family, children, and a woman that he was tied to, and that was for real. As much as I loved him, in the back of my mind, I wanted to be gracious about dealing with him. Demi had no respect or regard for me or mines. I didn't want to disrespect France, bring havoc, or become a homewrecker. So, I cherished the days that we spent together and was slightly guarded, even though the love that we had mirrored songstress Jazmine Sullivan's song, "Let It Burn." I swear I would play that song every day, over and over again, until you'd hear me screaming at the top of my lungs:

*"You feel that fire, just let it burn/There's no runnin' beneath your turn/Call me crazy, but I think I found the love of my life."*


As soon as Kenya got a whiff of me looking and feeling better, he tried to reappear at the house, calling me constantly, showing up at my job, and even having the neighbors watch the house to see who was coming and going.

There were no longer windows to my heart, and even though I still had love for Kenya, my spirit woman knew better. I spoke to Kenya about us moving forward with a divorce and learning to be amicable, maybe even friends one day, but my goal was to learn how to coparent. I wanted to show the children that even though things were not working out between us, we could still show them love as parents. Kenya wasn't going for divorce and refused it. He even wanted to go as far as to sign us up for marriage counseling to get guidance on how he could save his marriage with guru Iyanla

Vanzant who was coming to town. I was willing to go to counseling 'cause it was therapeutic, and perhaps she could let us know if what we had left was worth fixing.

He aimed to make amends, and he would call me constantly, asking for forgiveness, wanting to come back home and make things right. There was no love lost, but I had tasted peace of mind, a peace that I'd hear Black yogis describe. There was one part of me that yearned to give it one more try, but there was a wiser and more mature woman who felt that the engine had blown, and the car wasn't worth getting a new engine. It was as if our love had a recall. Although our love was so dope in the beginning, it had manifested into a cold disaster. Kenya was hopeful as we would talk from day to day, but I had a plan. I planned to get my health in order, save my money, restore my credit, and buy a house. I wanted out. I wanted out of the house and out of the memories and a new lease on life.

Ocean was working with my organization as a program director for our music program for at-risk youth. Things came full circle, and the music program was a lucrative contract that brought back my former staff, Kiana and Christian. He had picked up momentum, and he snagged his own place where Kenya's friend, Nate, and he became roommates. The apartment was spacious and came with great amenities, including a pool, gym, cookout area, and store. Dynasty and I would frequent Ocean's pool during the summer to unwind, and King would hang out with his uncle on the weekends. I was super proud of his growth.

Ocean had a front seat to my world because he lived inside of my house, and he watched my life crumble, but he also saw me rise and get my shit in order. Although he was my little brother, he saw the shit that Kenya was taking me through, and he hated it. He depended on me too, so he tried more to help me with the business and the kids. His only words to me were, "Cuh if you need me, let me know 'cause I will fuck that nigga up if he put his hands on you. It ain't nothing. I got you!" Ocean was a natural introvert, but he was no coward, and folks let that light skin fool them. Our family in California is associated with the Crip gang, and Ocean's father, Major, was a certified OG. Ocean didn't trust city-slicking East Coast niggas, and when he got tired of them, he would fly out and go home for a few days or a week to get that California love.

I was searching for happy, and I had found it for the first time in nearly 10 years. It was a happiness that reminded me of what it meant to sing in the shower, strut as I walked, dance to my favorite songs, eat ice cream on a sugar cone just because, and let my long tresses blow in the wind. Roca brought the spirit of happiness and shared the vibrations with me. I tapped into it. He was a friendly reminder sent from the ancestors that I was gonna be all right. I began hydrating, eating cleaner, and eating three meals a day. I began fucking until my hips spread, and my skin glistened. I finally found a Yoga practice where Black girls could find and own their very own magic. Between Yoga, exercising regularly, and going to church, the balance came. I set the intention. It was peace. Namaste.

# Chapter 25

*Sacred Love Notes*

We were naked in spirit and stripped of pride. Our relationship had become an open book for a crowd of close to 100 strangers in a small room seeking sacred love notes from Guru Iyanla Vanzant. Ms. Vanzant had chosen us as a backdrop to understanding the complexities of Black Love. Kenya and I had agreed to seek counseling through a local radio advertisement seeking couple's counseling. We decided that counseling was our last resort. We applied online and were humbled to find out that we were selected. We were nervous as hell once we realized that a live studio audience would join our counseling session, so we invited a friend of ours who was a licensed therapist named Jacob for therapeutic support. For the very first time, we were going into uncharted territories, and Ms. Vanzant had no cut cards. She asked the questions that we were silent about and resurrected guilt and shame like it was a pan of yeast. Her read on us reminded you of a candid grandma or a mean aunt, but she was an architect at healing, so we listened because we needed help.

"Beloved, I need you to move your chairs so that you are facing each other. It's gonna get real."

We adjusted our chairs, which sat high. You could spot our nervousness. I wore a black dress with a blazer and a 30-inch ponytail that gave life. Kenya wore a nice pair of gray slacks, a navy button-down, loafers, and his signature fedora hat. He appeared strong and confident. The camera crew gave us our own mics, and we sat at the edge of our seats, ready.

"Hey, beloved, your dress is short and cute, but we need to cover those legs. We don't have any covering, do we? You know what to do!" We laughed with the audience as she came right for me. I knew to keep it cute and camera ready for whatever popped off in the lion's den.

"So, what did he do to you?" She wanted real tea—with or without sugar.

"He cheated. He had an affair. He had a baby by another woman." You could see eyes bulging from the audience members. In a few seconds, we had their full attention, and Kenya was quite uncomfortable.

"He cheated and had a baby by a different woman? He defiled y'all bed? Lord, Have Mercy! Beloved, what do you have to say to that?" She faced Kenya holding her microphone.

"What I have to say is that—yes! Yes, I cheated and had a baby outside of our marriage, but I'm here because I'm sorry for what I have done and want to make things right."

She didn't buy it. I listened.

"You're sorry? No, you need to tell *her* that you're sorry. But when you stepped out on your wife, you defiled the bed. You broke the vows. You broke the covenant. Do you understand that in that decision that you destroyed the union between you and her?"

"She cheated too! She's not gonna tell you that." Kenya shifted the blame.

"I don't want to hear it. I don't want to hear it." She put her hands up in disappointment. "Beloved, did you cheat on him?"

"Yes, I did because he cheated on me first. I was a good wife to him. But I guess not good enough for him. What did he expect me to do?" Jacob was sitting in the front row, making eye contact with us and nodding to both of us, giving comfort.

"This is a mess. Look at her. You can see the hurt in her eyes. Look at her and tell her that you're sorry!" She played no games with Kenya.

He lifted his head with boldness and said, "Dream, I am sorry! I'm sorry!"

The audience didn't know whether to believe him.

"I take full responsibility, Iyanla. I am not perfect. I made mistakes. I didn't have anyone showing me how to be a good husband. I'm learning this. I never wanted to hurt her."

"You humiliated her!" Her voice went up a few octaves. "You brought another woman into your marriage. You *defiled* the marriage. You broke it with your decision." She scolded him as she paced the stage.

"Now, beloved Dream, look at him and say, 'You hurt me!'"

I burst out in tears and replied, "You hurt me! You hurt me! Why did you hurt me?" I began sobbing. Jacob was teary-eyed. You could see some of the audience members wiping their tears like they had been there too.

"Now, beloveds, this marriage as you know it is over!"

We both pushed back in our seats, and our spirits said in unison, "Hold up, Iyanla. We did not come here for you to close the shop down."

"Wha'chu mean the marriage is over?" Kenya got aggressive.

"I was married twice to the same man. The first round it was destroyed, and then years later, we married again when things were right. The marriage, as you know it, has now been destroyed because you allowed someone to defile the sacredness of your marriage. Once you did that, you tarnished your union. Now, what is next for you all? What do you want to do?"

"I want us to learn how to coparent and get along." I sniffled.

"You have children? How many do you have together?"

"We have one daughter together, but we raised three together. I want us to stay married. I came here to restore our marriage." Kenya was intentional.

"Restore? It's completely broken. Now, what you can do is focus on healing your souls. Raising those babies. And once you are healed individually, you can come back for a second go-round." Ms. Vanzant made sense, but neither one of us wanted it to be. It was safe to say that we were holding on to pieces of love.

"Now, look at him, beloved, and tell him, 'I am letting you go!'"

Iyanla Vanzant had officially lost her muthafucking mind. She went from a woman that I had respected to someone who seemed like she was using her gifts to exploit Black Love. We thought she could "fix our life," but clearly, she had another intention, and it was hard to read. Before I responded, I looked up to the sky and sought to hear God. Even the audience was in disbelief. Kenya was about to get out of his chair and cut the fuck up. I could see that the counseling session was about to go out the window and transform into an episode of reality TV. We were uncomfortable.

"I don't know about that." I paused for 5 seconds, taking a deep breath. I channeled my energy and saw that the audience was rooting for both of us despite Iyanla's guidance. Jacob put both his thumbs up to us as a sign to say that we were doing good under pressure.

"I am college educated, Ms. Vanzant, and I don't know if I should articulate my words like that. What I will say is that I am letting go of this!" My voice and my hands were shaking. The tears just couldn't stop. "What I will say is that I am letting go of this relationship because it is broken. I will see you again, Kenya, if it's meant to be. But we have kids, so I can never leave you." It was time for me to go. Iyanla was spiritually time traveling, and that was not the route that we were going.

"OK, beloved," she walked toward Kenya, "look at her and tell her that you are letting her go. Tell her now that you are letting her go!" she commanded.

"No disrespect, Ms. Iyanla," he stood up and stood his ground, "but that's my wife, and I am *never* letting her go! I am never letting her go. I would have to die to let her go!"

At that point, we didn't know if there were demons or angels amongst us. Iyanla Vanzant was walking a thin line between darkness and light. Kenya was a gangsta, and he wasn't trying to hear that shit. It wasn't holistic healing for us at that point, but the audience could tell and saw that we were organic, and nothing was scripted.

"Well, beloveds, what I will do is offer counseling services to you so that you can heal and work through everything. It's deeper than the time that we have, as you all can see."

Iyanla Vanzant saw that we weren't the type that you could troubleshoot in one session. We probably could have gotten our own spin-off.

"We thank you for coming, and our producers will be in contact with you soon." She ended the session.

Kenya smiled, and I smiled at him back. He grabbed my hand and ushered me out of the audience as people in droves came to hug us, give advice, share wisdom, and overall positive feedback. Some audience members wanted pictures with us, and others wanted a way to stay connected. We were grateful for the moment, and the show proved that we lost trust and respect, but the love wasn't lost.

"Iyanla got me fucked up, Dream! I'm not leaving you. They gonna have to kill me for me to leave you. It's not gonna happen."

Jacob came up to us and gave us a group hug.

"Whew, chile. You guys did really good, really good. She used a lot of therapeutic strategies that were intense, but just when she thought you were gonna fold, you stood your ground."

"Hell yea. This is my wife!" Kenya proudly raised our hands in the air. "Yea, I fucked up, but we gonna thug it out."

"I think we need a break, Kenya. We need to stay separated for a while and see what the future has for us. You need to get your life all the way together. For real. She is right. This, as we know it, is fucked up and all wrong."

"Give me some time to get myself in order. Please, Dream. Give a nigga some time, and I will get it right on the second go-round."

We all laughed to keep from crying as we took a ride to a local bar for happy hour. Kenya and I were overdue for a drink. We didn't need to overthink. We needed time to just be human without the titles and the heaviness. We had a few shots and used the time to catch up on our individual lives. Although what Iyanla Vanzant said felt like daggers to our hearts, Jacob said that he watched us realize with our very own eyes that the love was still there. Kenya and I had so much history that was beautiful, good, bad, ugly, and crazy. But it was our story, nevertheless. And if we could leave an unorthodox marriage counseling session in peace that was broadcast to the world, then, indeed, we had something sacred and undefinable. There was so much time lost, and we were missing out on each other's personal growth.

I bought a beautiful home in a nice corridor in town. It was a friendly community of predominately middle-class Blacks and retirees. The kind of neighborhood where you had to have a gardener and landscaper, and if your lawn weren't manicured, the neighbors would side-eye you. While the kids missed their old friends and our old neighborhood, they understood the need for peace in our lives, and the change was good. Kenya and I agreed that we had exposed them to too much negativity. They needed to witness positive and healthy relationships.

Kenya admitted that he was living out in VA with Demi, but insisted that he was looking for a higher-paying job that had benefits. He indicated that he wanted a thriving career and wanted to contribute more to the kids as their father because Dynasty was in elementary school, and Nia and King were in middle school. The difference between Nia and Dynasty was that Nia was his firstborn, and they were tied at the hip. Dynasty loved both of us. However, she had Kenya's heart, and in his eyes, she could do no wrong, and he would deem her as "the brains" of the operation. He saw Dynasty as a magical being and admired her for being super smart, talented, and cute. She had Kenya's whole face. There was no denying that she had more of his features than any of his kids.

Nia was a daddy's girl who always wanted to be with Kenya, no matter the circumstance. If Kenya were in a shelter, Nia would be right beside him. And wherever he decided to go, she was a "rida," and her loyalty was with her dad. Nia stayed with Kenya and Demi and was close to Sojourn. It was hard for her to convey her true feelings because she had spent nearly a decade around King and me, and then came Dynasty. She knew that her dad was married and had a baby by another woman, which was complicated for a kid. King was loyal to his mama, and as he got older, he was indeed my protector. King just wanted me to be happy, and nothing else meant more to him. Although King wasn't Ken's biological child, Ken was in his life since King was 4 years old and definitely helped me with raising him. Ken said that he might have had a son prior to meeting me that lived out in VA, but he called that son a "Maury" baby because the young lady he had relations with would never take a DNA test to confirm if he was the father. Ultimately, there was a disconnect between them because Kenya needed a real confirmation, and her allegations weren't good enough.

Ken had plans to move back to the city because he had job offers close to my house, and he was missing Dynasty, and Dynasty was definitely missing him. He asked if he could stay in my basement on days that he had work assignments near my house, and I was compassionate and saw fit that he could. Although I was falling in love with Roca, nothing meant more to me than family. My daughter needed her father, I needed the support, and in my mind, it was a pathway to healthy coparenting.

My priority was no longer a marriage. It was more self-care and orchestrating my life to where I was at peace and experienced happiness, however it came. I warned Kenya that in my new house he could not disrespect me, get high, super drunk, or have people coming to my house. He'd have to hold his own when he was there and help out with the kids. For the first time, I had order in my house, and it would stay that way.

While I watched Kenya try to right his wrongs, there was a dark side to him that he did not like to expose. There was a duality to him that I understood as a Black man in America trying to find his way to abounding joy, love, and safety. I knew his obvious battles with substance abuse, addiction, lust for women, and mental health, but there was even a darker side that he never wanted me to see. That dark side he would speak in code, and out of respect for the street code, I never knew what he was really into, and I never asked because I knew better. However, every now and then, he'd tell me about certain people in his circle that he did not trust, and he'd clear his name with me about any rumors that were lingering in the streets.

Kenya confided in me about snakes in his life that he believed were sent to devour him. I paid attention because there was no coincidence that it was three women who hung in a similar circle named Iniko, Zina, and Tayla. Kenya allowed these women to come into his life because they were familiar spirits that manifested themselves in the form of a "sis, sandbox, and homegirl." He believed that they would one day infiltrate him, so he wanted me to be on point and to pay attention, and I did. In the spirit realm, they were jezebels and sorcerers operating in the spirit of witchcraft. They were not only sent to manipulate him, sexualize him, and demonize him, but they were sent as a culprit of Delilah assigned to take Kenya's power away. Kenya made me aware that he was fighting hard to cut ties from the dark side, aiming fully to cross over and serve Christ. My spirit woman was interceding and stayed awake. God would give me the revelation.

I reflected on a conversation that Kenya would have with us at the dinner table.

"Listen, y'all, Daddy isn't gonna be here forever, so you better soak up game now." The kids looked puzzled as they ate and listened. "No, seriously, at the end of the day, I'm trying to get my life in order. I need you two, being the oldest, to stay in school, graduate, and go to college. I expect that you look out for your li'l sister. But knowing Dynasty is so damn smart, she'll probably be looking out for y'all." Dynasty giggled as she wiped the juice from her mouth. "It's hard out here being a young Black man. You hear me, King? Stay in school and let football take you all the way. Nia, find your passion. Find what you love and go with it. Your mom, she knows what her purpose is. She loves business; she loves helping the community and writing books. For the most part, she has her life figured out, and I'm trying to get to where she is. I don't have long." We were all quiet. He had been sipping on some Cognac, but his tone was different. He was serious. We were all looking like . . . Where is all of this coming from?

"What do you mean you don't have long? Stop talking crazy," I said, standing next to him.

"What I mean is that I think that I won't be here very long. Niggas are dying every day. People you know are snaking you out. I feel like niggas wanna kill me." He sounded paranoid.

The kids didn't know how to feel. They turned their bodies and watched his mannerisms.

"Just stay here, Kenya! Get on your feet. Get your life in order and stay sucka free. Don't go Uptown. Don't let niggas know your moves. Stay quiet and stay away from anyone you feel is a snake, and you'll be good."

"Yea, Dad, stay away from Uptown." Nia was adamant.

"Yea, Ken, stop going Uptown. Just stay here with us and do what you gotta do." King sounded like a grown man.

"Daddy, stay away from bad people." Dynasty was his conscience.

"Eh, Dream, you know you can't divorce me, right?"

"Why is that?" I smirked.

"You wanna be a boss? Well, you are gonna be the one to bury me a G. You are gonna run my whole entire funeral. And when I die, you are gonna cry, baby girl. You are gonna cryyyyyyyyyy!"

"What type of shit are you on? Why are you speaking on death in front of the kids? You are twisted, dawg. You trippin'." I had become annoyed with his twisted premonition.

"I'm preparing y'all. You don't wanna heed, then that's on you."

"Really? You crazy as hell, and you need to put whatever you drinking down. 'Cause them wine and spirits are getting to your brain. Anyhow, time to change the subject."

"I'm gon', man. I'll be back."

"Where you going, Dad?" Nia asked.

"Y'all good. I'm gon' to get some fresh air. Dream got y'all." He looked at his phone and went outside and hopped in someone's ride before we could even catch a glimpse.

He was strong and bold, self-centered, wild, and fiery. He was the truth when you weren't ready for it. Kenya was an Aries man, and his impulsive behavior would have him disappear for days, and we were simply immune to it.

Nia, from that day on, began staying most of her time at my new house because her mom was incarcerated, and Kenya preferred her to be at my house since he was going to work from there. Taja had her own demons, and I was never concerned about why she was going back and forth to jail because it really hurt Kenya that she didn't get her life together for her children. He would always get his daughter, no matter the circumstances. Nia also spent time living with Ken's grandma, spending time at Keema's, and on the weekends, her mother's sister, who was really cool, would come get her. Even though Taja never respected me, I always made sure that Nia was safe, clothed, ate good, played, got assistance with her homework—I tried to show her positive vibrations of a Black woman. All the kids went to school within a mile radius of one another, so the drop-off and pickups were smooth, and they were all older, which made things even better. We had no babies, and we could move to a unique beat in life.

Living in my new community had many benefits, and the main one was wellness. There were parks, tracks, and gyms to motivate me on my healthy lifestyle journey. I dedicated 4 days a week to the gym. I was becoming addicted to cardio and saw the results. Monday through Thursday, around 6:00 a.m., you would catch me at the gym, and if I were feeling inspirational, I would go on Sundays before or after church. The doper the playlist, the longer the inclines, and the more calories that I burned. Going to the gym was a friendly reminder that I never wanted to be prediabetic ever again. As I walked and jogged for more than an hour, my phone rang. It was my son.

"Ma, Kenya is here. He wanna know where you was at. You at the gym?"

"Yea, I'm at the gym. I'm wrapping up. Is he drunk?"

"Yea, a li'l. He loud as a mug, though. We all up. Everything good."

King was such a big boy.

"All right, son, I'm on my way."

If Kenya was drunk this early, I knew to get my ass home. The gym would catch me on another day. The house was just 3 minutes away. My intuition told me that Kenya would be in rare form.

"Look at Miss Important. Oh, now, you wanna work out? Why we can't work out together?" Kenya had a red cup in his hand as he stood at the top of the stairs.

"What's up? Where you been?"

"Out VA. Why you care?"

"Damn, I was just asking." I walked into the house. He walked behind me. The kids were talking amongst themselves.

"Why you wasn't working out when we lived at the old house? What, you was with your li'l boyfriend?"

"What? Really? I didn't work out at the old house 'cause you were stressing me out. Now, I'm trying to do what's best for me on my own. I don't need no one accompanying me to the gym."

"Yea, whatever! Man, when you gonna stop playing with me?" He aggressively got in my face giving me the stank face.

"Look, it's too early for drama. You need to drink some water and get out of my face, Kenya! Come on, it's a peaceful Sunday."

"Look, I'm gonna speak my mind regardless. You act like your shit don't stink. You got issues too. You got secrets too. You gotta a whole boyfriend, and you're married. It ain't just me!" He got louder and wouldn't stop. The kids peeked to see if we would escalate.

"You came here to interrogate me. Nigga, you had a whole baby on me. You was living the 'Secret Life of Bees' while I was grinding trying to build an empire, and you didn't even respect it. How long did you think I was gonna tolerate that shit?" I walked to my room.

"What you mean? I love you, girl! I made a fucking mistake, dawg! Niggas make mistakes all the time. Solomon did that to you. I fucked up and did that to you, and that nigga you dealing wit' is gonna do the same thing! It's not your fault. It's mine. I take full responsibility! But you not gonna hold it over my head!" He came right behind me.

"Since you wanna go there, you crushed me, dawg! You broke me! You humiliated me! Now, I'm getting my life back. I'm bringing order and balance, and now you checking for me. But you can't mend something you broke!" My mouth was on fire.

"Man, don't play with me, Dream! When you gonna stop doing what you're doing with that nigga? What, you infatuated with his beard? His SUV? He a South Side nigga. You think I'm a thug. *He* the muthafuckin' thug. You know he got a whole girl. You stupid!"

"I know a lot of shit. I know that Demi is ugly as hell. I know she fatter than me. I know she broke down and ain't got nothing on me. What were *you* thinking?" I went off.

"I don't know what I was thinking. She will do whatever I tell her to do." He had no real rebuttal.

"Well, there you have it. You settled. I didn't. But what I know is that you ain't gonna come in *my* house poppin' off and disturbin' my peace on a Sunday. You wild, Kenya! You trippin'. Now, you wanna do something? Give me some money for your daughters. Dynasty needs money for her dance tuition, and Nia needs things. Ain't nuffin' free."

"Money ain't nothin', sweetheart!" He began throwing twenties at me. "I got bread. I cashed my check. Here you go!" He handed me a handful of twenties, hitting the palm of my hand real hard.

"Thanks." I smiled.

"Naw, give me my money back!" He switched up on me. "You are unappreciative. You can keep some of that." He took three $20 bills from me and walked off.

"You are so petty. But all right, whatever."

He picked up Dynasty and sat with her on the porch. They were having their own conversation. She was the only one who could calm him down. The rest of the kids went outside and hung out with him.

"You love Daddy?" He began kissing her fat cheeks.

"Yea, Daddy, I love you. You and Mommy need to stop fighting." She was so wise.

"Yea, I know, but your mom makes Daddy mad. But I'm gonna listen to you. You got more sense than everybody. You gonna be Doc McStuffins. You know that, right?"

"Yes, Daddy." She leaned her head on his shoulder.

"Eh, Dream, let me take the girls with me." Dynasty sat on his lap.

"Hell no!"

"Whatchu mean, 'Hell no'? These are *my* daughters. I'm taking them Uptown!" He stood up belligerently.

"No, you are not! I'm taking them to a cookout. You are not taking Dynasty, you already know that, and especially Uptown. Nia, you can decide if you wanna go with your dad." I grabbed my fanny pack that was near the door. King and one of his friends that spent the night knew that things were gonna get ugly. The tension was high, and the kids knew exactly what to do when things were out of whack. They went and put on their shoes real quick and stood outside by my car. Nia looked torn.

"Dad, I'm gonna go with Dream. You don't need to go Uptown." She put her head down. She never wanted to disappoint her dad. He stormed into the house and grabbed a fifth of Cognac that looked like he drank half of it already. He took his gray baseball hat and two cell phones off the table. He wore a gray T-shirt, blue jeans with no belt, and stumbled outside. My neighbor, who he had befriended, started walking toward our house, which was a good distraction.

"So, you not gonna let me take them?" He was super loud.

"No, I'm not!" I shut the door and unlocked my car. The kids hopped inside.

"Dawg, you are gonna make me fuck you up!"

"Fuck who up? I tell you what. I'm getting in my car. We headed to Ms. Kim's cookout." I did not budge. I got in my hamster, locked the doors, and rolled up the windows. He was drunk, but he was still strong. He had never put his hands on me, but he was notorious for breaking something. He picked up a brick from the side of my driveway and motioned to bust my front window. I immediately called 911 'cause he was out of his mind, and I was afraid that he was gonna destroy the window with the kids in the car. When the operator came on, I spoke fast and to the point and told her I was in a domestic dispute that needed to be diffused. Kenya heard me and got irate and hit the window with his hand but didn't crack it.

"What's he doing?" King was getting mad. "As soon as I get a li'l bigger, I'm gonna knock him out! He's doing too much."

The girls were shaken.

"You called the police on me? The *police?*"

"Kenya, go 'head! Go 'head!" I was getting angry as I completely backed into the street.

"Fuck you, Dream!" He stood in the middle of the street causing a few neighbors to come out. My neighbor Country walked up on Kenya to try to get him to calm down.

"Fuck you too, Kenya!" I gave him the middle finger and drove in slow motion so that he could feel the sentiments.

Talk about 0–100, he was the only man in the world that could take me out of character, and he knew that. You could count on him to take the perfect day and turn it upside down. He was as bipolar as D.C. weather. There was no doubt that we both were still hurting. His muse was the liquor, and mine was in wellness. There was no cheap fix for broken people.

The kids were excited to go to Ms. Kim's cookout because it was on our old block, and they could hang out with their old friends. We all could use a break. Ms. Kim was a single mom, a hard worker, and a few years older than me. Her yard was the life of the party, and on the weekends, if the weather was good, she would be on the grill. She had the music popping, plenty of daiquiris and beers, a hookah bar, and a big screen to watch movies outside at dark. Ms. Kim dated Nate, who was Kenya's friend and Ocean's roommate. She could be messy at times, but overall, she was a good-hearted person who believed in a good time. If you got her wrong, though, she was as strong as an ox. She had height and was thick, and she would fight a nigga.

That night, the weather was perfect. We had a ball doing karaoke, and even Ocean joined us as we blended daiquiris, took shots, and sang the night away. We didn't get in the house until 11:00 p.m. Just as soon as I got the kids settled and asleep, I got a text from Keema.

Have you been on Kenya's FB page?

No. We are not friends on FB. Why? I texted back.

Someone posted RIP.

My spirit froze. I called her immediately.

"Yea, someone posted rest in peace."

"Why would they post that on social media? Can you message that person and see what's going on?"

"Yea, I'm doing it now." There was silence on both ends. "Oh Lord. They said Kenya was shot on Atlanta and S Street. We need to go there now!" Keema was talking fast.

"OK. OK. Lemme throw something on. I'm headed there now." We hung up. My mind was going blank. My eyes were seeing flashing lights. My adrenaline went into full throttle. Not knowing what happened to Kenya was causing me great vexation. I called my brother and asked him to come to the house immediately because

Kenya had been shot. My brother could tell in my voice that it was serious. He called an Uber and was at my house in 15 minutes. I stood at the door with my hair wild and a hat to the back. I couldn't fathom what was going on. My brother knew to lock up the house, protect the kids, and not say anything to anybody. His main concern was for me because I was a lioness going into enemy territory, not knowing if the lion had been captured or if I'd return.

# Chapter 26

## The Other Side of the Game

As I drove like a bat out of hell, I could feel the angels surrounding me. I called Jacob and explained to him that Kenya had been shot and asked him if he could ride with me to the crime scene—he was down. Jacob was a friend, but he was also a clinical therapist who could calm me down in the most traumatic circumstances. The more red lights I saw, the faster I drove right through them. Out of a sense of urgency, I called my biological father to let him know that Kenya had been shot and to pray for us. My father tried to get me to avoid going to a crime scene because he knew it was dangerous, but there was nothing that could stop me.

I pulled up in front of Jacob's house. He had a look of perplexity on his face. He took a deep breath and said, "Dream, we gonna be OK," and put on his seat belt. My heart was racing. The light at the intersection near his condo couldn't have been any longer. The police were at the corner, so I had to be patient. My final thoughts were to call Ms. P from the day care because she lived about 5 minutes away from where Ken was shot and could meet me there. In my heart of hearts, I needed to use my own street credibility to find out what happened to Kenya before I arrived. I called one of my old homies from Uptown, whose ears stayed glued to the streets to find out what exactly happened to Kenya.

LBoogie took a deep breath and said, "Dream, yea, it's true. He was shot Uptown. I just need you to keep your head up and take care of those babies, no matter what. Take care of those babies." I dropped the call and looked at Jacob.

"What did he say?"

"He told me to keep my head up and to take care of my babies." My eyes watered.

"Whew, chile. I'm here. I got you." Jacob was nervous.

My mind began racing. My spirit was leaping. I couldn't take it. My foot was heavy on the gas. I would run every red light until I got there. We pulled into the gas station at the corner of Atlanta Avenue and witnessed yellow tape, crime scene investigators, and detectives. Jacob, Ms. P, and her daughter stood beside me in utter silence. I ran straight to one of the officers.

"Excuse me, Officer. My husband-My husband was shot on this block. That was my husband!" My breathing was off.

"Calm down, miss. What's his name?"

"His name is Kenya Harris."

The officer acted nonchalant, like Kenya was just another nigga shot in America.

"Okay, listen. He wore a gray shirt, blue jeans, and a gray hat today. He didn't have a belt on. I'm his wife. My name is Dream Angelou Harris."

"Let me give this information to the detective. Hold tight."

I had the craziest feeling inside. It felt like an out-of-body experience. At that moment, things were surreal. Keema and Ryan pulled up in one car, Kenya's grandma and his mom, Macy, pulled up in another car, and Demi had the audacity to show up too. You could feel the tension in the air. We all stood apart. Nothing was right.

"What'd they say?" Keema walked up to me.

"I gave his description to the police, and he said that he would send a detective to us."

"Yea, they saying he was shot. I'm still trying to get the details."

A white and Latino detective walked up on us.

"Hi, are you the wife of Kenya Harris?" He spoke directly to me.

"Yes, I am." Jacob and Ms. P stood right by my side.

"I'm his sister. This is his mother and grandmother." Keema was aggressive and made it known that they were his kin.

"We'll talk to his wife, but you can come with us too."

"That's fine."

We walked with them a few feet and stood next to the detective's vehicle. They offered us to sit down. But my anxiety was too high, so I remained standing. Wasn't sure if Keema sat down, but we were there to listen.

"So, your husband, your brother . . . Kenya Harris was shot and died at the 900 block of S Street. I'm sorry to tell you that he did not survive." The detective looked us dead in the eyes.

I collapsed to the ground immediately. Life became pitch black. There were no stars. For the first time in my life, I felt like a part of my soul had died, and it would never resuscitate.

In one instance, there was a spirit of wailing like African women who prepared for mourning for their kings, 40 days and 40 nights. In one instance, Keema hollered like a battle cry, and soon as Macy and Grandma heard her, they knew that Kenya had succumbed. Their wails had arrhythmias. Their tears were dehydrated. Our cries were helpless. It was like the shit you saw on the 10:00 o'clock news. My friends immediately tried to revive me and pick me up off the ground.

"Come on, Dream. Come on, boo. You gotta get up for those babies!" Ms. P began shaking me with tears in her eyes. She had just lost her husband months prior, so she understood my pain.

"Come on, Dream. You gotta get off this ground. You got the kids to think about."

"Noooooo! Nooooo! Noooo! What the fuck am I supposed to do?" I began screaming.

"Dream, baby girl, I got you. I got you. Just hold me." Jacob used his strength and pulled me up, using his body for me to lean on. He held my hand and began speaking to me therapeutically. I couldn't hear. It was a nightmare. It was the worst nightmare ever. What would I tell our children? What would I say to Nia, his firstborn? How could I explain it to Dynasty? How would King feel? My head was spinning out of control.

"Listen, Dream, right?" The detective walked to me. "I know you are grieving and are at a loss for words. But as his wife, you will have to shift gears, unfortunately, and meet us downtown because this is a homicide."

"OK. OK. OK. OK." I was trying to get in control of my breathing. Yet, at the same time, why the fuck would I have to meet them at the homicide office? The detective handed me, Keema, and his grandma his card and circled the address.

"Meet us there shortly." They walked away swiftly and hopped in their cars. They had a job to do, and I had approximately an hour to cry, and then I'd transform into my wife duties. I had a flashback of Kenya's premonition when he was talking to the kids and me about his death. Every word he said would come to pass. And much as I hated it, he passed the baton to me. I had to boss up, orchestrate his funeral and burial, and if I had 5 minutes, I'd cry, but my heart would cry forever.

He died Uptown. The kids even told him not to go there. Yea, we were beefing, but I just didn't understand why he would act irrational and go into the Valley of the Shadow of Death. I expected him to be in my neck of the woods, at Keema's house, or out in VA. Our argument was meaningless. Couldn't get the time back. It was better to Love Yourz than not to have yours. All I could do is rewind the time in my mind.

As Jacob drove me to meet with the detectives, in my subconscious were flashes of the days, months, and years that we spent together. The moments kept flickering. I could hear the laughter between us. I smelled his aroma. It would never die.

The detectives boxed me in a room that looked like some shit you'd see on CSI. As they asked me questions about Kenya's characteristics, I realized that he had prophesied his own death. He enlightened me about the snakes that surrounded him. Even in his transition, his vibrations were in that room and communicated that he was murdered by a sandbox, a homie, or someone he considered a brother. His spirit operated like a medium, showing me as the detectives talked in circles that he was murdered because of envy, hatred, and fear. The detectives assured me that they would do their jobs until justice was served, but there was no relief in what they were saying.

It felt like an episode on POWER. The atmosphere was wicked. Jacob and Ms. P had really demonstrated their love for the kids and me, and Kenya would have loved them for that. It was nearly dawn, and Ms. P drove home, and I dropped Jacob off. Jacob had been my counselor, my homeboy, my foot soldier, and he needed rest. On the way home, I called Aunt Nandi and Uncle Marvin, I called Sanai and then my mama. I called my mama last because when she would hear my voice, she would know that if I had ever needed her, I needed her then.

As I pulled up into my driveway, Aunt Nandi and Uncle Marvin met me at the door. There were no words, only tears again. As I fell back on the couch, Ocean sat at the table with tears in his eyes. Although Kenya and he didn't see eye to eye on a lot, he dreaded to see me in pain; he dreaded to see the kids in pain. He and they would have something more in common. He knew what it was like to lose his dad, but he was an adult, and they were just children. Uncle and

Auntie surrounded me, rocking me on both sides. The weeping continued for hours. There were no words. They expressed that they had the kids and me, and like usual, they would always be here for us.

It was Monday morning, and even though it was a school day, the kids slept through their alarms like a breeze, which was unusual. I let them sleep. Dynasty was the first to wake up, and I directed her to get her sister and brother up to come upstairs because it was an emergency. Nia and King rubbed their eyes, yawning up the stairs as they both sat at opposite sides of the table. Dynasty sat in the middle, and I stood up like a queen who had lost her crown.

"I know you missed school, but it's OK. I needed you all to be here because it's urgent." I looked at Nia.

"Who died?" King blurted out.

"Did something happen to my dad?" Nia was in tune with her dad's spirit.

"Yes, your dad was shot yesterday at 6:25 p.m."

"Did he die?" Dynasty looked into my eyes.

"Unfortunately, he did. Your dad died. He didn't make it. I am so, so sorry." I walked straight to Nia to console her. She broke down. She sobbed and sobbed and sobbed. I embraced her and held her. She was a daddy's girl. She was his day one. She clung to him. All I could do was hold her. Then I extended my left arm to console Dynasty and King. King had tears uncontrollably falling down his face. He just kept shaking his head. Dynasty, however, was resilient. She didn't cry. It was as if Kenya's strength was fortified in her body. She began hugging her siblings and rubbing both of their backs. Her ministry was compassion, and it was unbelievable.

"Our dad died, but we shouldn't be sad because he's with the angels. He's in heaven. He isn't hurting anymore. He isn't sad anymore. Daddy finally got some peace." We froze and smiled. Her words were heavenly. She was indeed born before her time.

"Dynasty, man, she act just like Kenya!" King recognized.

"We gonna be good. Daddy is watching over us. Anyway, whoever killed my father, God is gonna kill him."

It almost killed me to have to tell the children that their father died. My soul had collapsed, and the burden was unbearable.

I spent days consoling, embracing, and loving on all the kids. I couldn't eat, sleep, and had no energy to do anything else but love on them. We were all that we had. The universe had shifted. The clouds were a combination of cirrus and stratocumulus, and you could feel that Kenya's soul was infinite. Our narrative was different. Our lives would never be the same. Each day was crooked, difficult, and on hard days, they were shattered. Every day, it was a group hug. All I had was my kids and a centimeter of sanity. My mama was on her way, and her presence alone would give me an extra dose of the strength that I needed to get by.

Grief came in phases, and once it hit me that as his wife, I was in charge of Kenya's affairs, including his homegoing and burial. Then I had to move from flight to fight and business mode. Out of respect for Kenya's grandma, who raised him, I went to meet with her for guidance. She made it crystal clear that the ball was in my court, but she put me in contact with the undertaker for the family. We looked at caskets, and she took care of reserving the funeral services at her family church and coordinating with her pastor. There was turmoil between his family and me over the years. However, it was maturity on my part to put things to the side and to run things past his grandma as I made decisions.

Although they painted me as this evil and mean-spirited wife, each day that I came to meet with Grandma, she realized that I wasn't so bad after all, and that I had nothing but love for her grandson. In death, people either unite and learn to forgive, or there was a showdown. Even Kenya's aunt Nita, who lived with Grandma, started to have a change of heart when it came to me, and in her own conviction, she secretly made amends and apologized for what she did to me. You could see in her eyes that she was broken that her nephew was gone, and it was hard for her to come to me just as it was hard for me to forgive her, but I did—life was short. Aunt Nita started gravitating to Dynasty, and strangely enough, baby girl liked Nita. Aunt Nita felt like Dynasty not only acted like Kenya, but looked just like him, and she yearned to spend time with her until they eventually had a bond.

Ken's father, Nelson, was utterly broken simply because he and Ken were starting to have a better relationship after having a strained one from him being an absentee father. Nelson vowed to support me and have my back, and his family, as a unit, donated toward the funeral.

Macy was grieving hard, and I had to respect it. Kenya was her only son, and she'd never get another one. She never cared for me, and I figured it was because I gave "gone with the wind fabulous," and you couldn't control me, but she could control Demi and supported Kenya's infidelity as long as she benefited. She wanted to pull rank and have a say-so about what went into the program without giving a penny. I gave her a li'l lead to satisfy her, but my mama was tired of her calling my phone, trying to call shots without an ounce of respect.

My mother secured all borders of my house. We were clear that we were dealing with a homicide, and Kenya's killer was still on the streets. Together, my family and close friends formulated a united front to ensure my safety and the safety of the children were implemented. My brother, Abel, Desire, Sanai, Cookie, Ms. Kim, and Frank ensured that they were at my house like clockwork in shifts just in case anyone wanted to jump out there. My cousin Britney, a high-ranking officer in the air force, had recently moved to the DMV. She was cut up and diesel and trained in warfare. She stayed ready, and she would get the strap before any nigga. She was a protective soul who cared dearly for my kids. She would watch the kids, take them places where they would have fun, and go shopping. Her spirit was calming, and on other days, she would gather them for a bite to eat and allowed them to process their feelings regarding their dad's passing. She really took to Nia and aimed to mentor her if provided with the opportunity. She would often share with Nia the pros of joining the military as an option for Nia once she graduated from high school.

Then I had my cousin Jimmy and his wife, Paisley, who were consistent with checking up on us, tightening up the house, and even catering food in lieu of a private dinner at my house. My *ohana* was solid, and as a result, I was getting ready to do something I'd never expect at 39 . . . plan my husband's funeral.

After meeting with a Black-owned funeral home, I'd learn how expensive, extravagant, and janky they could be. It was family operated, and you could tell they knew the funeral industry like they knew their name. The platinum casket that I chose was pricey, and the package that I chose was nearly $10,000. Their prices were inflated. Although they greeted you with a smile, they were crooked and billed me even until the morning of the funeral. I had no insurance policy on Kenya. He encouraged me years before to get a policy, but I thought we had time and didn't heed that advice, and now, I found myself paying out-of-pocket. In my mind, there was solace in giving every penny that I had to bury him. It was my way of communicating that I would love him forever, had forgiven him, and that it was indeed "'til death do us part."

Going to the burial was a feeling of nostalgia. At the entrance was a sista named Ruth, who greeted me with so much compassion. After we reviewed the terms and conditions of what it would take to bury Kenya, we put two and two together. She was the mother of a young lady that was in my mentoring program at MOV. Her daughter,

Jennifer, was gifted, humble, and easy to guide. She wanted to pursue the beauty industry, so I connected her with Desire to work as an intern.

One of my greatest fears was going into a cemetery alone. Growing up, we ran past cemeteries, said prayers if we drove past, and it was the place that you'd go to when you were real old. All I knew was that we were young and free, with our lives being cut short, and assassinated by people who looked like us.

Ruth guided me through the hills and valleys of the cemetery until my spirit connected to an area of mausoleums. She pointed and explained that the mausoleums in ancient times were symbolic in burial for Egyptian queens and kings. Each tier of the mausoleum had spiritual significance. The Egyptian mausoleums were architecturally defined with wings, a sprouting circle symbolic of the sun, and often a pair of sphinxes, where the female sphinx guarded the entry to the tomb. My goal was to get Kenya in a mausoleum, 'cause I believed anyone tied to me belonged to be entombed like royalty, and 6 feet under wasn't gonna work for my psyche.

In the center of the mausoleum was a tier called "Heart," which was at a perfect height so that Kenya's children could tap and reach him when it was all over. The mausoleum would cost close to $10,000, which was out of my price range, but God let me know that He had me, so I signed the burial agreement and went forth. I knew that the "Valley of the Shadow of Death" existed, but I feared no evil, for God was with me.

My mama put her ear to my bathroom door as I took a 45-minute shower, weeping the entire time, sobbing through a decade of loving Kenya wholeheartedly and preparing myself to say my final goodbye. In my mind, the tears were black, cascading over my cheekbones. I could have drowned in that water all day long, yet, I felt my mama transferring her energy to me like I transferred my energy to her when Major died. I was standing on her shoulders, and my great-grandma's shoulders, and sistas like Ms. P, who had souljah'd up, put on their big drawers and pulled that black veil on like a G.

My sistas were rooting for me. I had an army of good sistas who had lost their husbands and boyfriends to the streets. I finally understood the game, and like Erykah Badu said, I was on the "Other Side of the Game!" My big homegirl, Tee, from Bison University, came and styled Dynasty and me. She put me in a hip-hugging black dress with a black velvet blazer. She styled Dynasty with a cute leather skirt, tights, and matching leather shoes with a black cardigan. I wore my wedding studded-out stilettos for the second time and packed a cute kitten heel in my purse because I knew those shoes were beautiful, but you could only get 2 hours of wear out of them. Desire came quickly to touch up my hair with her heavy-duty flat irons. My mom adorned me with jewelry and crowned me with a black headband veil.

A caravan of sistas in their cars lined up beautifully in front of my house, awaiting me to get in my vehicle. My mentee, Ayden, drove me in my car. My mom and Dynasty rode with Desire, Ocean and

King rode with Ms. Kim. My vehicle led the way to Kenya's grandma's house, where the funeral car would greet us and take us to the funeral. I sipped on a cup of tequila as we rode to the house. My goal was to be so numb that I would have a very detached moment. It was clear that I would be present in body but absent emotionally. King and Dynasty walked into Grandma's house to get Nia and Keema's daughter, Ama, who was a young adult. Nia was holding a chocolate-brown li'l girl who had her head on Nia's shoulder. The toddler was wearing a tribute shirt for her daddy. It was Sojourn, and that was the very first time that I'd meet her. Dynasty and King were clueless about who she was, but when Nia introduced them to her, they immediately embraced her with a lot of hugs. I looked at her and said, "You wanna come with us?" She nodded yes.

I blurted, "I don't like your mama, but you are innocent, baby girl. Let's roll." Ama and Nia sighed with relief 'cause you could tell they were tasked to check my temperature. Sojourn didn't ask to come into the world. She was simply a product of the mess. I welcomed her. Kenya's father greeted the children and me as we all got into the funeral car. The kids were happy to be around one another as they could lean on each other for comfort and support.

The driver was a nice, young Black man who showed compassion and listened to me as I rambled about nothing. Kenya's dad was in utter pain, not saying a word. As we neared the church, Abel, Cookie, and Ms. Kim's uncle, Big John, called to let me know that the coast was clear and that undercovers were present. Big John let me know that some people were poppin' off about me being a few minutes late to the funeral, and he, without a doubt, checked any and everyone who had something to say. What they didn't know was that the police had to take necessary safety precautions because of the nature of the homicide before the kids and I could arrive.

There were so many people waiting when we arrived. It felt like we were burying a dignitary 'cause there were hundreds of people from all walks of life parting a sea, making a clear path for the children and me to walk hand in hand to the front of the church. At the top of the stairs were Mr. Light and Mr. Fab from Men of Valor, waiting to embrace me. They stood like guardian angels, and it was a confirmation of the radiant love that came from the brothas and the community, for I had supported so many families who were victims of gun violence, and that love flowed 360.

We all held hands. King stood like a prince holding my left hand, and Dynasty held my right hand. Nia held her hand, as well as baby Sojourn. We stood at the entrance of the processional, being led by a drum call . . . a drum call that reached from the villages of West Africa, navigating time and space, creating sacredness. A drum call for mourners, families, and friends that would communicate to the heavens that our hearts were too heavy to bear the trauma. The symphonic drum call echoed African queens whose kings were assassinated and were left to become *shujas*. We walked down the aisle to be surrounded by pallbearers who were strapped and ready for any infiltrator. We sat to the right of the church on the very first row. My family and comrades had formulated a great pyramid of protection surrounding the children and me, and they made sure that no one came close to me. My brother was directly positioned behind me, and my mama sat right next to me, along with the children and Vinia, a former student of mine. Vinia's daughter and Dynasty were playmates. I signed off days before so that Nia's mom, Taja, could get a pass from her probation officer to attend the funeral. Nia needed her mom more than ever, and Taja was there. As the drummers faded out, the message was sent into the universe. Kenya's body lay there in a fresh suit with his signature fedora, appearing stoic. The drum call was finished.

My soul broke.


The program was absolutely beautiful, and the obituary was designed by my good friend, Banneker, who went to college with me. Dynasty's dance troop did an amazing tribute dedicated to Kenya and his daughters, and my homegirl, Missy, sang melodically. To sit and watch the funeral was a nightmare before our eyes. You got the feeling that it was a celebrity funeral because hundreds of people attended, with no standing room. Young, middle-aged, and old people sat there. Kenya knew so many people from all walks of life, and he was loved by many. Family members and friends gave their reflections of a Kenya that those dear to him loved and understood. Spectators, haters, and you could sense, enemies, were among us. Some of Kenya's flings were sprinkled throughout the church, but what they learned was that he was married to a "boss," and they had to take several seats.

It was traumatic for his mother, grandma, and father to see their son for the very last time. It was beyond painful to watch the raw emotion of his children as they said their tearful goodbyes, but it was also sad to watch his very own comrades carry him out 10 toes up. The pallbearers held their composure, but they were torn like so many young Black men who lose their homies to gun violence. Kenya was always everyone's protector, but that love was not reciprocated to him.

As we were escorted to the funeral car, people in droves gave their condolences. God knew I needed strength, and as I looked up, I saw my father standing next to Britney, and in his hands, I collapsed. All I could hear was, "Lee, Lee, get her. Get her." He secured me, and I just cried like never before. I needed my dad to rescue me and protect me. I needed my dad to speak to me in a language that I understood. He held me, and as he and my mom got me in the car and started hydrating me with water, he affirmed, "Dream, baby, Daddy is here. I'm here!" I got in the car with the kids and together we rode to the private burial.

The burial was taxing to my soul. The color of the sky appeared obscure, the air had no breeze, and the atmosphere shifted into retrograde. Kenya's loved ones gathered poetically, yearning for justice. While we understood that we all lived and would all die, Kenya did not deserve to be assassinated. We surrounded the casket, holding on to every minute. Flashes of our time line came to me like visions. Remnants of the day that we met, flickers of the time that we would date, to our awesome moments on vacations, I did not want to let him go. Flashes of him dunking me at ocean beaches, throwing footballs at my back, and him getting me to swim out to the deeper parts of the waters . . . I did not want to let him go. Dinners, cookouts, ballouts, and fallouts, that time, yea, that time—I would never get back. I'd take the bad, ugly, crazy, and drunken in love time just to feel his heartbeat. In essence, Iyanla Vanzant was not a witch doctor. She was prophetically preparing us to let go, for the marriage was fulfilled even until the end.

The dove keeper read the symbolism of sending our loved ones off to glory. The children and Macy took turns of letting each dove go. Of course, I was terrified of the doves but happy to watch them fly. One dove was stubborn and paraded awhile, giving his final goodbye. The sun came out, and the grave diggers began preparing his body to enter the mausoleum. To watch his grandma, mother, cousins, and friends put their forget-me-nots into the vault was astounding.

The process of his casket entering the vault was mind-blowing. Dynasty fearlessly touched and kissed his coffin as they prepared to seal his body. Shocking the hell out of everybody, I took off my star-studded wedding shoes and put them inside the crypt. The grave diggers looked at me for final confirmation that it was okay to seal the burial chamber. I nodded. They began drilling and sealing every part of the catacomb until his final resting place was secured on all sides. In my spirit, Kenya had me play out loud on my cell phone his favorite song, which was "Smile" by the late legend Tupac Shakur and rapper Scarface. You could hear the song echo and the lyrics resonate, *"There's gon' be some stuff you gon' see/That's gon' make it hard to smile in the future/But through whatever you see/Through all the rain and the pain/You gotta keep your sense of humor."* His homies knew right then and there that Kenya was vibrating high as they bounced their heads back and forth to the beat.

I would walk away from the burial with a sense of peace, letting go of the man in my life who had the most authentic imprint. The sun surely peeked out and shined on me, and I knew that I had carried out his final request. I had more than exceeded my duties as a wife, but I honored him and established his rightful place as a Black King. As I walked away, peace filled the atmosphere. I could finally let him go into the ancestral realm. He would say to me all the time, "Eh, Dream, I'm the one who is gonna make you Stronger! It's gonna be me!"


Well, Kenya, you were right. You ignited the warrior in me, pushing this California Dreamer to greater heights than I could ever see, making me uncomfortable facing my own demons and causing me to fight like never before. You were right. We all got 'em. I didn't know my own strength, Kenya, yet, I embrace it now. My crown was crooked, but I adjusted it, and it has a fly tilt to it. Wow! I promised to tell our story, and I vowed: "'Til Death Do Us Part!" A Black Love Story imperfect in every way—but unbreakable and unbendable.

"Ouch, ouch," I hear you say . . .

We blazed a fire, dawg.

CPSIA information can be obtained
at www.ICGtesting.com
Printed in the USA
BVHW040628070121
597246BV00028B/615

9 780578 736310